YOUR MAGIC or MINE?

ANN MACELA

M PRESS ®

Medallion Press, Inc.
Printed in USA

Awards and accolades for
THE OLDEST KIND OF MAGIC by Ann Macela:

♣ The Heart of Denver Romance Writers 2006 Aspen Gold Winner for Best Paranormal Romance.

♣ Second Place for the Romance Writers Ink More Than Magic 2006 Contest for the Paranormal Category.

♣ Honorable Mention in the Paranormal Category of the Write Touch 2006 Contest of Wisconsin Romance Writers.

♣ Third Place for Best First Book in the 2006 Beacon First Coast Romance Writers Contest.

♣ Second Place, Mainstream/Single Title category—Texas Gold, East Texas RWA.

♣ Finalist, Cover Art—Anne Bonney, Ancient City Romance Writers.

♣ Finalist, Paranormal category—Published Laurie Contest, Smoky Mountain Romance Writers.

"Bravo, Ms. Macela, you have a hit on your hands and this should be an award-winning year for you! This author is a voice that can not be denied — her first published paranormal novel is distinctly defined, with refreshingly sharp nuances! . . . This is a phenomenal paranormal story that you must read! This comes with the highest recommendation from the reviewer. <u>IT IS A PERFECT FIVE HEARTS</u> — the story screams more sequels and this reviewer can not wait to get her hands on those!"

—*The Romance Studio*

★★★★★

Francie and Clay are two strong characters. The author brings them to life with her depiction of their growing relationship. Francie doesn't believe what Clay is telling her, and it becomes a fun-filled struggle for him to convince her. She is a great heroine – one this reader thoroughly enjoyed. She shows signs of stubbornness and vulnerability. Clay is a man who takes it for granted that his soul mate will fall into his arms. He is shocked by Francie's reaction, and at times, his responses to her are quite humorous. This couple was great together, and the chemistry was just right. Not only does the author give us a lead couple to love, the people surrounding them are winners too, from Daria to Tamara. They all add to the richness of the story. Run, don't walk to get your copy of DO YOU BELIEVE IN MAGIC? It is a fun and fast read – perfect for the beach or in your favorite spot for reading!

—*Susan T, Fallen Angel Reviews*

"DO YOU BELIEVE IN MAGIC? is a light romance, a good choice with which to while away an afternoon."

—*Lisa Baca, Romance Reviews Today*

"Well written with a great plot, believable characters and snappy dialogue, Ann Macela has yet another winner on her hands. Be forewarned though, it is almost impossible to set DO YOU BELIEVE IN MAGIC? aside for anything so be sure to have a day blocked out to do nothing but enjoy yourself.

This reviewer recommends DO YOU BELIEVE IN MAGIC? to any readers who enjoy contemporary paranormal romances. And while you are picking up DO YOU BELIEVE IN MAGIC? from your local book store be sure to pick up the first book in the series THE OLDEST KIND OF MAGIC and block out an entire weekend for yourself."

—*Shaiha, Love Romances and More*

"The sexual tension between Clay and Francie is HOT! … The pages sizzle with heat. The story is imaginative, fresh, and appealing…. The book has a surprise ending that will leave the reader cheering."

—*Fantasy Romance*

DEDICATION:

This book is for everyone who ever wished,
"If I could only cast a spell . . ."

Published 2008 by Medallion Press, Inc.

The MEDALLION PRESS LOGO
is a registered trademark of Medallion Press, Inc.

Typeset in Adobe Garamond Pro
Printed in the United States of America

ISBN: 9781933836324

10 9 8 7 6 5 4 3 2 1
First Edition

ACKNOWLEDGMENTS:

Thanks to my critique group plus Paula who read every word of this story and made wonderful suggestions for making it better.

Thanks to Drs. Charles Bacon, Tom Mabry, and Maureen Bonness. Dr. Bacon for his help with theoretical math concepts and Drs. Mabry and Bonness for their aid on the botany side. Any mistakes in my story are my own.

If I've taken liberties with any department or person at the University of Texas, I apologize.

I also have rearranged the building layout on Nob Hill in San Francisco and placed my HeatherRidge Hotel and Condominium on Sacramento between Mason and Jones, thereby displacing existing buildings. I hope the residents will forgive me for evicting them, even fictionally.

Thanks especially to Helen Rosburg and Medallion Press for taking a chance on me and my practitioners.

And, of course, to my own "Blue Mage," who puts some true magic in my life, Paul.

PROLOGUE

Him:

He ran. As fast as he could, through the tangled jungle, through the pouring rain. Chains of writhing vines reached for him as he sped by—or was the supple branch that brushed his arm a snake looking for its dinner? Booms of thunder so loud they shook the ground rolled down from the treetops. He almost stumbled on a fallen limb, but kept his balance by sheer force of will.

He halted his headlong dash and took shelter for a moment under a giant leaf. Thick bushes, huge, vine-covered tree branches, strange spiky or large-leafed plants pressed in on all sides. *Green* saturated the very air. The warm humidity, the earthy smell, the confining plant growths all increased his sense of claustrophobia and alienation. He definitely did not belong here. He chose another direction and ran again.

He had to get away, get out. But, where was he?

And which direction was out? He'd been running forever, he knew that much. The jungle had no end.

Or, was he running in a circle?

With a final bone-deep crash of thunder, the rain stopped, and he did, too. Only dripping water and his own fast breathing broke the silence. He was alone— exactly as he preferred.

Why then was he so forlorn?

Her:

She turned in a slow circle on the flat, sterile plain. Not a bit of vegetation, green or otherwise, in sight. Only brownish-gray earth and rocks. A true wasteland.

Wait. What was that? A rainbow, like light through a prism, sparkled on the horizon. She ran straight at it.

A tall building rose before her. A glass structure. A greenhouse! With lush, growing plants stretching up to the light. Exactly what she wanted, needed. Inside, she'd be safe, in her natural habitat.

She circled the building. No door. No operable windows. How was she supposed to get inside?

She beat her hands on the glass. It didn't move. She threw rocks. They didn't even scratch the shiny surface.

Was there anybody around to help her? She cupped her hands around her eyes, leaned on the glass, shifted to see around this fern and that tree. No one. She revolved in a circle again, searching the dusty plain.

She was totally alone—exactly as she did not want

to be. And as, she knew in her bones, she was not supposed to be. A wave of loneliness almost brought her to her knees.

Him:

He started walking again. What else could he do except keep going? He stumbled upon a gravel path, followed it through the shrubbery. In a few spots, the canopy of trees left little light to see by, and only the crunch of his feet on the small stones kept him on the trail.

The path existed, therefore someone—or something—had to have made it. Surely it led somewhere. To another person, to civilization.

He shook his head. The isolation was getting to him. He felt . . . almost lonely.

Ridiculous. He'd never been lonely in his life. Had he? No. Was he sure? Yes. Then why this niggling sense of doubt, this vague sense of needing someone?

What was that noise? It came from around the next bend. It sounded like . . . no, it couldn't be in this jungle . . . it sounded exactly like breaking glass.

Her:

She was beyond frustration. She'd tried every method she could think of, but she still couldn't get into the stupid greenhouse. She was thirsty, too, made even more so by the sight of water running down the glass inside.

Think. What hadn't she tried? She moved to a place

where the plants didn't press against the windows and looked inside again. Nothing except foliage. No evidence of human or animal life. She could almost cry. With a sigh of despair, she leaned against the glass wall . . .

And fell in.

Him:

He came around a bend in the trail into a clearing, and there she was, picking herself up off the ground. A woman. A naked woman. A naked, gorgeous woman with long, dark, curling hair.

She glanced around curiously, but didn't seem to be afraid or uncomfortable in these surroundings. In fact, she was smiling when she reached out to stroke a large elephant-ear leaf. When he walked forward, she turned to face him.

It wasn't easy, though he did manage to pull his gaze from her curves to her eyes—the greenest he'd ever seen. He was immediately ensnared, enthralled, enchanted.

No. His mind reasserted itself. He had to get out of here. He didn't want or need anyone. He had no time for a woman—even this one.

His body, however, had an opposite opinion and tightened. Hardened. Heated. Swelled.

Her:

Oh, thank heavens, she wasn't alone. A man was here. She had someone to talk with, to share the wonders to be found in the jungle.

He stopped about three feet away. A cloud blotted out the sun, the darkness under the trees increased, and she couldn't see his eyes. She cast a lightball and brought its power and light up through blue to indigo with violet streaks, her highest level.

How unusual. His eyes were light blue with a charcoal rim around the iris. As she watched, his irises expanded until only a thin line of blue remained. She'd thought light blue eyes were cold, icy, aloof. His, however, were more than warm, and her body reacted to their heat. She tingled all over, and her center hummed.

She glanced down at herself. She had no clothes on, but she wasn't bothered by her nudity. It felt natural somehow. She looked into his eyes again. He was staring at her as if he'd never seen a woman before. She asked, "What are you doing here?"

"I'm trying to get out," he replied.

"Why? It's the perfect place to be."

"I hate it. Do you know how to get out?"

He hated it? Her Eden? If he felt that way, better for everyone that he leave. "You only have to . . ." She realized that she didn't know. She wasn't even sure how she had gotten in.

"I've been following the path," he said.

She told him what seemed plausible and felt right. "You'll never get out doing that. You have to make the extra effort."

Him:

Extra effort? What did she think he'd been doing, going out for a stroll? He managed to jerk his eyes away from her and look around. Oh, great. The path had disappeared.

A distant rumble of thunder and a gust of wind caused him to shiver. The breeze brought with it a subtle menace. A dangerous evil was coming, he was certain. "We have to leave."

"Nonsense. We're safe here."

Crazy woman. No, they weren't. He couldn't abandon her, however. He had to protect her, no matter what her opinion.

He walked around the little circle of open space they were standing in. He couldn't see even a vestige of a trail leading away. Were they trapped?

A way out had to exist. She had come in, hadn't she?

He searched again. He was smart. He'd use mathematics to determine her route.

He cast whole equations he remembered from physics and calculating trajectories. He cast *computare limes* to calculate the path. He cast *comperire* to find it.

Nothing worked. He tried being physical instead of cerebral and pulled on leaves and vines in several likely spots. Everywhere he went, plants blocked him, seemed to be growing faster than he could pull them aside, seemed to be reaching for him.

More thunder rolled, reverberated around them, and the feeling of menace grew stronger.

His attempts were doing no good, and his anxiety was increasing. He stopped before her in the middle of the circle. She appeared unperturbed—to such an extent that he wanted to grab her and shake her. Didn't she realize the evil was approaching?

"We really must go," he said. "It's dangerous here."

She was definitely disgusted, but she gave in. "Oh, all right. Come with me." She took his hand and led him toward the largest tree.

Right in front of them, the leaves parted to reveal the path.

"Thank God." He was so relieved to see it he pulled her to him in a hug.

Only when their bodies touched did he discover that he was naked, too.

Her:

He had pulled her into his arms, and she realized they were both naked. Why had she not noticed that before? No matter. How wonderful to feel her skin against his, her soft breasts against his hard chest. She put her arms around him. A hug had never felt this exciting, this right, this blissful.

He ran his hand down her back, pulled her closer, lowered his mouth to hers . . .

Buuuuzzzzzzzzzzzzzzz.

As her alarm clock sounded, Gloriana came awake with a jolt, clutching her pillow and almost shaking with arousal. She was practically panting, and her heart beat like she'd run a marathon.

"Wow, what a dream," she muttered as she hit the button on her clock and flopped over on her back. Maybe she could fall back asleep and recapture the dream. She shut her eyes and concentrated on its last moments.

Just when she thought she'd succeeded, her dog jumped on the bed and pulled the sheet from her.

"Damn, Delilah," Gloriana said, but the hound only tugged at her big sleep shirt.

"Oh, all right, let's go for a run." Muttering about dogs that were too damn cheery in the morning, she headed for the bathroom.

The exercise restored her equilibrium, and she put the crazy dream out of her head. All she remembered was a heated look from pale blue eyes, and even that memory faded by the next day.

Him:

When he pulled her closer, she moaned, lowered her lids over her green eyes, lifted her rosy lips to his . . .

Mesmerized by the feel of her, he lowered his head to add taste to the mix. Her scent swirled in his nostrils . . .

And all he could smell was . . . dog breath.

He fisted his hand in her hair. All he felt was . . . dog fur.

A wet tongue licked his chin.

He opened his eyes to stare straight into Samson's red and white face. He was on the edge of his bed clutching the dog's ruff.

When Samson whined, Marcus let go and levered himself up from the bed. His muscles were tensely knotted, and the power the mysterious woman had in the dream revealed itself in his throbbing erection. He'd have to stretch carefully before his morning run.

Yeah, run. That's what he'd been doing all night.

He went through his day with a vague sense of unease hovering about him that dissipated by evening. By bedtime, he couldn't remember what caused it.

CHAPTER ONE

No!

No, no, no! The words banged their way out of her head and into her throat, and Gloriana Morgan clenched her teeth with a snap to stop her thoughts from tumbling out of her mouth.

Her shocked brain persisted in thinking them, however, and added even more behind the dam of her teeth.

No! This man could not be Marcus Forscher.

For her opponent in their debate of the issues surrounding the working of magic, she'd expected a practitioner so divorced from ordinary spell-casting he couldn't possibly acknowledge the methods of ordinary mortals. A man with his head so high in the mathematical clouds he couldn't speak in less than equations, as demonstrated by his articles on the subject. She'd also envisioned either a total math geek—scrawny, thick glasses, disheveled in jeans and a wrinkled button-down shirt, nerdy to the extreme—or an aged professor of the same variety with even thicker glasses and one of those jackets with leather elbows.

Instead, who did she have shaking her hand?

A six-feet-tall, very blond, tanned hunk with a square jaw, an aloof, down-his-perfect-nose gaze, and a slight cool smile. And those eyes—a chilly light blue with a charcoal rim around the irises—he used to inspect her from top to bottom and back before locking his gaze with hers.

The warm clasp of his hand caused even more of a jolt as little zings of energy traveled up her arm and tightened the hold she had on him—or was it the hold he had on her?

"How do you do, Dr. Morgan?" she heard him say in a low deep voice. The hairs on the back of her neck quivered.

Finally one of the zings reached her brain and shocked her mind back to the matter at hand. She unlocked her jaw and managed to force a polite answer past her lips. "Pleased to meet you, Dr. Forscher."

She carefully pulled her hand from his and let it drop to her side. Her palm still tingled and she fought against rubbing it on her skirt. Oh, God, her skirt. Her usual long, dark green flared skirt that went with her usual light green blouse and usual dark brown suede jacket. Usually worn for lectures in front of fellow botanists. She probably looked shabby—even nerdy—next to his impeccable navy suit and crisp white shirt. She paid little attention to fashion in general, much less the male variety, but his clothes all looked expensive with a capital *E*. At least he wore one vestige of nerd-dom—his red tie, replete with mathematical symbols.

She paused to take a calming breath before she turned to the man standing as the third point of their triangle.

Short, pudgy, balding, rumpled, fiftyish, and tweedy, Ed Hearst looked like what she had imagined for the editor of W^2, *The Witches and Warlocks Journal*, the publication of record for the magic practitioner community. Part newshound, part scholar, Ed was a man she should not underestimate. His shrewd brown eyes took in an enormous amount of information, his sharp ears caught every nuance in conversations, and his formidable powers of persuasion were responsible for her presence at the event.

Pushing his smudged rimless glasses up his nose, Ed beamed at them like a rabbit eyeing two particularly plump heads of lettuce. "I can't believe you two have never met in person. The debate has been going on for over a year and a half, and your offices are close by on campus."

"The mathematics and plant biology departments don't mix much," Forscher replied, "and I was a visiting professor at Cal Tech for the last calendar year."

"I've spent a great deal of time in the greenhouses lately," Gloriana put in. She'd never felt the need to look him up in person. What good would it do? Neither would change their stands on the matter. Why get into a pointless argument? She had better uses for her time.

"I appreciate your cooperation in putting together the event so quickly," Ed said. "We were fortunate you didn't have travel plans and the HeatherRidge ballroom here in Austin was available in the middle of March. We certainly couldn't have this discussion in a place that wasn't owned and staffed by practitioners. I realize two weeks' notice was short. Once I get an idea, however, I run with it, and holding the debate at this time will allow us to cover it in the next issue."

Gloriana kept her attention ostensibly on Ed, but she snuck a peek at the mathematician from the corner of her eye. Was something wrong with the man? He was still scrutinizing her with the most intense gaze—as if she were a type of plant he'd never seen before.

"So," Ed said, rubbing his hands together, "who wants to go first in the debate?"

"Let Dr. Forscher speak first," Gloriana said quickly. She needed the time to settle herself down. "His article was the catalyst to the letters."

"Is that okay with you?" Ed asked him.

Gloriana held in a sigh of relief when Forscher focused that laser-beam gaze on Ed.

"Fine," her opponent said with a quick nod.

"Then let's go." Ed ushered them up onto the raised platform where a table stood with chairs, microphones, and filled water glasses.

Gloriana took the right-hand seat and arranged her

notes as Ed sat in the middle and Forscher settled on the other end. She adjusted the microphone in front of her and scanned the ballroom. On this Saturday evening, the large ornate room with crystal chandeliers was filled almost to capacity with a mix of all ages and both genders. She could see her family seated off the middle aisle—her parents, her brother and his wife, and her sister and her husband—and she gave them a smile. Her father grinned and gave her a "go get 'em" gesture with his fist.

Ed waited until his photographer had snapped a couple of pictures and the audience had settled, and said, "Good evening, ladies and gentlemen. Welcome to our discussion on 'Spell-Casting: Past, Present and Future.' I'm Ed Hearst, editor of W^2. To my right is Dr. Gloriana Morgan, associate professor of botany, twelfth-level practitioner, and to my left is Dr. Marcus Forscher, professor of mathematics, eleventh-level practitioner. Both teach here at the University of Texas. Their curricula vitae are in the handout you received at the door.

"Last year, W^2 published Dr. Forscher's article entitled 'A Mathematical Basis for Spell-Casting,' in which he discussed the creation and use of mathematical equations and proof methods for working magic. Thinking in and applying math terms would, he suggested, standardize casting and result in a more efficient and effective process for all."

A number of people in the audience shifted in their

seats, but Gloriana couldn't tell if they were moving in agreement or opposition to the idea—or simply getting comfortable.

Ed kept talking over the slight disturbance. "That article drew more letters to the editor, both pro and con, than we ever received. When we printed a selection, along with Dr. Forscher's replies, we received double the first response. The tenor, the enthusiasm, and, yes, the intensity of the correspondents quickly convinced us we had an issue of substance and worth for the entire community. One of the most articulate proponents for maintaining a more traditional view of casting caught everyone's eye. At our request, Dr. Morgan wrote two articles on the subject, which we ran side by side with Dr. Forscher's."

Ed paused to take a sip of water before continuing, "From those debates in print came the idea of bringing the two of them together with other practitioners to discuss the theory and practice of magic. Their respective specialties make them excellent choices for such a discussion since Dr. Forscher's leads him into mathematic and magical theoretical research and Dr. Morgan's grounds her literally and figuratively in spells ancient in their origin and practical in their nature.

"We'll give each of our speakers a chance to express their ideas before opening the session to questions and comments. We're recording the session. Let's keep this informal *and* in order, shall we? Dr. Forscher will go first."

Gloriana picked up her pen to be ready to jot down points she might want to address. Although she had agreed to it, she wasn't sure she liked the setup at the table, but it had seemed a better choice than having to stand at a formal podium like two candidates running for office. Sitting in a row as they were here, however, she couldn't see her opponent without leaning way back and even then she couldn't see his face.

On the other hand, maybe that was a good thing; she didn't need eye contact on top of the effect of that deep compelling voice. A shiver ran down her spine while Forscher thanked Ed for providing the forum. She made herself sit up straight, take a quiet breath, and ignore the itch in the middle of her chest. *Concentrate on his words, Glori.*

"My ideas and recommendations started, as scientific investigations do, with questions," Forscher began. "What is at the heart of that which makes us practitioners in the first place? Many would answer, it is the ability to use magic in our everyday work. Given that, how could we practitioners cast better, more effective spells? Refine and understand the process and methods for casting? What factors, elements, go into a spell in the first place? How can we understand a spell mathematically?

"I drew on ancient and present masters for hard data and inspiration. What I learned led me to postulate a basic equation, one that would encompass the casting of every spell. The equation, which some call a formula, is on the back page of your handout."

Paper rustled as audience members flipped pages. Gloriana did the same. She had not looked at the pamphlet, thinking she already knew what was in it. Another assumption gone bad.

There on the last page was the infamous formula. How sneaky of him to supply it. What was the matter with her? Why hadn't she thought of printing handouts of her major points for the audience like she would for a class? She mentally shook herself. Not a thing to worry about at the present time. He was still talking.

"I realize," Forscher said in a self-deprecating tone, "developing the process for the use of the formula moves me from my purely theoretical base into the realm of what some call 'applied mathematics,' or mathematics that everyone can use. So be it. My thinking led me to speculate on the nature of magic reality and from there to create the equation, and it became clear that I had a foundation on which to build and from which everyone could benefit. Let's look at the formula."

Gloriana looked down at the page. It displayed the equation,

$$(s_T + L_s + L_p) * E_p * R * I = S$$

She drew little stems, leaves, and petals to make the last S into a flower.

"A cast spell contains six elements," Forscher said. "The last two may not be required, but the first four always are. You begin with the spell, small or lowercase *s*, you are going to cast. The exact spell depends on the particular, specific talent, sub *T*, of the practitioner. Capital *L* sub small *s* is the level of the spell being cast. Capital *L* sub small *p* is the level of the practitioner. In casting, these three 'ingredients' are multiplied by the amount of magical power or energy, capital *E*, the practitioner, sub small *p*, puts into the spell."

Gloriana felt her eyes almost crossing at the recital. Too many capitals, subs, and letters.

"For example," Forscher continued, "when casting the light spell *lux*, a small amount of energy input would create a dim light and more would create a brighter one. *R* refers to any ritual, gestures and the like, the spell requires, and *I* to any item used or required. The ritual and/or item provide energy themselves and act as multipliers on the casting to increase the potency or longevity or some other aspect of the spell. I used the asterisk instead of the normal mathematics symbol to show multiplication because there seems to be something else going on besides a straight multiplying effect. I haven't identified the 'something' yet. The result is the cast spell, capital *S*. Does everyone follow me thus far?"

Gloriana kept her expression neutral when she looked out over the audience as he paused. Several people nodded, a few shook their heads, and others frowned. She couldn't tell if they didn't understand or if they were disgusted at the idea. No one, however, said a word.

"As I said, the equation is a foundation," Forscher went on. "We need to do more work with the spell elements, defining and calibrating them. I maintain that eventually, by applying the formula, arranging the elements precisely in his mind and with his actions, a practitioner will be able to cast more efficiently, make better use of his energy, and generate more powerful spells. We will all understand the process completely. Spell-casting will become more coherent, more regularized, less haphazard, less risky."

He paused again, and when Ed leaned back, Gloriana managed to see her opponent's face in profile. He had a small smile on those perfect lips—a smile that sent a shiver of anticipation down her back. Would he repeat the words that had set off a firestorm?

"It's time," Forscher stated, "to move forward, to put the cauldron-stirring, potion-making stereotypes and unorganized, disorganized, nonproductive, energy-wasting methods of the past behind us. We must not look back, only forward, as we seek to understand our practice and wield it objectively, without emotion, scientifically, without messiness. Tradition—simply because we've always done something a particular way since the tenth century—has no place in the twenty-first. We can remove ourselves from the limits our history and our laziness have imposed upon us. We will enhance our powers and live up to our full potential."

Yep, there they were, the incendiary statements

that galvanized so much response. A ripple of sound and movement flowed through the room. A few people clapped—mostly younger men and women, from what Gloriana could see. Had she heard a few growls among the paper rustling and chair shifting? She glanced around but saw only poker faces. Nobody was giving away their opinions—yet.

When Gloriana faced Forscher again, he was looking back at her, the small smile still in place. Or was it a smirk? When her gaze met his and his expression changed to fierce, however, she could almost feel the glove smacking her face. The duel was definitely on— and she had a surprise for him. She was going to take the debate to a new level.

"Your turn," Forscher said, his voice low and husky.

Ed leaned forward again and blocked her view, breaking the contact. "Next we'll hear from Dr. Morgan," he announced.

Marcus Forscher made himself sit back in the chair and forced his eyes to the papers on the table. What in hell was the matter with him? One glance at Gloriana Morgan and he didn't want to look anywhere *except at her*. Euphoria had engulfed him—like he'd discovered a new proof for one of mathematics' oldest problems. He, who'd learned never to show emotion or other weakness, wanted to shout with joy.

He'd regained control of himself to speak, and when he'd finished, he'd given her an encouraging smile to indicate his goodwill toward hearing from her side. When she'd looked back, however? The impact of her dark green eyes had tightened his muscles almost to fight-or-flight level—and caused a definitely inappropriate reaction in his lower body. He'd barely managed to say two words.

Had she or someone else cast a spell on him? To make it difficult for him to debate? No, not possible. He was very sensitive to spells; he'd recognize it immediately. He pressed his fingers over his magic center at the end of his breastbone. No, his center itched some. Otherwise it felt fine.

Why hadn't he looked Morgan up on the university or the practitioner Web sites? Surely seeing her picture would have prepared him for the reality of that dark curly hair and those big green eyes. When, however, had he had the time, what with returning from California and being thrown into his teaching duties and his book deadline? No matter. Here he was—and so was she.

He scooted his chair around to be able to see her without Ed in the way. She was pretty, with her hair falling to her shoulders, heart-shaped face, and clear complexion. Slim but curvy, probably five feet five or so. Dressed in a scholarly fashion, the greens and browns suggestive of her botanical bent.

Morgan flashed a suspicious glance at him while stacking her papers. He almost grinned. She was going to be a worthy opponent. Her arguments and observations about magic theory had been well thought out, intelligent, and penetrating. Expecting no less at the moment, he was looking forward to the discussion, but he couldn't see how she could refute his hypothesis. It all fit together with mathematic precision.

"Here I am," Morgan began with a big smile, "a certified potion-making, cauldron-stirring practitioner, who delights in the craft and the feel and the subtleties of practicing magic, who revels in the traditions of our art, and who believes in the innate ability of us all to live up to our magic potential."

That drew a chuckle, and Marcus felt his lips twitch at her turn of his phrase. To gauge the effect of her words, he alternated his gaze between her and the audience.

"To me," she continued, "one of the pleasures of practicing magic is learning how to manipulate the forces all those letters in Dr. Forscher's equation stand for. To work magic in reality, not theory. To work magic until a spell becomes an integral part of me and I don't need to think of every single step. Making a spell my own, with my individual refinements. Practicing, practicing, practicing."

Marcus noted many nods, especially among the older spectators. She had some supporters, and he had expected that.

"No matter how great or small our potential power or level, or how simple or complicated the spell, or how difficult or easy the demands of our specific talent, casting a spell is a matter of art as much as precision, individual experimentation as much as following a precise recipe, and warm emotion as much as cold science. And, let's face it, as we have all experienced from teaching children, making magic is often downright messy."

The entire audience laughed. A few applauded. Marcus stopped himself from frowning, but *damn*. With only a few words, she had captured them. Practically the entire lot were hanging on her words. He'd never been able to accomplish that response unless he was with a group of mathematicians on his level.

"I'll admit," she said, "some of the spells and techniques I use have origins back beyond the tenth century and even farther, to ancient China and Egypt. Does that make them less potent, efficacious? Does the age of a spell in the hands of an experienced practitioner make it less efficient to cast?"

Several people—both young and old—shook their heads.

"Those ancient spells have been tested and refined by the greatest practitioners, and that knowledge has been passed down to us. Regarding emotion, who among us does not feel a thrill, a warm satisfaction, when casting precisely the right spell, exactly to the requirements of the job? Who is not driven to create new spells for the sheer joy of manipulating magic to make our professions easier, more useful, and, yes, more efficient? The practice of magic is not, has never been, static."

A few practitioners clapped for her statement. Their approval meant nothing. Marcus remained sure of his argument. It might feel good, but emotion had no place in the actual casting.

"I agree wholeheartedly with our ongoing spell research and development," Morgan stated. "As we enter professions that didn't exist even fifty years ago, we must have new enchantments for them. As our older professions change to meet the demands of the modern world, we need new wizardry. If Dr. Forscher's formula helps only one practitioner create only one spell to solve only one problem for only one profession, that's great! If it helps more, that's even better."

At last, Marcus thought, she's going to address what I'm really talking about—theory, not practice.

"Tonight I'd like to address a point about the issue that has bothered me from the beginning, but which has not really been touched on in the debate. I'd like to look at the larger, more general, more practical picture before it gets lost in the intricacies of the formula. Theory is all well and good. Working magic, however, is not easy or simple, as all of us can attest. Let us beware of thinking Dr. Forscher's formula, or others like it, will solve all our casting problems.

"Educational fads come and go. One method of teaching a subject, magic or not, can rise to the forefront and supersede all others—but not always to the benefit of the students. Such could be the case here. Urging, especially going so far as *forcing*, the use of the equation in all spell training and ignoring our tried-and-true systems could have unintended results," she said, a grim look on her face.

"Let us consider two situations, the first involving our young practitioners in whom magic has recently manifested itself. These people are working hard to master the concepts and manipulate the powers within themselves. We all remember the difficulty in our first spell attempts."

Marcus felt himself begin to frown at his opponent. *Forcing* use of his equation? Did she think he was advocating exclusivity? Where was she going with her idea?

"Trying to use the formula may help some and hurt others," she said. "For example, in the lowest level universal spells—where we all begin and where differing casting methods abound for each spell—a young practitioner learns to manipulate the energy within her and move that energy outward to cause something to happen. Five different people could, and probably do, have five different processes to accomplish the same result. Indeed, during training we stress the need to develop our own individual method.

"Will we let our 'messy' learning procedure continue, or will we try to impose a 'regularized' method? What if a young person cannot think in formula terms? Cannot at first separate the parts of a spell into discrete sections? Can't deal with manipulating all the parts at one time? How will we handle the frustration and feelings of failure sure to follow?"

Marcus frowned harder. She wasn't speaking to the point at all. She was a scientist herself, but she was appealing to emotions rather than the scientific worth of his equation. She hadn't done it in her articles. There she'd dissected spell-casting into its constituent parts with examples of different processes. And no mention of frustration or feelings. What was she up to?

His opponent took a sip of water and gazed out over the audience. Marcus tried to find the focus of her gaze—ah, there. An older woman with dark curly hair and a heart-shaped face. That had to be her mother. In fact, the younger woman next to her must be a sister. The older man and one of the younger men had the same coloring, the same nose. Her entire family must be here. A pang of . . . *something*—longing? loneliness?—struck him in the chest. He ignored it. This moment was not the time for him to succumb to emotion.

Morgan was speaking to her second point, and he concentrated again on her words.

"The second situation," she said, "involves casting at higher levels. I can speak with some experience here. My mother, a level ten, and I have the same basic talents with plants. Although we use them differently in most cases, many of our spells are the same. Enchanting is such a highly individualized art that even my mother and I, with similar talents and closely attuned to each other's powers, do not cast our high-level spells exactly the same, even those requiring precise ritual. We achieve the same overall ends—only their details may differ.

"Could we cast our spells truly the same, with identical results? We have experimented with Dr. Forscher's formula and found our enchantments remained slightly different in their amount of power, duration, results, and other aspects. The closest analogy I can think of comes from cooking. Two cooks make the same recipe, using identical ingredients, but . . . her meatballs taste better than mine."

No, she has it wrong, she hadn't, couldn't have, cast precisely, Marcus thought, as another chuckle rippled across the room.

"In conclusion," she said, "I applaud Dr. Forscher's ingenuity, creativity, and effort in developing his equation. I'm sure some practitioners will benefit greatly from using it. I agree, we all need to cast our spells as efficiently and productively as possible. All I ask is for those who want to drag us into the future or impose a casting regimen, please, consider the reality of working magic. It's a matter of art and mastery, a 'feel' for the forces within us, knowledge of and respect for our history, and above all, the combination of individual experimentation, experience, and emotions that result in great magic. Thank you."

The audience broke out in applause—or rather about half of them did, Marcus noticed. Several people stood with their hands up, a couple waving wildly for attention. Ed called for order.

There had to be a fallacy in her statements. True, in typical mathematical theorizing, he himself had not experimented in the real world, had not practiced his formula beyond a bare minimum. Some of his colleagues had, and they reported good results. His theory remained valid. The business about "forcing a casting regimen," however, was far off the mark.

"Let's settle down, please," Ed boomed into the microphone once more. "Everyone will have a chance. Hold up your hands, and I'll call on you. One of the ushers will bring a mike. Please wait until all of us can hear you before asking your question."

While waiting for the ushers to get to their positions, Ed pushed his chair back and said, "Nice job, both of you. I'm going to let the discussion go on until we start getting repetitions in the questions. Okay?"

Gloriana nodded and saw Forscher do the same. She wondered how he was taking her remarks. Before she could ask, however, Ed pulled forward and called on an elderly man in the front row.

The man stood and waited until the mike arrived. "I've been practicing magic, man and boy, for over seventy years, specializing in oil exploration. I've never heard of a general formula for all talents. If your formula is so great, why hasn't somebody thought of it before?"

Ed turned to Forscher. "This one's obviously yours."

"Perhaps someone did, sir," Forscher replied. "I found no record of one, however. From my research, I can tell you that before the seventeen hundreds and the Industrial Revolution, the number of existing spells was relatively small, and the differentiation among them was not great. When professions proliferated, likewise did the need for less general, more specific specialty spells, but everyone seemed to be wrapped up in their talents and even those at the highest levels didn't confer with others outside their own circle. No 'Renaissance man' like Leonardo da Vinci came forward to survey or study a number of different talents or to attempt a consolidation."

Ed called on a stylishly dressed woman in the third row on the middle aisle.

"I'm Loretta Horner," she announced as though her name should mean something to the group. "Dr. Morgan, I can't express how great my pleasure is in hearing you say what my husband and I have thought since we read Dr. Forscher's articles. In our view, 'regularizing' spell-casting with a formula will take away all our individual processes and force us into a lockstep parade. Our traditional methods are best."

A number of people applauded as she sat down. Gloriana nodded, but didn't say anything because Mrs. Horner hadn't asked a question.

Ed called on a younger man who looked more like what Gloriana expected a mathematics nerd to look like—thin, with round glasses, wearing jeans and a button-down blue shirt.

"I'd like to speak up for Forscher's equation and theory," he said. "I'm Bryan Pritchart, one of his mathematical colleagues, and I've played with the equation. It's a good beginning for more efficient casting. Of course, it's not perfected yet, and I can suggest a couple of improvements. We've been practicing magic the same way for too long. It's time to try the new." Some of the people sitting around the man clapped.

Gloriana snuck a glance at Forscher, who didn't look very happy at the man's statement—probably because he'd said the part about 'a couple of improvements' in a snide tone of voice.

"Thank you, Dr. Pritchart," was all Forscher said.

A large balding man in the middle back of the audience was next. The fellow rose and crossed his arms over his chest. "I'm against highfalutin folderol. The formula is too complicated, most people won't be able to follow it, and why should we try to fix what's not broke? I'm a level five, I raise cattle, and I don't have the time to think up an 'e-qua-shun' while gelding a calf or inseminating a cow, I can tell you that. Nobody is going to force me to do it, either!" He gave a sharp nod of his head and sat down to a couple of "you tell 'ems" and "amens."

"Sir," Forscher said, "nobody is trying to force anything on you or anyone else here. I'm offering a possible method for more efficient casting. It needs testing and refinement. You are free to try it or not, as you wish."

A young woman in an orange UT sweatshirt took the mike. "I don't understand you people who refuse to see Dr. Forscher for the genius he is. He's helping us understand the building blocks of magic. We need to look to the future, not back to the past. Tradition and the so-called tried and true ways are okay for you old practitioners. We young ones need more, especially for the new professions we have to deal with."

Gloriana heard "harrumphs" coming from several "old" practitioners. When Forscher thanked the student for her support, she flushed beet red.

A woman who could be the photo on a "Soccer Mom" poster was next. "Look here. I'm at best what you might call 'mathematically challenged.' Are you telling me I have to use math to prepare my children to become practitioners? When they have talents that have nothing to do with math?"

Gloriana watched Forscher frown. Like many theorists, he must have been so far into his equation that he didn't think of the practical or of people who could not or would not welcome his formula.

"No, ma'am, I'm not saying that," he replied. "It's a theory, an experiment at the moment. And you might be surprised how much math there is in everyday life."

Gloriana stifled a smile. He probably should not have made the last statement—or sounded quite as condescending.

Sure enough, the woman responded, "I'm not stupid

or uneducated. There's math in cooking and cleaning and making change and filling up the car. But that's arithmetic. What you're selling here looks like calculus to me. If you're cooking up a spell, then how much is a cup of power, tell me that?"

Almost everyone laughed at the exchange. Even Forscher grinned before replying, "That's what we need to study."

Ed pointed to a white-haired man sitting next to the stylishly dressed previous questioner. "I'm Cal Horner," he announced in a slow drawl. "Something's been bothering me about your all-encompassing equation, Dr. Forscher. There are all kinds of talents, and every one has a set of spells that goes with them. Everybody can't possibly cast a spell the same way. How do you expect to apply one equation to all of them? How can, for example, a plumber cast one of his talent's spells the same way a cook can?"

Gloriana suddenly recognized the names. He was a retired industrialist and she a society hostess from Dallas. The Horners had a reputation in the non-practitioner world for their conservative opinions on every issue imaginable. Were they making another stand here?

"I believe people can cast in the same manner, and we can apply the formula to all," Forscher replied, leaning forward with his elbows on the table. "In general. There may be corollaries to the original equation. That's one of the situations we must study. Suppose a plumbing spell and a cooking spell are fundamentally the same enchantment, but applied to different objects. Is a plumber heating solder different from a cook heating water? If you have a spell H for heat, is H for solder the same as H for water? The plumber casts H-open parentheses-solder-close parentheses and the cook casts H-open parentheses-water-close parentheses." He gestured the parentheses as he spoke. "Same spell, different targets, possibly different amounts of energy needed."

Horner looked confused. "I don't know . . ."

Gloriana saw confusion and puzzlement on a number of faces. Throwing parentheses and other such terms around was a sure way to lose his audience.

Before Horner could ask another question, Ed called on someone else, another man who appeared to be in his thirties.

"I, for one, welcome your ideas, Dr. Forscher," he said in a somewhat pompous tone. "I'm Mike Brubaker from the University of Chicago. We need more research into the broader universe of casting. What you're proposing fits nicely with mathematical theory. I can think of several spells that satisfy the definition of a mathematical object and in combination can be formed into groups and rings. For example, the simple *flamma* spell could be cast as a positive 'F' to light the candle and a negative 'F' to extinguish it. Also, *lux* can be seen as two spells, 'L' for the light energy plus 'C' for the cage it inhabits, and that's a group."

"Let's not get too complicated, here," Ed cut in quickly. "We're not all mathematicians." He pointed to a gray-haired woman who was holding up her cane, but the man who had identified himself as Bryan Pritchart took the mike when it passed him on the way to her.

"To carry Brubaker's theory forward, I think he's onto something," Pritchart announced as if he were conferring an award. "We need to identify essential and innate features versus those that are merely details or personal idiosyncrasies. We have to consider diffeomorphism and topology and . . . Hey!"

The woman whom Ed had called on snatched the mike out of Pritchart's hand. "It's my turn, young man," she snapped and pointed her cane at him, only narrowly missing the person between them. "You youngsters always think you're smart. You come up with these 'formulas' and think you've invented something revolutionary. Let me tell you, that is not the way people cast spells. We've been doing fine without the blasted thing for millennia. You ought to leave well enough alone."

"Look, lady," Pritchart said, grabbing the mike back. "Casting mathematically will be the wave of the future, and I don't intend to be left behind with the bunch of you geezers who refuse to accept the idea."

"See here, Pritchart, don't talk to Mrs. Shortbottom like that." Horner's voice came thundering out of the loud speakers as he appropriated a microphone from a nearby usher.

Gloriana jumped. Some audience members turned sharply, and a few snickered.

Horner didn't pause for breath. "She and many of us were casting spells before you were born and we're doing all right. Forscher's formula may look like manna from heaven to you. To the rest of us, it looks like a gift horse. Foisting it on practitioners who have no need for it is tantamount to forcing us to deny our heritage, to ignore our centuries of casting experience. I, for one, will have no part of it. Let's go, Loretta. If we can't carry on a decent conversation here, we'll leave." He handed the mike back to the usher and led his wife down the aisle to the doors at the rear.

"Oh, yeah?" Pritchart sneered, his lip curling as he watched the couple walk by.

"Yes, you, you . . . hippie!" Mrs. Shortbottom poked Pritchart in the belly with her cane and stormed off in the opposite direction while he doubled over.

That exchange brought half the audience to their feet, most of them with their arms raised and yelling for attention. Those seated started talking to their neighbors, some clearly arguing and waving the handout in the air. Several participants surged into the middle aisle in the wake of the Horners.

"Ladies and gentlemen!" Ed shouted and stood. "Take your seats and come to order." He pounded on the table for emphasis.

His attempt to restore order went unheeded. If anything,

the tumult increased.

Gloriana searched for her family and saw them making their way to the side of the room rather than into the center aisle. That space had filled with people. The cattle rancher was yelling into Pritchart's face, the soccer mom was fussing at Brubaker, and Mrs. Shortbottom was swinging her cane, taking no prisoners on either side.

"Practitioners! Come to order!" Ed called again into the mike.

Gloriana slid her chair back and looked at Forscher, who had a bemused smile on his face. As if he could feel her gaze, he faced her and said something.

When she shook her head and pointed to her ears to signify she couldn't hear him, he rose, came to her, and bent over to say in her ear, "See what you caused?"

"Me?" She pulled back enough to see his face. When she took her next breath, she inhaled his scent, a woodsy-and-pure-male concoction she felt fill her nostrils and muddle her brain. She shook her head to clear it and said, "The formula was your idea."

"Yes, but I said nothing about 'forcing' it."

She couldn't tell if he was angry or laughing at her. Either way, she was not going to take the blame for the debacle before them. "I simply brought out the ramifications you neglected to mention. You can't make enormous changes without looking at the entirety of your project."

Before he or she could make another statement, Ed

turned around and leaned down so they could hear him. "I think we've lost our audience. They're more interested in talking to each other than listening to us. I, for one, am not going to get in the middle. Security's here and will make sure nobody starts more than a verbal argument. Let's go out into the side hall."

Gloriana stood up and led the way to the entrance where her family was waiting. Everyone went into the hall and, when the door closed behind them, she gave a sigh of relief at the quiet. She introduced Ed and Forscher to her family.

"That went well," Ed said, a big grin on his face, after shaking hands all around.

"How can you say that?" Gloriana asked. "We almost had a riot." She flicked a glance at Forscher, who was also frowning.

"Nonsense," Ed replied. "A vigorous argument, that's all. We wanted to start a discussion. I'll say we did it."

"We did not really discuss the equation," Forscher interjected, sounding more than a little peeved. "Or its merits. The 'discussion' deteriorated from an explanation into an emotional, unreasonable brawl."

"What did you expect, that people would accept such a radical change in casting without question or protest?" Gloriana asked, her arms folded in front of her. She had been surprised at some of the reactions, but no way was she going to admit that to him.

Both Ed and Forscher opened their mouths to

comment. Before they could speak, another chimed in.

"Hearst! I want to talk to you." Horner and his wife hurried down the hall toward them, followed by several other audience members, including Mrs. Shortbottom and her cane.

"Damn," Ed muttered. "You all get out of here. I'll take care of him." He walked away to intercept the couple.

"Fine," Forscher said and faced the Morgans. "It was nice meeting you. Dr. Morgan, we'll have to continue our discussion another time." He bowed slightly and, pulling open the ballroom door, walked back into the still-arguing crowd.

Gloriana watched the door close and took a deep breath. At least the debacle was over. "Come on," she said, rubbing the itch at the end of her breastbone. "Let's go home."

CHAPTER TWO

Marcus shouldered his way through the crowd, stopping only to say a few words when he knew the person. He avoided the group around Pritchart and Brubaker. Outside the ballroom he took the direct line to the escalators.

"Marcus!"

The voice sounded familiar. He glanced around, stopped, turned, and walked back to the caller. As he shook the hand of the man he considered to be his mentor, he said, "George, I'm glad to see you. I didn't know you were here."

George Frederick Bernhard laughed. "Wouldn't have missed it. What a circus! Come on, walk me to my car. I don't want to get dragged into one of these arguments any more than you do."

"I always said you could read my mind," Marcus agreed and let the older man precede him on the escalator.

Absurdly pleased George had come, he looked his friend over during the silent ride down. The mathematician certainly didn't appear to be in his sixties. His sandy brown hair displayed little gray, his brown eyes were sharp, and his wiry frame moved energetically.

Once in the lobby, they walked together to the parking garage elevators. "What did you think of that so-called debate?" Marcus asked.

George snorted. "Some debate. Nobody really addressed your theory or its merits—"

"I agree."

"—but nobody talked coherently about the larger issues Morgan brought up, either."

"Everybody had their own agenda," Marcus said, pushing the elevator button. "Prick certainly did."

"Prick? Oh, yes, I'd forgotten Pritchart's nickname. He's still jealous of you, isn't he?"

"I have no idea what his problem is," Marcus said. "He's been an asshole ever since we were undergrads at MIT."

"From what I heard in that room, he wants the accolades for your work. He's trying to take over your formula and lead the charge into the future of mathematical casting."

"He's welcome to it if every discussion in public ends up like this disaster."

The elevator came and they rode up after determining the location of their cars, fortuitously on the same floor.

"What's with the Horners?" Marcus asked while they walked into the parking garage. "They came out of nowhere. I don't remember that name in the letters Ed received, and he did show me all of them."

"Your guess is as good as mine," George answered. "Their conservatism and opposition to new methods in all fields is well established. They've always pushed for a return to 'basic teaching'—whatever that is—in both magic and non-magic subjects. Here's my car." He pushed the button on his key ring, and the locks disengaged with a beep.

Marcus slapped the portfolio holding his speech notes against his leg—the sole expression of frustration he would allow himself even if he did feel like punching the wall. "What I really don't understand is why Morgan changed the focus of the debate the way she did. I hadn't mentioned the 'art' of casting, or 'emotions,' and I certainly did not mention 'forcing' someone to use the formula. She never used those terms in her articles."

"She was probably trying to broaden the scope of the discussion, make it into a conversation everybody could understand. Personally, I think she was right to do that."

Marcus blinked at that statement. George was on *her* side? He kept his tone level. "What do you mean?"

"You've seen how non-math people react to one of our discussions, especially when we're tossing around terms like Pritchart and Brubaker were doing?"

"Yeah. Total incomprehension or boredom or both."

"Exactly. We need to talk in words everyone can understand. Not let them dismiss your equation out of hand as incomprehensible. What will make or break acceptance of your idea is how it fits into the rest of magic theory and *practice*. People have to be able to use it consistently and correctly. I think you've done good work here. To incorporate it into the fabric of practitioner life won't be easy, however, with flame throwers like Pritchart antagonizing people on one side and hidebound reactionaries like Horner dragging us back to the Middle Ages on the other."

"I've been saying all along, and tried to make the point tonight, that the equation and its use need study. I never envisioned complete acceptance or complete denial without tests."

"I didn't, either," George acknowledged. "Maybe Ed can restore some calm to the discussion in the next W^2 article. Talk to Morgan. She didn't look happy about tonight's outcome, either. You might be able to come up with a united front."

"I'll think about it," Marcus said.

They parted with the promise to get together soon for racquetball or chess, or maybe both. As he climbed into his silver BMW, Marcus thought of their last games. In both, they were well matched, but he had the edge on the court. The chessboard was another matter, however. George was the only person besides his father who could defeat him regularly.

He pulled out of the HeatherRidge and headed for his home in the western hills. He'd take Samson on a run before bed. He needed to work off the tension he felt in the back of his neck and shoulders. That so-called discussion had not left him in his usual calm state.

Neither had the sight and sound of his opponent. And if that weren't bad enough? When he'd leaned over her to tease her about causing the near riot and her spicy floral scent had enveloped him, he had to stop himself from burying his nose in her hair and licking her neck to see if she tasted as good as she smelled.

What in hell was the matter with him? No woman had ever affected him that way, almost made him lose control. He wasn't going to let it happen again. He wouldn't take George's suggestion about talking to her, not on the phone or in person. Communicating by letters and articles was as close as he wanted to get to the woman from this point forward. With a little luck he'd never have to see her again.

A sharp little pain hit him in the middle of his chest. The whole mess was giving him heartburn. He rubbed the small ache before turning up the volume on his latest jazz CD. Yes, a run would definitely do him some good.

※❋✦✶❋※

Gloriana looked at her family seated around her mother's kitchen table at their herb and plant farm outside Austin between Smithville and LaGrange. Family gatherings had been infrequent since the holidays, and it did feel good to be back together. She didn't get over to Houston for a visit with Daria and Bent or Clay and Francie nearly often enough.

She had to admit, her family was a good-looking one. Her father and brother both tall, with black hair and those gray eyes—and the slightly hooked Morgan nose. Thank goodness she and her sister took after their mother. They really looked alike; in fact the only things separating her and Daria were her sister's short cap of curls and three fewer inches of height.

At least both Daria and Clay had married wonderful mates. Although a non-practitioner, Bent had fit right into the family, and Gloriana thought he was perfect for her sister. His reddish hair contrasted nicely with Daria's dark chocolate, too. Francie, whose practitioner capabilities had not manifested themselves until her mating with Clay, had been a surprise for them all. Also, Clay certainly had a beautiful mate—all six feet, thick blond hair, and centerfold figure of her.

Everyone was happily eating strawberry shortcake and rehashing the evening's entertainment, but Gloriana was getting tired of the discussion. She was looking forward to heading for her own house on the other side of the farm.

"I haven't seen Cal Horner in a long time," her father said. "He's as feisty as ever. Have you heard any news about him, Antonia?"

"He's been pretty quiet, Alaric," her mother answered. "I think he's been putting his efforts into non-practitioner matters."

"Who were those two young guys, the mathematicians?" Bent asked.

"A couple of hotshots with overinflated egos," Clay muttered. "I remember Pritchart from undergrad days at MIT. His nickname was 'Prick' and he lived up to it. Looks like nothing's changed."

"Mrs. Shortbottom certainly 'pricked' him," Bent said, and everybody groaned. Daria punched her husband in the arm. Bent grinned.

"Bernice Shortbottom's been a thorn in everybody's side except the Horners for years," her mother observed. "She thinks Cal and Loretta are the saviors of us all."

"I hate to admit it in the face of family solidarity behind Glori," Clay said, "but Forscher, Prick, and the rest of the mathematicians may have something with his equation. It may truly become *the* method of casting."

Gloriana could only stare at him while she made herself swallow the strawberry in her mouth. Whose side was he on?

Daria, who had nothing in her mouth, took up the gauntlet. "What are you saying? Who was talking the other day about the 'art' of casting a computer spell? It certainly wasn't me or your wife."

"Yes, who was telling me that I had to develop 'my own' casting process, not let myself be swayed by what others do?" Francie asked, waggling her fork at him.

Gloriana smiled to herself. Clay had always been the nemesis of his two sisters. It was nice to see Francie didn't let him get away with anything, either.

"I think there's room for both views," her father said. "If I heard Forscher correctly, what was lost in the yelling was his call for experimentation and study of the equation and its uses. He recognizes the need and said so. Glori, you said, also rightly, if one good spell comes out of the formula, that's great. I'll admit, and my attitude may be where Clay is coming from, the equation appeals to the math in me. It may help streamline some of my auditing spells for a company's books."

"And my computer spells," Clay agreed.

"That's good," Gloriana said, "as long as we look at the larger picture, too. Which is what I was trying to do, if you heard *me* correctly. Don't sweep out the proven and traditional simply for the novelty of Forscher's formula. People learn differently and cast differently. How many times are we told when we're first learning to 'protect our process'? And speaking of process, how are you coming on learning magic, Francie?"

Francie grinned. "Fine. Casting a spell still puts me in a state of awe when I think about what I'm doing, but it's great fun. It looks like my talents lie with computers, too, only more on the business applications side than the operating programs. Thank goodness. I have no desire to delve into systems architecture like Clay does."

"Have the genealogists traced your lineage for practitioner blood?" Alaric asked.

"Yes, they've found one source, a multi-great-grandmother, and they're having problems going back farther than her. Moreover, her children aren't in the registry at all. It's a tangled family tree."

"They often are, dear," Antonia said.

"She lived in a time and place of intense fear of black magic, and her family and descendants may have suppressed or denied their abilities. The consensus of opinion is that, since the talents were dormant in my line for such a long time, I might never have manifested mine without the mating."

"There's still much we don't know about our abilities," Antonia said with a shake of her head. "Have the teaching masters decided on your potentially highest level yet?"

"Show them your lightball," Clay encouraged.

"Okay, here goes." Francie shut her eyes for a moment, opened them, and held out her hand. A glowing green-and-blue streaked ball of light appeared, sitting on her palm. "That's as high as I've been able to push it."

"The colors put you between levels eight and nine. That's excellent news," Alaric said.

"Speaking of news, we have some also," Daria said.

She smiled at Bent, who took her hand and kissed her fingers. "We're going to have a baby!"

"Great!" Clay exclaimed.

"That's awesome." Francie clapped.

"Stupendous." Alaric reached over to shake Bent's hand.

"Honey, that's wonderful." Antonia stood up and came around to give Daria and Bent a big hug. After she sat back down, she stared at Alaric. "Oh, my goodness! You realize that means we're going to be grandparents!"

The look on her face caused everybody to laugh—except Gloriana.

"I'm going to be an aunt," she said softly, almost to herself. The news hit her like a tree branch had fallen on her. What was wrong with her? She should be, and was, very happy for them. Why was she so stunned? Almost sad? Even panicked? She picked up her iced tea and swallowed some, partly to wet her dry throat, but mostly to hide behind the glass while she thought over her peculiar reaction.

Daria gave them the facts: due in September, no idea if a boy or girl, no names picked out yet. Gloriana managed to sit through that and the following questions with a minimum of distress. When her parents indulged themselves in some reminiscences about their children's births, however, she wanted to run screaming. At least Daria and Clay didn't look too happy about the tales, either.

Her mother finally shooed the men out of the kitchen,

saying she knew they wouldn't want to discuss pregnancy details. While the guys went off to have a celebratory brandy, the women cleared the table and talked of morning sickness and gynecological matters. Or rather the other three did; Gloriana sat in a corner and concentrated on *enduring* the discussion. She didn't want to even think about the subject, but she couldn't tell anyone about her confusing feelings—they felt somehow traitorous.

The discussion went on for a half an hour before she could reasonably say good night and escape.

Thank goodness, she thought on the drive, she had built her own house on the farm a half mile away from the big house. As much as she loved her family, she didn't feel like being good company at the moment. First the debate or Forscher—or both—unsettled her, then Daria's news. If she didn't calm herself down, she wasn't going to fall asleep easily tonight.

A little itch started under her bra right over her magic center, and she rubbed it before pushing the button to open her garage. One thing about Texas, there were always bugs.

"Hello, Delilah," she said to the black and white basenji when she came into her kitchen.

The dog answered back with her customary yodel and became very interested in sniffing her shoes and skirt.

"I know," Gloriana said, bending down to pet her, "all those smells from all those people. I'm glad you're a barkless dog. I don't think I could bear yapping after the hoopla tonight."

Delilah grunted and leaned into her hand.

"Did you have fun with Mother today? How about a run? I'm too wired to go to sleep."

When Delilah heard the word *run*, she looked Gloriana right in the eyes and grinned.

"Come on," Gloriana said and led the way to her bedroom to change.

In five minutes she was jogging down the road to the greenhouses, leash in one hand, flashlight in the other. She wished she could use *lux*, but you never knew who might drive by and see the strange light. The air was cool, probably upper fifties or lower sixties, and fresh. She could practically smell the basil growing on her left and the tarragon on her right, and she inhaled deeply.

How she loved spring here in the middle of Texas—the chartreuse of the new tree leaves, the tender shoots of the vegetables and herbs showing their heads aboveground, the bluebonnets and Indian paintbrush carpeting the fields around the farm, the adult birds bringing their chicks to the feeders for the first time, the new calves and lambs trying out their legs, the sheer promise in the soft air.

Her magical botanical talent brought her close to the earth, its seasons, its flora and fauna. Her abilities to nurture growing plants, to help them blossom and set their fruits and vegetables, to use them for healing and well-being in people and beasts alike, were an intrinsic part of her. She couldn't imagine being without them, seeing the world . . . seeing the world like Marcus Forscher must—in terms of cold, hard numbers instead of intense colors, tastes, and fragrances.

The thought of the mathematician reminded her of her larger dilemma—her reaction to Daria's news. She couldn't decide why he seemed somehow linked to the situation. What was going on in her head to cause these feelings of restlessness, of anticipation, and, at the same time, of sorrow? She'd been fine until Daria's announcement. Happy the debate was over, happy she wouldn't have to see her opponent again, and then? *Boom!* One pregnancy in the family and she had to pick herself up off the floor.

Was she jealous of Daria? That her sister had a husband and soon would have a baby?

Nah, she knew how love worked among practitioners—especially the soul-mate-phenomenon part. She'd seen it happen with both Daria and Clay, seen them find their mates as all practitioners did, with a little help from the imperative, of course. She didn't expect to be interested in a man until the right one, her soul mate, came along. In fact, after the experiences of her siblings, she'd wondered off and on when she'd meet him. According to Mother Lulabelle Higgins, who'd predicted the event for all of them, it would be soon. Who would he be?

What about her reception of the baby idea? She'd never thought much about having kids before, had taken for granted she would, naturally, but she had to find the prospective father first, and there was certainly no suitable man on the horizon. Was she yearning for a child? She'd never "yearned" before.

Maybe it was simply spring, and her hormones were rising like sap in the trees. Maybe her response was simply her biological clock's alarm buzzing. She was twenty-nine, after all.

She slowed and stopped when she reached the T in the road where it branched to different sections of the farm. Her curly tail wagging, Delilah snuffled around the fence posts and investigated a small hole, probably the home of a burrowing animal. Gloriana took a firmer grip on the leash. Basenjis were sight and scent hunters, and she didn't want the dog to flush a nocturnal creature and take off in pursuit.

She breathed deeply and looked up at the blanket of stars above her. Whatever the answers to her questions were, she wouldn't find them there. It was time she took herself to bed. "Come on, Delilah. Race you home."

CHAPTER THREE

Four weeks later

"Let's take this show on the road, whatta ya say?"

Gloriana stared at Ed Hearst sitting at the end of the table in a HeatherRidge conference room in Austin on Thursday afternoon. The W^2 editor was as rumpled as ever but also jubilant.

Then she glanced across the gleaming mahogany at the man on the other side. Convinced her expression showed her negative reaction to Ed's outrageous proposal, she wished she could read Marcus Forscher. His face was set in stern lines that betrayed none of his thoughts. It didn't help that he hadn't even looked in her direction since they sat down.

His brown eyes gleaming behind his glasses, Ed rubbed his hands together and kept talking. "Since the journal came out on the first of April, we've received piles of mail. We have pros and cons and every shade in between. The Horners are bellowing, the mathematicians are calculating, and everybody, and I do mean *everybody*, is clamoring for more. You two have really struck a nerve among members of the community." He leaned back and gazed at her and Forscher as though he'd found the spell to make the journal double in circulation.

And . . . perhaps he had.

His enthusiasm didn't mean, however, that she had to go along with his scheme.

Ed pushed a stack of printed-out e-mails and regular correspondence across the table. "Look at these. I've had invites and requests from High Council members, teaching masters, people grouped together by talents, high-levels, low-levels, you name it. They all want to take part in the debate over spell-casting methods and magic education. We can hold meetings all over the country. Under the journal's auspices, we'll offer practitioners an opportunity to hear the latest research and talk about their own ideas. Those who can't attend the meetings will be able to read the transcripts. We're even thinking of Webcasting the sessions on the main practitioner Web site."

"Ed . . ." Forscher said.

"Ed . . ." she said at the same time. She noticed out of the corner of her eye the mathematician hadn't even glanced at the letters, and she, too, ignored the papers.

"I know, I know," Ed interrupted. "Both of you are busy, the school year is still in full swing, and you have obligations and commitments. But I've figured out a way we can satisfy our audience and still allow you your academic pursuits. You both told me earlier you weren't traveling during the summer, right?"

He didn't give either a chance to answer because he forged ahead. "So, what if we arrange meetings every other Saturday in a different city? Or maybe every Saturday for six or eight weeks and get it over with? You could travel there in the morning and come back the next day. Or even that night if there's a flight. It's not like you have to prepare a new talk for every place. Simply state the sides of the debate, answer questions, and I'll keep order."

At Ed's last statement, she heard Forscher make a sound very much like a snort. She managed to hold her reaction to a sigh.

"Okay, okay," Ed continued with a touch of chagrin in his tone, and he held up his hands in mock surrender. "I'll admit I lost it at the last one. However! At these meetings, not only will we be ready and will I maintain a civil decorum, we're also going to have sergeants-at-arms. I've covered all the bases. You have to say yes."

For the first time since she arrived, Gloriana looked straight at Forscher—right into his icy-blue gaze. When their eyes met, his expression grew even grimmer, sharper, more disdainful. She fought the ridiculous urge to smile; the situation certainly didn't call for an attempt on her part to soothe his feelings, or make the discussion more "pleasant," or give any indication of female "weakness."

Instead, she simply shook her head.

He followed suit with a slow negative movement of his.

"If it's money you're worried about, travel expenses, an honorarium, the journal is picking up the tab," Ed said. "You'll be amply rewarded."

"No," Forscher said in a low voice, but he didn't take his eyes from hers.

"No," she agreed as she watched his pupils expand until only a faint rim of blue remained.

"I think you'd better take a look at these." Ed pushed a couple of papers into their line of sight.

Gloriana was the first to break eye contact with Forscher to see what Ed had. She picked up the page nearest her while her opponent took the other. She gave it a brief glance before returning her gaze to Forscher. She'd let him go first.

Forscher frowned at his letter. "The banner at the top says 'The Future of Magic,' and across the bottom are the names of Bryan Pritchart, Michael Brubaker, and others. The text reads, 'As practitioners vitally interested in developing new spells and new methods of casting, we are banding together to alert our fellow warlocks and witches of a dire situation. The danger posed by those whose mind-sets are locked in the past is great and immediate. These people will destroy the ability of all practitioners to thrive in the twenty-first century. Join *The Future of Magic* and help us fight the reactionary, regressive doomsayers who would leave us and our children unable to practice magic in the world of today and tomorrow. Help us go where no practitioner has gone before.'"

He tossed it onto the table and leaned back in his chair. "Is yours similar?" he asked.

"The letterhead calls the group the *Traditional Heritage Association*," she answered. "Down the left side is a list of names with Calvin and Loretta Horner's at the top. The body of the letter says, 'Join us in our efforts to stop those who would ruin our precious practitioner way of life and destroy our traditions. These 'futurists,' as they call themselves, want nothing more than to leave us with no art, no warmth, no emotion in our practice of magic. They would reduce casting to meaningless numbers and lifeless symbols. They see no value in historical or individual casting methods. They would cram down our throats a regimented, complicated, difficult regime that will destroy our life, liberty, and pursuit of magic.'"

"That's what's going on while we're sitting here," Ed said, waving his hand at the letters. "Both sides are gathering their troops to do battle over an issue that should be thoroughly and calmly investigated and discussed. Marcus, nobody's really studying your equation or trying out its capabilities. Pritchart's trying to act like Captain Kirk on *Star Trek*, make off with your ideas, and put himself forward as the savior of the planet."

He turned toward her. "Gloriana, Horner and his cohorts are distorting your message. Neither of these groups is interested in a middle road, a large picture, or, to use the political term, a big tent that covers all. And if Pritchart is Kirk, Horner wants to sound like Thomas Jefferson."

Ed looked back and forth between the two of them and spread out his hands. "I ask you, do you want these people to hijack your ideas and theories? Do you want these people to speak for you, to split the practitioner community into fragments? When you can do something about it, make sure both sides are heard, give voice to a rational, deliberate way of looking at magic and its practice? Because I can tell you, that's what will happen unless we step in and bring some rational discussion to these charges."

Gloriana shut her eyes and took a long, slow breath in and out. When she opened them, she was staring directly at Forscher, who returned her gaze with a stone-cold expression. She was somehow surprised that a man so gorgeous could look so forbidding and severe. Even his blazer—a light blue one that matched his eyes—looked grim. At least today he wore a button-down, dark blue shirt with no tie. But still, next to his perfection, she felt like a field hand in her smudged khakis and a moss green polo shirt.

"Ed's right," he said to her. "It looks like we have no choice. Or I don't. I won't have Prick Pritchart stealing my equation or corrupting the studies for its use." His implacable tone could have chipped ice.

"I don't, either," Gloriana agreed. "Horner and his

bunch will throw us back to the Middle Ages and will certainly alienate everyone who uses numbers and calculations
in their spells—including my own father and brother."

"We need some ground rules," Forscher stated. "Ed,
you must keep order."

"No problem there," the editor said with a big grin
on his face. "Our sergeants-at-arms will be Swords."

"Swords?" Gloriana asked. "The Swords from the
Defenders who destroy evil magic items? The guys who
can throw fireballs? Isn't that a little extreme?"

"We're going to be ready for anything," Ed answered.
"The High Council and the Defenders Council both
offered their services. The councils recognize the worth
of what we're doing here and want to take the opportunity
you two have provided to help set policy for the next
century. They could set up meetings through their
auspices, but nothing will have the impact of genuine
grassroots debates and decisions. Since the Swords can
cast offensive spells that stop a man in his tracks, we'll
have order."

Gloriana looked from one man to the other. Ed was
eager, and Forscher was resigned. She and her opponent
were on the same side for a change. "Okay, count me
in, too."

"Good," Ed said. "Neither of you will regret it."

"I hope not," she and Forscher said at the same time.

CHAPTER
FOUR

About two hours later, Marcus pulled his silver BMW into his garage. His home in the hills west of the city had never looked so good. He was worn out from dealing with Ed and . . . that Morgan woman.

In the past four weeks, he'd put her completely out of his mind—if you didn't count some extremely arousing dreams. He knew he couldn't be responsible for his subconscious; he hadn't, after all, been on even a simple date for a while. He'd been too busy in California, and being back in Austin had been a nonstop marathon of holding classes, working with his grad students on their dissertations, and writing his latest books and articles.

He'd barely gotten back to normal before Ed and his traveling circus returned and wanted him to run away with them.

He entered the house to Samson's chortling greeting, a definite request from the red and white basenji to be let out of his crate, the sturdy wire-framed inside doghouse. He knew Samson didn't like being cooped up, but that was better than having him loose to get into things like closets, boxes, and cabinets. Marcus had learned his lesson early of how disruptive and messy a curious puppy could be.

He looked around the room before opening the door. Everything was in its place, neat, clean, uncluttered, exactly the way he liked it. One woman had called the white walls, light oak floors, and gray, beige, black, and white furnishings "austere," but it suited him. So did his collection of art photographs. When she brought him a plant with long thin green and white leaves, claiming it made the space "more cheerful," he'd put it out on his deck and forgotten about it after they stopped dating. He found it dead the following spring. Oh, well, if he wanted color, he had Samson for that. He opened the crate's door.

With a frown at his master to remind him of his displeasure, the red and white dog came out and stretched, graceful and almost catlike in his movements.

Marcus knelt down and held out his hand to rub Samson's wrinkled forehead. The dog, however, smelled his hand first and even licked it, making a grunting noise as he did so.

"What's gotten into you?" Marcus asked when he was finally allowed to pet the animal. What had Samson smelled? He hadn't eaten after lunch, and he'd washed his hands since then. He'd left the HeatherRidge and come straight home . . . but he'd shaken hands with Hearst and Morgan . . . Did the dog smell *her*?

He himself certainly had, that same mix of floral and spice she'd worn before. Despite the distance, her scent had pulled at him from across the table, like a flower attracting insects. Hell, if he were a bee, he'd be diving into . . .

Stop! A bee? A flower? What was the matter with him?

He hated to admit it. The woman affected him, aroused him, tightened his muscles to the point that he could barely move. He wanted to tangle his fingers in her dark curly hair, run his hands over her skin to see if it was as soft as he imagined, kiss those . . .

Samson bumped his hand, and Marcus came back to reality. Fat chance for all that.

From what he could tell, he did not have an attractive effect on her. She barely glanced at him, didn't smile, and looked as unhappy as he felt over their situation. Her lack of response was probably all to the good—it made it easier to resist her, to control himself. She—any woman—was the last thing he needed.

Here they were, however, trapped on an odyssey with Ed Hearst. He should look on the bright side. Maybe the controversy would run out of steam once Prick and the Horners had a couple of chances to fight for the spotlight. Then he could come home and get back to work on what counted.

Yeah, right. The arguments would probably go on forever. He'd be entangled the entire summer.

He gave Samson another pat before rising. To make sure Morgan wouldn't distract him or his dog again, he washed his hands at the kitchen sink and was drying them when the phone rang.

"Hello, Marcus," his mother said when he flipped open his cell phone and answered.

"Hello, Judith, how are you and Stefan?" he asked. As the words came out of his mouth, he suddenly remembered Gloriana Morgan calling her parents "Mother" and "Daddy" when they'd been talking outside the ballroom—names he had never used with his own parents. At their specific request, they had been "Judith" and "Stefan" as long as he could remember.

"Stefan and I are fine, thank you. He's off at a physics department meeting. I have an appointment with a possible new assistant professor here in economics in a little while, but have some free time. Are you busy?"

"No, I'm free at the moment," he said. He could picture her at her precisely organized desk in her office at the university in Massachusetts where both his parents were on the faculty. She'd be sitting upright—"No slouching, Marcus, it's so common," was her mantra—and look more like a business executive than a professor in her crisp suit with her hair neatly coiffed and her fingernails polished a muted pink. He looked down at himself and could almost hear her telling him to put on a tie and look more professional.

"I read the articles in W^2 about your formula and the reception it received down there in Austin. At the Boston HeatherRidge last Saturday, that's all they were talking about."

"Oh, really? What are they saying?" Good, some reports from the outlying regions instead of Ed's correspondents. Although not totally unbiased, his mother was an astute observer.

"Practitioners who are more, shall I say, 'mathematically or numerically inclined' are trying your equation in their casting. They say they need more precise instructions and calibrations, but believe it shows promise. Those who are not 'talented' in that manner don't want to try it or associate with those who favor it. I must admit, some of the former have been rather impolite, even indelicate, in their statements about the latter. A few of those against it have responded in kind, I'm afraid."

"Have the discussions gotten out of hand?" he asked, remembering how quickly the arguments had escalated at the so-called debate.

"No, everyone has been exquisitely civil in public. Of course, rumors are flying privately about who is no longer speaking with whom because of their discussions."

"Has anyone spoken one way or the other directly to you or Stefan?"

"Only those who favor the equation. They've praised you for the excellent work, as is certainly your due."

"Thank you, Judith." He knew her statement was the highest accolade she'd give him. He'd never discussed the equation or its development in depth with either of them, although he knew they'd read his articles. Stefan had said only, "Good job," his most effusive praise. Marcus could count on his fingers the times his father had said those words to him.

"But that's not the reason I called," she said. "Not the primary reason. I'm afraid we're going to have to cancel or postpone our usual Fourth of July gathering on Cape Cod this summer."

"Oh?" he said, while a feeling very close to relief flowed through him.

"Yes, the conference I usually attend in Helsinki has been moved to the end of June. Stefan wants to visit with some of his German colleagues, and we thought we'd see them during the first week in July."

"I'm sorry we can't make the Cape in July," Marcus said, infusing his tone with as much sorrow as he could. Which wasn't much, given the fact that the four or five days they spent together annually had grown more and more difficult for him over the years. They had almost nothing in common. It had reached the point where, outside of academic subjects and current events, they had little to talk about. He'd begged off visiting over the Christmas and New Year holidays for the last three years; they hadn't pushed him to reconsider.

"Would you like to meet us in, say, Berlin, instead?

I'm sure Stefan's colleagues could make some appointments with mathematicians for you."

He blinked at the tone in her voice. She sounded almost . . . wistful. He must be hearing things. His mother was never wistful. He pulled his thoughts back to his situation and said, "As it turns out, I'm not certain what my own schedule will be. The editor of W^2 wants to take the debate across the country, hold meetings in a number of cities so everyone can participate. Dr. Morgan and I would be the main speakers."

"Will that keep you from your regular research and writing? It's important you produce another article or two. Aren't you working on a book also? A real book, not that science fiction—"

"We'll only travel on the weekends, and I'm making good progress on my mathematical theory book and my fiction," he said quickly. He didn't want to discuss his other calling—his "hobby," as his parents called it. "I've already polished and submitted the articles I wrote in California."

"Good. You may have made full professor at an even earlier age than either myself or Stefan, but you can't rest on your laurels. You may want to leave the University of Texas someday and come back East. The more established you are in your field, the more attractive you'll be."

"Yes, Judith," Marcus said, indulging himself by rolling his eyes. Neither she nor Stefan would be thoroughly approving until he was on the faculty of Harvard or MIT. They never understood how he could be happy in Texas, of all places.

"Let me know your schedule when you have it, and I'll send you ours. We might go to the Cape after we return. If you have a few days, you could still join us." He heard some commotion on her end, then her voice continued, "Oh, it looks like my appointment is here."

"I'll see what the calendar permits. Give my best to Stefan."

"I will. Good-bye, Marcus." She hung up before he could even answer.

He closed the phone and looked at the dog. "No Cape Cod," he said.

Samson yawned, walked to the door, and looked pointedly back at him.

"Okay, let me change and we'll go for a walk." He had to laugh as he climbed the stairs to his bedroom. Sometimes he wondered who had trained whom in this household.

On the walk, Marcus paid no attention to the houses or the view from the hills overlooking the Colorado River while Samson pulled on the leash until an intriguing smell distracted him. Instead Marcus thought about his mother's phone call.

What was that old saying about dark clouds and silver linings? At least he didn't have to spend time on Cape Cod with his parents, hearing their opinions about his career, his place of employment, or his other, non-sanctioned activities. His alter ego Frederik Russell was doing fine, thank you, with six novels published to critical acclaim and good sales.

He also, however, did not want to spend time running around the country with Ed and his touring zoo. They hadn't determined even a tentative schedule for the meetings, although they had come up with a list of possible cities. Ed was going to check availability of the ballrooms in the HeatherRidges and propose a plan.

Bad idea. If he let Ed set the agenda, he'd lose control of the situation. Ed wouldn't stop at six weeks and six cities—not when they had identified twelve in their preliminary list. Not if the debates became hotter, and more people got involved. Swords notwithstanding, there would be more and greater fireworks with Prick and the Horners egging each other on. Of course, the excitement would create more demand. Result? Ed would run Morgan and him all over the country all summer. Perhaps even into the fall.

To accomplish his work, he needed calm and structure in his day-to-day activities. The fewer interruptions the better. He had been looking forward to long summer days of reading, thinking, and writing.

If the present was an indication, he'd have no peace. He'd already received a number of e-mails about his formula and that ridiculous debate. He'd refused to be drawn into arguments and had developed a standard answer referring the letter-senders to W^2. Once they started traveling, however, he could only expect the number of messages and demands on his time to double or triple. Hell, if he had time left for walking the dog, it would be a miracle.

Control. That's what he needed. Control of his own schedule, his own life. He'd dance to no one's tune.

Samson went still for a moment and stared at something next to a curve in the road. Marcus gripped the leash tighter. When the hound assumed that posture, he'd usually spotted an animal to chase. Sure enough, a cat emerged from behind a gatepost and started to cross the street.

The dog lunged against the chain. Marcus braced himself, held on with two hands, and said, "No, Samson!" At the sound of his voice, the cat took off running for the house across the road.

"Damn it, Samson! No! You are not hunting the neighbor's cat." Marcus hauled on the leash and used it to pull himself close to the hound, who was still trying to follow his supposed prey. For a relatively small dog, a basenji packed a lot of power, and Marcus held on tightly until the cat had disappeared.

"Come on, boy, let's go back." He tugged on the leash. Samson looked after the cat once more, back up at him, and gave an audible sigh, but he followed readily enough. In a few strides, he was out in front again.

"Control," Marcus said. Samson only flicked an ear

back and forth at the word.

Marcus shook his head. Samson was usually obedient, except when he spotted live, furry prey. Then his instincts and genes took over, and discipline was left by the wayside.

"Control," Marcus said again, returning to his thoughts before the cat incident. He needed to gain dominance, leadership of the situation, and reduce the tour to a minimum number of cities. Facing Ed by himself, however, might not give him the desired result. Ed was a manipulator par excellence. Look at how he'd played them today with those last two letters. He wouldn't give in easily.

Besides, the discussion was significant to the whole practitioner community and to the future of magic. Marcus couldn't back out entirely, and he certainly didn't want to be considered an obstructionist. Truth be told, he was proud of his equation and to be making a meaningful contribution to spell-casting. How could he arrange matters for his good but still see that his formula received the fair hearing and subsequent research it deserved?

What if he and Morgan approached Ed with a united front? After all, they were in the same boat. Both had obligations and plans important to their careers. She didn't want to traipse all over the country, either. If the two of them stood up to Ed with an agreed-upon plan, they should be able to push it through.

Yes, that idea offered distinct possibilities—and a chance of success. Smiling, he picked up the pace homeward. He had to arrange a meeting with Morgan. No matter his attraction to the woman and her lack of the same for him. He could control his body and his mind. He'd worry about his subconscious later. The little itch over his magic center returned, and he ignored it again. First he had to find the folder Ed had given them with the contact information.

❀✲✳✵❦

Although he called Morgan's office and left messages Thursday night and off and on the next day, Marcus wasn't able to get her on the phone. On Friday afternoon he called Ed to see if the editor had her personal numbers since she wasn't listed in the phone book. Ed supplied several numbers—a cell phone, a number in Austin for her condo, and another number for her farm phone.

Farm phone? Where did the woman live?

"Idiot, you should have done this earlier," he muttered to himself as he sat down at his computer and signed on to the private practitioner Web site. A banner headline on the home page told him to click on the button for the latest in the discussion over spell-casting. Not what he needed to read. He went straight to the registry.

There she was: Gloriana Violet Morgan, twelfth level, associate professor, botanist, biological scientist, with all her degrees and achievements. A color photo showed off her curly dark-chocolate hair and emerald green eyes. He stared at the picture for a few seconds, then read her impressive curriculum vitae.

"You might be a level greater than I am," he couldn't help saying to the picture, "but I made professor first." The knowledge brought him scant pleasure. He clicked on the contact-information button. The displayed data included the Austin condo address and phone number and the same for the Morgan Plant and Herb Farm. She must spend part of the week in the city and the rest on the farm. Probably did some research there also.

He clicked on the link for the farm. The home page introduction told him he was viewing the practitioner version; for customers with non-practitioner needs, he could click on another link. He perused the magic information. The Morgans grew certain plants to meet the exacting needs of their clients—for potions, salves, and certain spell requirements. They also offered a line of herbs, both fresh and dried, for chefs. He looked at the prices. They seemed steep to him, but what did he know about making potions? Or cooking, for that matter?

He looked at his watch. Six o'clock. Maybe he could catch her before dinner. He flipped open his phone and punched the numbers for her cell.

"Hello?" she answered, with a lot of noise in the background.

"This is Marcus Forscher," he said.

"Who? Oh, wait a minute." The noise got louder and sounded like the evening news, then faded. "Sorry about that. I had to turn the TV down. Who is this?"

"Marcus Forscher," he repeated.

"Oh. Yes. What can I do for you?" Her voice went flat with the question. She didn't seem pleased that he was her caller.

"I've been thinking about our situation with regard to Ed's plans," he stated. "From your expression yesterday, I gather you aren't looking forward to the crazy circus either."

He heard her sigh. "No, I'm not. I have research plans for the summer, and I'm sure you have the same. But I don't see how we can call off the debates. The subject matter is too important."

"I agree. However, I'd like to minimize the impact on us and exert some control over the process."

"How can we do that?"

"Let's meet tomorrow, come up with our own schedule, and present Ed with a fait accompli."

"We can certainly try. Where do you want to meet? I'm out at the farm and wasn't planning on coming back to Austin until Monday morning."

She didn't sound too happy about his suggestion—or it could simply be the idea of coming back to town. He could be accommodating—especially if it would influence her decision his way. "That's okay," he said, "I could come there."

"Here?" Her voice went up as though she didn't believe he'd come.

He heard another voice asking, "Who is that, Glori?"

"Hold on," she said. She must have put her hand over the phone, but he could still hear what they were saying.

"It's Marcus Forscher, Mother. He wants to come out here tomorrow to talk about Ed's plans."

"That's a good idea. Ask him to lunch."

"*What?*"

"You heard me, ask the man to lunch."

After several seconds of silence, Morgan came back on the phone. "Look, why don't you get here about eleven. We can talk and have lunch with my parents. They will want to hear our plans and might have some good recommendations." She sounded more resigned than pleased to be making the invitation.

"Thank you. I'll look forward to seeing your parents again." He was going to ask for directions when Samson's whining and glances from him to the door and back took his thoughts in another direction. Oh, what the hell, he might as well ask. "By the way, would it be all right if I brought my dog? He could use the fresh air."

"Fine. Do you have a pencil? Here's the directions." She gave him explicit instructions and timing. "Oh, and one more thing? We dress very casually here."

"I'll see you tomorrow. Good-bye," he said and hung up. Her last comment struck him as curious. Sure, his parents had taught him how to dress. "Looking like an ivory tower bum is not the way to instill confidence in business donors," his father had said. His mother made sure he understood fine tailoring. What did Morgan think he wore on the weekend in the country? A suit and tie?

※✦✶✦※

Gloriana hung up the phone and couldn't help wiggling when a shiver ran up and down her back. She looked down at her arms. Goose bumps. She rubbed them vigorously.

What was it with her reaction to that man? Hearing his low, deep voice had been the last thing she expected when she answered the phone. She could still feel his words reverberating in her skull. They seemed to set off little zings of energy right in her magic center. She switched from rubbing her arms to rubbing her breastbone; it helped only marginally.

So, he wanted them to make their plans for the debate. Certainly a united front was a good idea. Ed would steamroller them if he could.

What would it be like to have Forscher visit the farm? Mr. Perfect on her turf? Staring at her with those icy blue eyes, studying her like she was a mathematical problem he was trying to solve.

She'd have to watch herself and not play those female games she despised—where the woman tried to jolly the guy out of his grim demeanor, tried to coax a smile, as if having a pleasant face would change the attitude behind it. Not that she did that normally, of course. No, he was going to have to take her as she was. If they were going to debate, they'd do it as equals.

Even though, except for his "cauldron-stirring, potion-making" crack, she had no complaints about his treatment of her, she'd still be on guard. The man was an academic in a predominantly male field, and she'd met plenty of others in that situation who clearly thought they were beings of a higher order. He might revert to type if she let him get away with it.

What kind of dog would he have? A man who obviously prized control would have an exceedingly well-trained animal, probably a German shepherd or maybe a Lab. What about a Border collie—no, too exuberant, too happy a personality. She looked over at Delilah lounging on the floor by the door. Certainly not a basenji with their unpredictability, mischievousness, and definitely minds of their own.

It would be interesting to have him here, she decided. See what lurked under his shell. Maybe she could get beneath that hard surface, loosen him up, see if he was all grim and unrelentingly hard or not so bad once he relaxed. See if she could melt the look in his eyes.

Although . . . why on earth would she want to do that? They didn't have to be friends to work together. She wasn't attracted to him, was she? How could she be?

A handsome man with practically golden hair and striking blue eyes was a fine thing to contemplate, even fantasize about, if she was in the mood. She'd never been one to squeal about movie stars; visual perfection gave no clue to the real person. She was more interested in a man's views, his ideas, his aspirations, his down-to-earth common sense, and her attitude was evident in her choice of male friends and colleagues.

She hardly knew Marcus Forscher, and what she had seen and heard and read from him had not been conducive to wanting to know him better. They were never going to agree about the art and emotion of casting. She might be willing to agree to disagree, but he appeared to be incapable of seeing any value in her side.

No, she wasn't attracted to him.

"Earth to Glori," her mother said. "You've been standing there staring out the window for five minutes. Is he coming?"

"Oh. Yes, he's coming."

"Are you all right? You look a little confused."

"I'm fine." She rubbed her chest again. It had started itching when her mother spoke.

"Did a bug bite you? Do you need some ointment?"

"No, Mother, no bug. My clothes are chafing some. I'll go call Daddy for dinner."

"Yes, do that," her mother said, stirring the pot of spaghetti sauce.

Gloriana wondered a moment at the speculative

glance her mother gave her, but turned her attention to where her father might be. The itch had gone away.

CHAPTER FIVE

Saturday morning precisely at eleven, Marcus pulled up in front of the ranch-style, sandy-colored brick house. He'd followed Morgan's directions carefully, driving past the customers' entry gate to the farm and coming in at the smaller road marked "private." He parked in the graveled area next to the road, climbed out of the car, stretched, and looked around.

Fields of growing plants spread to all sides, while her front yard held a lush, dark green lawn, four large live oaks, a couple of bird feeders, and mulched beds bursting with multihued flowers. Two wooden picnic tables with benches and several lawn chairs sat in the shade of the trees. He could smell new-mown grass and some sort of floral fragrance—he didn't have a clue what it was. Or what the flowers were, either, but they were pretty and cheerful.

Samson whined from the backseat of the BMW sedan. "Okay, boy, let's get you out of there." Marcus unhitched the leash from the seat belt slot and removed the harness. "I know you don't like the contraption," he said while Samson jumped from the car and shook himself. "If we have a wreck, you won't like flying through the window, either. Remember, behave yourself, or it's back on the leash."

Samson trotted beside him up to the front doorway, which held screen and wooden doors, both shut. Marcus rang the doorbell.

The curtain behind the glass fluttered and he caught a glimpse of dark curly hair. Morgan opened the door and looked at him through the screen mesh.

Every thought in his head flew away when their gazes met—and locked. He knew his mouth was open and words of greeting were forming in his throat, but he had to concentrate on breathing as his whole body came to attention.

She didn't move, either.

A sharp "Yip!" pulled his gaze downward. The screen door opened, propelled by a dog, a black and white basenji, of all things. The dog darted out and headed straight for Samson, who yodeled a greeting. The two animals circled each other, sniffing and nuzzling. They looked back at the humans, next at each other, and started trotting, then running down the walk and out onto the road.

"Samson!" he bellowed as he took two steps after them.

"Delilah!" Morgan yelled as she came outside.

The hounds stopped at the edge of the nearest field, grinned over their shoulders, and headed for the horizon like they were chasing antelopes on the plains.

"Samson!"

"Delilah!" She put two fingers in her mouth and let loose a whistle that almost took the top of his head off. "You come back here!"

The dogs kept running.

"Oh, for heaven's sake." Morgan stood there with her fists on her hips watching until the hounds vanished behind the plantings. Turning to Marcus, she said in an exasperated voice, "I wish you'd mentioned what kind of dog you have. Delilah is fine around more placid dogs. When she's with one who likes to run, well . . . you saw the result."

"Delilah? Your dog's name is Delilah?" She hadn't even told him she had a dog, but he wasn't going to press the issue. What good would it do?

"Yes. And yours is Samson?" She shook her head. "Oh, that is too cute for words."

"Will they be all right? Samson has seldom been loose to run like that—not in an unconfined space." He gazed down the road. No hounds came into view.

"Don't worry. Delilah's out all the time. I'm sure she'll bring him back safe and sound," Morgan said with a slight smirk.

"I hope so," Marcus heard himself say, but his

attention was suddenly on her, not Samson, as she stood in the sun and her green eyes took on a deeper, darker hue. She had said they dressed casually, and she certainly had. He couldn't stop his gaze from running from her somewhat battered running shoes, up her old faded jeans, and to her scooped-neck light-blue T-shirt with a blue-and-white-striped cotton shirt on top. The jeans showed off her great curves and the scoop revealed creamy skin leading toward . . .

He jerked his scrutiny back to her face. *Control*, he ordered mentally and concentrated on maintaining a blank expression.

Morgan had a strange look on her own face for a second. Then she opened the screen door. "Let me pick up a couple of files, and we can go over to my parents' house. We can thrash it out together, and they might have some good ideas, too."

He followed her into the house.

She said, "I'll be right back," and vanished around a corner.

Passing a formal dining room on his right, he walked through a wide foyer into a large living room. From where he stood, he could see, also on the right, into the kitchen over a high counter bar with stools on the side. A round dinette table and chairs sat in a bay window on the back kitchen wall. The living room held a long, deep red couch and two blue upholstered easy chairs, arranged in a seating area facing the fireplace. An impressionistic-style landscape of flowers hung over the mantel, its vibrant colors seeming to glow, even in the muted daylight that came through the sliding doors on either side of the hearth. An entertainment center took up the wall opposite the kitchen.

The whole room looked "comfortable," somehow welcoming . . . or it would have if it hadn't been so messy.

Magazines and books rose haphazardly in two stacks by one of the chairs, an afghan throw and pillows sprawled on the couch, and framed photos almost spilled off the mantel. He could see newspapers, stacks of student papers, and some mail on the kitchen table. A scattering of miscellaneous objects, including a wide-brimmed straw hat and a pair of much-used gardening gloves, decorated the bar counter. Under the long, thin table behind the sofa lay a tennis ball, a chew bone, and a rubber duck, evidence of Delilah's residence. He wondered how Morgan could live with all the clutter—especially how she could find anything.

He was surprised that she didn't have more plants than a couple of small spidery ones in pots on the bar and a tall pine sort of tree in the corner by the sliding glass doors that led to a deck. But, she worked with plants all the time; what did she need with more?

Morgan came around a corner from the hall to his left with some file folders in one hand and her purse in the other. "I'm ready. Why don't we take your car? Go on out the door. I need to set the alarm."

He went out the front door and watched while she closed it, opened a panel in the wall, and punched some buttons. "Why all the precautions? I thought people in the country never locked their doors."

"Crime is reaching into the country these days," she replied, shutting the panel. "With customers wandering off the beaten path, we've found it better to be safe. My brother, Clay—you met him at the debate—is a computer genius, and we all have the most up-to-date security you can imagine. We have the usual protective house spells, too, but they can't call the sheriff or alert us if there's trouble at one house and we're all at the other."

He opened the passenger-side door for her, and she sat and swung her legs in. As he came around to the driver's side, he scanned the horizon again. "No dogs," he said, sitting down and putting his seat belt on.

"They'll truly be fine. I promise. Look at it this way," she said with a smile. "If a tired basenji is a happy basenji, then both of them will collapse at our feet and sleep when they come back. You won't have to walk him at all tonight."

"That's one benefit, I suppose," he said and started the car. A saxophone wailed a jazz melody out of the speakers, and he turned the radio off. "How long will they be gone?"

"Go left and follow the road, and right at the T. You'll see the house in the distance. I'm sure the dogs will be back in an hour or so. That's Delilah's usual running time." She glanced into the back when something jingled. "A harness? For Samson?"

"Yeah, it keeps him more or less in one place. Sort of like a child's safety seat."

"What's the covering on the seat? I like the idea."

"It's a fitted custom cover. It was either that or try to rig towels, and those never work. It gives him a soft bed and keeps the leather safe."

While they talked about other pet paraphernalia and he drove, Gloriana took the opportunity to surreptitiously study her guest. What was it that caused her totally inappropriate reactions to him? Every nerve ending in her body had fired when she opened the door and gazed into his eyes. Instead of icy, the look he'd given her had been definitely . . . hot. No, scorching, and she'd felt it all the way to her toes. It was a miracle she'd managed to stop herself from jumping a foot straight into the air.

Then, after the dogs escaped, he'd almost caught her ogling him. She'd retreated into the house and used the time gathering her files to calm down. Surely she could control herself better. Another peek wouldn't hurt.

"We dress casually," she'd told him. What had she had expected him to wear? Probably pressed khakis and a starched button-down oxford cloth shirt. Instead, what did she have sitting next to her?

A blond hunk with a rangy build and broad shoulders that didn't need padding, dressed in a dark blue

T-shirt, well-fitting jeans with a belt buckle embellished by the math symbol for pi, and running shoes—all of which were in pristine condition. Inhaling a scent of man and faint aftershave and watching his long fingers caress the steering wheel as he turned the car, she had the sudden urge to run . . . her hands over his toned body.

Calm? Where did she get the idea she was unperturbed? She pulled her gaze to the passing fields and gripped her purse and files tighter. She'd been composed at the meeting with Ed, but Forscher had been across the table a couple of feet away, not merely a few inches. Unfortunately, there was no one, not even a dog, to divert her thoughts or reactions here. She looked out the windshield. The house was coming into view. Thank goodness, she'd have her parents for buffers.

"That's some house," Forscher said as he pulled up in front and leaned forward to peer through the windshield.

"What? Oh, yes, it is. Only the front half is the original Victorian structure. It was called 'The Bays' because of all its bay windows. My parents bought the property before we kids were born. The house was in deplorable shape, so they didn't try to restore it to a former historic grandeur, only make it livable. Besides, Mother had certain cooking requirements in the kitchen."

She climbed out of the car and looked up at the tall two-story, white frame building, trying to imagine how he was seeing it for the first time. The wide porch, the hanging pots of red, white, and blue petunias, the huge old oaks surrounding the structure, all seemed to welcome visitors. She loved the place, but she was also happy to have her home—and her adult privacy.

"Interesting effect with the tower on the corner," he said, joining her at the bottom of the front steps after he grabbed a briefcase from the backseat. "Especially with the witch's hat roof."

"The room under the hat on the second floor became the playroom, later the study hall and rec room for us kids after my parents built their new master bedroom on the back. It's a great place to sit and read. Very atmospheric when a storm's coming in."

He paused at the top of the porch stairs and looked out over the fields again. "Still no dogs."

"It's all right, really," she said in as reassuring a tone as she could muster. She knew he was worried—she certainly would be in his circumstances. "I know all the places Delilah goes, and they won't get in trouble. Besides, we have staff working the store and its area. They'll keep an eye on the dogs if they run over there."

"Well . . ."

"Come on, let's give them an hour of freedom, and then we'll go looking." She preceded him through the double doors and into the wide hall where the smell of a baking apple pie permeated the air.

"Mother, we're here," she called while she walked down the foyer past the stairs and into the kitchen.

"Hello, dear," her mother said, lifting the pie from

the oven. She put it on a trivet on the counter, closed the oven door, stripped off her padded mitts, and came over to hold out her hand to their visitor. "Welcome to our home, Dr. Forscher."

"Thank you. It's a pleasure to see you again. And please call me Marcus," he said, smiling as he shook her hand.

Only vaguely did Gloriana hear her mother say to call her Antonia. All her attention concentrated suddenly on their guest. She'd never seen him smile at anyone—if you didn't count that smirk he directed at her during the debate. Forscher's smile, even aimed at another, changed the man almost by magic from forbidding and stern to warm and thoroughly approachable.

How fascinating. How appealing. How . . . She refused to finish that thought.

"Hello," her father said as he came into the kitchen. She watched Forscher and her father go through the greeting ritual and agree to call each other by their first names. Again the smile and the charm.

But when he faced her, his face settled into that intent, almost "hunting" look she'd seen on Delilah when the dog had picked up a prey's scent. How did he make such an abrupt transformation? Why? Was the man a chameleon? Had he cast a spell on her?

That thought jarred her out of her trance to find everyone else looking at her.

"Shall we go into the study?" her mother asked in the tone of voice she used when her children had not been paying attention.

Gloriana followed her mother and the men across the entry hall into the large book-lined room that was the family meeting place. Her father ushered them to the table in the large rectangular bay, and she hurried to the window side. That way she would have over four feet of smooth oak between herself and the mathematician. If distance helped her keep calm around him, she'd maintain the separation.

"When Glori told us the purpose of your visit," her father said, "I gathered some information on the cities on Hearst's list." He waved at the maps, printouts, HeatherRidge brochure, and calendar in the middle of the table.

"Thank you, Alaric," Forscher said, opening his briefcase and taking out some files and his personal data assistant. He shuffled papers as he spoke. "I have some ideas for discussion. From our reactions to Ed's plan and our brief conversation yesterday, I think we can agree that we need to gain some control over the circus, or we'll never get our work done. Is that correct?"

He raised his eyes to hers at his question. She was ready for him this time, and she maintained her equanimity. Although . . . her magic center gave a little flutter, almost of anticipation, and she had the distinct impression the ice in his gaze was melting.

She put those extraneous thoughts aside to answer carefully, "Yes, I believe the questions we've raised are important and worth discussion across the practitioner community. Nobody, however, needs *us* to lead the inquiry. Although I have no objection to helping launch the subject, I refuse to become anyone's poster child."

"You may already be one," Alaric interjected. "You, too, Marcus."

"What?" she and Forscher said together.

"I was online a little while ago and checked to see if the THA or the FOM had Web sites up. Sure enough, they do. Each has a picture of the three of you from the debate. The THA has an individual one of you, Glori, with quotes from some of your articles to bolster their arguments. The FOM has the same for you, Marcus."

"Is that legal?" Gloriana asked. "Implying we agree with them? Using us to further their cause?"

"I doubt it matters, one way or the other," Forscher said with a grimace. "We certainly can't take them to court and make the discussion public to the non-practitioner world. I doubt the High Council could help, either. The damage has been done. We must make our position clear through the debates however, assuming Ed and the Swords can keep order."

"Ed should let us put an article or two in the journal," she added. "But first, we need to decide the cities we'll visit and the dates. The sooner we get it all over with, the better."

"Yes, twelve is out of the question. You'll be traveling from the end of the semester straight into the next school year," Antonia agreed. "So, how many?"

"No more than six," Forscher said.

"Let's say five and keep the sixth for a fallback," Gloriana said. "Ed's the type who will say one or two more than we do because he likes to negotiate everything."

"You're right," Forscher replied, "and let's spread it across the whole country. How about Boston?"

They discussed the merits of each city on the list with the help of her parents, who had been to and knew practitioners in all of them. They finally decided on five cities: Boston, Atlanta, Chicago, Denver, San Francisco, with Washington, D.C., for a negotiating giveaway. The tour would start the second Saturday in June and go straight through the month and into July with no breaks. Luckily the Fourth of July fell in the middle of the week, and they wouldn't have to skip a weekend. The actual order of travel would depend on the availability of the halls.

Forscher consulted his calendar on the PDA and nodded his head. "Yes, that schedule should accomplish our purposes and Ed's. I'd like to get it pinned down quickly, before he makes HeatherRidge reservations he can't cancel."

"Then let's call him," Gloriana said. "I have all his numbers." She flipped open a file.

Her father fetched the phone from his corner desk and set it to speaker mode. Gloriana dialed.

"Ed Hearst," the editor said when he answered.

"Hi, Ed, this is Gloriana Morgan. I'm sorry to bother

you on a Saturday. I have Marcus Forscher with me, and we'd like to make a proposition about the debate plans."

"Okay, I was planning on calling the HeatherRidges on Monday, so let's hear it."

"We suggest visiting five cities," Forscher said before Gloriana could continue. She didn't care particularly for his assuming control of their presentation, but she kept her mouth shut. She wasn't about to give Ed the idea they weren't together in their thinking.

Forscher read off the list of cities and the proposed timetable. "The tour must be over by the middle of July. Later than that interferes substantially with our individual plans and is completely unacceptable, not to mention possibly detrimental to our careers."

"Only five cities?" Ed asked, and she thought she could hear a twinge of exasperation in his voice.

"That's correct," Forscher said. "Such a schedule will allow you and the councils to assess if the project is worth continuing. Our participation should not be necessary after those meetings." He looked at Gloriana and raised his eyebrows. "Do you have anything to add?"

"No, I think you've covered the salient points." She leaned back in the chair and crossed her arms. She suppressed a smile; Forscher could certainly sound stuffy in his polysyllabic way. On the other hand, he also sounded like he wouldn't give an inch.

"Five cities is simply not enough," Ed countered. "The demand is too great and the subject too broad for only a few meetings to satisfy it."

"That may be," Gloriana jumped in before Forscher could. "But we will have done our part by drawing everyone's attention to the discussion. Ed, magic education is a huge topic, and our future methodologies won't be settled in five or fifteen or fifty meetings. Every single practitioner should take part. We have no interest in being the spokespeople for either extreme, and neither of us likes being caught in the middle."

"That's why we need you," Ed said, "because you're not on the extremes. Besides, you're both articulate speakers and you think fast on your feet. At the moment, you're the only ones who can keep the discussion focused. Marcus, you want people to experiment with your formula and to offer more precise casting methods, even for low-level spells. Gloriana, you want to keep magic practice individualistic and open to the myriad of abilities across the practitioner spectrum. Isn't that so?"

"Damn, he's good," she muttered to herself and smiled in admiration of Ed's negotiating abilities to go right to what they most cared about. She, however, wasn't going to give in to him.

When she looked across the table, the mathematician had a distracted expression on his face. He blinked and focused when she raised five fingers in front of him and mouthed the words, "Five only." He nodded and held up his five fingers.

"That may be so," he said to the phone, "but we still

have obligations to fulfill to the university and others. We will be happy to submit another article or two for the journal. That, however, will be the extent of our contribution. Five cities, Ed, no more."

"I can't talk you into six?" the editor wheedled. "It's only one more."

"No," she and Forscher answered simultaneously.

"I'll need at least two articles, one to run before we start, and the other when we're done. They should be joint articles, too."

"Let's leave the issue of a single joint article or concurrent ones up to us," Gloriana said. The thought of actually sitting down and writing an article with the man, spending so much time in close proximity, made shivers run up her spine. They were cooperating at the moment because they had the same overall purpose—limit the mess. While trying to write the thing, all they would do was argue, she was certain. More time wasted in the process.

She didn't explain her reasoning, but it appeared she didn't have to because Forscher nodded and said, "We'll take care of it."

"All right," Ed grumbled and was silent for a moment. When he spoke again, his enthusiasm had returned. "This setup can work. I'll e-mail you with the article deadlines and the dates for the five cities as soon as I have them on Monday. These debates will be good for all of us, especially the general practitioner community, you'll see."

She and Forscher said good-bye to Ed, and she punched the button to hang up.

"That's that," Forscher said, putting up his PDA with finality. "I think we have what we asked for."

"And it's time for lunch. Marcus, there's a powder room across the hall if you'd like to wash up. Oh, Glori," Antonia said as she rose and pointed toward the door, "you didn't tell me we had another guest."

Everyone looked in the direction of her finger. Two grinning basenjis sat on their haunches and yodeled in greeting.

CHAPTER
SIX

While he washed his hands before lunch, Marcus used the time to calm himself. He'd been so relieved to see Samson again, he'd almost grabbed the hound and given him a big hug.

Not that he'd had the chance, however. Samson had immediately fawned all over Morgan, even flopping over and presenting his belly for scratching, something he seldom did, even for his master.

Of course, Delilah had checked him out—in a thoroughly ladylike manner. She'd said hello and leaned into his petting, even given his hand a lick.

All the while, Morgan had knelt by his dog and grinned, an "I told you so" look on her face.

At least the negotiations had gone well. They'd gotten what they wanted out of Ed. Morgan was right—they didn't need to write articles together. Not only could he not see them agreeing on their approach, he wasn't sure he could hide his attraction during an extended period of time alone together.

For the present he simply had to eat lunch, make pleasant conversation with her very nice parents, work out a few more details with her, and he could take Samson and go home.

He walked out into the entry hall and looked around. The Morgans may not have attempted a true historic preservation, but the house was handsome with its dark oak floors and pastel plaster walls. He peered into the large living room. No real Victorian period pieces there to speak of, simply comfortable-looking furniture. Although not to his more austere and contemporary taste, of course, it was nice just the same. Similar to that in Morgan's house. The place was also neat. The daughter must not have inherited her mother's housekeeping gene.

He turned to the dining room on the other side of the entry. His mother would like the room. The Queen Anne dining table, chairs, and buffet were beautiful and elegant, especially when combined with the crystal chandelier. The table was not set, so they must be eating elsewhere. He heard voices in the kitchen and headed in that direction.

He came through the kitchen door in time to see Antonia hold out a dog biscuit to Samson. Before he could open his mouth to ask her not to give the dog a treat, Morgan spoke softly from directly behind him.

"It's all right. I have a deal with Mother. Only one

doggy cookie for Delilah a day. Mother's a sucker for a hungry animal, no matter the species. She'll try to stuff you, too." She walked around him before he could answer her.

Antonia noticed him as Samson took the treat politely from her hand. "Have a seat right over there, Marcus," she said, pointing to a chair at the circular table set into another bay. "Is iced tea all right with you? We have soft drinks, milk, beer, and wine also."

"Tea is fine." He sat, put his napkin in his lap, and used the opportunity to look around. The large kitchen was a cheery place, with white, glass-doored cabinets and maple countertops, pots of herbs growing on the windowsills, and polished copper pots hanging from the rack over the island in the middle. He was surprised to realize how comfortable he felt, despite the fact that he had never eaten in any kitchen except his own; his parents were dining-room people.

Alaric brought over the bread he had been slicing and put it on the table, went back to the counter for a platter of tomato slices, green leaves, and light yellow slabs of cheese, and sat down next to him. Morgan poured tea into ice-filled glasses, added a sprig of mint to each, and placed the glasses at each setting. She took the chair across the table from him.

Antonia came to the table with a big bowl, which she placed on the mat in front of her plate. "We're having chicken salad, Marcus, I hope you like it. The bowl's heavy, so if you'd all pass your plates, I'll serve the first helping."

"I'm sure it will be delicious," he murmured as he watched Antonia plop two large spoonfuls of salad on his plate. Morgan had been correct—her mother was trying to stuff him.

"The tomatoes and basil are straight out of our greenhouses, and, everyone, tell me what you think of the cheese. I'm trying a new brand," Antonia continued.

"Oh, good," Morgan said, "you made my favorite brown bread, Daddy."

"There's another loaf if you want it," he answered passing the plate to her.

Everyone concentrated on serving themselves as the bread and tomatoes went around the table.

Marcus scrutinized the mound of chicken salad in front of him. It didn't look like what he was used to. The dish had more than simply chicken, celery, mayo, and hard-cooked eggs. There were those flat snow peas he'd always found tasteless, and some cut-up white bits he couldn't identify, along with black olives, sliced carrots, chopped red bell peppers, and little green flecks of herbs. A faint whiff of mustard came to him also.

Not his usual fare of a hamburger and fries. He mentally sighed. He'd have to be a good guest and eat it all, no matter how it tasted. He loaded up his fork and took a bite.

Flavors exploded in his mouth and melded together in a sensation crunchy and creamy, piquant and smooth, cool and warm all at the same time.

He swallowed quickly and took another bite. The second was even better than the first.

He chewed, swallowed, and smiled widely at his hostess. "Antonia, I misspoke when I said I was sure it would be delicious. This is beyond delicious. It's absolutely great. How do you make it taste so good?"

"Welcome to eating at Chez Antonia," Morgan said in a low voice from across the table.

"Thank you, Marcus. It's my magic, of course," Antonia answered with a smile and a wink. "Don't forget to have some tomatoes."

The meal passed in a gastronomic blur for Marcus, to the point that he hardly heard and barely participated in the discussion about their plans for the farm—something about building a restaurant and offering cooking classes. He ate not only what Antonia had originally served, but another helping besides. The chewy, warm brown bread and the tomato dish, drizzled with olive oil, were perfect compliments.

"I must admit," he said as he used the bread to sop up the last of the salad, "I haven't eaten this well in ages."

"Do you cook for yourself much?" Antonia asked.

"No, only simple meals," he answered. "Steak, hamburgers, scrambled eggs, that sort of thing."

"Your parents didn't teach you, or you don't care for it?"

"No, my mother doesn't cook much, my father not

at all. We had a cook and housekeeper when I was very small. When I was school age, I went to boarding school and was home only on vacations. We often traveled during the summers." He went on to tell them about his parents, their professions, their university, his calling them by their first names—a departure from his usual reticence, but he couldn't stop himself.

Antonia and Alaric did seem interested and asked more questions. Morgan didn't speak, only drank her tea and flicked glances at him from time to time. He concluded by saying, "The traveling was very educational. Judith and Stefan always made sure I met some of the most prominent scholars in whatever my interest was at the time."

"See, Mother, we always told you how much better educated we'd have been if you and Daddy hadn't made us kids work the farm during the summer," Morgan said with a smirk. Then she added with an overly sad face, "I was a grown woman before I saw Disney World."

"Poor baby," Antonia said and patted her hand in mock commiseration.

"Marcus, don't listen to her laments," Alaric said. "Glori, you'll give him the idea y'all were indentured servants. Besides, if you hadn't been working with your mother, we wouldn't have discovered your talents at an early age. That not only gave you a head start on progressing through your spell levels, it allowed you to complete your degrees in record time."

"Okay, Daddy." She rolled her eyes. "I lived it, re-member?"

"Besides," he continued in a serious tone, "times were tough. We needed the cheap labor. I do wish y'all hadn't eaten us out of house and home, though. We would have shown a profit sooner."

She jabbed a finger at him as she said, "If you hadn't cooked the books, we would have received our full al-lowances."

Marcus watched the interchange with a certain amount of surprise and confusion. Cheap labor? Eaten too much? Cooking books? To eat? No, that's right, Alaric was in accounting. He was even more astonished when father and daughter broke out in a parody of "Six-teen Tons" that ended with a harmonized version of "I owe my soul to the Mooorrrgan Stoooorrre."

While Morgan and Alaric hugged and laughed, An-tonia scolded, "You two behave. There's no telling what kind of impression you're making on our guest." She turned to him. "Don't believe a word they say, Marcus. How about some pie?"

Dessert lived up to the enticing aroma that had greeted him when he stepped into the house. After one-and-a-half—well, okay, two—pieces, he truly was stuffed. He took a final sip of coffee and wondered how far he'd have to run to work it all off.

"At least five," Morgan said to him. "Maybe ten."

"Five what?"

"You looked like you were calculating how many miles you'll have to run to compensate for all the calories you consumed. Depending on your metabolism, five to ten miles or lots of spells at the top of your level. Trust me, I've measured it." She grinned at him.

She had a teasing twinkle in her eye, but he didn't doubt the truth of her statement. Or the fact that he'd like to pull her across the table and see if she tasted as good as her mother's chicken salad.

He ruthlessly forced his mind back to the matter at hand. "I believe we still have to cover what we're going to say in our presentations and in that first article."

"You two talk elsewhere, and Alaric and I will clean up the dishes," Antonia interjected as she rose. When Morgan picked up her plate, Antonia took it out of her hand. "Go on, shoo."

Marcus followed Morgan out of the kitchen and into the living room, where they settled in the "tower" seating area, she in an overstuffed chair and he on the love seat. The dogs came with them and curled up on the rug between them.

She said something about the prospective articles and making reasoned arguments, and he made an appropriate response—or he guessed he did. His mind went off on a tangent about how soft her hair looked and how her eyes twinkled when she had a mischievous thought. Then she mentioned focusing the conversation at the debates, and all he could focus on was her breasts plumped over her crossed arms.

He hauled his mind out of the gutter and suggested composing a list of questions to pose to the audience. She liked that and smiled. His gaze went to her lips. What would it be like to kiss her? Kiss her? Oh, no. A shiver of panic raced up his backbone. His reactions to her were getting totally out of hand. Before he lost all control, he had to get out of here.

He quickly agreed to make up lists, exchange them, and send them to Ed. When she couldn't think of other issues to discuss, he grasped the opportunity to leave. All three Morgans, plus Delilah, walked him and Samson to the car.

After thanking Antonia and Alaric for their help and wonderful lunch, he made one more mistake: he turned to Morgan and looked directly into her eyes. An inexplicable urge to stay, to get to know her better, to see if she'd tease him again struck with a sharp jab to his solar plexus, but he managed not to gasp. He shook himself mentally. If he couldn't stop acting like a complete fool over his attraction to her, he'd go through even greater hell at the debates.

He covered his confusion by attending to Samson's car harness. Alaric made sure he knew the fastest way back to the highway, and finally Marcus was able to drive away. In his rearview mirror, he could see Samson twisting to watch their hosts.

Breathing a sigh of relief, Marcus idly scratched the

itch over his magic center and resolutely started planning his list of questions for the debate—a subject sure to keep his libido under control.

CHAPTER SEVEN

Gloriana watched the car until it disappeared. When she turned around to go back in the house, she discovered her parents both looking at her with those calculating expressions that usually signaled trouble. What had she done to warrant a "discussion"? She'd been particularly nice to the man. Cordial. Polite. Even though he'd tried to take over the negotiation with Ed. At least he'd gone along with her idea for separate articles, and they hadn't fought about "regularizing" spell-casting. She'd even been able to look the man in the eye and not think of ice—or anything else.

She started up the path after her parents.

"Marcus Forscher seems like a nice young man," her mother said as they walked to the house.

"Yes, very bright and quite personable," her father said as they climbed the stairs to the porch.

"I do wonder about his childhood, though," her

mother said as they went inside.

"Yes, boarding schools at an early age, and calling his parents by their first names," her father said as they walked into the kitchen.

"I can only imagine what he usually eats. I had the distinct impression he was very apprehensive when he tried his first bite of the salad," her mother said as she sat down at the table.

"Probably doesn't like 'fancy' food. No telling how all that boarding school and restaurant food affected his eating habits," her father said as he also took a seat.

Gloriana put her hands on her hips and glared at them. "Will you two stop?"

"Stop what?" her mother asked, a look of innocence on her face.

"I'm sure you have something to say about Forscher, so spit it out. You discussed what a 'nice young man' he is and what his parents must be like while we were in the living room. Okay. Fine. I agree with everything you've said. But we're still polar opposites when it comes to the practice of magic and probably a bunch of other things. He's uptight, and I'm informal. He's theoretical, and I'm hands-on. His head is in the clouds, and mine's in the dirt. No matter what, however, I'm going to have to work with the man on these crazy debates, and I don't expect it to be easy. So, say what you have to say."

She stalked over to the dog's water bowl, picked it up, filled it with water, and put it back down. When she straightened up, her father pulled out a chair and motioned to it. "Have a seat, Glori, we think you may not have realized something."

Uh-oh. They looked concerned, truly concerned. What could they be talking about? She sank into the seat. Delilah came over and put her head in her lap and she rubbed the dog's head and behind her ears. "What? What haven't I realized?"

"Did you notice the way Marcus looks at you?" Antonia asked.

"Sure. That disdainful expression, like he's not sure what I'm going to do or say, and he has to watch me like a hawk? The icy one where he hardly cracks a smile? The one where he's about to hand down a death sentence, or maybe he smells something bad? Those looks? So what? The man doesn't like me much. He's arrogant and aloof. I can still work with him. Lord knows, I've worked with worse." If he acted like his ol' buddy Prick and didn't metamorphose into Mr. Congeniality or get close so she could smell his tantalizing scent . . . or look directly into his blue, sometimes-not-icy eyes . . .

"Glori?"

At the sound of her mother's voice, she came back from wherever she had been. She blinked, focused, sat up straight, cleared her throat. "That look?"

"I don't think you're reading him correctly," Antonia said.

"Do you have any idea of the expression in your eyes

when you look at him?" her father asked.

"When I look at him? I try to keep a blank or polite expression on my face. At the meeting with Ed and today, I considered us to be in negotiations. I can't afford to go all 'girly' and expect to be taken seriously. Daddy, you know I make a lousy 'sweet young thing.'"

He chuckled. "That you do, sweetheart."

"So? What's in my eyes? On my face? What are you two beating around the bush about?"

Her parents sighed simultaneously. Alaric sat back and said to Antonia, "You explain. You're better at these discussions than I am."

"Coward," her mother muttered. She sat straight and assumed that this-is-the-way-it-is expression all the Morgan kids feared. "All right. Here's what we're thinking. The way you and Marcus looked at each other reminded us of how *we* acted when *we* met. It was uncanny. It wasn't disdain in his eyes, Glori, it was lust."

"Lust? Oh, please, Mother. The man's cold as a glacier." She shook her head vigorously to reinforce her statement. "I'll admit he's gorgeous, but he's still icy. Lust? No way."

"A man doesn't go all gooey when he's aroused," Antonia said. "He goes hard—all over. Not simply in one part of his anatomy."

"Mother! I understand the basics." She could feel a flush creep up her neck into her cheeks. "And I don't go all gooey when I look at him."

"No, you look more like a kid in an ice cream store—exactly the way your mother did. Like you can't believe what you're seeing, and you really like it," Alaric said.

"Meanwhile he looks like he's spotted his mate—exactly the way your father did," Antonia added.

"Wait a minute here." Her gaze went from one to the other and she started adding up the clues. Forscher was "in lust" for her. She liked what she saw. What was the word her mother had used? *M-m-m* . . . That could only mean . . .

"No!" An electric shock ran through her body, and she slammed her hand down on the table. "No! That man is *not* my soul mate! He *can't* be!"

"Why not?" Antonia asked.

Gloriana stared from one parent to the other and back. Her mother and father had gone mad. She had to come up with reasons against their ridiculous assertion. This time, however, she, who usually had an answer for every harebrained notion, couldn't think of one word to say. She shut her eyes, gripped her skull between her hands, and rubbed hard.

Fortunately, neither parent said a word.

Finally, after a minute of almost pulling her hair out, her ability to think returned—sort of—and she managed to start talking. "Be-be-because . . . we don't even like each other. We have nothing in common! We think differently. I'm concrete and tangible, grounded in the real here and now. He's abstract and hypothetical, in the theoretical stratosphere. He's all numbers and symbols and I'm all . . . something else. Sure, I use chemical symbols in my work, and numbers, too, but not at his level. Look at that equation! How much farther from the way I practice and view magic can he be?"

Okay, that was a start. She wasn't grasping at straws. Why else? "More importantly, we hold philosophically opposite views on the practice of magic. I'm not sure if I even like him as a person. Soul mates are supposed to think alike, like the same things, especially each other. He's perfect. Even his jeans have a pressed crease. I'm always playing in the dirt and getting it all over me. I'm sure there are other anomalies—like music, for instance. When we were in his car, he was tuned to a jazz station. I have absolutely no interest in jazz."

Okay, here came the clincher, she was certain. "The soul-mate rules say mates are supposed to be compatible in every way. Daria and Bent and Francie and Clay certainly are. Forscher and I are not. How on earth can we be soul mates?"

"You're both in academics and have basenjis," Alaric offered.

"Hardly enough, Daddy, to base the rest of my life on."

"I'm going to give you the same advice I gave your sister," Antonia said. "Get to know the man. That's part of the process. Before and after the debates, spend some time together. Talk about yourselves, your goals, your likes and dislikes, books, music, movies, politics, all that.

See what's inside of the shell he's built around himself."

Gloriana looked from one parent to the other again. They clearly believed what they were saying. With them staring at her, however, she couldn't think, could hardly breathe. She had to get out of there. If leaving meant she was a coward, so be it. She stood up, pushed back her chair. "I understand that you mean well, but I can't process this information. You just put my brain on overload. It's the craziest idea I've ever heard. I'm going home. Thank you for lunch. Come on, Delilah, let's go. The walk will do us both good."

"Please, Glori," her father said, "promise me you'll think about it."

"Okay, Daddy. I'll do that. I'm not going to jump to any conclusion, however, yours or mine."

Her mother followed her out of the kitchen and gave her a big hug at the door. "You know we want the best for you."

"Yes, Mother. I understand." Weariness settled over her bones. With all she had to think about and accomplish in the next few weeks, why did the burden of a soul mate—and Marcus Forscher, of all people—have to happen, in her busiest time of year?

❋❋❋❋❋

"Finally, done." That evening Gloriana put the last paper in the pile of graded student work, entered the grade in her computer listing, and leaned back in her chair to stretch. By sheer force of will, she'd concentrated and graded every paper in her two graduate courses. What was she going to do next?

She rose, picked up the stack, and took it to the table where she usually laid out the student papers by class. For once, the table was bare of others waiting for her attention. She looked around her home office. She didn't feel like browsing the Internet, or looking at e-mail, especially what she'd been receiving about the debates, or even doing some of her research.

Her stomach growled, and she glanced at her wristwatch. Eight o'clock already? She headed for the kitchen. Delilah was sprawled on the rug by the fireplace and didn't even twitch when Gloriana went by. Yep, a tired basenji was a good dog, from her point of view. She bet Samson was zonked out, too, especially if he wasn't used to the freedom of running off a leash.

What was Samson's master doing? Had Marcus Forscher realized the predicament they might be in? No, he couldn't have because they weren't . . . that word. She refused to even consider the notion that her parents were correct.

They couldn't be.

How could she and Forscher ever come to terms about spell-casting, much less to the togetherness soul mates enjoyed? The pleasure of being in each other's company, the just-between-us jokes, the sheer joy in their

eyes when they looked at each other—all that she'd witnessed in her brother and sister and their spouses. She
could only imagine what the intimacy between mates
must be like in bed . . .

"Stop thinking," she ordered out loud and started
putting a sandwich together. When it was ready, she carried it and a glass of wine to the living room coffee table
and sat on the couch. She turned on the television—a
commercial, of course, came on immediately. She took a
big bite of her sandwich and flicked open a horticultural
magazine lying on the table.

She wasn't paying attention to the program until she
put her sandwich down to flip the page . . . and heard a
man with a low, deep voice say, "Oh, my darling, we will
be together forever." She looked up to view a clinch to
beat all clinches. In response, her breasts tingled, and
her magic center vibrated like a plucked cello string.

Not what she needed to think of, much less witness! If she hadn't had a mouth full of food, she'd have
screamed. She grabbed the remote and clicked channels
until she found some old cartoons.

Between the magazine and Bugs and Elmer, she
managed to finish her sandwich.

What next? She sat back on the couch and drummed
her fingers on her knees. It was too early to go to sleep.
She'd eaten, so she wasn't going to go for a run. Dead-
to-the-world Delilah offered no distraction. She didn't
feel like cleaning the house; she'd done that yesterday.

She absolutely, positively did not want to sit here and think about Marcus Forscher.

Or, oh, God, *soul mates*.

But wait. What did she really know about soul mates or the whole phenomenon? How they found each other? About the imperative that brought them together? The SMI, as Clay called it? She'd never really discussed it in detail with other family members—not since she and Daria had that conversation where they'd concluded it didn't exist. Yeah, right. Then Bent came along and blew their theories to smithereens. She'd helped explain magic to Francie, and Daria, as the one with the experience, had taken over the imperative explanation.

She wasn't going to bring up the subject with her mother—not after their earlier conversation—but she had another source. She rose from the couch, took her dishes into the kitchen, poured herself another glass of wine, picked up the phone, and punched the buttons.

The phone rang on the other end. "Hello?"

"Hi, Daria, it's me. Do you have a few minutes to talk? I have some potentially important questions."

Her sister must have picked up something in her tone of voice because Daria hesitated before saying, "Here, talk to Bent while I move to a quiet place."

"Hey, Glori, how are the plants?" her brother-in-law asked.

"Fine. How's your garden?"

"Blooming like crazy. You and Antonia did your

usually wonderful job on our landscaping."

"You're our urban test site. It better look good after all our hard work," she teased.

Another phone was picked up and Daria said, "Thanks, Bent, I've got it."

Gloriana exchanged good-byes with Bent and heard his receiver hang up.

"Okay," Daria said, "what's going on?"

"Mother and Daddy think Marcus Forscher is my soul mate."

"What? How? When?" Daria practically shrieked in her ear. Her next words were considerably calmer, and Gloriana could almost hear the click when her sister went into consultant mode. "How did they arrive at this conclusion?"

"He came here today to discuss how we might control the debates and make sure we can still get our research and writing done before fall." Gloriana sighed. Might as well tell it all. "Our parents say that he and I are looking at each other the same way they did when they first met. He concentrates on me the way Daddy does on auditing—you know that laser-beam look he gets. Personally, I think Forscher is icy, hard, and disdainful. Regarding my looks, I'm not 'looking' any way at all. You've been a negotiator, determined to make the best deal. You have to keep a poker face."

"What's Forscher like as a guy?"

"It's the strangest thing, Daria. When he's not

staring at me, he can be Mr. Congeniality, charming, handsome, with a smile that wrapped Mother around his little finger. If that's not enough, he liked her chicken salad—ate enough to stuff a buffalo. She thinks he's great. Do I need to explain more?"

"What's he interested in, besides spell-casting by formula and theoretical math, that is?"

"I haven't the slightest . . . No, wait, that's not true. He likes jazz. He has a dog, a basenji, no less, named Samson."

"Samson? Oh, honey, you're doomed." Daria started laughing like she'd been sniffing the catnip her two cats liked.

"Ha, ha. I'm serious, Daria. I need some help. What if they're right? What's it like to meet your soul mate? What happens next? Am I truly stuck with him if he's the one? Can I fight it?"

"Whoa, Glori. Slow down. First of all, when I met Bent, my magic center started itching like crazy. I found out later his did, too. Francie and Clay had the same problem, and remember, Francie didn't like Clay, either, at first. Have you been itching?"

Uh-oh, that didn't sound good because, with Daria's question, a huge mosquito took a bite out of her magic center. She ignored it—and the question—to ask another. "What next?"

"Let's simply say the attraction builds. You don't have the problem Clay and I did when we met Francie and Bent—Marcus Forscher is a practitioner, so he's been taught about soul mates. Brother dear and I had to convince our mates about both magic and soul mates, and it wasn't easy for either of us."

"I remember all too well." She smiled at her memory of Francie's reaction.

"As for fighting it . . . I don't think you can, or not without serious injury," Daria said skeptically before continuing in a blissful tone, "Besides, the first mating makes up for all problems."

Gloriana did not want to discuss her sister's love life—too much information, for sure—but she had to ask, "What about the first mating? You go to bed, have sex, and it's done."

"Mother never really explained this. It's a *process*, not a one-time thing like I thought originally. Also, it's much more than 'having sex.' It's definitely making love. For both of us couples, the bonding took several, uh, 'matings' to take effect. Bent and I realized it had happened when we touched each other's magic centers and felt like we'd been struck by lightning. Francie told me they touched centers and had colored lights swirling around them that came together practically in a nova."

"How many matings to bonding?" Not that she cared, because she wasn't going to tie herself to Mr. Iceberg. She told herself it couldn't hurt to have the facts.

"Oh, at least five or six. Maybe seven? I really don't remember. When it happened—*Wow!*"

"What else can you tell me?"

"About your 'fighting it' question? Watch out for the imperative. The SMI can be vicious if you don't give in. It didn't bother me too much, but Bent said he felt like he'd been shot when he resisted, and Francie was sure she had a bleeding ulcer. Clay said it messed with him even after he'd given in to it, and that happened before Francie said yes."

"Oh, joy. What pleasant times to look forward to in the middle of the damned debate. I wish I'd never written that idiotic letter to Ed. No sense regretting that, I guess. Maybe I can still hope Mother and Daddy are wrong."

"I doubt it. Remember, Mother took one look at Bent and said he was the one."

"Thank you so much for that recollection."

Daria must have heard the grim sarcasm because she chuckled. "I'm sure it will all work out."

"Yeah, right. Do me a favor in the meantime and don't tell Francie or Clay, especially Clay, about Mother's revelation. He's looking for a reason to get back at me for everything I said when he and Francie were going through the process. I'm sure you'll tell Bent, but swear him to secrecy, too, will you?"

"Okay, I promise. I can understand your hesitation, particularly when you and he seem to have little in common. If Mother's prediction comes true, however, you'll still be all right. Remember what Daddy says, 'Being soul mates just gets better all the time.'"

Exactly what she needed to hear, Gloriana thought as her mouth twisted wryly. Daria would go on about the glories of "soul mate-ness" for hours if you let her. Time to change the subject to the one sure to distract her older sister. "So, how are you feeling, Little Mama?"

They discussed gynecology and obstetrics and pregnancy until Gloriana thought she'd scream. She finally hung up the phone with Daria's admonition—and where had she heard it before?—to get to know the man.

"Yeah, right," she muttered and left the kitchen. Thinking she'd simply read in bed, she grabbed a couple of professional journals off the kitchen table. Delilah still didn't move. Some loyal companion she'd turned out to be, her affections stolen by a flashy red and white male.

As Gloriana lay there later, totally unable to concentrate on the scholarly articles, a wave of loneliness washed over her. Its source? There could be only one: she envied her sister with her soul mate and a baby on the way.

She would find her own soul mate, one day. She knew that as surely as she knew she could spell plants to make them grow. Her mate didn't have to be Marcus Forscher. These debates would be a good chance to meet all sorts of possible soul mates. She'd keep her eyes open, take advantage of the opportunity.

A little pin poked her in the breastbone.

"Oh, stop that," she ordered before turning out the light. She resolutely closed her eyes and concentrated on her next-day tasks until she fell asleep.

CHAPTER EIGHT

After a restless night and dreams of an emerald-eyed, chocolate-haired woman that left him aching with need, Marcus thought of begging off the invitation to his mentor's for dinner and a chess game on Sunday evening. Despite a morning spent unaccountably unable to concentrate, he decided to go. Seeing George and his wife, Evelyn, might take his mind off . . . other things.

With a warm smile, Evelyn, a well-rounded woman in her early sixties with light brown eyes and graying brown hair, opened the door at his ring. After he entered, she gave him a big hug. "It's good to see you again, Marcus. We need to get together more often."

In contrast to her high-powered, energetic, twelfth-level, professorial husband, Evelyn was a laid-back, fifth-level practitioner and a public school first-grade teacher. She exuded calmness and competency, and Marcus felt more himself—in control—immediately.

Ever since George had brought him home for dinner right after his arrival on campus, he had looked upon the two of them almost like a second family—or perhaps more than that. With the Bernhards' son and daughter long out of the nest and living far away, George and Evelyn had in essence adopted him. Indeed they helped him to stay "balanced" in a way he couldn't define—or didn't want to.

"I agree." He returned the hug, held it for a moment, curiously reluctant to let go. "You're looking good."

"And you look tired," she replied as she closed the door. "The end of the year always keeps you professors hopping, and with the debate on top of that, I hope you're taking time to relax."

"Evelyn," George called from deeper in the house, "bring him back here. He needs a drink, and I do, too."

The dinner went pretty much like all their time together did—lively talk about the university and politics, both legislative and academic, sales of Marcus's latest sci-fi book, and, of course, about the debate. They both wanted to hear his side of the event and the subsequent controversy.

Marcus related the tale of the meeting with Ed and his visit to the Morgan farm—leaving out his attraction for his opponent, of course. Some things were nobody's business except his. He concluded, "I think we have the situation as much under control as we can get it. If Ed can only keep order and we choose the audience participants carefully, we should be able to get through the events with a minimum of fuss."

"I hope so," George said with a speculative expression, "but I doubt it will be that easy. Not if the first debate was any indication for the future."

"I wish I could be there," Evelyn interjected. "A few of the calming spells I use on my students might be in order."

"Honey, the Swords won't allow spell-casting," George said and patted his wife's hand.

"Maybe they should," she replied. "Contentious people in a group can regress to the equivalent of my first graders who haven't had their naps. Enough unpleasantness. Let us have some dessert, and you must tell me what Antonia Morgan served for lunch and what their house looks like. I use their herbs and spices all the time."

After dinner, Marcus and George retired to the study where the chessboard was waiting. "Next time," George suggested, "you'd better take pictures of the Morgan place and ask for the recipes."

"Yes," Marcus groaned. "I have no idea what was in that chicken salad."

"Men never do, according to Evelyn. Here, pick a color." He held out his fists with a pawn in each. Marcus chose, took the white, and they began to play.

Some time later, George said, "Checkmate."

"What? How did that happen?" Marcus blinked at the board. Damn. He'd waltzed right into the other man's trap.

"All right," his mentor said, "what's the matter? Something's bothering you. After the first ten minutes, you haven't been concentrating. I didn't think you were worried about the debates, or are you?"

Marcus leaned back in his chair and rubbed the itch at the end of his sternum. George had won in record time. Where had his mind been?

He'd been gazing at the painting above the mantel as he usually did when waiting for George to make his next move. The picture, portraying members of George's family from the early eighteen-hundreds sitting around a picnic table in a colorful garden, was pleasant enough. He'd seen it often and no longer paid attention to it, but he'd found if he looked away from the board for a while, he could more easily see new possible moves when he faced the chess pieces. Tonight one of the women had drawn his eye. She wore an emerald green dress, and her brown ringlets fell about her face in artful disarray.

Although the painted image looked nothing like her, he had been imagining Gloriana Morgan in that picture.

And his thoughts had gone right after her.

George glanced at the picture, then at him, down to his hand, and back to his face. "No, I don't think it's the debates. It's Gloriana Morgan, isn't it?"

Marcus felt his face grow warm. He carefully clasped his hands loosely on the table, but kept his gaze on the board. "What about her?"

"How old are you, Marcus?"

The absurd question caused him to meet the older man's eyes. "Thirty-four. Why?"

Grinning, George said, "Don't you think it's past time for you to meet your soul mate?"

"What?" The question shocked Marcus so much he jumped to his feet and had to grab the chair to keep it from falling over. "My soul mate? Who? Morgan?"

"Yes, Gloriana Morgan."

"Oh, no!" Marcus turned his back on George and stalked to the window. Because of the darkness outside, all he could see was his reflection on the glass. He watched himself take deep breaths and rub his itching breastbone while he tried to regain his equilibrium.

George had gone senile, right in front of him. That was the only explanation for such a ridiculous notion. Either that or the older man was teasing him—yeah, that sounded better than senility. George was trying to shake him up the way he sometimes did, claiming it did a "youngster" good to lose control once in a while. He wasn't going to let it happen this time, however.

He sauntered back to the table, sat down, spread his arms wide, and shook his head. "Okay, George, you got me. Good joke. I overreacted. That's what you wanted me to do, wasn't it? I have to tell you though, I don't find anything funny in your question."

"I'm not joking," George replied and held up both hands when Marcus opened his mouth to protest. "Hear me out."

"Hmph," Marcus grunted, and he shut his mouth and crossed his arms.

"Despite the very large role she plays in the upcoming events, you barely mention Gloriana by name. When you say her last name, your voice changes its timbre, its crispness, becomes deeper. Also, almost every time, you rub your magic center."

As George said the last two words, Marcus fisted his hands to keep himself from scratching that persistent itch. "So?"

"Don't you know, one of the first signs of the soulmate imperative is an itching or hurting magic center?"

"That's ludicrous." Wasn't it? He'd never heard of that before. Certainly his father hadn't mentioned it in their obligatory discussion on sex and soul mates when he was thirteen—a discussion never repeated with either parent.

"You look tired. Not sleeping well? Or having dreams that leave you aching?" George paused and smiled, but he seemed to be looking inward to himself more than at Marcus. "I remember when I first met Evelyn. I was a senior in college and, man, did I have X-rated dreams about her."

A vivid memory of the night before flashed through Marcus's mind, and his body hardened in an instant. He even had difficulty forming the words to deny George's assertions. Finally he managed to say, "Morgan can't be my soul mate. The phenomenon is all about instant attraction, total concentration on the mate to the exclusion of everything else, and a whole boatload of similarities between them. None of that applies here. Leaving out the dogs and our teaching professions, we have little in common, especially with regard to magic. We're not concentrating only on each other or excluding our friends. We're doing our jobs and this damned debate. We've hardly seen each other. Hell, she's not even attracted to me."

"Are you sure?"

"She hardly ever looks me in the eye, she always has an expression like she's playing high-stakes poker, and she doesn't want somebody to guess what she's thinking. Furthermore, she never gives off those little signals a woman does when she's interested—smiling, asking personal questions, coming a little bit closer than necessary—that sort of flirting."

"Every time you've been together, there have been other people around, and you've been discussing the debates, where you and she are on opposite sides. Maybe she simply hasn't had the opportunity. Haven't you been alone with her at all?"

Marcus was about to shake his head, but remembered . . . "Only when I picked her up at her house to go to her parents' place yesterday. Samson met her basenji, Delilah, and the two of them took off running. They were out of sight before I could move. All she did was smirk and tell me her dog would bring him back safely.

If she was attracted to me, I certainly didn't see it."

George grinned. "Samson and Delilah? Both basenjis? Oh, that says it all right there. She's your soul mate, no doubt about it. I wouldn't worry about lack of overt attraction. She's probably one of those witches who's slow to react—or maybe *you're* the one who's not giving *her* signals."

The conversation had gone from ridiculous to bizarre and was headed toward grotesque, Marcus decided. It was time to bring it down to reality.

"Listen, George, you know how I feel about the whole soul-mate business. For all the good that people claim it brings, from my point of view, the damn imperative is a menace. You know what it did to me and my parents, and that I don't want to deal with it. In the present situation, I think you're wrong. My reaction to Morgan has a simple explanation: I need to get out more on dates. For the moment, if you don't mind, let's change the subject. You're white this time. Let's play the game."

George studied him for a few seconds, and Marcus could almost hear his mentor analyzing the facts, arranging them in a logical progression. He braced himself for an argument, but the older man picked up the chess pieces and said only, "I'm here if you ever want to discuss it."

Walking Samson later that night, Marcus thought over what George had told him.

Morgan was his soul mate? He'd never even considered the idea up to now—never saw his attraction as part of the soul-mate phenomenon. Was he blind? No, nor ignorant, nor unaware. Why hadn't he thought of the possibility? Because she wasn't, of course. Couldn't be, for all the reasons he'd given George. No way. No way in hell were they soul mates. *Soul mates!* The absolute last thing he wanted. Or needed.

No, he'd resist the very notion to his dying day.

Then there was Morgan, the woman herself. How simple things would be if she wasn't a practitioner. He'd be free to take her to bed with no repercussions. It was his bad luck to be attracted to a woman he couldn't have. Female practitioners never had sex except with their soul mates, and when they did . . . Bam! Bonded for life.

To the exclusion of all others. Even . . .

No, he'd continue on his plan to have as little to do with Morgan as possible.

A small pain struck him in the chest, and he groaned. It subsided when he rubbed. That wasn't a pain in his magic center—more likely his dinner settling. The whole business was giving him heartburn, and not of the amorous type, either.

CHAPTER NINE

Monday afternoon, back in Austin at her condo, Gloriana finished the paperwork for her last class. Her only remaining task was to hand in the grades and other reports, and she was done for the school year. She leaned back in her desk chair and stretched, pushing and pulling against it to loosen tight muscles. She'd take Delilah out for a run in a while and blow her mind clean of the mishmash of weird thoughts she'd been plagued with ever since her parents said the words *soul mate*.

First, her e-mail. She flipped on her laptop, and when the list displayed, she groaned. More on the debates. Weeding through the senders, she took care of those related to her school work and moved on to those from friends. A couple of the latter offered her a place to stay if she came to their cities on the tour; she declined with thanks.

Second, the debate messages—quite a number since

she'd ignored them over the weekend. To those who signed their names, she replied with her standard message referring them to Ed Hearst. The rest she deleted after skimming the contents.

Hmmm, one from Loretta Horner pledging Traditional Heritage Association support in "your courageous battle for traditional magic." Ugh. Gloriana sent her thanks for the good wishes and reiterated that they were in a discussion, not a battle. Whatever she said, she was certain Loretta would pay absolutely no attention to reason, nevertheless, she felt she had to try to remind her of the original purpose. Keep the channels of communication open, if possible. She read over her message several times to make certain neither the Horners nor their adherents could "lift" part of it to make her sound as if she was on their side.

The next one didn't have a name in the sender column, only some numbers. "Debate" was the subject. The message was written in a bold purple font: "Horner's Harpies Are Half-Baked Henchmen Whose Hope Is to Heave Our Practice Back to the Hackneyed Habits of History."

Somebody really liked the letter *H*. She chuckled at the "half-baked henchmen." The remainder of the message glorified the benefits to be found in the "Futuristic Formula." No mention of the formula's originator, she noted, but plenty of the Future of Magic and Bryan Pritchart. Neither did the sender identify him or herself. Delete.

Most of the messages, from both THA supporters and FOM adherents, were unsigned. "Cowards," she muttered. At least it was quick to go through them. By the time she reached the end of the list of forty or so, she needed either a nap or a drink to recover from the onslaught of poorly written prose.

One aspect of the letters she hoped did not signal a trend: the tone of the last few on both sides became more strident, slung more mud, sounded angrier, less rational. Assuming the worst—each side moving in the direction of the last letter writers—it would become more important than ever to keep control and order in the debates.

Meanwhile, she had questions to work on to focus the discussion. How can we help each individual practitioner cast in the most efficient and powerful manner? How can we transmit to our young people the scope and beauty of magic? She worked on the questions after dinner and went to bed feeling good about her progress.

The next morning she sent a copy to Forscher, who responded in an hour with his questions. His were more explicit, more focused on his formula and the need for experimentation. She was reading over them when the phone rang.

"Hello, Gloriana," Ed responded to her greeting. "I have Marcus Forscher on a conference call with us. I thought you two would like to hear the schedule I've put together."

"That's fine with me," she said.

"Okay here," Forscher's deep voice acknowledged.

A shiver ran down her spine at the sound. "Stop this," she mumbled to herself.

"Pardon?" Ed said.

"Nothing, I moved something on my desk." She rolled her eyes at the lie.

"Here's the schedule, beginning the first weekend in June as you requested. We'll go every weekend for five weeks. Boston first, Denver, Chicago, Atlanta, and end with San Francisco. We've reserved the largest ballrooms at the HeatherRidges and arranged for TV feeds to other rooms if necessary. I'm starting a registration page on our Web site.

"So we don't have audiences loaded with the same people every time, we're limiting attendees in the main room to people who live in the area and the immediately surrounding states. It's not first-come, first-serve, either. We'll choose randomly from those who register on our Web site or by mail. Only those in the main room will be able to actively participate. I'll be careful whom I pick to comment. We want to ensure a balance."

"Good idea," Forscher said. "I didn't think of that."

"Neither did I," Gloriana echoed. "Are you anticipating objections to the plan?"

"It doesn't matter. I have approval and support from the heads of the High and Defender Councils. Our shared goal is to have as many different people as possible take part or at least attend. Nobody wants to listen to Horner or Pritchart for five weeks in a row."

"They'll manage to infiltrate somehow, I think," Gloriana said, "and my e-mail indicates they have followers all over the country."

"Mine, also," Forscher added.

"Believe me, we know," Ed answered with a groan. "They're inundating us with mail and phone calls."

"We have some questions to ask the audience that might lead to our gathering real data and good suggestions," Forscher said.

"Yes," Gloriana interjected. "We thought if we could focus on the discussion, we might be able to stop some of the speeches."

"Sounds good," Ed remarked.

"We also thought we might give both sides only three minutes at the beginning of the first meeting to say whatever they wanted to say," she said.

"I like your ideas," Ed replied. "Let me make a suggestion. Rehearse your statements, questions, and answers. Practice with each other. You need to be focused and clear. You're both used to public speaking, so that's not a problem, but I've seen a message lost when the messenger was too wordy or too obtuse or too long-winded."

"I think that's a good idea," Forscher replied. "I'd like to be ready for various contingencies."

Gloriana didn't agree. They both knew what they wanted to say, she had too much work to do to waste time, and the main problem would be keeping order. Ed was the one who needed rehearsing. She couldn't get out of it, however, without appearing to be an obstructionist. After all, she did have to work with both of them over the weeks to come.

If she was stuck, she knew she didn't want to rehearse with Forscher alone in a room—too much proximity for comfort—so she said, "We'd do best with an audience to critique us and do some role-playing. I'm sure my parents would agree. Is there somebody you can ask? Say, meet out at the farm?"

"Yes, I have a colleague and his wife who might be willing to help out."

"Great," Ed said. "I'll take a look at your questions and see what I can add. You two rehearse, and I'll send the details for the trips."

"I'll call my parents as soon as we end here," Gloriana said. "How about next Saturday or Sunday?"

Forscher agreed, and they all promised to send e-mails when they had more information.

Gloriana hung up the phone and took a deep breath. Her parents and his friends should make enough of a buffer between them to keep the soul-mate business from rearing its head.

She called her mother, who was happy to help and who, of course, told her to invite everyone for lunch with rehearsal to follow. They chose Sunday, and Gloriana was to find out the names of the friends for her mother. Austin had grown fast in recent years, and the Morgans could no longer say they were acquainted with most of the practitioners in the area.

Gloriana dutifully promised to report all and hung up before her mother could say a word about . . . that awful term. What had she and Daria called it when they were erroneously deciding it didn't exist? Oh, yes. "X."

"X" could wait. She had work to do.

❧✶✳✶❧

"You've done what? Who's coming?" Gloriana stared at her mother on Friday morning. She'd driven out to the farm intending to spend as much time as possible in the greenhouses. She had reports to write on the progress of her research, and she wanted to see how her mother was coming along on a variety of the parsley-like *gotu kola* they'd recently imported from India. She'd found Antonia puttering around with the plants in her greenhouse for experimental herbs.

"Your sister and brother and their spouses will be here tomorrow. Daria called to ask about a recipe, and I told her what we're doing. It seemed to me that the more in the audience, the better. Clay will make a good representative for the math people and that Pritchart fellow. Daria and I can hold up the Horners' side." She indicated the plant before her. "Isn't it coming along nicely?"

Gloriana ignored the dark green leaves. "Forscher's

bringing his fellow math prof, whose wife is an elementary teacher, so we'll have more than enough . . ." Her voice trailed off when she realized her protests were in vain. The Houston four were coming, period. "Okay, fine. We'll have our own town hall meeting. I told you I think a rehearsal is a big waste of everybody's time. I do have one serious request. *Please* don't say one word about that soul-mate 'thing.'"

"Of course not, dear, that's your business."

Her matter-of-fact tone should have reassured Gloriana, but the look on her mother's face was a little too innocent. She gave her a squinty-eyed glare. "You haven't told them already, have you? Or Daddy hasn't told them, has he?"

"I did not mention the words *soul mate*. Neither did your father."

"Good." She knew Daria wouldn't break her promise to keep quiet. Maybe her secret was still safe. In fact, the extra guests might be a benefit, placing more of a buffer between her and Forscher. She wouldn't have to do more than participate in the rehearsal and let the others keep him busy. The thought cheered her up, and she could turn her attention to her mother's new project with enthusiasm.

CHAPTER TEN

"Get in the car, Delilah," Gloriana said to the hound on Sunday morning after she arranged the blankets on the front seat of her Mercedes convertible. "We're driving today in case I have to come looking for you and Samson later."

Delilah grunted and jumped into the bucket seat.

Gloriana shut the door, came around the car, and slid behind the wheel. She pulled the blanket tighter between the seat and the middle console before starting the engine. "Looks like we need one of those doggy covers like Forscher had," she said. "Maybe one of the harnesses, too. You wouldn't be able to jump out when I have the top down."

Delilah only whined as if to say, "Let's go."

"I hope I'm presentable—for his friends, I mean," Gloriana muttered as she approached the first turn. She had on her new pair of khaki chinos—no dirt smudges—

and a dark green, short-sleeved, summer cotton sweater. She'd even put on jewelry, silver drop earrings inlaid with malachite and a necklace with a matching pendant.

She simply wanted the day over with. To have to face Forscher, his friends, and her family while thinking—or trying not to think—about the whole situation was almost too much to bear. Nobody had said a word last night about the dreaded "X," but a certain tension simmered under the conversation. She knew they all knew, no matter what her mother had or hadn't told them. They'd all be scrutinizing her and Forscher. Her brother especially would be watching for some tiny tidbit, some minute fact or statement or blunder with which to tease her.

She'd warned her father about her lack of enthusiasm and his need as "Ed" to keep order, even firmly stated that she'd walk out if the rehearsal degenerated into a debacle. He'd scoffed at her fears, said they all had her best interests at heart, and promised to watch out for Clay. All she could do was hope for the best.

One conclusion cheered her as she pulled up in front of the big house: her supposed "X" had no idea they might be in the clutches of the SMI—or she hoped not. In fact, they might truly not be "that thing" to each other, no matter what her parents claimed. He certainly wasn't calling her, asking her out, pursuing her the way Bent and Clay had with Daria and Francie. Therefore, they weren't, and she had nothing to worry about. She wasn't about to be shackled forever to someone who was her direct opposite.

Thinking optimistically, if everybody behaved themselves today and concentrated on getting through this idiotic rehearsal, she could be back in the greenhouses by late afternoon. Free, at least for a while.

She and Delilah had barely climbed out of the car when the dog came to attention and looked toward the road to the highway. Gloriana quickly grabbed her collar and gazed in the same direction. Two cars, one of them Forscher's silver sedan, appeared, and Delilah began to yodel and tried to lunge at the vehicles.

"Hold still, girl." Gloriana dug her heels in and held on with both hands. "Sometimes I think I should enter you in the tractor pull at the county rodeo."

Forscher parked and got out. "Hey," was all he said as he opened his back door and reached in to Samson, whom Gloriana could hear whining. Within seconds, the hound was free, and Gloriana let Delilah go.

The dogs yodeled and nuzzled hello to each other, but didn't run off. Instead, they stood still as if politely waiting for the other guests.

Not perceptively looking any happier than she felt, Forscher came to stand by her while the other car parked. Of course, he was still Mr. Perfect, today in a crisp dusty-red button-down shirt with the sleeves rolled up and black casual pants with a sharp crease. The sun caught the almost silver highlights in his blond hair, and she had to shut off the trite comparisons to gods and surfers her mind conjured up. He wore sunglasses, so she couldn't see his eyes. She could, however, feel his gaze, that strange mix of ice and fire.

She suppressed a shiver. *Just nerves*, she told herself.

The older couple exited their car and, when Forscher didn't move, Gloriana went to greet them. At least *she* had been taught to be polite. "Hi, I'm Gloriana Morgan. Welcome to our farm."

She shook hands with George and Evelyn, who said to call them by their first names. Delilah and Samson trotted up to say hello. George said, "You must be Delilah!" and he leaned down to let her sniff his hand before petting her.

"Hello, Marcus," Evelyn said and gave the man a hug when he finally came to them.

Forscher took off his sunglasses and did his chameleon bit, but Gloriana could tell he wasn't faking the affection he felt for these people. Neither were they pretending. Her family came out on the porch and the next few minutes were full of introductions. She stepped to the rear and followed everyone into the house.

During the buffet lunch, Gloriana snagged a chair at the extended dining room table between Daria and her father before her mother could make seating assignments. Forscher was across the table and down. Good. She didn't have to try to make conversation with him.

After the usual first minutes of tasting and complimenting the chefs—her mother and sister had done most of the cooking—talk became general. Gloriana concentrated on her fajita salad and the others' conversations. Daria discussed education with Evelyn and their father. George and her mother had their heads together, and she was pointing to a dish, so they were probably talking about cooking. Forscher and Clay reminisced about MIT and the infamous "Prick," while Bent and Francie listened.

Good. All was serene. Or was it?

The mathematician was clearly in "charming" mode again. Francie shot an eyebrows-raised glance between him and Gloriana and back again. She waved her hand at her face in a fanning motion and mouthed, "Wow." Gloriana rolled her eyes at her sister-in-law and shook her head. Some women were pushovers for a pretty face, she fumed behind her iced tea glass.

When Daria whispered in her ear, "Yum," and nodded at the man, Gloriana seriously considered pouring her tea into her sister's lap. She refused to even glance at Clay; she knew he was grinning.

"All right," her father said when it looked like everyone had finished eating, "I'm going to suggest we have dessert after our debate while we're discussing the results. Let's get our rehearsal under way."

⁂

Everyone adjourned to the living room. Her father, Clay, and Bent had the room already set up, with chairs arranged auditorium-style and a table and chairs for her, Forscher, and Alaric. Daria and Antonia, representing the THA, sat to her right; Clay and George, the FOM on the left; and Bent, Francie, and Evelyn in the unde-cided middle.

While the audience settled, Gloriana pulled her father close and whispered, "Let's concentrate and get through this, Daddy. Clay has that look like he's plan-ning something. We don't need another circus."

"Don't worry, I'll watch out for Clay. We'll have a nice, decorous rehearsal. You'll see, it won't have been a waste of time."

Alaric explained the rules: opening statements by Gloriana and Forscher, three minutes each for the THA and FOM, questions from the speakers, order to be pre-served at all times. Did everybody agree? Everybody nodded.

Forscher began with a short statement explaining his equation and both the need for its study and the fu-ture benefits likely from its use. He did not repeat his "cauldron-stirring" comment from the past, but he did call for looking forward, reducing emotion, and develop-ing a scientific casting method.

When he finished, he did not look at Gloriana at all. No smirk. No icy glance. Thank goodness.

In basically a shortened version of her previous

remarks, Gloriana discussed spell-casting in terms of art, joy, and tradition, agreed new professions required new wizardry, and asked all practitioners to keep open minds. She urged them to synthesize all methods into the one that worked the best for themselves as individuals.

Alaric called on Daria for the THA side, and Clay interrupted. "Why should they go first?" he asked, rising with a scowl on his face and his fists on his hips. "Who decided that?"

Gloriana was happy Clay was only acting, because when her truly angry brother stood up to his full six feet five, he was a formidable force. She glanced over at Forscher who, to his credit, didn't appear intimidated. In fact, he didn't even blink. He did, however, frown and say, "We didn't think of that reaction."

"Objection noted. We'll tell Ed to have them flip a coin first," Alaric said, writing a few words on his legal pad. He looked at his watch and pointed. "You're on, Daria."

Clay sat down and Daria stood, looking thoroughly prepared with notes in hand. "I am here today to speak for all those who treasure our historical, traditional methods of casting spells," she said and proceeded to lay out a coherent and organized argument for the THA side. At two minutes thirty seconds precisely as reported by the moderator, she sat down to applause from Antonia and the three in the middle. A couple of low growls came from Clay and George.

Gloriana suppressed a smile. Her sister should have

been a lawyer instead of a management consultant. If only the Horners and their people would be succinct and reasonable.

"Now for the FOM," Alaric said.

Clay rose with that smart-alecky, here-comes-trouble expression she remembered well from childhood. "We at the Future of Magic are greatly concerned about the backward-looking activities of our more tradition-minded practitioners," he began with a pompous tone. Then he proceeded to make an emotional argument about unemotional spell-casting, combining the traditionalist's fear of the new with the joys of scientific efficiency and regularization.

Gloriana couldn't resist smiling at Clay's antics. His so-called arguments sounded good, but had little real reasoning behind them. More invective than substance— probably what they could expect from the FOM.

Alaric said, "Time," at the end of three minutes. Clay kept talking.

"Your time is over, sir. Sit down," Alaric said again, and he rapped his pen on the table.

Clay stopped talking, grinned like an evil demon older brother, and sat down. He and George high-fived each other.

"Next we're going to try questions and proposals from our panelists. If you audience members wish to comment, raise your hand, and I'll call on you. You'll be limited to two minutes each." Alaric wrote something on his paper, and muttered, "Stopwatch for Ed. You go first, Glori."

"I'd like to start at the most basic, a bedrock principle. Casting is an individual art. How can we help the individual practitioner discover the best way for him or her to cast with the most effect?" she asked.

Alaric recognized Evelyn who said, "I'd call for the teaching masters to study how each practitioner learned casting and to apply that knowledge in a curriculum tailored to the individual."

Good idea, Gloriana thought. As she'd looked into the matter, she'd been astounded how little even teaching masters knew about harnessing the energy within to cast that very important first spell. Once he or she had cast one spell, the rest seemed to follow, or that's what had happened with Francie. She herself couldn't remember not being able to cast.

George spoke next. "We *futurists* believe full development of the Forscher Formula will make casting considerably simpler and more straightforward. The traditionalists, with all their talk about emotion and art, are only confusing both the issue and many practitioners." He went on to extol the virtues of a single method for casting—without all the unscientific talk about art and emotion—until Alaric called time.

Gloriana could hear the implied approval for the FOM supporters and the disparaging sneer for Horner's group, and she struggled not to laugh. George was certainly getting into the spirit of the occasion. She felt her mouth tighten when she realized he hadn't really addressed her question. On the other hand, his response was probably what they could expect.

Francie held up her hand, and Alaric nodded. "Speaking as one who came late to magic practice, I have to say, it's *hard* to cast a spell. I had to try several methods before I found one I could use. I'm definitely a novice, and I don't think I could use the formula, or even its terms. On the other hand, seeing that flame appear right on top of a candlewick is absolutely exhilarating and totally emotional."

"Are you being a traitor to your husband's cause, woman?" Clay thumped his hand on his chest as if from a mortal wound.

Francie stuck out her tongue at him, and Bent laughed.

"Order," Alaric said and tapped his pen on the table. "Let's go on to the next topic. Ask your question, Marcus."

"My question concerns the equation itself," Forscher said. "A number of you believe it has value. How can we specifically study its application to determine its best use?"

"I think—" Clay said.

"Wait to be called on," Alaric admonished. When nobody else held up a hand, he said, "Okay, you have the floor."

"Thank you," Clay said. "I propose a committee of high-level mathematicians and teaching masters to calibrate the requirements for low-level spells in basic general disciplines. We can already measure internal energy production. It's simply a matter of teaching a bunch of guinea pigs—uh, test subjects—to cast at precise outputs. It should be no more difficult than teaching people to read."

"I can speak to that." Evelyn raised her hand, and Alaric nodded. "Teaching reading is not easy. Children learn by different methods. For some, phonics works, for others, the 'whole word' approach is best. Because something comes easy to one person doesn't mean it will to another. I would not like to see anybody pushed into one method or another—reading or spell-casting."

"I thought the formula was even harder to use because you have to remember what all the letters and sub-designations mean and how much energy application is too much," Antonia said.

Gloriana couldn't help smiling this time. She remembered the problems her mother had—but her mother was such an intuitive caster, especially after years of casting. Trying to use the equation had seriously disrupted the flow of her process.

"Wait to be recognized," Alaric cautioned.

Antonia gave him one of what Gloriana considered her "mother looks" until he said, "Go ahead."

"Remember, I tried the formula, and I had trouble," she continued. "Some young people can't grasp algebra or haven't even gotten to it yet in school. How can they think about the equation while struggling to manipulate the diverse parts of a spell, especially to control their power use?"

"Oh, that's easy," George spoke up, then stopped. "Whoops, I forgot. Am I recognized?" Alaric waved at him and he went on with a grin, "Put the process in a rap song."

"What?" several people asked.

"Sure." George rose, began to speak with a rhythmic beat, and accompanied his words with hand gestures.

"You take your talent, you take a spell.

You add your level, you stir it well.

Pour in some power, but not too much!

Mix it precisely, keep a light touch!

Watch your hands, don't let them roam,

Focus on a crystal, if you need one.

Concentrate, concentrate, and when you're done,

Abracadabra! Alacadun!

A ball of light shines like the sun!"

Rainbow colors spinning around inside it, an orb of light appeared in his hand.

Gloriana smiled. George evidently had hidden abilities. She shot a glance over at a frowning Forscher. Couldn't the man take a joke about his "baby"?

"Hey, I like that," Clay said. "How does it go again? 'You take your talent . . .'"

"You take a spell," George continued.

"You add your level, you stir it well," Clay added the

next line and mimicked George's hand gestures while Bent began to beat time on the arm of his chair.

"Pour in some power," Francie almost sang.

"But not too much!" several people stated emphatically.

"Mix it precisely," Evelyn added.

"Keep a light touch," Antonia admonished, wagging her finger.

"Concentrate, concentrate," everyone in the audience shouted.

"And when you're done . . . Abracadabra! Alacadun!" George finished, "A ball of light shines like the sun!"

Sparkling lightballs in rainbow colors materialized in the hands of everybody except non-practitioner Bent.

"Order, order!" Alaric rapped on the table with his knuckles while the audience laughed and batted the balls around like toys. Clay rolled one along the floor, and Samson chased it into the hall.

Gloriana sighed. Her prediction of chaos was coming true right in front of her, and it wasn't only Clay acting up. She glanced over at Forscher, who was shuffling his papers with a resigned expression. She could empathize—he wanted a real discussion of his formula, not another circus.

"Daddy," she said and put a hand on her father's arm, "let's get on with it."

He nodded and spoke louder. "Let's come to order, people. The question is how to study the equation to determine the best way to use it."

"Thank you," she heard Forscher say softly.

"Let them have their committee," Daria said with a gracious smile.

Gloriana came to attention. She knew that tone; her sister had laid a trap.

"Why are you giving in so easily?" Clay glared at Daria, then his eyebrows shot up. "Oh, I see. You think the whole idea will get buried, don't you? Send it through Council channels, let everybody talk and talk, and nothing will get done. What's that old saying? In a bureaucracy, all channels lead to the Dead Sea?"

"No, of course not," Daria replied, "I believe the notion should be studied—thoroughly. In the meantime, let the rest of us muddle along in our blissful ignorance, happily casting our spells as we always have."

"I'm more interested in the result," Evelyn interjected. "What happens when some of us can't use the equation—not won't, but aren't capable, can't think or cast in those terms?"

"I won't be stifled by a strict formula," Antonia stated with a sharp shake of her head.

"Mother, you aren't stifled by recipes, either. You make them up while you go along," Clay protested. "Think how efficient you'd be if you used it?"

"Sometimes, son, it's not efficiency that results in a good meal—or a good spell," she replied.

Touché, Gloriana thought and sighed. They were getting off the subject. She poked her father in the arm.

"Daddy, we need to stay on track."

"In a minute," he said, "I want to see where this is heading."

"Think how a low-level practitioner would benefit from using the equation," George suggested.

"What if they simply couldn't use it? They tried, but they couldn't think that way or make it work?" Francie asked. "I'd be devastated and think I was a total failure."

"You're not a failure, honey," Clay said.

"That's not the point," Evelyn put in.

Gloriana watched in dismay as everyone started talking at once and to each other. Then Bent, of all people, started chanting George's rap ditty, and Francie joined him. Clay said something about "stodgy, old-fashioned" casting. Antonia said she'd show him stodgy and wiggled her fingers. Her mother's favorite illusion of rose petals filled the air, and they swirled in invisible currents when Francie accompanied the beat with hand and arm movements.

George joined the chanters and cast multiple lightballs that danced through the petals. Evelyn shrugged and cast the illusion of a dunce cap which she settled firmly on her husband's head. Daria asked Clay how she, who couldn't spell anything except herself, would have learned to cast when trying to fit into a rigid mold. Clay's answer was lost amid the uproar.

Her father—finally—called for order, but gave up after about fifteen seconds and joined in the rap.

"Oh, hell," Gloriana muttered. The event was breaking down exactly as she'd feared—in chaos and fiasco. She turned to her father and tugged at his sleeve until he stopped rapping. "I give up, Daddy. Nobody is taking us seriously. This rehearsal is useless. It's worse than a waste of time—it's no help at all. I warned you, and I'm not going to stay around and play. I'm out of here."

Shaking her head in frustration, she rose and marched out of the room. The hounds followed.

CHAPTER
ELEVEN

Marcus stared at the confusion of rose petals, multicolored lightballs, and gesticulating, talking, singing people. He had never envisioned the rehearsal falling apart as it had. The Morgan family was clearly crazy, but George and Evelyn had joined in the debacle, too. What a mess. They'd never get anywhere after this uproar. It was the first debate all over again.

When Morgan walked out, he felt a moment of panic. She was leaving him alone in anarchy.

No, she wasn't going to do that to him. He wouldn't let her. He wasn't going to be stuck with these lunatics.

He stood and stalked into the hall. A burst of laughter and clapping followed him. The front door stood open, and the dogs were on the porch, so he went out to join them.

Morgan had opened her car door. She was truly leaving.

"Wait!" he called and heard the word come out in

a croak.

She stopped and stared at him over the closed top of the dark green convertible.

"Take me with you." God, he sounded pathetic. He didn't care. He had to get out of there, and they needed to talk about what happened. "Please."

Her eyes met his for a long moment before she nodded. "Get in."

Samson and Delilah beat him to the car. When he opened the passenger door, she was spreading a blanket over the back seats.

"Come on, you two, in the back," she said.

After the dogs climbed in, he settled into the front seat and fastened his seat belt. He didn't know where they were going, and he didn't care.

When she started the engine, a country-western song blasted out of the radio speakers. Some guy was singing about a woman who was T-R-O-U-B-L-E. Marcus couldn't stand country-western, but at least the words certainly fit his situation.

She backed out onto the road. "Hold on," she said, changed gears, and stepped on the gas.

The car leapt forward like she'd hit the afterburner on a jet, and he grabbed the armrest as the acceleration pressed him back into the seat. She slowed—barely—for a right-hand turn and hit a high speed on the straightaway. He glanced backward. The dogs had their heads out the open windows and seemed to be enjoying themselves.

"Where are we going?" he managed to gasp out over the music.

"Over there." She actually took a hand off the wheel to wave in a direction off to the right.

On the horizon, he saw a tall building literally shining in the sun. Other, lower buildings stretched out from its right flank and reflected the clouds. The farm's greenhouses, he surmised before her fast cornering jerked his gaze back to the road. He took a firmer grip on both the armrest and the seat belt.

A couple of white-knuckled minutes later, they pulled up before the larger structure. Blessed silence fell when she cut off the car engine. With shaking hands, he released the seat belt and pulled himself out of the car. He was surprised his legs still held him upright after that ride.

"Do you always drive that fast?" he asked. He wasn't sure if he was angry or astounded as he stared at her across the roof of the convertible.

"Fast? That wasn't fast. I barely hit fifty. Besides, the sooner we were away from that riot in the living room, the better." She gave him a mischievous grin before waving at the building in front of them. "Well, what do you think?"

He faced it and looked up . . . and up. From the ground to a peaked roof it stood at least three stories high. The bottom third of the glass structure was tinted a light smoky brown, and he couldn't really see inside. Leafy branches pressed against the upper panes like they were trying to escape. "What is it? A greenhouse on steroids?"

About to unlock the door, she glanced back at him. Her green eyes sparkled, and she chuckled. "I never thought of it like that. Come in and see for yourself."

She turned the key, but before opening the door, she shook her finger at the dogs who had followed them from the car. "Okay, you two, remember, no chewing on the plants."

"Are the plants poisonous in there?" he asked, suddenly apprehensive.

"I don't use herbicides or pesticides, and some of the plants are mildly toxic or have a few thorns. Delilah comes in all the time, and she leaves them alone. If Samson was a puppy, I wouldn't let him in. Otherwise, I don't want my specimens to have teeth marks. It really will be all right." She walked into a small vestibule between the outer door and an inner one. When he had closed the first door, she led the way through the second.

He followed her into a world with heavy, humid air smelling of earth and faint floral fragrances, with multiple shades of green punctuated by spots of red or pink or white or purple, with large and small ferns, bushes, trees, and vines. A narrow pathway, overhung with leafy branches, led deeper into the jungle and quickly disappeared. At ground level, the lighting was soft and shady, filtered by the trees; above the boundary of the tinted glass, the sun shone brightly on the treetops. He could hear water running somewhere.

"Welcome to my tropical paradise."

Her words brought his gaze back down to her. Dressed as she was, the green sweater matching the emerald of her eyes and blending with the background, her dark hair flowing around her shoulders, she could almost be a creature of the forest. Or the jungle, rather. He, however, felt distinctly out of place, practically on another planet.

"This is my playground. It's for pure enjoyment and is not connected to either the farm operations or my research. When I come here, I can block out the rest of the world." She grimaced. "When the so-called debate degenerated into chaos, I decided I'd better get out of there before I screamed like a banshee and made a fool of myself. It seemed to be the appropriate place to come for some peace."

"I'm glad you did," Marcus said. "Left, I mean. It gave me the excuse to do the same. What happened to everybody? They all seemed to go crazy."

"I'm not surprised. I feared Clay would start something, if for no other reason than to uphold his reputation for family teasing. I warned Daddy, and he assured me he'd keep order. Hmph! Some order."

Marcus shook his head. "Clay wasn't the primary instigator. George holds the honor with his rap song. Putting him and your brother together was like throwing two firecrackers into the fire. For reasons I've never been able to fathom, George delights in 'shaking me up' from time to time. He claims it's good for me."

"Our rehearsal never had a chance, did it?"

He could only shake his head again. She sounded and looked so disappointed, his hands itched with the desire to take her in his arms to comfort. Or maybe simply to hold her. Hell, even when confused and unsettled by a ludicrous "debate" and a terrifying ride, his damned attraction to her pulled at him like she was a magnet and he a pile of iron filings. He refused to think it could be more than his libido reminding him of its existence. Certainly not what George had been talking about. He needed to change the subject.

To distract himself, he started looking around. Her house had been practically devoid of plants, he remembered. The building and its contents more than made up for that lack. "What are all these?"

"Do you have plants or a garden?"

"No. Except for tending to Samson, I'm too busy. I told my landscaper to put in native trees and the like to cut down on the upkeep. Never had an interest in gardening, either."

"Oh. Then let me give you the nickel tour. The path runs through a series of S curves, to maximize the growing area and put us close to the plants. To my left is an allspice tree from Jamaica. Over to the right a cinnamon tree from Asia . . ." She walked him along the winding gravel walkway pointing out ferns, flowering bushes, trees, a stand of bamboo. The dogs disappeared into the foliage ahead.

Marcus was grateful, but a little surprised that she used common names in her explanation, not the long Latin ones he would expect of a botanical scientist. He had never heard of some of them, others he vaguely remembered seeing somewhere. All appeared to be growing with abandon. He could only marvel at the size of some of the elephant ears—at least, he thought that's what they were, even if they were blue in color.

He was beginning to feel the vines reaching for him, when they emerged into a small clearing where the path widened. Light streamed down from above and highlighted brilliant reds, pinks, and blues in flowers and leaves. After the darkness of the green tunnel, the profusion of color and light was almost blinding. A cooling breeze made the humidity bearable and rustled the leaves. On the side wall rose a huge tree with large branches arching over the open space. The lower branches, almost within his reaching distance, had no tree leaves and teemed instead with foliage with stiff, shiny, spiky leaves.

"Is all the vegetation natural?" he asked. "That can't be a real tree. Its trunk doesn't extend through the wall."

"No, I fudged some and copied what some zoos have done in artificial rainforests. The biggest trees are fake and serve as hiding places for wiring and plumbing or platforms for the vines and bromeliads. The epiphytes can grow practically anywhere since they don't put down roots like other plants. If you look closely, you can see the braces holding up the long limbs."

He studied the false branches overhead. They certainly appeared natural with the vines coiling around and draping off the horizontal. One of the vines had a funny color—sort of a mottled brown. He followed it with his eyes until he came to an end. What was that triangular shape? Were those eyes?

"Uh, I thought you said there was nothing harmful in here. What about that snake?" He pointed to it.

"Snake? Oh."

He heard her chuckle, but didn't take his eyes off whatever that was lurking above.

"That's Sassy, the cybersnake,"—she emphasized the hiss of the S sounds—"my brother's contribution to my garden. He's named for an African tree bark that's poisonous. 'Can't have an Eden without him,' Clay said. He's rubber."

He took his gaze off the snake to look at her. She had that mischievous glint in her eyes and quirk to her lips again.

"He's computerized, of course. Clay rigged him to move and even fall down on people. There's a remote control to activate him." She glanced at her watch. "Come this way."

She crossed the clearing, and he followed her down the serpentine path through another twisty, leafy, even narrower, more thickly planted tunnel into a much bigger open area with more shrubbery, flowers, and trees on its edges and a lawn in its middle. They had reached what looked to be the rear of the building. In the right corner against the clear back wall rose a black stone formation about ten feet high. A gurgling waterfall splashed down its rugged sides to land in a pond with lilies and a background of tall skinny stalks topped with pompoms of green skinny leaves. At the other end of the pond close to a stand of bamboo, a stream vanished into the bushes.

Against the side to his left stood a wooden structure raised about a foot off the floor and covered by a roof made from palm fronds. A double-wide chaise lounge, a coffee table, and two lawn chairs sat in the middle, and what appeared to be a shed formed the solid back wall.

Marcus breathed easier. The jungle wasn't devoid of civilization. In fact, the cabana might be a good place to sit and think. Despite the humidity, the space was not uncomfortable.

A loud booonnnnnggg suddenly rang through the building.

Marcus jumped as the sound reverberated off the walls and he felt it resonating in his chest. "What was that? An alarm?"

"A notification. Let's get under cover." She stepped up onto the cabana floor and sat in one of the chairs.

He took the chair next to her. Delilah jumped onto the platform and yodeled at Samson, but his hound was busy sniffing around the pond's edge.

"What's going to happen?" he asked, wondering if a floor show would erupt from the pond. Given her family, he'd better be prepared for the worst. "Samson, come here."

The dog ignored him—until a sound like thunder boomed, and rain began to pour down. Samson yelped and made a beeline for the protection of the cabana.

"Delilah doesn't like water, either," Gloriana said with a smile while Samson shook himself dry.

Marcus frowned at her.

She must have thought he was angry because she said in an apologetic tone, "It really is a rainforest. I have some towels in the pump room behind us, if you want to dry him off."

"No, he'll be fine," he answered as the rain increased in volume. He looked up. The palm frond roof did its job; not even a drop permeated the barrier.

Neither spoke—they would have to shout to be heard over the rain. She didn't look at him, so, seated where he was to her right and slightly behind, he used the time to study the woman. She appeared to be checking out her jungle, focusing on points around the area, until she closed her eyes and gave a deep sigh. The inhalation caused her sweater to tighten across her chest, and the movement drew his gaze. He felt his body stir. Maybe it had not been such a good idea to come with her to her wet paradise.

After several minutes, the rain abruptly stopped, and silence surrounded them, punctuated only by the gentle sound of water, either dripping from the leaves and the cabana roof or gurgling down the rocks into the pond. She opened her eyes and looked at him—with an expression he couldn't read, and the intensity of her gaze shook him to the core.

With an effort, he broke the eye contact and stood, walked over to the edge of the platform. He had to clear his throat before he could speak. "You have the rain on a timer, I presume?" It was an inane comment, but the best he could do at the moment.

"Yes. The water circulates in a closed system." Her voice sounded breathless at first, then evened out as she talked. She explained the complicated drainage and nutrient system and finished with, "The arrangement is so efficient that we lose very little to evaporation."

Marcus peered up at the barely visible piping high above him, then down to the waterfall, pond, and profusion of flowers and foliage. Her rainforest was both high-tech and primeval. He understood the mathematics of her system almost intuitively. At the same time, he felt distinctly out of place in such an environment, like he was truly in the middle of an ancient jungle.

"How long have you been working on it?" he asked, merely to keep the conversation going.

"Three years. I was hoping to spend more time here this summer, but with the debates . . ."

"Three years? That's all? Some of these plants are enormous. Did you need a crane to lift them into the building?"

"Most were small enough for one or two people or a forklift to pick up when we put them in place." She looked at him with a quizzical expression for a moment before her face cleared. "You don't really know what my magic is or does, do you?"

"I assumed it was all about plant chemistry, manipulating DNA and the like to come up with new species variants and pharmaceutical compounds."

"That's only part of it. My real magic manifests itself in helping plants to grow. When whole specimens, not simply seeds, come to me from all over the world, they're usually in distress from the handling. I use my magic to keep them alive and help them prosper." She rose from the chair and walked past him down the steps over to one of the bushes. "Come here and I'll show you."

When he stood beside her, she pointed to a branch. "Here, take hold gently right below the leaf. Go ahead, it won't bite. It's a poinsettia."

Relieved, he looked down at the branch in his hand. He knew that plant because he always brought Evelyn and George a big one for the holidays. The branch he held was almost all green leaves with only a few tiny red ones at the top. The true flowers, the yellow nubs in the center at the end, were more suggestions than actual fact.

"Watch," she said.

He felt a humming, but couldn't tell if it was in the air or coming from the plant. His fingertips tingled as though something under the skin of the branch was vibrating. Nothing else happened for a few seconds.

He shot a glance at her. She was concentrating on the leaves. He did the same. He was about to ask what to look for, when suddenly the leaves began to grow, especially those at the tip. Before his eyes, they grew at least an inch and turned a deep scarlet. The yellow flowers became round balls. The whole branch quivered—or was that his hand shaking?

"That's all I'll do for the moment," Gloriana said. "I don't want to stress the plant unduly."

Marcus looked from the branch to her and back again. Most of the magic he'd ever come into close contact with had been intellectual—manipulating formulas, or designs, or numbers in the mind. Sure, all practitioners handled energy, and he'd been able to cast *lux* since he was a small child. He'd seen how Evelyn could calm people, but had no idea how she actually managed the feat. He knew some physicians could speed healing—somehow.

He'd never actually witnessed someone manipulate another living thing like that. It wasn't telekinesis. It wasn't light energy. He ran his fingers over the leaves. It certainly wasn't an illusion. It was physical magic. He'd actually felt the power flowing, causing a change of recognizable proportions. He could almost believe he'd seen a secret of the universe revealed.

"How do you *do* that?" He didn't bother to hide the wonder in his voice. His bulging eyes and dropped jaw had already given him away. "You must be working on the molecular level."

"I assume so. I've been helping plants grow forever, and I don't have to dissect my spells. Never did, as a matter of fact. I think about what I want to happen, focus, mentally cast the *crescere* spell for growth, add some energy, and . . . the leaf grows." She shrugged. "I'm an intuitive caster like my mother. That's why I had such trouble trying your equation and what I meant by the 'feel' of magic."

He stood gazing down at her, torn between the need to know more, to solve the puzzle of how she caused the plant to grow and the desire to pull her into his arms and work some magic of his own. He wondered if she could teach him how to cast *crescere*, then almost laughed at the idea. Of course she couldn't. Or rather, he wouldn't be able to learn it. He didn't have that talent. Her magic definitely wasn't his.

In fact, what he had seen should be reinforcing his conclusion that they weren't soul mates. Their magics were totally opposite. Hers, the ancient, female, basic enchantments the witches of old must have used, literally grounded in the earth. His, the new, predominantly warlock, cerebral, flying in the stratosphere of the mind. They had nothing in common. His attraction was an aberration. The soul-mate imperative was not working correctly for him. What else did he expect from a child of his parents? The imperative screwed them up. Why not him, too?

Stifling a groan as his center spiked with heat and he wanted to touch her so much it hurt, he retreated a step. He needed to get back among people before he lost control of himself. "Should we return to the house? Surely things have calmed down by now."

Morgan seemed to shake herself. "Yes, I hope so."

They walked through the leafy tunnels again, followed by the dogs. The greenhouse felt even more like an alien environment than it had when he entered, and he was glad to come out into the fresh air, even if it was a hot breeze.

"Do me a favor, will you?" he asked, letting the dogs into her car. "Take it a little slower, and turn down the radio."

"Don't like country-western? I'll do both, but the hardest will be to slow down. That's what Clay always asks when he rides with me," she groused. "What is it with men when they aren't driving?"

She complied with his requests.

CHAPTER TWELVE

"Look who's here," George said when they walked into the dining room. He had a smile on his face that distinctly reminded Gloriana of her brother when he was plotting against her.

"Have some cherry pie and coffee," Antonia said.

Gloriana sat down at one of the two remaining seats—right next to each other—and glanced from one face to the next. Her brother looked mischievous, but he often did. Francie did, also, and that wasn't usual. Daria was concentrating on her pie and winked at her. Bent and Evelyn were talking about his company. George was grinning at Forscher, who settled in the adjoining chair and seemed to be ignoring the older man. Her mother busied herself serving the pie. It all seemed basically normal—too normal.

"Where did you go?" her father asked.

The question blew her thoughts away. "We took a

tour of the jungle." She decided not to bring up the re-hearsal debacle; she'd sound like a whiner.

No one mentioned the event at all, in fact. George asked her about the rainforest, and Clay talked to Forscher about mathematics. When dessert was done, the Bernhards said it was time they headed home, and Forscher agreed.

As she watched the cars drive away, Gloriana breathed a sigh of relief. At least the visit was over and Forscher was gone. She glanced at her parents, who were climbing the front steps. Should she bring up the re-hearsal? It wouldn't do any good to berate her father for failing to keep order. She couldn't even blame Clay, al-though she'd really like to.

Maybe they had learned something from the uproar. Everybody had been talking, voicing their own person-al views, obviously more interested in the subject than in following the rules. The topic might simply be too volatile for rational discussion. If so, Ed and the Swords would have to keep close control at the actual debates.

She followed her parents into the kitchen. The Houston four were cleaning up the dishes, and, when she appeared in the doorway, they all faced her. Each one was smiling—too sweetly.

"What?" she asked. Little warning tingles shot up her spine.

"Did y'all have a good time at the greenhouse?" Clay asked in a too-innocent tone.

"Why?" She squinted at him and braced herself.

"Getting to know your 'opponent' better?"

"What are you talking about?"

"Well, seeing as how you two are destined to be to-gether . . ." he answered.

Both Daria and Francie said, "Clay!"

"Daria, I asked you to tell no one," Gloriana said from between her clenched teeth.

"I didn't!" Daria said. "Clay announced it when we were clearing the table."

"I speculated," Francie put in, "but I didn't say a word, either. I thought you'd tell us when you were ready."

"Glori, it sticks out all over the both of you," Clay stated in his most condescending, big-brother manner. "He was scratching, you were trying not to, and when you looked at each other, your expressions were so hot, your ears got red. I can put together the clues as well as the next practitioner."

"Oh, for crying out loud." Gloriana glared at her family. How bad was this teasing going to get?

"George gave me the idea," Clay continued. "He said something about it before we started the debate. It was his idea to . . ." He shut his mouth abruptly.

"Idea to . . .?" she coaxed with a come-here gesture. Clay shrugged like he had simply been speculating, but she wasn't going to let him off the hook. "Keep going, brother dear."

"Yes, you'd better explain it all, son," their father said, obviously trying not to smile.

Clay shrugged. "I happened to mention how you had warned Dad to keep order. We decided to see how much chaos we could cause—after all, you can expect it in the real debates. When I said you would probably walk out if things got too rambunctious, George suggested that you and Marcus could use some time alone together. I asked why and he said he thought the two of you were soul mates. I gather Marcus isn't too happy with the idea."

"*He's* not happy?" Gloriana reached out to hold on to the door frame for strength to stand when it hit her that Forscher might be aware of their situation. He didn't like it, either? What did that mean?

"So, we pushed the envelope a little. You can't lay blame totally on me and George. Everybody joined right in with no coaxing. Don't forget, you made the decision to leave. We didn't chase you out the door." He crossed his arms and assumed a self-righteous expression.

All Gloriana could do was slump against the door. "Oh, my God," she muttered.

Her mother came over to her and gave her a hug. "Don't worry so much. Everything will work out, dear."

Gloriana glanced from one face to the next. "Yeah, right." Her family meant well, even Clay. Hadn't she been thinking that the real debates would be much worse than the pretend one? Maybe she should have stayed and fought it out.

Too late now—an expression she'd been using too much lately.

"Thanks for your help, I guess," she said. "I'm going home. I don't have the strength to talk about what anyone did or didn't do. You made your point. The first debate is next weekend, and I have a lot to do before then."

Despite her intentions, she didn't get away until after the exodus of the Houston bunch. In her car, she immediately turned the radio off. The last thing she needed was a song about unrequited love, requited love, love gone wrong, love gone right, or any country-western staple, especially not Johnny Cash singing "Ring of Fire."

Marcus Forscher. Her soul mate. No. *Alleged* soul mate.

What was she going to do about him? In the green-house, she'd felt the compulsion at least twice to throw herself into his arms, stretch out on the chaise with him, and discover how perfect he truly was. Keeping control of herself hadn't been easy.

When she'd showed him her plant manipulation skills, he'd had such a look of horror on his face. Was it truly horror? Or maybe simply amazement. He didn't seem comfortable in her world, she was sure of that fact. Whatever it was, he certainly wanted to get out of there after her demonstration.

Where did all it leave her? He knew about "X" and

the possibility they were "X," and so did she. He hadn't said a word, she wasn't going to. He hadn't made a move, she wasn't going to, either.

All she had to do was get through the next five weekends, they'd both go back to their routines—where they never saw each other—and the whole thing would blow over.

Wouldn't it?

As if in answer, her magic center gave a lurch, then a flutter. She had the distinct impression she could hear laughter.

CHAPTER
THIRTEEN

"I'd like you to meet our Swords, John Baldwin and Grace Cabot," Ed said after he'd welcomed Gloriana and her parents to the private dining room in the Boston HeatherRidge the following Saturday. "John's on the Defenders Council and will be with us at every event. Grace is head of the Defenders for New England."

"It's nice to meet you," Gloriana said as she shook hands. While Ed introduced her parents, she looked the three over. Short, balding, sturdy Baldwin practically radiated magical power and an air of command. Cabot combined the look of "old money," refined and elegant, with a no-nonsense attitude.

"We've heard the tapes from Austin, and we've devised a plan for order," Baldwin stated. "We have a Sword in each overflow room, and Grace and I will be in the ballroom. I don't anticipate problems."

"I hope not," Gloriana said. "Our rehearsal at home

showed that simply discussing the subject can be volatile, even among friends and family."

"We're ready." Ed grinned and stage-whispered, "We made sure Mrs. Shortbottom and her cane are not in the main room." He continued in a normal voice, "We also insisted Horner's and Pritchart's entourages stay separate from each other."

Before anyone could comment further, the door opened, and Forscher walked in with a couple who had to be his parents. A sharp not-quite-pain-not-quite-thrill hit her in the center, and she only barely suppressed her gasp. To calm herself down, she studied his parents. It was clear how Forscher had come by his dress habits.

An older version of his son, the father had darker blond hair and blue-gray eyes. The Forscher men had the same carriage—their perfect posture showed off their impeccably tailored navy suits. The only difference in attire was the elder's red-and-blue-striped tie versus the younger's solid light blue—matching his eyes. The tall, slim, honey-blond woman had on a beautifully tailored, ivory-colored suit with camel-and-ivory spectator pumps and a brown alligator clutch purse. Gloriana didn't recognize the name brands by sight, but the shoes alone proclaimed a serious attitude toward fashion.

The chic ensemble made Gloriana feel frump-ish, even though she wore a new suit in the dark green she preferred. To go with it, she'd let her mother bully her into buying a pale blue-green silk blouse with an embossed fern pattern. She stood a little straighter and told herself she had nothing to be ashamed of, including her plain-brown medium heels.

She glanced at Forscher and caught him frowning at her. Her magic center began itching when their eyes met. She resolutely ignored the aggravation. It was nothing compared to the dreams she'd been having. She'd begun to think they needed to talk about the situation—but only if he would be the one to bring it up. God, she was turning into a coward.

Forscher brought his parents over to the group and introduced everyone.

"Dr. Morgan," his mother said as she shook Gloriana's hand, "I'm looking forward to the debate. You and Marcus have certainly stirred up the practitioner community."

"Thank you, Dr. Forscher," Gloriana said, unsure if the woman was pleased or annoyed at the result of their articles. Judith Forscher's smile was polite, not quite reaching her sapphire-blue eyes. Her gaze was not overtly inspecting, but Gloriana felt thoroughly scrutinized—and possibly found wanting.

She was suddenly thankful her parents had decided to make the trip, even over her initial objections. They had claimed she'd need the support. She still thought she could handle whatever the debate brought. Having them here as a buffer to the Forschers—all the Forschers—would be helpful, however. In the meantime, she had a position to uphold, and she straightened her spine and assumed her professorial manner. Nothing done or said could ruffle her composure when she put on those imaginary robes.

"Too many Ph.D.'s," Ed announced. "Let's use first names, shall we, or I'll be terminally confused. And let's eat so we'll have time to enjoy the meal."

Gloriana sat down at the round table between Ed on her left and John Baldwin on her right. Conversation was polite, general chitchat for a while, until people began talking to those next to them. Baldwin reassured her of their resolve to maintain order, and they shared a laugh at his reaction to the antics of the first debate.

She snuck glances at the Forschers when she could. Marcus Forscher was talking mostly to Ed on his right rather than to his mother on his other side. He called her Judith at one point, and Gloriana shook her head mentally at the thought of calling her mother by her first name. It felt funny even to think of it. His father was answering a question from her father.

Did his parents have an inkling about "X," she wondered. When she found out Forscher's family would be at the predebate dinner, she made her own parents promise not to say a single word, not even a hint. Forscher himself was still sending shivers up her backbone when he looked at her, but nobody seemed to notice her discomfort.

When Ed and Forscher were talking and Baldwin was speaking with her mother on his other side, Gloriana watched Judith out of the corner of her eye. The woman appeared perfectly calm, composed, and serene. When she looked at her son, however, her expression immediately became softer, more approachable, and Gloriana could see the pride in her eyes. When Ed asked her a direct question, something to do with the national economy, however, it faded, and she became a professor again.

❊❉❊❉❊❉

After dinner, Marcus followed Ed and Morgan into the ballroom and up on the stage. The room, larger than the one in Austin, held over five hundred people. The stage was higher also, and he had a clear view up the center aisle all the way to the entry doors. Two large screens hung from the ceiling on either side of the stage, ready to display the speakers. Four camera operators and several men with microphones lounged against a side wall, and he could see more people in the camera booth above the doors. On stage a sound technician completed his check and conferred with Ed.

Marcus plopped his black leather folder on the left-hand side of the table. He searched for and found their parents sitting over at the right near some side doors. Good, Alaric was making sure they could leave if a disruption occurred. He watched Morgan wave at them, and he rubbed the small pain behind his breastbone by pretending to straighten his tie. Despite his attraction, he still couldn't believe she was his soul mate.

Certainly not.

No matter how hot his dreams or painful his center or active his libido.

He hadn't said a word to Judith or Stefan about soul-mate possibilities. No sense in stirring those deep waters. His parents were leaving for Europe in a few days, so after tomorrow he wouldn't have to worry about them hearing rumors. Her parents hadn't given him an indication they suspected it, either—which was fine. Neither he nor Morgan needed any interference or matchmaking.

Especially from George, whose phone calls he had not returned. Even though he himself knew they could *not* be soul mates—not after what he'd seen of her magic in the greenhouse, he also knew his stubborn friend wouldn't give up on the idea. Thank God George and his parents didn't correspond.

He looked over at his parents again. He had arrived late last night and had lunch with them today—with the main topic being their usual polite discussion of his career. Stefan encouraged him as always to look for a position among the Eastern universities. Judith only asked him if he was truly happy—a surprising departure from her normal comments.

The four parents seemed to be getting along. They actually shared a laugh when Alaric swung his arm in a wide arc, then poked a finger at his father.

Morgan stepped up next to him, and he felt his

nostrils flare when her scent reached him and swirled around in his lungs, practically making him dizzy. At least he wasn't repeating the reaction he'd had when he first saw her in the dining room—the response he'd had to use his note folder to hide. He thrust his itching hands into his pockets to keep them from reaching out to touch her.

She didn't seem to react to their nearness, but simply waved a hand at the foursome. "Looks like Daddy's telling tales again."

"Mrs. Shortbottom, no doubt. Let's hope he doesn't have some new ones at the end of the evening."

"Amen to that." She took a step away and placed her dark green portfolio on the table by her chair.

Ed finished with the technician and came to stand with them. "We're going to open the doors and start as soon as people are settled. Tonight we're asking the audience to fill out a questionnaire about the event, including their opinions on the issue. It's not scientific, but should give us some ideas for the future meetings and let us hear from those who didn't ask a public question. If you'd like, we can go over them after the debate."

Both he and Morgan nodded in agreement as the ushers opened the doors. A few people rushed to the front and claimed front-row seats. Others followed more sedately, and it wasn't long before the seats were filled.

Morgan, Ed, and he remained standing and identified people they knew for each other. Prick sat on the left in the middle on the aisle, with a couple of other mathematicians from local universities Marcus recognized. The Horners marched down the center and took seats in the second row on the right. Morgan waved at a trio of women, clearly friends of hers. In their black Sword robes, Baldwin and Cabot took their positions, one to each side in front of the stage.

Marcus turned to Ed. "Do both sides understand the rules?"

"Yes, I spoke personally with Pritchart and Horner and made the situation absolutely clear." He hauled a large timepiece out of his pocket. "I have the stopwatch Alaric recommended. Are we all set?"

Marcus exchanged a glance with Morgan, who shrugged and said, "I'm ready."

"So am I," he replied.

Ed grinned. "Then it's showtime."

CHAPTER FOURTEEN

"Therefore, we at the Traditional Heritage Association call upon all practitioners to band together against this attempt to destroy our time-tested spell-casting methods," Calvin Horner stated, his voice practically quivering with indignation and certitude. "We don't need change simply for the sake of change. We don't need the Council or anyone else telling us how to do our business. We must stop Forscher's pernicious formula now, or we will certainly pay later. Thank you." He sat down to much applause—from the right side of the hall.

As he looked out over the audience, Marcus concentrated on keeping a straight face. Daria had done a much better job of explaining the THA position at the rehearsal. Horner played to his supporters, appealing to emotion, to scare tactics, and to thinly veiled sarcasm about the "Fomsters," his name for the Future of Magic crowd. Of course, the man did not even consider studying the equation in an unprejudiced manner. No, he wanted to bury the "abomination."

Marcus glanced at Morgan. While he would have liked to stare at her, doing that made his body react and his thoughts go off on tangents, so he kept his attention on the speaker. From her body language, it appeared she was doing the same.

She did seem to be unhappy, also. They had tried to establish a neutral tone, both basically repeating their opening remarks from the rehearsal. She had even agreed with the need to study his equation. The applause had been polite.

After Horner came Prick, from the left side. The participants had divided themselves up spontaneously, with the FOM on the left and the THA on the right. Where were the people in the middle of the question? He made a note to speak to Ed about a different chair arrangement.

When Horner first stood up to speak, he had taken a microphone to the front below the stage and faced the audience. Very clever, Marcus thought, to give the impression of being in charge. Prick must have come to the same conclusion, because he walked down the aisle from his seat in the middle to take a stance where his opponent had.

"You don't have to be a mathematician to see the worth of using a precise, clear, modern approach to spellcasting," Pritchart said, and Marcus began to hope the man would present a better, more coherent argument than Horner had. His wishes were dashed, however, when Prick continued. "Horner's 'Traddies' would have us believe we cannot formulate a general theory of the casting universe. I say we can and must, or be doomed to outmoded, inefficient, anachronistic casting methods that will only keep us from reaching our potential."

Marcus gritted his teeth and kept his face blank while he listened to Prick appeal to the very emotion he was denying existed and, even more infuriating, act like he had been the equation's creator. Finally Ed called time, and Prick smirked his way back to his chair amid much applause.

Fortunately, the question-and-answer parts of the program went smoothly, as the audience responded to the questions he and Morgan posed and asked some good ones of their own. A number of participants agreed with the need to study the formula and clarify how one determined the amount of power and other elements in the spell. A few adherents from each camp had their say, but for the most part everyone acted politely—if you didn't count the "if looks could kill" stare downs and pointed remarks from time to time.

Finally, after a few summation comments, Ed declared the session at an end. Marcus and his parents and the Morgans gathered together in the room where they had eaten supper.

"We and the Forschers are going out for a drink," Alaric said. "Why don't you two come with us?"

"Ed's bringing back the evaluation forms everybody filled out tonight, Daddy," Morgan answered. "I'd like to see those first. After that, I'm going to bed. I'm exhausted. I'll call you in the morning."

"Thanks, I'm going to take a rain check," Marcus said. "I have an early flight tomorrow. I'd better say good-bye. It was a pleasure to see you and Antonia again." He shook hands with her parents before walking over to his own.

"Good job, Marcus," Stefan said. "Listening to those blowhards on either side makes me wonder about the state of education and the ability to create a logical argument in this country."

"Thank you, Stefan," he answered and basked for a moment in his father's highest praise before adding, "I'm not looking forward to the remainder of the circus."

"You'll do well," Judith said and gave his arm a squeeze. "We'll follow your triumphs on the practitioner Web site. I'm sure our European colleagues will have many questions about the debates."

"Come on, Judith, I could use that drink." Stefan shook Marcus's hand. "You'll demolish those idiots, I'm sure."

Judith gave Marcus's arm another squeeze. Then she surprised him by stretching up to kiss his cheek. "We'll miss you on the Fourth of July."

"Me, too," he replied and fought an impulse to hug her. He had to remind himself that she didn't like to be "mussed," and lowered his arms, which had been rising of their own accord. He glanced over at the other family and saw Morgan get and give big hugs from her parents, and a little twinge of something that might have been re-gret—or jealousy—flickered through his mind.

He watched the parents leave, but before he could say anything to Morgan, in came Ed and John, their arms full of papers.

"Here are all the evaluations," Ed said, placing the stack on the round dining table. "Let's divide them into categories of Traddies, Fomsters, and neutrals to begin with. Watch for the agree-disagree scores, too. They may help you decide where the writer stands."

"That sounds reasonable," Gloriana said and sat down across the table from Forscher. She had watched him and his parents out of the corner of her eye and won-dered briefly at the reserve they all showed. Didn't even give their son a hug when they weren't going to see him for months. Thank goodness those stiff and starched people weren't her parents.

Ed and John divided up the forms, Ed indicated where to put each category, and they started reading.

"Here's a good one," Ed said about three minutes later. "*All you people and your ideas remind me of is the government trying to force us into categories that don't fit us. THA wants us this way; FOM wants us that way. My wife dragged me here tonight. I have no time for it. I'm only trying to make a living.*' He doesn't like anybody."

"I'm sure there are many who feel the same way,"

Gloriana said. "Too busy to want to bother learning new methods."

"Apathy or disinterest. That's what the THA is counting on," Forscher said, "and why FOM is trying hard to be incendiary."

Gloriana met his eyes when he said the word *incendiary*, and her magic center must have taken the word to heart because it immediately grew warm. She snapped her gaze back to the paper in her hand. Don't look at him, she admonished herself. She was only encouraging the imperative.

After a few minutes, she glanced at the piles of paper. The FOM and THA sides were about equal. The middle pile was noticeably smaller.

"Uh-oh," John said. "Here's one that's definitely not apathetic. *What is wrong with you people? Forcing us to change the way we cast is worse than idiotic! It's criminal! Who do you think you are? You all should be banned from spreading such blasphemous ideas!* Oh, my. Blasphemy yet, and with lots of exclamation points. Agrees totally with all the THA statements and is totally against the FOM ones. He signed it, too, so he's not hiding—Gordon Walcott."

"That's one of Horner's, all right," Ed said. "One of his inner circle. Walcott will be taking Horner's place in the next debate."

"He sounds more radical than Horner." Forscher grimaced. "Precisely what we need."

Gloriana sighed and kept reading. Two forms later, she came on one written in big black letters. "Here's an even angrier one from the FOM side. *'The THA is pathetic! The Traddies are crazy to stand in the way of progress! They should all be buried because they're already brain-dead!'* The writer makes no attempt at an argument and gives the opposite scores from the one John read."

"Is there a name on it?" Forscher asked.

"Yes. The handwriting is atrocious, but it looks like . . . B-something . . . Dorf? . . . no, Dortman."

"Ah, Brad Dortman. He's been one of Prick's sycophants for quite a while. I'm only acquainted with him from conferences and a couple of articles. Not very impressive in either his writings or his manners."

"Who's speaking for FOM next time?" John asked.

"Brubaker," Ed answered. "I hope he doesn't go off into math never-never land like he did in Austin. We'll lose half the audience from sheer incomprehension and put the other half to sleep."

"We may have another problem. Look," John said with an ominous tone in his voice. He held up a sheet that had been written with a black marker. The message stood out in stark words. *"Stop these debates! Let Magic Alone!"*

"Here's its counterpart." Forscher held up a page with big red letters. *"To Hell with the THA!"*

"Wonderful," Gloriana muttered and picked up the next in her stack. Thank goodness it held a sensible statement.

They continued their study, occasionally reading aloud when a unique comment emerged. Not too many did.

"Let's see what we have here," Ed straightened the piles after all the forms had been categorized. "About equally divided. I'll have these scored and get back to you during the week."

"Only four seem to be rabid," John noted. "Let's keep those to ourselves. No sense in giving someone ideas."

"I'd like to see more comments from the middle," Forscher said, "but I realize how difficult it is to get those. The people who choose to respond on these forms do select themselves to answer, usually because they have an axe to grind. Therefore, we're not getting a scientific sample on which to base our conclusions."

"We realized that," Ed said, "and the High Council conducted a survey last week and will repeat it after the debates are done. We'll have the results next week."

Forscher nodded. "During the debate, I did think of one possibility that might help us identify the undecided and uncommitted. What if instead of a single center aisle, we have two, and give those people a middle place that doesn't tie them to either viewpoint—or give the THA or FOM adherents any chance to intimidate them."

"I like that idea," John said. "If I have to maintain order, the farther apart the two groups are physically, the better. My staff in the auxiliary rooms said those audiences were rowdier."

"How much rowdier?" Gloriana asked. She wasn't

looking forward to a repeat of the first debate.

"Mostly only loud comments or applause. A few catcalls, some cheers. Nothing beyond that. The Traddies and Fomsters gathered in separate rooms, and the chances of a fight were practically nil."

"I'll make a special appeal next time for those in the middle to tell us their views," Ed said.

On that note, they adjourned. As she picked up her folder and her purse, Gloriana made the mistake she'd warned herself against. She looked across the table straight into Forscher's icy blue eyes. His gaze became warm, then hot, and a corresponding warmth, then heat spread from her center to her fingers and toes—and pooled in her middle before descending ever so slowly to a spot between her legs.

She covered the spot with her portfolio in a reflex she didn't remember making until she broke eye contact—with difficulty—and stepped back from the table. When she looked at him again, Forscher was on his feet and moving in her direction, his expression stark and predatory.

She kicked herself mentally to force her brain into gear and headed for the door. Over her shoulder, she said, "Good night."

Ed and John both said good night and headed in different directions.

"I'll escort you to your door," Forscher said with such finality in his tone that she knew her protest would be futile.

CHAPTER FIFTEEN

They walked to the elevators in silence. In the mezzanine lobby several Fomsters and Traddies were arguing while a black-robed Sword stood silently by the registration table. The belligerents called to them, but Forscher ignored the request to join the fray, and she followed his lead.

The elevator came, and they entered. Gloriana pushed the button for her floor and asked, "Which one are you on?"

"The same. I'm in 1217."

"I'm in 1215." She faced front and shot a quick glance at him. His body also faced the door, and he was looking straight at her. His gaze captured hers and held it. She felt a distinct falling sensation and wondered briefly if a bug in a carnivorous pitcher plant had the same experience when it went to its doom. He leaned toward her, slightly lowered his head. She was actually turning to him and raising hers—she couldn't stop her body from moving—when the elevator halted and three people entered. The necessity to step back broke the spell.

Oh, my God, she thought as she retreated to the side and stared at the door, the button panel, the floor numbers display—anywhere except at him. Ignoring her and Forscher completely, the new passengers discussed a problem family member—something about inappropriate spell-casting.

Finally, they reached the twelfth floor and emerged into the hall while the three behind them chatted away. She wasn't sure if the silence that fell when the door closed was helpful or not. With her mind in such a muddle and her body not obeying her commands, what could she say to him without making a fool of herself? Walking down the corridor, she didn't look back, certainly didn't make eye contact—she wasn't going to get into that situation again. They came to her door, and she pulled the key card from her pocket. She was about to swipe it through the slot when his hand covered hers.

"We need to talk," Forscher said in that low voice of his that vibrated through her like a wind through the treetops, leaving her nerves, like the leaves, quivering.

Gloriana took a deep breath and let it out. He obviously knew about their situation. Maybe they did need to get it all out into the open. She'd have to make sure she kept her distance—and control of her body.

"Yes," was all she trusted herself to say. She pulled

her hand from his and inserted the card.

He opened the door, and she walked in, thanking Ed silently for booking her a suite and glad she had left so many lights on. The last thing she needed with him here was a darkened room or a bed in plain view. Not that dim lights would set an intimate mood or that she meant to use a bed, but . . . oh, hell, she didn't know what she meant.

Struggling to control his raging libido, Marcus followed her. Back in the dining room, when their eyes met, all he could think about was how she'd taste, how good she'd feel, how good *he'd* feel when they met skin to skin without the hindrance of clothing. No, he told himself, not *when*. Not even *if*. They weren't going to do that. The last calamity he needed was to bond with her, to make her, in fact, his mate. He didn't even want to imagine that intolerable situation.

He thought he'd regained power over himself after that, but when she'd stood up and prepared to leave, he had to, simply *had to* go with her, see her safely to her room. Which was ridiculous on the face of it; no danger lurked in the corridors of a HeatherRidge hotel.

If all that wasn't bad enough, in the elevator, standing close enough to smell her, he'd almost pulled her into his arms. He had actually been leaning down to kiss her when those people entered and broke the spell.

The spell. Here he was, back to being enchanted, under the command of an outside entity. No, unacceptable. They had to talk this circumstance through, had to come to some accommodation with the damned imperative or the damned attraction—if that was truly all it was—or they'd never make it through the remaining debates. And he'd probably go stark raving insane from wanting her.

She placed her purse and folder on a side table, walked over to the chair and sofa grouping and stopped with the coffee table between them. She didn't look him in the eye, only down at her clasped hands, and said, "Yes, we need to talk. How do we begin?"

"Let's cut to the chase. It's the soul-mate phenomenon and imperative we need to talk about. Do you concur?"

She sighed, grimaced. "Yes."

"Are we attracted to each other? I am to you."

She hesitated, looked a little angry, a little dismayed. He understood those feelings all too well. He breathed again when she finally admitted, "I am to you, too."

"That raises the next question: Are we under the influence of the phenomenon? George tells me that I am, and he thinks you're my mate—on no real evidence or proof, I might add." He tossed his folder on the coffee table, took the two steps to the sofa, but didn't sit. There was no way he could possibly make himself comfortable. Every muscle in his body was strung as tight as Samson's leash when he was holding the dog back from running.

"Do you think so, too?"

He couldn't tell from her flat tone what she thought. Best to state his opinion in the same manner. "I don't honestly know. I seem to have the symptoms, again according to George. It could be simple attraction because I've been too busy to date for months and you're a beautiful woman."

She took a deep breath, and the movement drew his gaze first to her chest, then to her still clenched hands. She was obviously also tense. Her next words, however, brought his eyes back to her face. "My parents are saying we are, also with little evidence. My sister delineated the telltale signs—the itch and following pain in the magic center, the dreams, the, uh, reactions when in the vicinity of the other." Her face flushed a delicate pink when she said the last words.

"I can't come to any conclusion," she continued. "Most of these responses could be normal male-female attraction, even though a witch isn't supposed to feel it for anyone except her mate. The imperative could have its wires crossed. My biological clock could also be driving my reactions. It could be our hormones and age acting against us—the mating instinct, but the human one, not the practitioner. From everything I've ever heard about practitioner soul mates, that you and I could be . . . we're . . . Oh, it seems absolutely impossible. We're totally *different*."

He felt a small bit of relief. Surely if they had come independently to the same conclusion, they could solve their problem. "I agree. We don't view or work magic the same—diametrically opposed to each other, in fact. I'm sure there are other differences like music, sports, politics, teaching methods, lifestyles, probably even our basic thought processes."

"I like country-western music; You like jazz. I like football and basketball; You like . . ."

"Baseball. I'm more conservative politically.; You're . . ."

"A yellow-dog Democrat. I'm an intuitive caster, and you . . ."

"Prefer a more structured approach. I like order and a minimalist approach in my home."

"I'm all about clutter and chaos, but it is an orderly chaos. That we both have basenjis and are runners must be purely a coincidence," she said with a wry smile. "My father puts great store in the dogs, and my mother, would you believe, in the way we look at each other."

"Am I correct in stating that neither of us wants the other for a soul mate?" As the words came out of his mouth, a sharp pain sliced through his chest and would have brought him to his knees if they hadn't been locked. He shook his head to clear his vision.

Gloriana grimaced and waved a hand at their problem. "I'm not against the concept. I have too many examples of its benefits in my own family. I have to admit, I've been expecting to meet mine since Daria and Clay have met theirs. However, I can't imagine spending the rest of my life with someone who's a total opposite, with whom I have little in common. I'm not sure we can communicate or understand each other on the level soul mates seem to."

She shook her head emphatically. "I do not believe in the old saying, 'Opposites attract.' That seems to me more like a recipe for disaster in a marriage. Even worse would be for either one of us to feel coerced into the mating."

She finally looked at him, and the sadness in her eyes made her statement even more poignant.

"I don't want a soul mate, period." The words felt like ashes in his mouth, but he had to tell her the truth, make it clear he wasn't the one for her under any circumstances.

"Ever?"

"Never. It's nothing against you, believe me. It doesn't matter why," he added to forestall the questions he knew she'd ask.

She frowned at him for a long moment before asking, "So, given your determination and my feelings, what do we do? Where do we go from here?"

"The question to me is how to prove that we're only attracted to each other and not ensnared by the phenomenon. That we aren't coerced by the imperative. That we're not, in fact, soul mates."

"What if, despite the attraction, we really are, or the imperative thinks we are—which is the same thing, I guess. It's not going to be easy to discourage. I've seen my brother and sister go through the process, and the SMI can be vicious when thwarted."

"SMI?"

"That's what Clay calls the soul-mate imperative."

"Ah, right." As he nodded, the ventilation system

blew her scent his way, and he couldn't stop from taking a step closer. He made himself take a step back. "If we are, then we come up with a plan. First, how do we tell if it's simple attraction or the imperative?"

"According to the practitioner databases, there are only two ways to tell if you're under the SMI influence. The first is to try to cast a spell on the other person, since mates can't cast spells on each other except for healing or defense. The second is to try to make love, and if you're not mates, you won't be physically able to consummate the mating."

She made a face. "The only spells I can cast on another person are healing ones, so if you had a headache and I healed it, my success would tell us nothing. I'm not willing to use the other method—that's simply too dangerous. I assume you don't have a fancy mathematical equation for a test."

"No, I don't. I never thought I'd need one. I can't cast spells on a person at all. My talent involves manipulating mathematical formulas and equations—in my head, in the air, or on a surface. And that second method, no way." He ignored the twinge from his center—and lower down. *Mind over matter,* he reminded his libido.

"You arrange symbols, work equations in the air?" She seemed incredulous.

"Sure, watch. Here is an example of Bertrand's postulate, the details of which I won't bore you with." He pointed, and numbers and mathematical symbols floated in the air where they could both see them as though they were on a wall. "Here's the proof."

He pointed and waved, and the proof unfurled before them, like a computer screen scrolling. When he looked at Morgan, her eyes had become enormous.

"I can try out different variables by spell. Here's the idea I'm working on in my latest article." He cancelled the first display and put up his latest work.

"If I test it with these . . ." His proof spread downward. "If I change some values and recast the spell . . ." The figures and symbols changed, added some, and rearranged themselves. "It proves that no counterexample to my postulate is possible."

"Or, more simply . . ." He ran through a couple of simple arithmetic and algebraic problems for her. Again numbers and letters shifted, multiplied and divided themselves. He canceled the display. "That's the way I work."

"That's not a simple illusion spell, is it?"

"No, in fact, I layer spells within spells. Think of them as 'what if' statements. If this, then that, but if this other, then that other. Working out the proper combinations and logical progressions can be quite tricky. Layering basic spells will be my next topic in my spell study. I had to start with the simplest equation first, of course."

"Oh," Morgan said, sounding somewhat stunned. She closed her eyes for a moment, rubbed her forehead, and, when she opened her eyes again, frowned at him. "Anyway, back to our primary topic. I'd never thought of the SMI until Daria found Bent, and Francie and Clay got together, and it's been hard *not* to think of the possibility when I'm around them. I never envisioned needing a test, either."

As it often did when he was thinking about a problem, the mathematical part of his mind conjured up several possible equations and solutions, but he didn't voice or display them. Theory wouldn't help them. They were faced with the need for a practical experiment, something that would yield concrete proof. "Maybe we need to approach our problem scientifically."

She raised her eyebrows. "How?"

"How did your siblings know they had met their soul mates? Before the first mating, that is?"

She looked off into the distance for a few seconds before saying, "In both cases, they and their mates fit the norm—thought the same way, had the same interests, all that *sameness*. Business for Daria and Bent, computers and basketball for Francie and Clay.

"Daria said the physical attraction was very powerful. She didn't believe in the SMI's existence at first, didn't even consider it a possibility when she first met Bent. The realization took a while to sink in, and by the time it did, she was in love with him. She was more worried about his reaction as a non-practitioner. Because he is not one of us and had no clue in the beginning and she was taken unawares, however, their story may not help us.

"As for Francie . . . she was resisting Clay for non-SMI reasons, but when they kissed, she said all the will to oppose him drained out of her. She described it like being possessed by an alien who had taken over her mind and her body. She couldn't string two coherent thoughts together. She had no idea what was happening to her, but she couldn't overcome it, no matter how hard she tried."

"Maybe that's our test."

"What, to kiss?" Her big green eyes opened wide, and she backed up a step.

"Can you think of another?" He felt his center warm and wondered if a kiss was, in fact, a good idea. What other test did they have that would let them escape unscathed? He took two slow steps forward. He only had to reach out a hand to touch her.

Gloriana watched his approach warily. Her emotions and thoughts were rioting in all directions. Confusion over the SMI—was it or wasn't it at work, pushing them together? Hopelessness over her inability to understand what he had showed her about his magic, including how he did it—had he really put spells within spells?

She was awash in feelings. Sadness over the idea of being coupled with someone she couldn't understand and who couldn't understand her. Puzzlement over his statement about never wanting a soul mate—and a little sorrow for him, too. Indignation over his rejection of her—accompanied by recognition that he wasn't really rejecting *her*, but being forced into a situation without his consent. Empathy over their predicament. Relief over bringing it all out in the open.

And excitement. Oh, yes, excitement and anticipation, centered in the middle of her body and making every cell in it come to attention.

She stared into his eyes, where his pupils had expanded so much she could see only a little bit of blue between them and the dark rims of his corneas. His gaze went from warm to hot to sizzling in a heartbeat.

Her blood heated in response; she could feel it rushing to sensitive places.

When he stopped six inches away, she had to raise her face to look at him directly. And that falling sensation came back and made her almost dizzy.

To brace herself, she put her hands on his lapels. She could feel his heat through his suit coat, and she could smell him—that woodsy-and-pure-male concoction she'd noticed at the first debate. It contributed to her vertigo, and she resisted the need to clutch for support.

He'd asked a question. What was it? Something about her thinking of another test? She needed to give him an answer. When she licked her suddenly dry lips, his gaze dropped to them, then returned to her eyes. *Concentrate, Glori. Speak.*

"No." She had to push the word out of her throat.

"No?" What could have been disappointment

flashed across his face.

"I mean, n-no, I can't think of any other choice," she whispered.

"Good," he whispered also and lowered his lips to hers.

Clouds drifted over her mind and fogged her ability to think. Her eyelids lowered of their own volition. All that operated was her sense of touch—concentrated on her lips.

He brushed his mouth across hers—once, twice, as lightly as a feather and as softly as a rose petal. On the third, he stayed, a beguiling, unhurried caress. She felt his hands clasp her waist, and his tongue trace the seam between her lips. She opened and tentatively touched tongues.

And the sun went nova.

And she was engulfed by the resulting shock wave.

He swept into her mouth, taking possession, and she exulted. *You're his,* a voice said in her mind.

He's yours, it said when he retreated, and she followed to stake her claim on him. Their tongues dueled, teased, tasted.

She vaguely felt his arms wrap around her in a vise-like hold, but she wanted, *needed* to be closer, and being there felt so *good*. She knew her hands moved up to fist in his silky blond hair. One of his slid down her back and pulled her hips to his, inside his open coat.

Ah, that was better, and better still when she tilted her pelvis—pressure where she needed it.

She heard him groan. She heard herself hum.

This was where she *must* be, in his arms, closer, kissing—oh, how the man could kiss—hugging, touching, holding.

It wasn't enough.

The heat pouring from him warmed her, right through her suit, right to her bones.

She slowly rubbed her front across his.

Ah, better still.

Another groan, another hum, as he responded with a rub of his own, lower down.

Oh, best!

He was holding her so tightly she couldn't breathe. She didn't care.

She wanted *more.*

Finally one or the other of them—she wasn't sure, probably both—ended the kiss. Bowing her head to his chest, she gasped for air. He rested his head on hers and did the same. She could feel his heart pounding. Hers thumped in unison. A vague hum with no origin droned around them.

Slowly they both relaxed their grips, and she thought she could feel each and every muscle unwinding.

She brought her hands back to his lapels. He moved his to her waist again.

Still breathing heavily, they each took half a step back. The hum disappeared.

It was only when Glori looked up at him, saw the tension and starkness in his face, the blazing blue of his eyes, that her mind started to work again, her brain regained the ability to think.

"Ohhhh," was all she could say, however.

He opened his mouth, shut it, cleared his throat, and said hoarsely, "I think we have a problem."

She nodded, swallowed, tried again. "That was more than one alien. It was an invasion by a whole army."

He took a deep breath, let go of her waist, stepped back a full foot until they weren't touching at all.

Immediately cold, she hugged herself and sat down on one of the armchairs before her shaky legs collapsed under her.

He walked around the coffee table and began to pace in front of the windows.

She watched him for a moment, but when he said nothing, only stopped to stare out at the city, she pulled herself together. It was either calm down or fling herself into his arms again, and that would lead to a place neither of them wanted to go—where they'd take the second, more potent test for soul mates. He was the one who wanted to talk and who came up with the kiss idea. Did she have to force words out of him to discuss the mess, make sure they were still in agreement, and decide what to do next? Sure looked like it.

She took a deep breath, sat up straight, and forced the intellectual, scientific part of her brain to work. "All right, what happened? We performed an experiment. What did we learn?"

He turned back from the windows, rubbed a hand over his face and around to the back of his neck. "That it's not simple attraction between us."

"Agreed." She put her hand on her magic center. It didn't itch; in fact, it didn't hurt for the first time in days. It seemed, instead, to be humming. "How do you feel?"

"Like I've been kicked in the head. Like an equation fell off the board and its pieces are lying all over the floor, laughing at me for assuming I knew what I was doing." He ran his hand through his disordered hair, then finger-combed it like he was trying to restore order.

She mentally smirked for being the one to disturb his perfection, but this was not the time to mention it. He hadn't understood her question. "No, really, how does your *center* feel?"

"My center?" He looked at her blankly before moving his gaze down to his chest. He rubbed the spot. "It doesn't itch. It feels . . ."

"What?"

"Smug. The damned thing feels *smug*." He almost spat out the words.

"Mine's humming."

"Wonderful." His voice dripped with sarcasm.

She rolled her eyes. He had wanted a "scientific" experiment. How come she was the one interpreting the results? A theoretical mathematician evidently couldn't deal with practical empirical data.

They didn't need an argument on an extraneous

subject, and she kept her tone even as she would have when explaining her reasoning to a student. "Therefore, we can conclude our experiment, our test, proved we're under the imperative's influence. We have an altered situation, one changed by the new information. We need to decide our course of action."

After seeming to give himself a shake, he walked over and sat down on the couch. "Also agreed. Our new situation . . . But first, what hasn't changed? I still don't want any soul mate, and you don't want one who's radically different from you."

"I don't see how so many differences can work in a mating, and above all, I want a man who wants to be with me. However, in this situation, what *we* think or want doesn't matter. The reality is that *the SMI* will be pushing us to come together."

"What can we expect when we don't? More itching and pain? Something worse? What did your family say?"

"All they mentioned was the first two. Since the non-practitioners didn't have the slightest idea an outside force was at work, they thought they were developing ulcers. For all four of them, basically the imperative made their lives uncomfortable, but they weren't incapacitated, unable to work, or function in general."

"What are our options? What happens if we reject the imperative, decide not to give in to it? At all. Ever."

He didn't know? Was he serious? The look on his face told her he was. "Didn't your parents tell you about it?"

"Stefan gave me the standard talk, and I decided that I wasn't going to let it happen to me, ancient force or not." He shrugged. "Never thought about it after that."

"According to my mother, you reject the imperative—and your soul mate—at your peril. You will never be happy—*ever*—if you do. You'll die a bitter, miserable person, totally alone."

"Better that than . . ." He shut his mouth abruptly, then muttered, "Never mind."

Better misery than . . . what? Something else was going on with Forscher, and she knew she wouldn't be able to get whatever it was out of him at the moment. Not the way he slammed that "never mind" door in her face.

He stood up abruptly. "I don't want to accept that outcome. I don't doubt your mother, but I'd like corroboration, details. During next week, why don't we both research the situation, see what our alternatives are."

"Fine." She couldn't keep the exasperation out of her voice. However, as closed down as he seemed to be, she doubted that he heard it. "I'm not going to be in Austin. We can also evaluate our reactions to being apart. We can meet at the debate in Denver and discuss our findings."

"Okay. I'll see you next week." He picked up his folder, walked to the door, looked back to say "good night," and left.

"Good night," Gloriana said to the closing door and scowled at his abrupt departure. Looked like they were both rattled, although he more than she. *Wonderful*— she felt her mouth tighten as she gave the word a sarcastic twist in her mind—she didn't want to be the only one suffering here. She did, however, want to discuss their plans more fully, especially to discover the reasons behind his rejection of the entire soul-mate concept.

One certainty: she wasn't going to get answers tonight. She hauled herself out of the chair, turned out the lights, and made her way to bed.

CHAPTER
SIXTEEN

Lying in bed later, Gloriana reassessed her calculations. There was no other interpretation for their reactions during that kiss. The imperative had them in its clutches.

So, what to do?

She had to keep her head on straight, not fly off the handle as she usually did, according to her brother. If she was arguing with Clay, she'd attack to force his reasons out. Not a good approach to Forscher, as closed as he was. He'd lock himself deeper in his cave, and they'd get nowhere. Better to remain calm. Be ready for any outcome.

What did she want that outcome to be? Truth be told, she did want a loving mate and children. She expected it. Having a family was part of being a practitioner. She'd never thought about it much until her sister and brother had both found their mates in the course of a year. If she let it, the idea consumed her thoughts.

Daria's pregnancy must have stirred up her own hormones, her own latent desires. Why else the panic she'd experienced at the news?

She wasn't against having a mate, only this particular one. She didn't even understand his magic. When he'd displayed his equations and proofs, it was like looking at gibberish. She knew chemical and molecular formulas and diagrams, but his math was *way* out of her league. She knew he understood it, down to each little sigma and plus-or-minus sign.

How he manipulated his mathematical illusions was another question. Were they true illusions, the same kind she used when she created the figure of a panther around her? Complicated illusions could take a long time to build. Ones that performed like computer spreadsheets—change one variable and see the effect ripple through it—were far beyond her expertise.

She'd never seen her father cast a spell like that with his auditing and accounting techniques. Furthermore, her mother understood what her father did, even if she couldn't cast his spells. Daria understood Bent, and Clay understood Francie. Shouldn't she expect the same?

What did her inability to understand mean for her being with Forscher? Soul mates were supposed to be helpmates, too—able to offer support and encouragement. How could she when she couldn't offer even an intelligent comment about what he did? On the flip side, how could he help her when he seemed almost frightened of her magic?

They hadn't discussed the emotional side of the situation, either. Oh, she'd experienced practically every emotion possible in the course of their discussion—especially before, during, and after that kiss. But what was he feeling? The kiss had certainly affected him physically. Emotionally? He'd reverted to the intellectual, emotionless man he'd been from the start. She could almost see him build the walls to shut in his feelings—and shut her out.

Yet she had always been about feelings, emotions, passions, as much as she'd been about the intellectual pursuit of her profession. To deal with him, she'd have to keep her emotions out of the equation—oh, how she was coming to hate that word—and talk in his terms. Be logical, practical, composed like he was, or he'd never hear a word she said. Keep her head on straight and, most importantly if he was going to reject her, guard her heart against the imperative's efforts.

What on earth could have caused him to be that way? He came from a soul-mate family. He had the same sort of parental example she did. Soul mates always loved each other, and that love always encompassed their families. How could he not want to be a part of it?

That brought her back to the basic problems. How could two such different people possibly be mates, but how could she convince an invisible, magic power that it was making a mistake? If she did, would another soul mate appear? Who knew?

He, on the other hand, was implacable, completely against having a soul mate, her or anybody else. Worse, he didn't appear to be someone who easily changed his mind.

Where did all her thinking leave her? If they were mates, she was damned if he rejected her, and damned if she did the rejecting.

Either way, she'd never have what her brother and sister had—a mate who loved her as much as she loved him and the possibility of children.

She almost wept at the thought, and her center vibrated in sympathy. Then it hummed—a distinctly encouraging feeling. She put her hand on the spot, and a pleasant, soothing tranquility settled over her.

In her floating state, she began to wonder what her children with Forscher would have looked like, how the combinations of hair and eye colors would have worked out. She fell asleep mentally constructing a possible family tree like biologist Gregor Mendel had done for common pea plants.

Marcus refused to let himself think about his—or their—predicament even after he returned home and re-trieved Samson from the boarding kennel. The hound was definitely unhappy about being left with strangers instead of his usual stay with George and Evelyn. Too bad. He knew he'd have to face his friends soon enough, but not right this instant. Not yet.

Evelyn, however, smashed his resolve to atoms when she called and ordered him to dinner on Wednesday, no excuses accepted.

So, he went, luxuriated in her hug, drank some of George's superb scotch, and discussed the debate, which they had watched on the Webcast.

"How did the evaluations go?" George asked over Evelyn's delicious pot roast. "I'm always leery of those on-the-spot forms."

"Ed e-mailed me today with the quantitative results. If you leave out the extremes, ninety-two percent of the respondents want more discussion. A few said they had actually tried the formula, and one reported trouble with the 'ingredient measurements.'"

"That's been one of the problems from the beginning," Evelyn said. "Did anything new come out of the comments?"

He wasn't going to worry them with the four rabid replies, of course, so he simply said, "Nothing that I could see."

"All the information's really out there already," George said, "what with the articles and reports and the Webcast. If we practitioners act like we usually do, we'll hash and rehash the issues until some real research is done on how to apply calibration to magical power. After that, we'll talk some more."

"We caught a glimpse of your family and the Morgans in the audience," Evelyn put in. "Your mother looks as beautiful as ever. How are they?"

"They're fine. Yesterday they left for Europe—a little vacation, a conference for Judith, meetings with colleagues for Stefan."

"What about Gloriana?" George asked, his tone innocent and his eyes full of glee.

"She's fine."

"Well?"

"Well, what?"

George chuckled. "What about her being your soul mate?"

"George, I told you not to tease the man," Evelyn scolded.

"I'm not teasing, honey. I really want to understand."

Marcus looked from one to the other. Evelyn and George had been his friends and mentors for years and had helped him in immeasurable ways. They had stood behind him in ways his parents never had. He owed them some explanation—but not the complete one.

"We didn't have much opportunity to see each other in Boston and only talked for a few minutes. We both think it's possible, only not probable. We're extremely different, nothing like soul mates are supposed to be."

"The only difference you have to worry about is that you're a man and she's a woman," George stated. "Everything else is window-dressing."

"You know how I feel about the entire soul-mate business—" Marcus began.

"Yes, I do. Must I remind you again that you are not your father. Gloriana is certainly not your mother, and you have no reason to believe you or she will act like them."

Marcus opened his mouth to protest that reasoning, and shut it again without uttering a word. George simply didn't understand the situation. He hadn't lived it.

"George, don't badger Marcus," Evelyn said. "Finding your soul mate can be difficult and confusing."

"So, what are you going to do about it—try to deny the imperative?" George said mildly, his tone clearly meant to assuage his wife.

"We're not sure yet. We both have reservations about the choice of the imperative."

"Oh, Marcus, you can't reject your mate. Terrible things will happen." Evelyn's face was creased in worry lines.

"What? What will happen? What, *exactly*?"

"If one mate rejects the other, they both suffer. As long as the rejecter lives, the other will never find a replacement. I've only heard of one instance of rejection between practitioners. The one rejected, a woman, committed suicide after ten years of loneliness and imperative pain. The man who rejected her actually married a nonpractitioner, and that marriage failed in a very short time, as you would expect."

"Is that fact or anecdote?" Marcus asked.

"I had it on good authority," Evelyn answered, "but I'm not absolutely certain."

"From everything I'm hearing about our 'ancient force,' it ranks right up there with the most horrendous torturers of all time," Marcus said.

"That's only if you resist," George responded.

"What about free will?"

"The reality of the practitioner world contains the imperative," George stated. "We can change it no more than we can change any other reality. To use a math example, you'll always find the roots of a quadratic equation with the formula: 'As long as a doesn't equal zero, then ax^2 plus bx plus c will *always* equal zero.' Nothing you say or do will change that reality. For the soul-mate reality, the same applies. If you'd relax and enjoy it, you'll be fine. The imperative doesn't make a mistake."

"Let's change the subject," Evelyn interjected before Marcus could respond to George. "Tell me about the dinner at the HeatherRidge."

At home that evening, Marcus worked through the practitioner database looking for imperative information. The next day he went over to the Austin HeatherRidge to use their library. He wasn't very successful in either endeavor and could only hope Morgan had been able to find more than anecdote and legend in her searching.

They had to find evidence that the—what did Morgan call it? Oh, yes—the SMI could and did make mistakes. Then they had to discover how to make it change its mind.

For the rest of the week, his center didn't itch or hurt, and he was able to keep the memory of that kiss at bay by overloading himself with tasks, problems, and duties. His dreams, however, betrayed him. Every morning he woke, arms—and other body parts—aching, with an enormous sense of wanting to hold and be held. Telling himself he needed uninterrupted time to work and hoping also for relief from the imperative's pressure, he flew to Denver on Friday night.

CHAPTER SEVENTEEN

Gloriana sat there in the Denver HeatherRidge ball-room on Saturday night willing herself not to scream. It had not been a good day. First a rainstorm in Austin made the plane late and a wreck on the Denver freeway delayed her even more. She'd rushed into the private dining room as everyone was sitting down to eat.

Dinner was pleasant, or at least the food and conversation were. Forscher was there, of course, looking as perfect as ever. By contrast she felt disheveled and slightly unprepared. Damn, why did she always feel off-kilter with him around? Well, duh, because of the SMI, of course.

He walked with her into the ballroom and in a low voice the others couldn't hear, said, "Meet in my room after we look over the evaluations? I'm in 1080."

"Fine. I'm in 1081." She breathed easier when they were sitting on the stage with Ed in between them. Her center was quiet, thank goodness.

She might still scream after all. Mike Brubaker was speaking for the FOM and boring everybody to death with high-level math terms and complicated explanations of power calibration. It was not a way to win friends and supporters. At least Pritchart had injected humor and sarcasm into his three minutes.

Gloriana looked out over the audience. She liked the setup, however. Ed had followed Forscher's suggestion of dividing the room into thirds. He had organized it with the middle much larger than the two sides, and it certainly made a difference. The people declaring themselves FOM or THA filled their sections, but did not appear as imposing as when there was only one division. In fact, some neutrals had dragged chairs to the center to avoid sitting with one of the factions. Most looked bored. She shared their sentiments.

Finally, Brubaker sat down after Ed called time twice.

To the front strode Gordon Walcott, Horner's second in command. Tall and very thin, his stiff carriage and his haughty expression proclaimed his arrogance, confidence, and superiority. He took the microphone from the usher and stood for a long moment looking down his sharp nose at the audience before speaking.

"Ladies and gentlemen, we at the THA are here to warn you. We warn you of the pernicious, malicious, destructive danger that will be foisted upon the practitioner community by this wicked heresy of a so-called magic formula for casting spells. Pritchart, Brubaker, and their cohorts would have you believe that, to cast properly, you must follow an overly complex, elaborate, incomprehensible set of symbols. They would have you follow their path, which will only lead to confusion, difficulty, and chaos. They would have you teach your children to cast their way—the only way, according to Pritchart. The THA is here to tell you that you do not have to follow them, you do not have to believe them, and you can find support and guidance against the insidious threat with us."

The man has the delivery of an old-time preacher, Gloriana thought, watching the FOM section bristle with indignation. The THA supporters were smiling, clearly pleased with their champion. The middle sat there, their faces showing such a variety of reactions, it was impossible for her to gauge their opinion as a whole.

How interesting that Walcott was blaming Prick, not Forscher for the formula. She glanced at Forscher, but he was staring straight ahead with no expression.

Walcott went on to denigrate and castigate the formula, the Fomsters, and anyone who agreed with them. From time to time, a Traddie would shout, "Amen, brother," or one would clap.

Over on the Fomster side, a grumbling murmur rose.

The two Swords, John Baldwin and Bill Morrow, shifted their positions—Baldwin to stand before the FOM side and Morrow to put himself between Walcott and his opponents.

"In conclusion," Walcott said, in tones of fire and brimstone, "if you follow the siren call of these miscreants, the practitioner life we love will perish, and spell-casting will be reduced to robotic methods that will doom us to an existence without richness, without simplicity, and without freedom. You must deny these blasphemers their victory. Only if we stand up and stand together will we save magic itself!"

The Traddies rose, cheering. A few people in the middle did, too.

The Fomsters rose, booing and yelling. Someone threw something at Walcott.

A flash lit the room, and bright blades of frozen lightning suddenly appeared in the hands of the Swords. Morrow's glowing indigo weapon intercepted the missile, which burst into ashes. It had only been a wadded-up piece of paper.

"Silence!" roared Baldwin in a voice that shook the room, and the crowd immediately hushed.

In the silence that followed, Gloriana was surprised to find herself on her feet, pulled behind Forscher. She had no recollection of moving, much less his taking her arm, but her heart was beating rapidly, like she'd run a mile. Ed was likewise out of his chair and in front of both of them. She tugged against Forscher's hold and stuck her head around his shoulder so she could see what was happening.

"Sit down!" Baldwin ordered. He pointed his long silver sword at a Fomster in a "Math Rules!" sweatshirt and added, "All except you."

Everyone in the audience sat, except the young man. Gloriana, Ed, and Forscher remained standing.

"Do you deny you threw that object?" Baldwin asked. The thrower turned the color of milk and shook his head.

Gloriana wiggled her arm. Forscher didn't let go entirely, but did allow her to stand by his side. Both he and Ed were watching the Swords. She instead looked at Walcott, who had not moved a muscle. The THA spokesman wore an extremely satisfied expression.

"Security, please escort that man out and hold him in your office," Baldwin said. After two guards had removed the thrower, the Sword faced the Fomsters and brandished his weapon. "We'll have no more such outbursts here. Is that clear?"

He glared at them until most nodded. He marched over to the Traddies' side and repeated the question. When several looked indignant, he waited with a stone face and a ready sword until they, too, nodded. His gaze swept the room. "That order stands for everyone. If you cannot be civil, leave now."

A number of the audience in the middle smiled with what appeared to be relief. Nobody left.

Walcott raised the microphone like he still had comments to make, but lowered it when Baldwin pointed his weapon at him.

"That goes for you, too," the Sword said. "Keep your incendiary, provocative remarks to yourself. Your time is up."

Walcott gave Baldwin a venomous glare and said nothing. He handed his microphone to an usher and sat down.

Baldwin and Morrow, who held their swords in two-handed grips, spread their hands apart, and the shining weapons vanished. They took their original positions before the stage. Baldwin looked up at Ed. "It's all yours."

Gloriana and Forscher exchanged a glance that told her he wasn't going to apologize for pulling her behind him. Not that she was asking him to. His touch had felt warmly protective in the midst of the confusion. He released her, and they resumed their seats.

Ed remained standing and picked up his mike. "I want to see Pritchart and Horner up here after the session," the editor stated. "I remind everyone of the rules printed in the handouts and on the practitioner Web site. Our meeting is for rational, reasoned debate and discussion. If you can't do that, if a spokesperson for either side can't abide by the rules, you won't be allowed to speak. Anyone causing a disturbance will be banned from the proceedings altogether."

He scanned the audience for a moment. Both Fomsters and Traddies were silently sullen. Ed sat and pulled his microphone to him. "All right, we'll ask some questions to get the discussion going. Those of you who wish to comment, hold up your hand and wait to be called on. Glori, you go first."

Gloriana arranged her notes before attempting to speak. The commotion was over, and the comedown from the adrenaline rush made her hands shake. She took a deep, calming breath to settle herself. Ed was right to bring the discussion back to its real purpose, even if it felt like an anticlimax after all the excitement.

She read her first question, the one calling for suggestions for the best way to discover how each practitioner could cast most effectively. A member of the middle audience offered an answer, and the rest of the debate ran as scheduled, although everybody was more than a little on edge.

At its adjournment, the three on the stage rose and stood with their backs to the departing audience.

"Man, I'm glad that's over," Ed said. "John and I are going to meet with the two fearless leaders and lay down the law: no inflammatory speeches, only reasonable debate. You go with Bill back to the dining room. I'll have the evaluations delivered there, and you can get started on them. Okay?"

Gloriana, Forscher, and Bill left the ballroom by a side door and walked to the dining room through the service corridors. She was happy to reach a spot where they could relax without people watching their every move.

"What a circus!" Forscher grumbled and took a seat

at the table.

"Feelings are running higher than I expected. I thought we were going to have to stun the FOM for a minute," Bill stated.

"Walcott incited both sides deliberately, and afterward he looked extremely satisfied with the reactions," Gloriana said. "I'm glad you and John were there to keep order. That's the first time I've ever seen a Sword in action. What's your weapon made of?"

"It's pure harnessed energy," Bill replied. "I basically fried that paperball with electricity. We can't 'fight' with them as though they were actual physical swords like in the movies. We can shoot an energy beam from the point that acts like a laser and cuts through practically everything, including weak magical shields. That's how we destroy evil magic items."

"Do you choose the 'style' of the sword? I noticed yours and John's don't look alike."

"Yes, I chose to create a sword that looks like a medieval long sword. John's is larger, more like a claymore."

Before Gloriana could ask another question, one of the ushers entered with the evaluation forms. She thanked him, took the forms, put them on the table, and sat down. "Looks like our work has arrived."

Marcus watched her divide the large pile into three equal ones. When the commotion started and the Swords drew their weapons, he'd wanted to throw himself at her, to cover her before those lunatics could hurt her. Only

John's quick assumption of control had stopped him from dragging her out of the room completely.

He shook himself mentally and turned to Bill, who sat down also. "Did John tell you what we found last week?"

"Those threatening replies? Yeah. Do we expect more?"

"After that uproar we experienced, I do. Why don't we do a quick flip-through and see if any stand out?"

"Good idea," Morgan said and handed out the stacks.

The three of them looked through all the forms and spread the questionable ones out on the table. They were categorizing by faction and threat level when Ed and John came in.

"I'll tell you about the meeting in a minute. What do you have here?" Ed asked as he and John sat down.

Marcus explained what they had done. "We have a total of eighteen 'rabid dogs.' Ten for the FOM and eight for THA. None of them are signed, of course."

Ed picked up a page and read aloud, "'*You Idiots and Philistines are dragging us back to the Middle Ages! We're not going to let that happen. Accept the formula or Else!'* He doesn't say what 'else' means."

"Here's one from the THA calling Fomsters heretics, blasphemers, whores, Communists, and pointy-headed liberals," John said with a chuckle. "He can't seem to make up his mind whether to be biblical or political."

"Here's one telling us to '*Rot in Hell! If you follow through with this disaster, it will cause such a cataclysm that you all will be destroyed,*'" Morgan read. "It's not clear which side wrote it—it's more of a universal condemnation. Does feel more Traddie, though." She placed the page away from the others.

"Whatever happened to the old idea of rational discourse?" Ed wondered, before becoming serious. "I made an executive decision and told Pritchart and Horner that we were going to change the format. There will be no more 'opening statements' from either side. We'll still open with your remarks, Marcus and Glori, and go straight into questions and comments from the audience. We're not going to have a repeat of tonight, whether it's being terminally confused by someone like Brubaker or being insulted and threatened by a fanatic like Walcott."

"I agree completely," Marcus said.

"Me, too," Morgan nodded. "How did they take your declaration?"

"Both complained, of course. When they mumbled about free speech, I told them they could say what they wanted in answer to a question, so long as it wasn't inflammatory. We will not allow a riot or name-calling or personal attacks. They need to concentrate on persuading people to their side, not frightening or forcing them. Pritchart and Horner nodded, but I don't know if they'll follow instructions."

"Who is Walcott?" Gloriana asked.

"He's been part of Horner's inner circle for some time," John answered. "I looked him up after he signed that evaluation. From what he's said and written, he's even more conservative than Horner. Lives in Waco, I believe, and is often seen in Dallas in Horner's offices. He's also an eighth-level with a talent for organizing political campaigns and is the brains behind Horner's endeavors. He's evidently decided to come out from his support role into the limelight."

Ed ran his hands through his thinning hair and looked at Marcus and Morgan. "We've got to get out in front of the situation here. Use the opportunity, both of you, to speak to the necessity of working together. Marcus, maybe you could explain the formula again and apply it to a simple spell. Glori, why don't you talk more on how you cast spells. Look for common ground. Let's all be extremely specific. If we give people concrete examples, maybe we can get away from these sweeping generalities. I'll try to pin participants down more on the exact meaning of their comments with the same end in mind."

"Let's also emphasize the need to study and test the equation," Marcus said. "My major request is getting lost in the rhetoric."

"How do you feel about Pritchart?" John asked. "It appears to me that he's trying to take all the credit for your work."

"Botanist Alexander von Humboldt," Morgan interjected, "is supposed to have said, 'There are three stages in scientific discovery: first people deny that it is true, then they deny that it is important, and finally they credit the wrong person.'"

"That's typical Prick," Marcus answered. "I thought he had learned his lesson in grad school when nobody would collaborate with him. Idiot. He doesn't bother me."

"His tricks bother me," Ed said with a scowl. "I'm going to start calling it 'the Forscher Formula.' We'll take a rule from advertising—repetition helps people remember."

"How about calling it F-Squared?" Morgan asked with that mischievous grin of hers. "Or maybe Forscher's Famous Formula—F-Cubed."

Marcus couldn't help groaning. "Oh, please, no. The last sounds like a patent-medicine, snake-oil concoction."

On that note, they adjourned.

CHAPTER EIGHTEEN

To avoid both factions, Marcus and Morgan used the service corridors and elevators to reach their floor. As they walked down the hall, he congratulated himself on avoiding an elevator ride like the last one.

When, however, he ushered her into his suite, he caught a whiff of her scent. Breathing deeply to hold her fragrance in his lungs, he watched her drop her purse and folio on a chair and roam the suite's living room. Neither the dress or the jacket she had on could be considered "sexy," but the way her body moved under them made him wish . . .

Easy, take it easy. He put down his folder and walked over to the floor-to-ceiling windows, where he stared at her instead of the city. Her restlessness betrayed her tension. Indeed, they both needed to relax before they could discuss their situation reasonably.

To get them both talking, he asked, "How are you?

What happened to make you so late tonight?"

She stopped pacing and faced him. "It rained in Austin, and the plane was late, and a wreck on the way from the airport delayed me more. When did you get here?"

"Yesterday. I find that changing locations sometimes frees up my thought processes. I wrote quite a bit last night and today—finished an article, in fact."

She nodded. "I like to do the same thing. I get some of my best ideas in waiting rooms."

"Probably something about a neutral atmosphere." Like they were in here, another bland hotel suite. Maybe it would help them come to a conclusion. "How did your research go on the imperative? I found few hard facts, only reams of legends and anecdotes. Evelyn told me one tale she had 'on good authority,' but without names. I never found it officially recorded, however, and I even went to the practitioner library."

"I didn't find anything new, either," Morgan said with a shake of her head. "Mother was no help. Of course I couldn't tell her exactly why I was asking. There's another good source, however, an old witch called Mother Higgins who lives in LaGrange. Before Daria met Bent, she told Mother that all three of us would be finding our soul mates soon. Unfortunately she's in Las Vegas for a week playing Texas Hold'Em. God help those poor gamblers who think she's simply a sweet little old lady. I'll try to find her next week. Maybe she knows more. After that, we'll have to ask for an interlibrary loan or go to the really large holdings ourselves."

"I'm hoping we won't have to go that far. The last thing we need is for someone to discover our . . . predicament in the middle of the debates. We don't need that kind of publicity."

Her eyes grew wide, and she shook her head. "No, no, no. And not a word to Ed, either."

"How's your magic center been? Mine's quiet." The words were no more out of his mouth than a razor-edged pain hit his solar plexus and made him gasp.

"Oh! Oh, damn!" she said at the same time, pressed both hands to her stomach, and doubled over.

The ache lessened to a dull thumping in time with his heartbeat, and he went to her side. "Are you all right?"

"I-I think so." Her face pale, she straightened slowly, but wobbled a little.

He took her arm. "Maybe you should sit down."

She glanced up at him, down at his hand, and back to his eyes. "Let go."

"I'm simply trying to help you. You looked faint." What did she think he was doing, accosting her? He released her.

"No. That's not my point. I'm all right. Are you hurting?"

"Yes. Not like from the first strike, though."

She held out her left hand. "Take it and tell me what happens when we touch."

Mystified, he put his right hand in hers. The pain

went away. "I'll be damned."

He let go, and the pain returned. "You, too?"

"Yes. The SMI is playing with us."

"We were fine until a moment ago—when we mentioned our centers." He grimaced, took her hand again. "The damn thing must spy on us. This is unconscionable!"

She raised their joined hands. "What do we do now? We can't hold on to each other all the time. I can handle the torture when it's mild, not a hard blow like that. What can we do to get the imperative to stop or at a minimum to reduce its attacks?"

"Let's go back to my original question. My center was quiet all week—still a little smug, but quiet."

"Mine was also, although it hummed a few times. If I thought of you or that kiss, it radiated . . . I'm not sure what I'd call it—*happiness*? Certainly a sense of pleasantness and well-being."

He reviewed the week in his head. Whenever he thought of her, and especially of kissing her, he experienced more than a simple pleasantness. He'd hardened like granite. Rather than divulge his reaction, he simply said, "Me, too."

They stared at each other. So close, he thought, they were so close, he could see himself reflected in her leaf-green eyes. So close, he could fill his lungs with her spicy floral scent. So close, he could rub his thumb over her soft hand. So close, if he bent down . . .

"I have an idea," he murmured, wondering only

briefly about the origin of his notion. The world had narrowed down to him and her, and suddenly nothing else mattered.

She looked at his lips and back to his eyes. "What?"

"If last week's kiss made the imperative leave us alone, what would happen if we tried it again? Maybe some respite for the next few days?"

"You think . . .?" Her eyebrows rose, her eyes widened, and she licked her lips.

"It's worth a shot, don't you think?" he asked, stifling a groan when her little pink tongue moved across her bottom lip and left it glistening.

"I guess . . ."

Although she didn't look convinced, he'd take her answer as a yes. The opportunity was—somehow—too great to pass up. Eyes slightly open, he touched his lips lightly to hers, saw her eyelids drift shut, and felt her mouth open. Closing his eyes, he ran his tongue over her lower lip to taste—mmmm, good—then dipped it in and met hers.

And the earth moved.

And the building swayed.

He had trouble maintaining his balance when his equilibrium failed and lava-hot fire flashed through him. The only thing in the universe keeping him upright was her, and he held on tight to her hand.

Searching for steadier ground, he took the kiss deep, right down to bedrock. She tasted like ambrosia, but it wasn't enough. The floor under him was still shaky. He needed a firmer hold.

He spread his legs and slid his left arm around her waist. Splaying his hand across her back, he pulled her into his body. As he did, a low hum surrounded them and pulsed to the beat of his heart. Ah, that was better, and better still when she pushed his open coat aside, ran her right hand inside it, and clutched the back of his shirt.

She's yours. The words reverberated in his head. *You're hers.*

Then she kissed him back, and a tremor more cataclysmic than the first struck.

She had to be caught up in the same turmoil because she let go of his hand and shoved her own past his coat to join its mate behind him.

Threading his fingers through her thick hair, he cradled her head and settled her more firmly against him. Good, an even better anchor.

Together they'd withstand the seismic upheaval.

He tightened his arms. She did the same. Her hands on his back kneaded his muscles. Oh, God, how had he ever gone this long, done without her embrace— so sweet, so true, so wonderful?

She was pliant, soft against his rigid body. What would she feel like . . .? He had to find out.

She whimpered when he loosened his arms, and she hummed when he slipped his right hand from her hair to her shoulder to her arm. As if she could read his mind, she pulled her left hand out from his coat and rubbed it up his chest and around his neck. The shift in position cleared his way to his objective.

Carefully, inch by inch, he tugged her jacket to the side until he could reach inside it. He let his hand linger on her waist for a moment before bringing it up her rib cage to under her breast. He could feel her heart thudding. His beat matched hers.

He softened their kiss and slowly raised his hand to cover her breast. The dress material was thin, and he could feel the outline of her bra and her tight nipple pushing against his palm. Oh, so lovely. Worth taking a moment to savor the softness and the weight.

She went still, drew back until her lips were barely touching his. She seemed to be waiting for something.

For him.

He fondled; she sighed. He kneaded; she moaned.

When he rubbed her nipple with his thumb, she pulled his head down to her and captured his mouth, pressing her hips into him at the same time.

Right against his arousal. Oh, yeah. Right where she was supposed to be.

He didn't question that certainty, but gave himself over to the sheer pleasure of her mouth, her body, of *her*.

Gloriana held on tight. She couldn't get enough of him, couldn't get close enough, couldn't touch him or be touched enough. His hand on her breast was sending lightning bolts of excitement through her, the vibrating hum was making her skin tingle, and she could feel her bones melting. Her foggy brain didn't help. She wasn't even sure she was breathing.

She did know exactly how exquisite it felt to be holding each other, to stroke his muscles while they moved beneath her hand, to rub his body with hers, to be engulfed by his scent, enthralled with his taste, ensorcelled by the man himself. It was magic of the highest kind.

Slowly, slowly, they ended the kiss. Gradually they let each other go. Gloriana couldn't tell who stepped back first, but when they were no longer touching, she didn't know whether to laugh or cry from the combination of pleasure and sorrow lodged in her chest. All she could do was to press her fist to her center.

"Are you all right?" Forscher asked, his voice low and raspy as he rubbed his own chest.

Hers was no better when she answered, "I think so. That kiss was worse than the first, wasn't it? More . . . more . . ."

"Yes. More everything. How's your center? Does it hurt?"

"No, not exactly. My description makes no sense, even to me. It feels both full and empty, all at the same time."

"Mine's not hurting. It's not right, either—I think it matches your description." He held out his hand. "Let's see where we stand."

She laid her hand in his, observed the result. "My

center's humming."

"Mine's smug again." He released her, put his hands on his hips, looked down at the floor, and shook his head. "Damn."

She forced her mind into gear and was relieved to note that her bones had solidified and she could stand without trembling. "Look, maybe that did what we wanted it to. Maybe—"

A pounding on the door to the suite interrupted her.

"What the hell?" Forscher stalked to the door and pulled it wide open.

There was nobody there.

He stuck his head out and looked up and down the hall. A piece of paper was stuck to the door, and he pulled it off. He stared at it for a moment, then gazed over at the door to her suite directly across from his. Disappearing for a moment, he returned with another sheet, a companion to the first. "You need to see this."

"What is it?" Gloriana asked. He handed her one of the sheets. The dark red laser-printed letters leapt off the page.

Stop Destroying Magic!!!
Accept the Truth!!!
End the Debates Now!!!
Or You'll Be Sorry!!!

"Mine's identical," Forscher said.

"But which side is behind them? The message could

be taken either way. The truth could be the formula and the 'new' casting method or the old one we're all used to."

"Good question. I wonder who else received one." He pulled his cell phone out of his pocket and hit the speed dial. "Ed, this is Marcus. Some flyers were stuck on our doors . . . Yes, that's right . . . She's here with me . . . That's what they say."

He was silent for a minute, and Gloriana could hear Ed's voice, only not make out the words. Before she could ask Forscher to put his phone on broadcast, he said good night and hung up.

"Ed said he received one of them, too, also stuck on his door and delivered by a door pounder. He's with John and Bill at the moment. The flyers were posted in some public areas also, but no one saw who did it. The Swords will check the security tapes, of course."

"What are we supposed to do for the immediate future of the debates?"

"Stay on schedule, according to Ed. He and John are taking the threat seriously, although it could be a prank—or a simple way to stir people up."

Gloriana frowned. Exactly what they didn't want— more aggravation. "There's nothing we can do about these idiots ourselves. What about our personal problem? Did we accomplish what we hoped for? My center's quiet. All I can suggest is to see how the week goes and continue our research."

"I don't have another suggestion. When are you

going to see the old witch?"

"I'll call her on Monday. Is there a specific question you want me to ask her?"

"Yes. See if she knows why there's so little information about soul-mate rejections."

Her nerves still jangled from their kiss and the abrupt interruption, and she needed some time to herself to get over both of those events. She nodded agreement and turned to the door. "I'll say good night, then."

"Wait. Let me see something first." He opened the door, stepped out into the hall, and looked both ways.

She followed. The hall was empty.

"Do me a favor," he asked when she used her key card on her own door. "Let me check out your suite."

"Is that really necessary? Do you think someone has gotten in? The threat's that serious?"

He frowned, looked uncomfortable. "Simply humor me, okay?"

She stopped herself from smiling. Two kisses and he decided he had to protect her? She opened the door and waved him in. "Go right ahead."

She stood in the doorway while he went through the rooms and walked back to her. "All clear. Ed wants to meet us at seven for breakfast. When's your flight tomorrow?" he asked.

"Eleven."

"I'm on the same flight. I'll see you at breakfast. Good night."

She closed the door after him and looked through the peephole. He was still standing there. She locked the dead bolt and the security chain with two loud clicks. When she looked again, she saw only his closing door. The man was definitely in protection mode.

Although he had checked out her suite, she felt spooked enough to go through the rooms—and the closets—again. No sign of disturbance appeared, and she breathed an absurd sigh of relief.

She wasn't going to worry about the prank, she thought while she washed her face. The real question concerned her soul mate. Her center was quiet, but it should be.

That kiss! Talk about an exhausting experience! Considerably more powerful than the first. She shivered as she remembered the feel of his hand on her breast. She'd read enough books with graphic kissing and love scenes to think she knew what to expect. Wow, had she been wrong! She could still feel the effects in every one of her female body parts.

She climbed into bed determined to blank her mind so she could sleep peacefully. It wasn't easy.

It also didn't work, she decided when she packed the next morning. Oh, she'd gotten to sleep all right—where her subconscious took over. She woke with impressions of dreams of children and him. Her body tingled and ached from the way the dream Marcus touched her.

Wait a minute. *Marcus?* She'd always thought of

him as Forscher. Suddenly he was Marcus? Oh, God, she needed to call him by his last name. Somehow that was essential if they were going to convince the imperative they weren't, couldn't be, mates.

Her center gave a little flutter, but subsided. She had no idea what that meant, and she had no time to worry. She had to meet Ed and Mar—no, *Forscher* for breakfast.

✿✦✳✿✦✳✿

Marcus eyed Morgan sitting across the aisle from him on the plane home. She was reading what looked like a scholarly journal and writing a note in the margin. When she tapped her lip with her pen, he almost groaned when his memory of her taste came back to him in a rush.

He glanced down at his computer where he was proofing—or attempting to proof—the article he had completed yesterday. It looked like gibberish to him. Who was he kidding about working? He wasn't concentrating worth a damn. He saved the article and shut down his machine.

Tilting his seat back, he closed his eyes. Lord only knew, he needed sleep. Last night's erotic dreams had woken him several times, and lying awake had not been much better. His mind continued to replay that kiss. And remember the bliss he found in her arms.

No woman had ever affected him like that with what should have been a simple kiss. Was all that the SMI's doing? How much of it was the woman herself? He had to admit, if she weren't a practitioner, he'd still be attracted to her—and actively working to get her into his bed.

She was smart—not merely intelligent about her profession, but her talent and magic itself. He could understand now why she brought up the larger picture about spell-casting; he hadn't looked beyond his own equation. She had good ideas and questions for the debates. She was fun to be with. She certainly had a pointed wit. F-Squared or Cubed, indeed.

Their kisses left him breathless and wanting more, and more . . .

No, stop this line of thought.

He should think about the prank. Who could be behind it? Ed had no real news to impart at breakfast. The security cameras caught a couple of people, men, from their estimated heights, in gray robes with raised hoods putting up the posters, pounding on doors and running for the stairs. The robes came from the training rooms in the basements, and everyone had access to those.

Nothing short of a full search would uncover who wrote and printed the flyers. Since the Denver HeatherRidge, like its sisters across the country, was a combination of individually owned condos and a hotel, it would be difficult, if not impossible to search all the rooms, invading the privacy and property of others, without hard proof.

Who might be willing to go to such lengths to discourage discussion of his formula? He had no clue what went on among the Horners and THA members or who the major players were, except for Walcott. The Traddies were certainly against change, period, but how reckless were they?

As for his fellow mathematicians? Prick was milking the situation for every ounce from which to take credit. By stirring up opposition, he might think he would make himself more important, more prominent. Brubaker? No, not Brubaker, who blabbered on in "math speak" until he bored everybody, his colleagues included, to death. Dortman had written that rabid note at the first debate, and he hadn't made a peep at the second. He wouldn't make a move without Prick's okay, either.

Nobody else came to mind. Nobody of any substance. All he could do was keep his eyes and ears open and let the Swords do their job, as Ed suggested.

After all, it wasn't like he didn't have enough to think about. Especially about the woman sitting not four feet from him. What was he going to do about her—his supposed *soul mate*? He still didn't want to believe the imperative. Why didn't the phenomenon leave him alone? He, who had sworn as a teenager never to go down the soul-mate path. He, who had borne the brunt of . . . No, better not rehash the past.

What counted were the present and the future. He'd made a good life for himself, full of success and accomplishment. He enjoyed his academic work, and his career writing science-fiction allowed him other outlets for his creativity. He could look forward to many productive and satisfying years.

As for a need for companionship, he had friends. Evelyn, George, some colleagues, a few other authors. He dated from time to time. He had a dog. What more could a man ask for?

As if in answer, his center seemed to sink in on itself and leave a gaping hole in the middle of his chest. He rubbed it—the friction seemed to help.

All his conjecture was getting him nowhere. He was simply theorizing ahead of his data. He had to be patient, do the research, and hope Morgan's talk with the old witch bore fruit. His chest settled down and didn't seem so empty. Maybe he was hungry.

The captain announced they were approaching the Austin airport, and he stowed his computer. He glanced over at Morgan, who smiled at him before hauling her bag out from under the seat and packing her journals. He tried to smile back, but didn't think she'd seen him.

After they landed, he followed her up the Jetway and into the terminal. In baggage claim her parents were there to greet her with big hugs. He ignored the hiccup his center made at the sight of family closeness and was about to slip by the Morgans with a wave, when Antonia called his name, and he walked over.

After exchanging greetings, Antonia said, "Why don't you come back to the farm with us for supper, Marcus. We have plenty and we'd love to hear how it went from both of you. What excitement! I've never seen a Sword in action."

Morgan looked a little stricken at the suggestion, and it was no hardship on him to decline. The less they were together, the better. Besides he had a good excuse. "Thank you, but I have to pick up Samson from George and Evelyn. I'd already arranged to have dinner with them."

While they waited for their luggage, Marcus walked with Alaric, answering questions about the debate. He could hear Morgan doing the same with her mother. Fortunately, his bag was among the first off the plane, and he was able to say good-bye and leave.

As he was walking away, however, Morgan came running after him. "Wait," she called, and he stopped. "I'm going to say the bare minimum to Mother and Daddy about those posters. I'd like to tell them nothing, but I don't think that will work. A lot of people saw the things."

"You're right. I'll do the same for George and Evelyn, in case they compare notes with your parents. George might come up with the names of others in the math world who are candidates for the prankster."

"Good idea. My parents might have more information

about the Horners and their supporters too. Okay, good-bye, until next weekend."

"Don't forget to tell me what Mother Higgins says."

"I won't." She turned and walked back to her parents.

He watched her go, and that damned hole opened up again in his chest. "Oh, stop this nonsense," he told it as he headed for the parking lot.

CHAPTER NINETEEN

Gloriana called Mother Lulabelle Higgins on Monday and went to see the venerable witch on Wednesday. She liked Lulabelle a lot, had learned many spells and potion recipes from the healer, and trusted her to keep confidences. Please, let her be able to help them.

In mid-morning, Gloriana pulled up to the simple frame house on an oak-tree-shaded street in LaGrange. The garden was filled with multicolored flowers, especially roses, daisies, and zinnias, and Gloriana smiled at the cheerful blossoms while she climbed the steps to the broad porch.

"Hello, dear," Lulabelle said, opening the door before Gloriana could knock. "Come on in. How are you and how is the family?"

"We're all fine, Lulabelle. How are you? You're looking well. How was Vegas? Did you take those gamblers to the cleaners?" She gave Lulabelle a hug.

Lulabelle grinned, patted her tightly curled, silver-white hair, and pointed to her T-shirt, which proclaimed "Poker Diva" in sparkling crystals. "I believe I taught a couple of them a lesson."

Gloriana followed the old witch to the kitchen. The house was immaculate as always, and the air was fragrant with the smell of freshly baked chocolate. Lulabelle moved fairly briskly, her slim body ramrod straight. A stranger would guess she was seventy, maybe seventy-five. Gloriana could only hope she looked so good when she was seventy, much less Lulabelle's ninety-some-odd years.

"I've made some brownies for us. My doctor says to indulge my tastes, and I'm following his orders. What would you like to drink with them?"

"Milk, of course," Gloriana answered. "Here, let me get it. The same for you?"

"What else? The glasses are in their usual place."

"The big news is, Daria's going to have a baby," Gloriana said as she poured the milk.

"No, you don't say! That's wonderful. I'll have to call her soon."

They each chose a brownie from the plate on the table and took their first bites.

"Mmmmm," they both hummed.

They chitchatted about her family and Lulabelle's until their first brownies were reduced to crumbs.

Lulabelle wiped her lips after a swallow of milk and looked straight at Gloriana. "You said you had some soul-mate questions, dear. Have you finally found yours?"

Gloriana sighed, played with her napkin, took another sip of milk. She knew her inquisitor would not let her rise from the table without telling every detail. "I don't know. I've met a man, a practitioner, and we're attracted to each other, but he's extremely different from me. We have practically nothing in common, we hardly speak the same language, we don't understand each other's magic, and it gets worse from there."

"Start at the beginning, Glori. Let's take it a step at a time."

"You remember how I was involved in that debate over how to cast spells? Everything started there." She proceeded to tell Lulabelle the entire story.

When she came to the kisses, the first test portion of them, Lulabelle smiled. When she mentioned their idea of assuaging the SMI with the second kiss, Lulabelle started laughing.

A little miffed at the old witch's reaction, Gloriana waited until her laughter subsided and said, "So, that's where we left it. What do you think? Did the imperative make a mistake? Can we change the SMI's mind? Are we stuck? What happens if we don't mate? Have you ever heard of practitioners who did reject their mates? Not legends or tales, but in reality, with facts that can be checked? We're serious here."

"Oh, my dear, I'm sure you are. That particular tactic is a new one to me and quite startling." Lulabelle grew serious. "Let me think out loud for a minute, starting with your last question. I've known, actually made the acquaintance of, only one practitioner who refused his soul mate. It was back in the nineteen-fifties. He belonged to a highfalutin New York City family, and his soul mate was the daughter of working-class parents. Oh, the horror and shame of having someone like her as their son's mate! He came from a long line of very blue blood, and the imperative had always paired their members with others of the same sort. His family was outraged and threatened to disown him if he married her.

"He, poor boy, did not have a very strong backbone and was greedy to boot, and he rejected her. I met him about ten years after the rejection. He was in terrible shape, had gone through two wives—non-practitioner, of course—and had taken to the bottle. He came to me for healing and told me his story. Although I helped him as much as I could, nothing was going to alleviate the pain and heartbreak the imperative was causing him." Lulabelle stopped to take a sip of milk.

"I saw him again about a year after that visit," she continued, "and he was even worse off. He'd actually found his mate—she'd moved out of town after the rejection and never married—and he asked her to marry him. This time *she* didn't want anything to do with *him*! Told him she'd come to terms with her life being without a mate, the imperative wasn't bothering her at all, and he should crawl back into his hole and pull it in after him. I suggested he try to change her mind—it's never too late if you're both alive—but we lost touch after that. I never knew what happened to either of them."

"What a sad tale," Gloriana said, her hopes for a happier ending plummeting. "What were their names? I'd like to look them up if possible. Ma—uh, Forscher and I want to check them out."

"William Robert Rhinedebeck was his name. I think hers was something like Gladys Kowalski or Kaminsky."

Gloriana pulled a piece of paper out of her purse and wrote down the names. "That's the only actual instance of rejection you have personal knowledge of?"

"Yes. I've heard the tales, of course, about horrible ends, suicides, even murders."

"Murders?"

"Where the one rejected kills the one rejecting, or one of the rejected kinfolk takes on the task."

"Oh." She wouldn't have to worry about that, thank goodness. None of her family would go after Forscher with a shotgun. Although, come to think of it, Clay might consider his computers fair game. "Do you have an idea why there's so little in the records about soul-mate rejections?"

"Probably because they're rare. Except for the one I am personally acquainted with, all the rest of the stories are older than I am and seem to be more like cautionary fables. I don't think we even bother with them anymore when telling you children about the imperative. You and

Marcus are the first people I've ever heard of to resist because you think you're incompatible. I will see what I can find out about this Rhinedebeck fellow, though. There may be more to the story."

"Thanks. But to get back to my other questions, has the SMI, or more correctly the phenomenon, ever made a mistake? Ever changed its mind?"

"I don't think so. Not where the two mates are concerned. Rhinedebeck and the woman were, in fact, soul mates. I've witnessed many matches between different classes, races, religions. I'm sure there have been other outraged or disappointed or upset families because people will act like jackasses, given an excuse. I've seen mates intensely attracted to each other and those who hardly appear to be mates at all. I've never heard of two potential mates being attracted one day and having no connection the next, as though the imperative took it all back." Lulabelle reached for another brownie.

Gloriana poured them both more milk. "Forscher says that he doesn't want a soul mate, ever. He has nothing against me, per se. He simply decided long ago it wasn't for him. He wouldn't discuss why he feels that way."

"What are his parents like? That's usually where our conclusions about mates come from."

"Stiff, formal, both professors, very proper, immaculately dressed. They seem well suited to each other. At their request, he calls them by their first names. His mother's proud of him, I could see that when she looked at him. I couldn't tell how his father felt. My parents got along with them okay, but they get along with everybody." She took a bite of another brownie. At this rate, she wouldn't need lunch.

Lulabelle stared into the distance for a minute before saying, "Glori, I think you have to get to the bottom of Marcus's refusal to accept a mate. He has to have a reason, and a very good one, to fight the imperative. You're never going to be able to be together until you do. That brings up other questions. Do you like the man? Can you see yourselves together? Do *you* want to be together, to be his soul mate and have him for yours?"

Gloriana moved her glass in circles on the table while she considered her answer. That really was the question, wasn't it? Such a jumble of ideas, notions, and impressions ran through her head that she couldn't settle on a decision.

Finally she said, "I honestly don't know. I like him, but I can't tell you why—probably the phenomenon at work. He's so perfect, always looking like a magazine ad. I guess he can't help that. When we're together, I feel like that character in the comics who always has a dirt cloud surrounding him.

"He's certainly smart, both about his profession and his magic. He can be charming. I wish he would loosen up a little. On the other hand, given his parents, he probably hasn't had much experience with 'going with the flow.' There's a part of me that wants to try to penetrate that wall he has around him, but that may be my perverse nature—much stimulated in my formative years by my big brother."

"Speaking of loosening up, are you aware that Marcus Forscher is a fiction writer besides being a professor?" Lulabelle asked.

"No. What does he write?"

"Science fiction. A couple of my grandsons and great grandsons are fans of his. He writes under the name Frederik Russell. From what they've said, the books are good space adventures, lots of intergalactic wars, and the like."

"I never would have guessed it. I'll ask Clay if he's heard of him. He and Daddy read that stuff."

"Surely there's more you can say about the man, Glori. What have you been able to agree on?"

She took a thinking break to finish off her milk before speaking. "We've complemented each other in our negotiations with Ed over the staging and during the events themselves. Like a man, of course, he often tries to speak first and for me, and I'm holding my own there. We're agreed upon the need for a study of magic education and seem to have arrived at a mutual consensus that encompasses both our views.

"I'm still confused. I am attracted to him, of course. The imperative's stirring up emotions and thoughts I never knew I had, while down at bedrock, I can't see spending the rest of my life with someone with very little in common between us and especially with a man who, except for an outside force, doesn't want to be there in any way, shape, or manner." She had to twist in her seat at the thought of that.

"What about the fact that we're really different about our philosophies of casting spells and working magic? He had a look of sheer horror—or maybe it was distaste—when he saw me give a growth spurt to a poinsettia. He showed me how he plays with these theoretical math proofs, and I couldn't even formulate an intelligent question. Our dogs may like each other, but you can't build a life on that. I feel in my bones we have other differences than the ones we know about—music, politics, and the fact that he doesn't have a single plant in his house. I have no idea what he thinks about children, except that he probably doesn't want them or he'd want a wife. How do you live with someone like that, much less be their helpmate, their soul mate?"

Lulabelle patted her hand. "Dear, that's where I think you're worrying about something that doesn't really matter. I've seen mates who were wildly different from each other on the surface, yet got along wonderfully and built strong, healthy families." She paused, a shrewd gleam showed in her eyes, and she asked, "How are you taking the news of Daria's baby?"

"Fine." When Lulabelle shot her one of those "oh, come on" looks, Gloriana shrugged. "I'm willing to admit the news threw me for a loop at first, and it has made me wonder about a family of my own. Yes, I'd like one. All of a sudden, I'm thinking of it at least once a day, where before all our problems, the notion never crossed my mind once a year. The question has become, how can I have one when my soul mate says no? I have no idea what it would take to change his mind."

"Meanwhile the imperative is pestering you, and you're both trying to keep it at bay with a kiss from time to time. Is your method of appeasement working?"

"So far it seems to be. No pain since I came home." She put her hand on her center. Nothing, not a hum, not an ache, not a twinge.

"How far do you plan on taking your pacification attempt?"

"What do you mean?"

"I'll bet the imperative is going to up the ante, raise the stakes, make you more miserable in its attempts to bring you together. It's also probably going to intensify your 'interactions.' How far into the first mating are you expecting to go?"

"How far?" Gloriana blinked at Lulabelle. "You lost me. What are you talking about?"

"You're aware that the first mating is a process. It's not wham, bam, and you're bonded." She waited until Gloriana nodded before continuing. "Be very careful if you two decide to make love with the idea of convincing the imperative to leave you alone. You may find yourself bonded."

"I did ask Daria about the process, and she said they made love a bunch of times before being bonded, like six or seven."

"I believe the average these days is between five and seven. In the eighteenth and nineteenth centuries, it was four to five, and records say fewer still if you look farther back in time. Remember, those are averages."

"I don't think I have to worry about an accidental bonding," Gloriana said. "Neither Forscher nor I want to take it that far. We already rejected that test. The SMI's quiet. Maybe we fooled it."

"You may be more alike than you realize. You're both intellectualizing the process, when it's all about emotion and passion, the heart, not the brain. I'd like to be able to tell you simply to relax and enjoy the mate and the mating, but I do understand your difficulties. Be careful, dear."

"We will," Gloriana answered, wishing profoundly the whole disaster would simply go away. She had nothing against emotion; however, when it wasn't reciprocated? Disaster.

"All our talk reminds me of my mate," Lulabelle said with a sigh. "Jimmy's been gone for twenty years and I still miss him."

"Oh, I didn't mean to make you sad with my questions,"

"None of my memories make me sad, Glori, especially those of Jimmy. They've become old friends. I'm looking forward to you and your mate, Marcus or not, sitting here in my kitchen eating brownies. By the way, before you leave, I have a transplanting problem."

Gloriana stayed to help repot a large ficus tree, thanked Lulabelle for all her help, and headed home. Big & Rich were singing "Save a Horse (Ride a Cowboy)" and she was congratulating herself on finally having some facts to deal with, even if she didn't like the idea of the SMI upping the stakes. When she reached the farm boundary, her center started itching.

She glanced down at her chest. "You be good and stop that. We're doing the best we can. You simply have to accept the fact that you made a mistake."

Her center rumbled and grumbled. She had probably eaten too many brownies.

※✦✲✶✬✥

By seven that night Gloriana was in pain.

At nine she called Ma—no, Forscher.

"What happened?" he asked after she identified herself.

"I saw Lulabelle Higgins today."

"No, that's not what I mean. My center's driving me crazy."

"Yours, too? Mine's aching."

"Mine's sore and giving me little shooting jabs every so often since this afternoon. What caused it to start? Did something change? Did you learn something from the Higgins woman?"

She didn't like his distinctly accusatorial tone. Did he think she was to blame for the imperative's capriciousness?

No way, José. "I have no idea why the SMI is giving us grief all of a sudden. Yes, I did learn something."

She told him what Lulabelle said about the Rhinedebeck rejection and her warnings about taking their appeasement attempts too far. She said nothing, however, about his adamant refusal of a soul mate or her own ambivalence. If she was going to get the truth out of him, she knew she would have to force it, and she wouldn't try over the phone where he could simply hang up.

"Okay," he said at the end of her recital. "I'll investigate Rhinedebeck, too. Did Higgins give you details about those suicides or murders?"

"No, she said those were practitioner legends, as far as she knew. Cautionary tales for the young, that sort of thing." Gloriana paused. "Uh . . ."

"What?"

"What's your center doing? Mine stopped hurting."

He was quiet for the longest time.

"Are you there?" she asked.

"Yeah, I'm here. The damn thing is sitting here, doing nothing. No aches, no pains."

"Why don't we get together to compare notes after the meeting Ed called for two o'clock?"

"Fine," he said.

They exchanged good nights.

Marcus glared at the phone in his hand and then at his chest. The second he had punched the hang-up button, his center had started aching again. Not quite like it had been before she called, but definitely a presence.

Morgan's news had not been particularly good. Not particularly bad, either. If the old witch could be believed, and he was going to check out that story for himself, Rhinedebeck had successfully opposed the imperative. Marrying non-practitioners had been a stupid move, of course.

It also sounded like the woman had come out all right. She must have, if she rejected Rhinedebeck when he came begging. The SMI had apparently left her alone and concentrated on the man.

He himself would do neither—marry a non-practitioner or go crawling back to his soul mate. He'd live a solitary life and do no harm to anyone. If the damn thing made him ache for the rest of his days, that was a small price to pay.

Morgan would be all right—much happier, in fact, without a mate who didn't understand her or her magic, especially a man who didn't want to be a soul mate to begin with.

The thought had barely left his head before the next thing Marcus knew, he was on his knees and holding his middle with both hands. A dull knife had attacked his diaphragm, his lungs—and his heart. It took an eternity for the excruciating pain to subside enough for him to switch to a sitting position.

Samson came over to give him a lick to say, "I'm here and your buddy," and Marcus put an arm around the dog and held on for a while. When his center finally returned to its former dull throb and his body stopped shaking, he tried to finish what he had been doing, but he couldn't concentrate, even to read. He gave up and went to bed.

Between the on-and-off torture and the dreams, it was a long night. When the morning dawned, Marcus surprisingly felt better. The pain had lessened considerably. If he carefully kept all thoughts of the situation out of his mind, he was able to work. It wasn't easy. By bedtime, he was thoroughly exhausted.

"If you're going to attack me tonight," he mumbled as he burrowed into his pillow, "good luck."

CHAPTER TWENTY

Late Saturday afternoon, Gloriana sat in a back corner in the inner garden courtyard of the Chicago HeatherRidge. Trees offered dappled shade, and petunias, peonies, and daisies bobbed their blooms in the breeze. The warm, flower-scented air felt especially good after the frigid air-conditioning. A fountain bubbled nearby, and a few sparrows hopped around the tables, begging for crumbs. One bold bird landed on her table, cocked its head, and looked her up and down.

"Sorry," she said, "all I have is iced tea."

The bird flew away when Mar—no, *Forscher* walked up and sat down next to her. He was his usual perfect self in his starched khakis and a button-down light blue shirt that matched his eyes. His hair looked like burnished gold in the sun. Gloriana stopped her fingers from brushing at the smudge on her jeans she'd picked up discussing a problem silver birch tree with the head gardener. At least her red Morgan Farm knit shirt was clean.

Forscher waved at a waitress by the bar across the courtyard and pointed to Gloriana's glass and to himself. The waitress nodded, and he sat back in his chair. "I don't understand why Ed was in such a hurry to meet. The survey results were identical to the last one, except that seeing the Swords in action was a big hit. We're not doing much differently about disturbances—a few more security people scattered around, of course. The only real change is letting Horner and Prick back in the main room."

"Personally, I could do without the pyrotechnics," Gloriana said.

The waitress brought Forscher his iced tea and refreshed hers. While he drank, Gloriana continued, "We've been getting some thoughtful comments from audience members. The teaching masters are making everyone think about how children learn. I wish Evelyn were here to add her experience."

"I'm happy she isn't," Forscher said, "because that means George would be also, and I would rather not go through that rap song again."

"You have a point." She was going to ask about the couple when she felt a pinch in her middle. Wonderful. She rubbed the spot.

Forscher looked at her hand and pressed his fingers into his solar plexus. "Hell. Here we go again."

"My center had been hurting off and on ever since

we talked, but it stopped when I walked into the meeting room. Now it's back." She rubbed harder.

"Mine, too. Did you find out anything else about the Rhinedebeck matter? I didn't."

"No, neither did I. I did find a number of Rhinedebecks in the practitioner registry, so the name is still with us."

"Are they related to the one we're interested in?" He didn't look very happy about the possibility.

"I didn't get into the genealogical files—didn't have time. Lulabelle didn't call with news, one way or the other."

"Maybe we'll both have time next week. I have to tell you, I'm ready for the next three debates to be over. It's impossible to get everything accomplished with no weekends."

"I agree," she sighed. "Delilah isn't too happy with my absences, either."

"Neither is Samson. He loves staying with Evelyn— she spoils him, but he's raring to run when I come home."

She was going to suggest he bring the dog out to the farm where both hounds could wear each other out, when he suddenly bent over.

"Damn!" He slowly righted himself.

"Did it hit again? Ouch!" She barely stopped herself from curling into a ball.

He held out his hand across the corner of the table. "Let's see if the remedy works like it did last time."

She put her hand in his, the pain stopped, and they both sat back with relief.

Gloriana tried not to think about how good touching him felt, even when it was only with one hand. Especially when he closed his fingers around hers. Warmth spread up her arm and through the rest of her, and contentment followed. She could feel her center hum, a faint, almost tickling vibration. She knew he was looking at her, but she didn't return his gaze. She didn't want to get caught up in him in a public place. She lifted her glass and took a sip.

She felt his thumb move across the top of her fingers, the back of her hand. She snuck a glance sideways. He was staring at her hand, like he'd never seen it before. He leaned over it, raising it at the same time, looking like he was going to smell it . . . or kiss it . . .

"Hey, Forscher!"

They both jumped and snatched back their hands.

"Oh, shit," Forscher muttered, staring across the courtyard at the man coming toward them. "Prick."

"Marcus, Dr. Morgan, I certainly didn't expect to find you here. And Marcus, what are you doing, conspiring with the enemy?" Pritchart gave them both what Gloriana was coming to think of as his trademark—a smirky grin. His T-shirt read: "Mathematics is the life of the gods." It was easy to see where Prick thought he belonged.

"Dr. Pritchart," she said in acknowledgment.

"What do you want, Prick?" Forscher asked in a weary tone.

"I came over simply to say hello, tell you what a good

job you're doing."

"Thanks."

"Dr. Morgan," Pritchart continued, leaning over with one hand on the table to speak softly to Gloriana, "I have to say how sorry I am that you're on the wrong side of the issue, advocating the Traddies' opinions. If you want to see the light, come talk to me. I'll be happy to explain the equation. With my expert help, you might be able to make meatballs as good as your mother's."

She almost moved her chair to back away from him, but she knew he'd follow her. She wasn't about to show any weakness to this agitator. "Thank you, Dr. Pritchart. I'm not speaking for either side, and basically, neither is Dr. Forscher. We want the best for our young practitioners and magic in general. What do you want?"

Before Pritchart could answer, a hand fell on his shoulder. "What are you doing, Pritchart, harassing my most important supporter? Or plotting with the leading opponent to the THA position?" Calvin Horner chuckled in one of those false, hearty ways meant to show he was kidding.

"Mr. Horner, nobody's plotting, and nobody's harassing," Forscher said. "Dr. Morgan and I were simply enjoying a moment of calm before the debate. We certainly hope neither of your groups is planning a repeat of last week." He said the words mildly enough, but Gloriana could hear their underlying edge.

Horner, with a shark's smile and a sanctimonious

tone, ignored the warning. "Of course not. If you remember, it was the Fomsters who threw that missile.
Thank goodness the Swords were able to keep them from
attacking our THA people."

"It was only a piece of paper, hardly dangerous.
Walcott certainly provoked it. Give me a break,"
Pritchart scoffed.

"Gentlemen, cease and desist," Forscher ordered and
stood up. "Save your comments for the debate."

Gloriana rose with him. "Yes. We're not the people
you have to convince. We'll see you tonight."

She and Forscher walked away from the strange two-
some. When they stopped at the bar and paid for their
drinks, she could feel Horner and Pritchart's gazes follow
them out of the courtyard.

Forscher took her hand again in the elevator. Neither
said a word until they reached their suites, once again,
directly across from each other.

"Do you think they saw us holding hands?" Gloriana
asked.

He raised their clasped hands and looked at them
like he hadn't even realized they were doing so. "I hope
not. We don't need someone asking us about our personal relationship on top of everything else."

He put his free hand on top of hers, and the now-
familiar warmth spread through her. Little fingers of
contentment stretched out over her brain, urging her to
relax and enjoy. She, however, kept her mind on the

issue by sheer force of will. "Did you get that bit when Horner said I was his most important supporter?"

"Yes, and I'm the leading opponent." He rubbed her hand and ran his thumb over the pulse point in her wrist.

She felt her heartbeat increase, but persevered. Resistance was possible. All she had to do was look at his hair, his ear, his jaw, anywhere to avoid his eyes. "And refuting the labels will only fuel the furor."

"I'm afraid so. Did you see Walcott over by the bar?"

"No, I didn't. How long was he there? That man gives me the creeps."

"He wasn't there long, and he left when we stood up. He glared at me like I was the devil incarnate." Clearly disgusted, Forscher shook his head. She noticed that he didn't meet her eyes, either.

"I was, uh, thinking about calling Prick on his assumption of your equation." Despite her determination, she was beginning to lose track of what she was saying, and she carefully watched his lips form his next words. She couldn't afford to miss what he said.

"You would only have prolonged the discussion, and Prick would have denied it. He's always been more than willing to stab his colleagues in the back while pretending to be their friend. He likes to use others to do his dirty work, too."

How did the man keep his concentration? Hers was fraying rapidly. She put her free hand on top of his, did some rubbing of her own. "So, he's a coward."

She finally gave in to the impulse and looked into his eyes—a mistake as usual, because he was gazing straight back into hers. She heard him say, "Yes."

She had no comeback. Neither did he.

She had no idea how long they stood there, staring at each other, holding hands. Her center hummed while warmth spread through her from his touch.

He tugged her a little closer, and they were leaning toward each other when, down the hall, the elevator dinged, and a couple emerged and walked off in the opposite direction.

Gloriana came to with a start and a gasp. She took a deep breath and stepped back, pulling her hands from his. He let them go.

"I'd better get ready for tonight." The words came out in a whisper. She dug out her key card and hurriedly opened her door. She turned back to him once she was inside.

"I'll knock on your door when it's time to go to dinner." His voice sounded rough, low, raspy, sexy as hell.

"Good. I'll be ready." She gave him only a quick smile and shut the door. Breathing a sigh of relief, she walked into the bedroom. If she'd stood there much longer, she'd have been in his arms again. Not a good idea when they still had the evening to survive.

Not a good idea, period. She had to stay away from him. The imperative stole her mind if she didn't.

⭐✦✶✷✦⭐

Thoroughly relieved the event was over, Marcus followed Morgan into the dining room after the debate. The entire evening had been an ordeal he didn't want to repeat.

First was dinner and sitting across the table from her, watching her talk with the others, including the Chicago Swords, Laura Wheeler and Johanna Mahler, who would be in the main hall with Baldwin. His center jabbed him off and on during the meal. The others probably thought from his fidgets that he had a digestive problem or a nervous condition.

He had a nervous condition, all right. Named Gloriana Morgan.

Glori, what a perfect name for her. Even if she was driving him crazy.

He'd wanted to punch Prick out in the courtyard when the jerk had leaned too close to her and fed her that line about talking to him to see the light. Asshole.

Then came that episode standing in the hall simply looking at each other. His center had been absolutely quiet, but the feeling of rightness about holding her hand permeated his every cell. Who knew what might have happened if they hadn't been interrupted? He shook his head to clear it. Those kind of thoughts led to madness.

The debate, for once, had gone very smoothly. Having a few magic-teaching masters and other non-magic educators had helped focus discussion. The Traddies had made their points mildly, and Walcott had been absent. Prick's henchman, Brad Dortman, had tried in his usual inept manner to say something provocative, but his words and delivery had fallen flat. He was so pathetic, the Swords didn't even ask him to leave.

All during the time, however, Marcus had been aware of Gloriana Morgan—he knew every move she had made, every time she pushed a wayward lock of hair behind her ear, every time she'd made a note, every time her body moved under that prim suit, every time she'd smiled at a man. Especially the last one.

Glori, Glori, have mercy. Maintaining distance was becoming incredibly difficult. Despite his unwillingness, hell, his outright refusal to go along with the imperative, despite his adamant repudiation of the ancient phenomenon, the damn thing was paying no attention to him. Fighting the pull to her was devouring an enormous amount of his energy and rapidly becoming impossible. What was he going to do when it conquered him?

No, *if* it did. *If*, not when. He couldn't, he wouldn't, surrender.

He knew Gloriana was having the same problems. She'd tried not looking him in the eye, but when she did, he'd seen her pupils dilating. She couldn't look away any more than he'd been able to. He'd heard the old saying about drowning in someone's eyes and thought it only a literary cliché—no longer. He wanted to dive right into the dark green. She'd held his hand, and he could feel the warmth flowing between them. Warmth that swirled and pooled . . . and made it impossible to say a word.

Glori . . .

No, *Morgan*. He had to remember to call her *Morgan* in his head. She probably thought of him as *Forscher*, copying the way most profs referred to each other. He'd noticed that neither he nor she ever called the other by name directly. They'd adopted the same defense and distancing mechanism. It was getting harder and harder, however, to maintain the contrivance. Harder still to pretend disinterest in the presence of others. Impossible to maintain the distance when alone.

Her light-gray suit was perfect business attire. Instead of depressing his attraction, it only spurred on his wondering if her underwear was utilitarian and what he'd find under that thin blouse.

And his mouth watered.

And when he came close enough, her scent practically made him dizzy.

And while he followed her, he had to remind himself not to watch too closely the sway of her hips and the glimpse of her legs under her pleated skirt. The urge to touch grew with each of her strides.

He wondered if hitting himself in the head would clear his obsessive thoughts. Probably not.

The question was rapidly becoming not if he could resist the *imperative*, but if he could resist the *woman*.

He looked elsewhere, around the room, hoping to find another view as interesting. One didn't exist.

He could at least put the table between them for a physical barrier, and he took a seat on the opposite side from her. Their gazes met and held, and he fought the urge to crawl across the expanse of white linen and . . .

His intention must have shown in his eyes, because hers widened and she glanced quickly down at her hands. When she raised her gaze again to his face, he felt like he'd been caressed by a flame. He didn't know green could be so hot.

Before he or she could say or do anything, however, a grim-faced Ed came in with an equally unhappy John Baldwin.

Good. Marcus forced his mind to concentrate on the papers in their hands.

"More posters," Ed announced and spread out a collection on the table.

"Same operation—gray robes, impossible to tell who they were—only tonight they did their dirty work during the debate," Baldwin said, "and with a difference."

Marcus looked down at the flyers. Some were identical to the originals last week.

Stop Destroying Magic!!!
Accept the Truth!!!
End the Debates Now!!!
Or You'll Be Sorry!!!

Others were blatantly partisan. "The Fomsters are evil and will destroy us!" versus "Only the FOM can save magic's future!" "Traddies will doom us to the magic of the past!" versus "Only THA can maintain our heritage!"

"Looks like everybody's getting into the act," Morgan said.

"Here's the one on your door, Gloriana." Baldwin held up a white page with red and black lettering. "Join our noble THA cause or be cast out!"

"Cast out? Of what?" she asked. "If they mean the Traddie group, that's fine with me."

"Here's yours," Baldwin said to Marcus.

It proclaimed—in more red and black—"Join us. FOM will prevail!"

"So, what's the verdict?" Marcus asked. "Are we in danger? Are these real threats, or is someone simply blowing off steam?"

"I wish we knew," Baldwin answered. He ran a hand over his face. "Tonight was quiet. We had three overflow rooms and, while there were the usual cheers and boos among the Fomsters and Traddies, they were all behaving themselves."

"I thought we had an insightful, interesting session tonight," Ed said.

"I agree, and we finally had intelligent discussion of methods for testing the equation," Marcus said. "In fact, a couple of the masters gave me new ideas for calibration."

"Maybe they're beginning to listen to our calls for

moderation and study," Glo—uh, *Morgan* remarked.

"We can hope so," Baldwin nodded. "In the meantime, we'll increase surveillance during the next session in Atlanta. Oh, I meant to ask, did either of you receive threats or posters through the post office mail lately?"

He and Morgan shook their heads.

"My e-mail is full of all kinds of letters, but nothing like what we've seen here," she said. "I simply refer them to you and the Council, Ed."

"Mine, too. I forward them and delete them from my e-mail."

"Tell us if you get any weirder than usual. We'll see you next week. Have a safe trip home," Ed said. He and Baldwin said good night and left the room.

Marcus and Morgan stared at each other for a long moment.

"Let's get out of here," he suggested finally. "We still have to decide what to do about our problem during next week."

CHAPTER
TWENTY-ONE

On the way to their suites, Gloriana tried to think of something new they could do about their situation. Hunt for more information on the Rhinedebecks, but that wasn't new, and what good would it do? He'd rejected her, and she'd rejected him, and they ended up apart. Would she and Ma—no, *Forscher* suffer the same fate?

She knew *suffer* was the correct word.

The SMI was applying more and more insistent, unrelenting pressure on her and, she assumed, on him. Sitting on stage, she'd been conscious of his every word and gesture, despite Ed sitting between them. Walking beside him to the dining room afterward, she'd felt each time he breathed, and his glance—now tactile in its intensity—had sent a hot shiver up her back when she preceded him through the door.

When they'd sat down . . . thank goodness Ed and John had come in. She'd felt like launching herself across that table, grabbing him by that perfect tie of his, and . . . and . . .

She clamped down on her rampaging imagination as they entered the elevator. She faced front, and he punched the button for their floor. An older couple followed after them and commented on their enjoyment of the debate. She and Forscher, yes, *Forscher*—she remembered for once—thanked them for the compliments.

When Gloriana asked which side the couple favored, the woman laughed. "Oh, we're in the middle. We have six children and could really have used a standard approach in the beginning to get them started. In the end, however, they proved to be quite different from one another in talents and casting methods that, well, one size definitely didn't fit all."

"Interesting," Forscher said. "I didn't consider such a situation. Thank you for the insight."

Arrival at the couple's floor ended their conversation, except for good-byes. When the door closed, Gloriana said, "None of the teaching masters suggested a standard beginning leading to infinite individual methods, either. I'm certain it wouldn't work in every case, but it's worth talking about."

"We'll bring it up at the next debate," he said as he took her hand and intertwined their fingers.

The familiar warmth his touch generated flashed through her body, and only with difficulty was she able to keep her body facing front. He'd acted so matter-offactly that she was sure he hadn't been conscious of his action. She snuck a glance—he was watching the floor numerals change.

They exited at their floor and walked down the hall, hands still linked. When they approached their suites, he said, "Let's go to yours."

He released her hand to insert the key card and open the door.

Gloriana breathed a sigh of relief as she dropped her folio and purse on a chair. She took off her suit jacket and laid it on the chair back; when she was near him, she was warm enough without it. Straightening the lilac silk shell over the waistline of her gray box-pleated skirt, she walked to the windows before turning to face him. "I don't know about you, but I'm happy to be out of the spotlight. I feel like somebody's always watching me when I'm in the hotel common areas."

"I'm the same way." He placed his folder beside hers, followed her to the windows, and looked out at Chicago, not at her.

He was standing close enough to touch, certainly to smell. What was it about the man's scent? No flower had ever smelled so alluring. Her center began to hum.

No, it wasn't him. She had to remember, the SMI was causing her reaction. Her center vibrated faster and radiated . . . satisfaction? Of course it was pleased. They were together.

Forscher was staring out the window and frowning.

Why didn't he say something? Once again, he'd gone into that silent state, and she had to be the one to start the conversation. They couldn't merely stand there. The imperative was too active, applying more pressure, determined to have its way by whatever means necessary. It was better, more prudent, much safer to discuss their problem, try to come up with a plan of action. Maybe talking would calm the SMI down, too.

"So, where do we go from here?" she asked.

"More research, I guess." He didn't look at her, only crossed his arms tightly over his chest. The expression on his face was positively grim.

She wasn't going to let his negative body language distract her. "Atlanta's practitioner library is the depository for the entire Southeast, and all the holdings in New Orleans have been moved there. I understand it also contains copies of a great many European sources. Maybe we should go a day early next weekend and see if they have data on the imperative. I could call and ask them to pull relevant documents before we get there."

She felt her center twinge, a sharp little jab to remind her of the SMI's displeasure about their goals. She ignored it.

"That's fine." His voice sounded strained, as though he was forcing the words through gritted teeth. "We simply have to find an answer, a way out of the imperative's ridiculous trap."

"Are you all right?" she asked when he closed his

eyes and grimaced.

"Damn!" He bent over suddenly, holding his middle, and went down on his knees.

"Ma—Marcus? What's wrong?" She knelt, too, putting her left hand around his back, and holding onto his right arm with her right hand.

His face contorted, he groaned and began rubbing his breastbone like he wanted to push his fist through it.

"Marcus, what's the matter?"

"Imperative," he gasped out. "Hit me . . . like this . . . the other day."

He was obviously in awful pain. What could she do? A healing spell wouldn't work on the imperative—she knew, she'd tried it on herself. She held him tight, although it didn't seem to help. He groaned again, and his muscles were like granite under her fingers.

She had to do something and tugged on his tie to loosen it. He seemed to breathe easier. She began to rub his chest under the tie and above his left hand, still pressing into his solar plexus. He was so warm, his body so stiff. "Does that feel better?"

He nodded, swallowed, took a deep breath. "Don't . . . don't stop." He moved his right hand around her back and held her closer. His eyes were still closed, but he raised his head, inhaled and exhaled, and said in a stronger voice, "Better."

She spread her fingers on his chest and applied more pressure, sweeping from one side to the other. After a minute, she could feel the steel-like hardness of his muscles soften a little. He was breathing better, too.

A few moments later, he straightened up on his knees, opened his eyes, and looked down into hers.

That sinking sensation hit her again, and she couldn't look away. His pupils expanded, and she could practically feel hers doing the same. She vaguely noticed her hand sliding down his chest.

Until she touched his magic center.

Intense heat flashed through her, all the way to her toes. She pressed her hand to his chest—whether to aid him or warm herself, she wasn't sure. Her mind couldn't seem to grasp the concept—any concept. She was losing her thought processes again, she knew that much, and she didn't care. With the heat had come a tremendous euphoria. She was flying.

He covered her hand with his, and her very cells rejoiced. When he turned his hand around and pressed it to her center, the heat doubled and redoubled. Her heartbeat speeded up, but instead of her blood rushing to her head, it raced to other, much more sensitive places. Desire and longing stole her breath. If she hadn't already been kneeling and holding on to him, she would have collapsed—or truly flown.

"Glori," he murmured, as his lids lowered over his darkened eyes, and his mouth descended to hers.

As their lips touched, immense need and voracious want welled up inside her and destroyed the slight vestige of opposition her muddled mind attempted to make. *He* was what she *needed*, and *he* was what she *wanted*, and *he* was what she *must have*.

She met his plundering tongue, dueled with it, returned his kiss with some plundering of her own. She heard him groan; she could feel her body vibrating. A low hum permeated the air.

Closer, she had to be closer. She worked her hand out from between them and slid it up to his shoulder and around his neck. Speared her fingers through his hair and held him to her.

Something was still missing—until he moved his hand from her center around to her back and held her even tighter, shifted so they were plastered together from chest to knees.

And their magic centers aligned.

Mine!

Raw energy blazed—hot, fierce, stunning. She could feel its aura shimmer around them. Only his arms kept her upright.

Magical power—elemental, primal, untamed, undisciplined—rushed from her to him and back, buffeting them like a hurricane's gusts. She held him tighter, somehow sure in the knowledge they'd ride out the storm—together.

Their kiss grew deeper, wilder, hungrier. She tasted his need, his desire, and reveled in them. He'd awakened a part of her she didn't know existed, a part demanding hot-blooded, compelling, reciprocated passion. She exulted in the discovery. She wanted the kiss to go on forever.

When he suddenly raised his head and moved back slightly, she whimpered, tried to pull him to her again, but he wouldn't let her. She opened her eyes to see his face—so stark, rigid, and severe above hers, his eyes mirroring the want she knew shone from hers.

The earth suddenly tilted as, with one arm behind her shoulders and the other at her hips, he laid her on the carpet. He braced himself above her on straight arms, and for a long moment, they stared into each other's eyes.

Even barely touching him, Gloriana could feel the exciting, arousing, burning power flowing between them. It was too much. It was too little. All she could see was the man before her—her man, and she would have him.

She grabbed his perfect tie and tugged.

"Glori," he said again and, coming down on one elbow, lowered his body to hers.

"Glori," he whispered and kissed her.

Their previous kiss had been potent and electric. This one shattered her senses. She couldn't see, she couldn't hear. She had only touch. She gripped his soft hair and his silky tie to hold him to her, then ran one hand under his coat and slid it over the fine cotton of his shirt and along the hard muscles of his back. Only he was real in the void—an anchor to cling to.

When he put a hand on her shoulder, another sense

reawakened—she could feel. Feel his fingers trace her collarbone, skim down her middle—where her center hummed as he passed—and around to her side, up and over her swollen breast. Feel through the silk of her blouse his fingers fondling, kneading, claiming. Feel his leg between hers, pressing into that aching place at the junction of her thighs. Feel his caress move from her breast down to her hip, down her thigh, and up under her skirt. Feel him pause at the top of her thigh-high stocking, stroke her bare flesh, spread his fingers over her leg and gently squeeze. Feel him move higher.

He cupped her, and her body jerked of its own accord, settled when he was still, arched when he pressed a finger to that most sensitive spot. She moaned when he pressed again and every muscle in her clenched. She couldn't help pushing back against his hand. Lightning flashed through her body, and she arched again, ground herself against his fingers to relieve the yearning ache between her legs.

Without removing his hand, he lifted his body away, drew back from the kiss. She protested, raised up, tried to hold him until he said in a low, raspy voice, "Glori, look at me."

She opened her eyes, stared into his. Only a thin rim of blue showed around a dark center.

"Glori, do you want this? Do you want me?"

There was an element in his tone she couldn't identify, so she ignored it. Instead, she tried to comprehend his question. Didn't he know every cell in her body was screaming for him? She did, however, have the answer. Her voice was scratchy like his when she said, "Yes, Marcus, I want you."

Quickly he shifted to her side, sat up, tugged her panties down and off, and raising her skirt, bared her to his gaze.

Gloriana watched expressions of such wonder and possessiveness wash across his face that she felt no embarrassment. On the contrary, she trembled with longing for his touch. He stretched out his hand and cupped her again, sliding his fingers through her curls and along her sensitive folds. His caress only caused the ache between her legs to grow stronger, more insistent, and she squirmed against his fingers in hope of finding relief.

Her movement must have acted like a trigger, because he changed position to kneel between her legs, and tore at his clothing, finally pushed his trousers and underwear down.

Before she had more than a glimpse of his erection, he pulled her legs around his hips, leaned over her on stiff arms, and positioned himself at her entrance.

He locked gazes and asked again, "Do you want me, Glori?"

"Yes, Marcus, I want you." As the words left her lips, she felt in her bones she'd given him the right answer. She was his.

He lowered his head and kissed her while he pushed

into her, slowly, inexorably.

She arched to him, used her legs to pull him closer. She could feel herself stretching, but if there was pain, it was lost in the glorious wildfire rushing through her. Oh, yes, right here was where he was supposed to be.

When he was completely inside her, he drew back and looked into her eyes again.

"Yes," she whispered.

"Yes," he whispered in return.

Marcus stared into her darkened green eyes for a long moment. Satisfaction and exultation and lust raged through him. He was right where he needed to be, inside her. Where he was meant to be. She wanted him, and he was hers.

She was so scalding hot, so tight, so slick around his throbbing cock. Where she was meant to be. He wanted her, and she was his.

Being in her eradicated the excruciating torment in his chest that had brought him to his knees. But the pain had been replaced by something else—a want, a yearning, a need for release, for completion. He felt building within him the compulsion to move.

Control. The word skittered through his heated brain and he acknowledged its worth. He had to be careful with her. It was her first time, after all.

Slowly, so slowly, he retreated. Slowly, ever so slowly, he advanced. Once. Twice.

On his third thrust, she crushed his coat lapels with

her hands, dragged his lips down to hers, and used her legs to pull him into her—all the way.

She tightened the muscles surrounding him.

And his control disintegrated.

The world dissolved in a rush of fire and energy and magic as he thrust into her again and again, as she arched to him again and again. Faster and faster.

He broke the kiss—they had to breathe.

She moaned a "No-o-o-o," and captured his mouth again.

Power intensified, built within him, raced between them, and finally burst in a simultaneous climax that lasted forever.

And ended in a sweet oblivion.

Marcus came to his senses lying on her, breathing like he'd run a marathon in a minute's time, with the most marvelous euphoria he'd ever experienced. He was still inside her and could feel her aftershocks—small contractions that rippled through both of them. Heaven.

When his breathing slowed, he realized he must be crushing her and levered up on his elbows. She opened her eyes. When their gazes met, she had a dazed look. As he watched awareness return to her, he felt the world crash in on him.

Oh. My. God. What had they done? What had he done?

CHAPTER
TWENTY-TWO

Gloriana blinked at the man above her. What was he doing up there? What was she doing down here on the floor? She frowned, searching her mind for memories.

He moved back, and she felt him pull out—*out*—of her body. He lowered her skirt, drew up his pants, zipped, and buckled. Before she could assimilate those facts, he said something. She had to concentrate hard to understand.

"I'm sorry. That shouldn't have happened," he said.

Sorry? What was he talking about? She pushed herself up on her elbows and looked down at her body, with her splayed legs and him kneeling between them. He retreated until she could bring her legs together and sit up.

"Holy . . ." she muttered. She didn't raise her eyes to his, but she had to clear her throat before she could ask, "What happened? You were hurting, and I was rubbing your chest . . ."

"And you touched my center, and all hell broke loose," he finished. "I couldn't stop kissing you, and when our centers came together . . ."

"I couldn't get close enough to you, and I wanted you badly . . ." Her voice quavered slightly on the last words. She could hardly believe she'd said them, but their truth vibrated through her.

"As I wanted you."

She ran her fingers through her hair and took a deep breath. She finally looked him in the eyes. His blue gaze was definitely warm, and some other emotion lurked behind the heat. He turned his head before she could identify it.

Memories came rushing back. "My mind simply shut down after that. I remember impressions of heat and magical power . . . and need . . . and then you were . . . and I was . . . ecstatic."

"I managed to remember to ask you . . ." He sounded hesitant, unsure, not like himself at all.

"And I said yes," she stated firmly, and he seemed to relax. She tugged her skirt down some more and shifted her legs underneath her.

He stood, seemed a little wobbly at first, but steadied and held out a hand to help her up.

Her knees shook as she rose, and he put his other hand on her arm until she said, "I'm okay."

"I'm sorry," he said again after he let go of her. "I never meant for it to go this far."

"Me, either." She ran a hand through her hair again; the curls disobeyed her attempt to calm them.

She glanced down. What was that by her feet? Oh, no . . . She felt her face grow hot when she bent and picked up her panties—her white cotton bikini panties. Not exactly the sexiest things to be wearing to . . . to whatever that was. Damn, she had to get her mind working.

She looked up to see him staring at the panties with the oddest look—sort of a sexy longing, if that was possible. Wadding them into a ball in one hand, she put them behind her back.

"The imperative certainly upped the ante," he said. "We have to talk about what happened."

"You're right." She nodded and sighed. At least his mind seemed to be functioning. She, however, needed some space. "Give me a little time to myself first, please."

He blinked at her for a few seconds, finally said, "Right. I'll go over to my suite and be back in a few minutes. Is that okay?"

She nodded again and started for the bedroom.

"Take all the time you need." He picked up her key card lying by her purse. "I'll take this with me to get back in easily."

"Fine." She stopped in the doorway, looked back over her shoulder, and said, "I'll see you in a few minutes."

She shut the door behind her and, eyes closed, leaned against it for a moment. Discombobulated and bewildered, that's what she was. She opened her eyes and looked at the panties in her hand. Embarrassed, too. And something else . . . but what? No matter, she didn't have time to think about it. She wanted a shower.

She threw the panties into her dirty-clothes drawer and quickly stripped. Leaving her clothes scattered on the bed, she walked into the bathroom. As she closed its door, she found herself face to face with her reflection. Her body didn't appear different from the way it usually looked.

It certainly didn't feel like her old one.

She felt somehow more alive, more vibrant, more . . . *something*. Until she finally looked into her own eyes in the mirror.

Satisfied, that was the "something." *Satisfied*.

"Marcus." When she said his name out loud, the satisfaction grew until she was literally tingling all over and almost dizzy. Her condition had to be similar to eating one of the more potent euphoria-producing plants.

She also felt sticky and sweaty. Muscles in unusual places ached, and even though they'd touched in only two places—very significant places—she could still smell him, even taste him.

First a tooth brushing, then a shower, that's what she needed.

With the hot water beating on her, she washed thoroughly while her thoughts seemed to float—until she rubbed the soapy washcloth between her legs.

Oh. My. God.

What had they done?

They'd mated!

No, no, no. Mating wasn't possible. Practitioners were not capable of having sex with other practitioners—unless they were truly soul mates. It was the one true test of being soul mates. She and Marcus had agreed that particular test was too dangerous to try.

But they'd actually done *it*. They'd had successful sex. Oh, didn't that change everything? What were they to do about their problem now? All their protestations and plans had been kicked into the next county.

So, what was she doing standing here? He'd be returning any minute.

She hurried to finish her shower and throw on clean underwear and the jeans and shirt she'd worn earlier. A brush through her hair did nothing to tame the wet curls; at least she wasn't dripping. She slid her feet into her flip-flops and opened the bedroom door.

Wearing his afternoon clothes, Marcus was entering her suite. His blond hair was darker, still wet, so he must have showered, too.

They stared at each other for a long moment—until they each took a deep breath and broke the connection. She could feel her center humming.

They couldn't stand there looking at each other all night. To get moving, she fell back on the manners her mother had drilled into her. She walked into the suite's kitchen and said over her shoulder, "Have a seat. I'm going to have some water. Would you like something?"

"Water would be great."

Pleased at her ability to sound normal when feeling the opposite, she took a couple of water bottles out of the fridge and filled glasses with ice. Thank goodness he hadn't followed her into the small space. They didn't need to be physically close to each other again.

He sat on the couch, and she placed the glasses and water on the coffee table. When she sat in a chair across from him, she almost gasped when certain muscles protested. They both opened the bottles, poured, and drank.

Gloriana put her glass down first and contemplated her strategy. Best to address the situation head-on, she decided. She propped her elbows on the chair arms and clasped her hands in front of her. When he had also placed his glass on the table, she looked straight at him and stated, "We have a problem. A big problem."

He leaned back against the couch, his arms stretched out to either side along its back. His expression was grim, his gaze guarded, but his voice mild when he spoke. "If I understand correctly what happened, the imperative took over our minds and bodies and/or aroused us to the point that we became a man and a woman at their most primitive. We had no other thought or recourse except to have sex."

Gloriana almost snorted. Wasn't that exactly like a man, especially a professor? Reduce a totally emotional event to a cut-and-dried statement that didn't even begin to consider the ramifications of the situation. Lulabelle had warned them about intellectualizing too much. Here was a perfect example.

"Wait a minute," she said, holding up a hand to stop him from speaking. "That's beside the point. The problem is that we had sex successfully. *We mated.* Therefore, we must be soul mates, and the imperative has *not* made a mistake."

His mouth dropped open, his arms crossed in front of his chest, and he stared at her as though he'd been punched right in the stomach. His face went completely white.

"Do you have another explanation or theory?" she asked. "The rules say that a male and female practitioner who are not soul mates cannot consummate the union—they are not physically able. Period. *Having successful sex is The Big Test.* If the imperative was wrong about us being mates, as we've been thinking, we wouldn't have been able to do it."

He'd closed his mouth, still looking astounded and appalled. After several seconds, during which she could almost see him analyzing her words, looking for a way out, and finding none, he took a deep breath and spoke softly, "You may be right."

Oh, wonderful. Denial. Not this time, buster. "What do you mean, '*may be*'? Am I right or not?"

He grimaced and rubbed both hands up and down his face. "I'm not sure we should go that far. Nothing about the whole fiasco has made sense. It may still be the imperative dictating our actions."

"That's bull and you know it," she said. "If we weren't soul mates, we wouldn't lose control like we did under the compulsion to mate. Maybe the imperative hasn't been *forcing* us to do anything. It simply gave us a shove."

"Some shove." He crossed his arms again and pulled them tight to his body. "The entire situation is abhorrent to me. Not only am I involved in something I swore I would never be a party to, it's making me into someone I don't even recognize. I have never, ever lost control of myself like that. In my book, what I did to you was akin to rape. I apologize again for subjecting you to that experience."

So, that was what he'd been afraid of. She'd let him off that hook, but not the other. "Marcus, that wasn't rape. We both wanted it. Badly. Get that thought out of your head."

"All right. I'll accept that you don't consider it rape. The imperative, however . . ."

He wasn't listening to her—or rather he wasn't hearing what she was saying. She'd try another approach. "Look at it another way. Is it really the imperative controlling us, or are we using the SMI as an excuse? I never heard a word about the phenomenon *creating* soul mates. It recognizes them somehow, and the imperative gives them a nudge when they come together. After that, the desire to become mates takes over. We came together, the attraction kicked in, and bang, we mated."

Where he had been inscrutable before, now she could trace every emotion across his face. Relief that she didn't think he had raped her. Horror at her next suggestion and its ultimate conclusion.

"I hate to agree, but I have to admit, you have valid points," he said in a hoarse voice, like he was forcing each word reluctantly past his lips. He was looking everywhere except at her. Finally he brought his eyes—fear and dread still present—back to hers. "Your line of thinking brings up the other mating rule—no artificial barriers. Assuming that was a mating, no matter what the usual averages are, could we be *bonded* with that one episode?"

She stared back at him while her thoughts flew to Daria and Francie. "No, I don't think so. My sister and sister-in-law told me their bonding, the actual decisive act, was transcendent, almost an out-of-body experience. While what we went through was strong, I don't think it was *that* powerful." She paused to assess herself before saying, "I don't feel differently toward you."

He relaxed with a whoosh of air from his lungs. "I don't either—to you, I mean."

"There is one point I simply don't understand. From everything I've learned and every instance I've seen, the soul-mate bond is all about love. The two mates love and cherish each other. The feeling increases they grow closer. I can't see how what we're going through has anything to do with love, though. The only emotion in evidence is lust. Where's love in the equation? I certainly don't feel like I'm 'in love.' Do you?"

He was quick to answer. "No, I don't. I feel manipulated. I'm willing to agree that we would have been attracted to each other even if we weren't practitioners, but we are. Practitioner mates certainly never need much coercion."

Typical man—he *still* wasn't listening and was back to that "forcing" idea, so she tried again. "Is it *really* coercion? Or are we simply overcome by the soul-mate attraction and doing what comes naturally? Oh, I'll admit the SMI's aggravating us, but it doesn't do that when we hold hands or kiss. How do you feel this minute, this second? Not in your head. In your body. I feel pretty damn good."

He gave her a thoroughly black look.

"Well?" she pushed.

"I feel . . . satiated," he mumbled.

"No aches or pains?"

He shook his head, stared at his hands.

Another matter raised its head as her brain made connections. "Uh-oh."

"What?"

"No barriers. I never activated my birth control spell."

"You could be *pregnant*?" If it was horror in his eyes before, now they held total terror.

"It's highly unlikely," she reassured him after a swift calculation of dates. "To be on the safe side, however . . ." She hurriedly cast the spell and felt the correct effects.

"There. Nothing to worry about."

"Are you sure?"

"Yes." When he didn't look completely convinced, she repeated, "Yes, I am sure."

He sat there like a lump.

"Okay, what next?" she asked, hoping to get him talking again. "We're soul mates. Where do we go from here?"

He frowned, but she couldn't tell if it was at her questions or the situation. "It appears from the Rhinedebeck tale that we can successfully refuse both the imperative and the mating. In that episode, the blame and the consequences came down on the man, not the woman. That's fine with me. There's no reason you should suffer at my intransigence."

"Let's be scientific here and look at the facts," she retorted. "One instance like Rhinedebeck does not make a trend. That couple hadn't mated—according to the evidence we have. Don't forget, the imperative is already giving me pain, too. Why won't it continue to do so? If you reject me, there's no guarantee that I'll ever have another mate. What am I supposed to do? Go out and find a non-practitioner to marry, like he did? I don't think so."

He glared at her. "Are you saying you *want* me to give in?"

"No. I simply think we have to consider *all* the possibilities for why we're in this jam."

"What's left to consider?"

"Why you're implacably against the concept in the first place."

His face went blank as he sat straight up and crossed his arms over his chest again. "That's my business and mine alone."

"It certainly looks like 'your business' has put us both into a mess of major proportions. All of our other disparities can probably be negotiated or handled or ignored, even the totally different approach to magic. Lulabelle says she knows a number of couples who have lots of diversities and contrasts. Maybe we ought to give the process a chance."

He said nothing, but didn't seem able to meet her eyes.

Okay, she'd try yet another tact. "At the beginning you suggested approaching our exploration scientifically. How can we do that when you're withholding what may be the most important variable—the reason for your refusal?"

"I can't see that my dislike of the whole concept has any bearing. Something—the phenomenon and its imperative enforcer, the universe, whatever—has decided we're soul mates. I refuse to give in to those dictates. I'd feel the same, no matter what. It's nothing against you personally. It's become a matter of principle to me. I do not want and will not take a soul mate. Becoming mates would be a disaster for both of us. There must be a way out of our dilemma."

Moving the man off his "principle" was like trying to move a giant redwood tree with her bare hands. What else could she do but keep trying? "How do you prove that your reasoning is sound unless you put it to the test?"

"All our talk is getting us nowhere," he said and stood. "Let's research deeper into the whole subject of soul mates and touch base during the week before we leave for Atlanta. I'll go on Friday to put in some time at the library there."

She stared at him. What could she say to those statements? He was totally walling himself up. She truly did want to scream.

He met her eyes for only a few seconds before walking to the door and opening it. "I'll talk to you in Austin."

She watched him leave and close the door after him.

Coward. The man was a coward.

And she was willing to bet real money that he was over across the hall packing to leave tonight.

Lily-livered, sniveling coward.

She smiled to herself. She knew what she had to do—the same as with her brother when he wouldn't tell her important information.

Ambush him.

Not until he had reached the sanctuary of his suite did Marcus allow himself to react. Once inside, however, he began cursing and pacing, using every foul word he could think of over and over until he ran out of breath and vocabulary. How could he be so stupid not to have recognized what happened when the two of them came together? Because he'd been so afraid he'd raped her that he hadn't seen the larger picture.

Soul mates! He and Gloriana were, in fact, soul mates!

Despite all his determination never to have one, all his care never to be even in the vicinity of eligible female practitioners, what had happened? A catastrophe.

No matter that having sex with Gloriana had been the most powerful sexual experience of his adult life. No matter that when he had been sitting there talking about the situation, he'd felt the most powerful yearning to take her in his arms and tell her everything would be all right.

Because it wouldn't. It couldn't.

He knew himself. He could fight his true nature and his family history, but he knew how it would all come out. Glori—vibrant, beautiful, funny, intriguing Glori—would be more than disappointed in him as a lifelong companion. She'd be crushed, sad, confused, and frustrated. She'd end up hating him, soul mate or not.

Better to refuse to go along with the imperative before they were deeper in the emotional morass. She'd get over him. The practitioner gods would surely grant her another mate.

Another mate. That meant another man would be the one to hold her, to kiss her, to take her to bed, to wake up beside her, to father her children.

Those thoughts almost doubled him over, and not from imperative-caused pain. No, more from an intense ache of jealousy and a mighty surge of possessiveness. *She was his*, damn it.

No! Stop thinking! These thoughts lead to madness. Get out of here before you do go crazy!

Yes. He'd leave tonight. Go home, where he was in control of his life—and alone.

He stalked into the bedroom, dragged out his luggage, and threw his things into it. He almost laughed at the thought of how his parents would react to his haphazard packing. Within five minutes he was on his way to the concierge. There had to be a plane out of Chicago tonight. Hell, the place had two airports. He'd go to Dallas, Houston, anyplace with a connecting flight to Austin. He'd spend the night in the airport if he had to.

On the plane early the next morning, after a night spent pacing the halls of O'Hare Airport, Marcus tried to sleep. Despite his exhaustion, it wasn't easy. His stubborn brain kept reliving those moments with Gloriana, their passionate kisses, the mutual resonance of their magic centers, the absolute thrill and wonder and, yes, satiation of their lovemaking.

No, not lovemaking. Sex. That's all it was.

His body and his magic center said differently, of course, and he was doubly glad he didn't have a seatmate as his unrepentant cock responded to his thoughts.

George and Evelyn were surprised to see him when he went to pick up Samson, but he managed to mumble something about not feeling well, and they let him go without asking real questions.

Marcus took Samson for a walk, then headed for bed. Once lying there, he decided he could survive the coming week and the next debate. He wouldn't have to see her again until Saturday. There'd be lots of people around. If he was never alone with her, he didn't have to worry about a repeat of their previous "togetherness." Furthermore he would not, definitely refused to, think of her or their problem until he saw her Saturday night. That determination relieved some of his stress, and he was able to concentrate on math proofs until he fell asleep.

CHAPTER
TWENTY-THREE

"Come on, girl," Gloriana called to Delilah as she walked out of her house on Wednesday morning, "Let's go to town. You can visit with Samson while I take on his master."

The basenji chortled at her and climbed into the car.

Gloriana strapped the hound into the harness she'd ordered on the Internet—a duplicate of the one Marcus had used on Samson. She headed for the highway singing along with Shania Twain on the radio, "I'm Gonna Getcha Good!" Delilah yodeled a couple of times in accompaniment.

As she drove to Austin, she plotted her moves. She was mad, damn mad, totally, thoroughly, completely mad. She didn't have words for her anger at Marcus Forscher, not to mention the entire soul-mate process.

At Marcus for his obstinate refusal to discuss the reasons behind his rejection of a soul mate. How else were they going to get to the bottom of their dilemma? He was the one who said, "Let's look at the situation scientifically." Scientifically? Hah!

She was also angry at the soul-mate process, particularly the SMI, for reducing her mind to such mush that she hardly knew what she—or he—was doing when she lost her virginity. That was one event at which she had wanted to be fully present, mind and body.

Oh, the memories of what happened had come back to her, and she'd relived every touch, every kiss, *everything* over and over, but that wasn't the same as being consciously there in the moment. It certainly wasn't the same without Marcus being there, touching her, kissing her, *everythinging* her.

She hadn't discussed the soul-mate revelations—especially not their mating—with her parents. Her mother had given her a couple of questioning looks. Thank goodness she hadn't broached the subject beyond asking how Marcus had been at the debate. Gloriana hadn't called Lulabelle, either. After all, what could they do? This mess was between her and Marcus.

Soul mates. She'd thought long and hard about the concept in general and her soul mate in particular. Okay, there was the phenomenon—practitioners always found their soul mates—and the imperative, which made sure they got together and "nudged" when they dawdled.

She'd thought about her brother and sister and how they'd gone through the process of finding and accepting their mates. Leaving all the *sameness* between mates aside, it appeared that lust—an enormous, all-consuming physical attraction—was the trigger.

Overwhelming desire certainly captured a person's attention; she was proof positive of that. Despite her mother's explanation and Daria's reports, she had still been unprepared for the intensity, confusion, and power of her feelings.

Maybe a warlock—or any man, for that matter—needed lust to fix his attention on a woman. Despite his protests, Marcus had given every indication of being fixated on her. All those looks from him had been sexual interest, not intellectual derision. Attraction, not repulsion. Desire, not disdain.

All well and good, but what about witches, specifically herself? The kind of astonishing physical attraction between them was new and exciting to her. She'd dated in high school and college from time to time, nothing intense, more because everybody else was doing it and she wanted to go to the parties. She and her boyfriend had usually parted amicably when she lost interest—or he pushed too hard for sex. The imperative at work, she knew, although at a much lower activity level.

For the present and the future, however . . . what did she want?

Love. She wanted to love and be loved as she'd seen with every practitioner couple she knew. All her family, parents, siblings, aunts and uncles, cousins, good friends, all were surrounded by, immersed in *love*.

A mate. She wanted a mate to share her life with, to have children with, to grow old with.

Children. Daria's announcement must have started her own biological clock ticking—or awakened yearnings she was unaware she had.

What did she want? She wanted *It All*.

Her center hummed happily when she recognized and accepted the truth of her decision.

She shook her head at herself. A few weeks ago, none of these wants ever crossed her mind. Now they consumed her attention, her life. She should have expected such a reaction from Daria's experience. Indeed, their mother had told them that the imperative discouraged witches from thinking about their mates and the consequences until they met them.

The situation was almost laughable. Daria had complained bitterly about the "arranged marriage" aspect of the phenomenon. Having seen the results for both her sister and brother, Gloriana had to admit the compelling attractiveness of the situation, however it came about.

So, what was she going to do?

If Marcus was her fate, so be it. She'd accept him. Whether it was the soul-mate phenomenon itself or its enforcing imperative or both pushing them together, it didn't matter. Not one iota of fact or fiction existed to suggest that either made a mistake in the pairing. Not ever in all of practitioner history. Soul mates were soul mates. Period.

Could she have *It All*? Wasn't *It All* part of the soul-mate definition? Would *It All* come naturally if she and Marcus spent more time with each other? Got to know each other? Came to love each other? Her father always said being soul mates got better all the time. All the evidence answered yes to her questions. She needed to have faith in the process.

Was she in love with him already? Well, she wasn't sure about that. She didn't really know him, certainly didn't understand him. They'd had very little time together, no chance to share everyday life, to discover those little things about each other that were lovable. They certainly hadn't been on a simple date. She'd been almost afraid of being with him, but more because of the attraction she'd been feeling and the misunderstanding of what he was thinking than their dispute about magic.

Marcus. What about her soul mate? What was he really like? He had many positive qualities. He was intelligent. He was honest—he'd been up front with the fact that he didn't want a soul mate, even if he wouldn't tell her why. She'd assume he had loyalty and honor since she couldn't imagine being paired with someone who didn't. Dedication to his career, too. As a fellow professor, he certainly understood the demands and needs of the job, and she wouldn't have to explain when she spent hours in the greenhouse. Conversely, she'd understand when he did whatever he did to create new theorems or equations or proofs.

What about negatives? Stubbornness, the tendency to be overbearing, the inability or refusal—take your pick—to hear what she was really saying, the refusal to discuss love or any emotion. Wait, couldn't those traits be applied to all men? Oh, the burden of having to live with them.

Then there was the practice of magic, of course. In the discussions, the majority of the audience seemed to be reaching an equilibrium whereby all forms of practice were accepted, with none in the forefront. What she'd been afraid of, forcing one style or another on young practitioners, wasn't going to happen. She might have been wrong to think his formula would be that forced style, but the Traddies weren't right to exclude the new, either.

They did practice magic totally differently. Maybe they couldn't understand how each other's talents worked. Did that really matter? Talents were individual, tailored to each vocation or profession. No one could practice them all. She couldn't create an energy weapon the way a Sword could. Why should she be able to do or need to understand what Marcus did, and vice versa? She'd been overreacting to think they had to practically be able to cast each other's spells.

One other thing: his "Mr. Perfect" appearance. He had to be immaculate in everything—his surroundings, his work habits, his lifestyle. She was unable to remain spotless when working with plants and was perfectly happy to live and work in a mild chaos—fairly clean, but cluttered. They'd have to arrive at a middle point somehow.

Could she count on a sense of humor? She hadn't seen much evidence. On the other hand, maybe he did have one. How else could he live with a basenji?

One matter, the most important one, was absolutely, positively clear. Trust. If they didn't trust each other, they couldn't have *It All*.

Trust. A little word with a big meaning. Soul mates knew neither would let the other down, they could rely on each other in all circumstances, they could express and expose their darkest secrets, deepest longings, craziest ideas, and still be loved unconditionally.

Did she trust Marcus? Oh, that was a very good question. She must, to some extent, or even the SMI couldn't have forced her to have sex.

Did he trust her? No, not even as much as she did him.

Did he trust himself? An interesting question—yet another to which she had no answer.

Everything came down to his refusal to talk. If he wouldn't share himself, his one big secret, "his business," at the crux of his obstinacy, and *get over it*, she wouldn't have a true soul mate, wouldn't have that oneness, that unity of spirit, body, and soul that she not only wanted, but needed. Not only desired, but craved.

Whatever "his business" was, it had to be important and extremely personal to him. Some powerful aspect of the phenomenon that turned him against the concept and the reality. From his reactions, getting him to open up would be difficult. She refused to think it impossible.

After all her thinking, what did she have to do? What was her plan to make him tell her why he was adamantly against having a soul mate?

Take him by storm. Move through his defenses and reduce them to rubble. Leave him no recourse. Laying on a little guilt trip wouldn't hurt, either.

How nice that the best, the most effective way to accomplish that objective would also take care of her anger with the process itself.

She started laughing while the plan unfolded in her head. Delilah looked at her curiously, and Gloriana gave the dog's head a rub. "You take care of Samson, and I'll take care of his master."

❋✳✴❋✽

Gloriana pulled up to Marcus's house about eleven. The homes here hidden behind their two- or three-car garages and minimal front yards. On both sides of the street, they rose two or more stories to take advantage of the vista. Given the slope of the ground in these hills above the Colorado River, he probably had a very nice view out his back windows.

The cream-colored stucco building appeared as she had expected to find in the neighborhood and from his uptight personality—contemporary, sleek, austere. The landscaping made effective use of native plants that wouldn't need watering or much gardening effort by the owner. That's right, he said he'd had it professionally done.

With few windows facing the street, the house also reminded her of a castle fortress—and its owner, a medieval baron determined to protect himself from the rabble hordes. She knew he was here; he wasn't at his office, and this had to be the only other place he thought he could retreat from the world.

"Look out, Marcus," she said while she and Delilah walked down the flagstone path toward the dark gray door, "here come the barbarians."

After making sure her full, knee-length, red-and-blue-striped skirt hung correctly and her scoop-neck, red blouse was buttoned straight, she rang the bell. Samson yodeled from the other side, and Delilah answered him. She heard Marcus telling him to calm down, and the door opened.

Her adversary, her nemesis, her *mate* stood there in jeans and a T-shirt with both panic and shock on his face. The rest of him, however, was perfect, pressed, and shaven. Even his hair was combed. Of course.

"What . . . what are you doing here?"

"I'm here to see you. We are going to talk, Marcus Forscher, whether you want to or not." As she spoke, she poked him in the chest with her finger until he backed up and she and Delilah could enter. The dogs took off for the back of the house.

Gloriana breezed past him and walked down the entryway, past stairs on the left both up and down, past a dining room on her right, and into a large living room stretching the width of the house and with windows overlooking the hills. She noted two curly tails disappearing down the staircase to a lower level. She dropped her purse on the beige sofa and looked around.

Yep, the interior met her expectations, given the style of the house—pale hardwood floors, white walls, a minimal amount of furniture, earth tones in the upholstery and scattered rugs, black and white art photos instead of paintings. Spotlessly clean. No mementos, family pictures, little collectibles. Absolutely no clutter, not even a dog chewie. Did anyone live here?

Then she spotted it on a window ledge, and it drew her immediately. A small variegated ivy in a dark green plastic pot. The only plant in the place, from the looks of things. The kind you buy in the grocery store. Automatically, she stuck a finger in its dirt.

Of course. Dry as a bone. She picked it up and turned back to Marcus. He had closed the door and come into the room, but he still looked shocked—and grim. He said nothing.

She spied the kitchen to her left, so she carried the ivy there and watered it. Nice dark gray granite counters, she noted. She opened the white cabinet doors until she found his dishes—white with a thin black rim. What did the man have against color? She preferred her Fiesta Ware. She took out a small plate and set the ivy on it and the plate on the wide windowsill behind the sink. "There you are," she told the plant. "You've had a long drink, and you'll be fine."

Eyeing her warily, Marcus was standing in the kitchen doorway. Saying not a word, he backed up to let her into the living room. She gave him a brilliant smile when she passed him.

She roamed around the room, perusing the books on a shelf, studying the large landscape photo—Ansel Adams?—above the fireplace, and fluffing one of the dark brown throw pillows on the beige leather couch. Let him fill the silence.

"What are you doing here?" he asked again.

Finally the man spoke! She faced him, put her hands on her hips, and grinned. "I'm here because we have to talk. We are going to talk. I am not giving you a choice. But first . . ."

She sauntered toward him, ran the last four steps, and leaped on him. He staggered but caught her. His arms closed around her. Oh, yeah, it felt good.

Legs wrapped around his hips, she grabbed hold of his hair and looked him in the eyes. "Hello, soul mate."

"No, we—" he started to say. She used her hands to shake his head, then held it still.

"Yes," she said.

And she kissed him.

Marcus tried to say something more, but it was damned difficult with her tongue in his mouth. And her legs around him and his arms around her. Oh, hell, she felt, and smelled, and tasted so good. So right. So perfect.

So, he kissed her back.

Despite the warning bells going off in his head.

Because his cock had sprung to attention and was clamoring for release from his jeans. For release, period.

Because the last three days had been torture. Erotic dreams had haunted his sleep, vivid memories of the episode in her hotel room had surfaced every time he stopped consciously concentrating on something else, and, to top it off, his center had plagued him painfully unless he was thinking of her.

All right, he had finally admitted *out loud* to the fiendish SMI, he wanted her. Their mating had been ecstasy. More powerful than any sex he'd ever had. His protests had made no difference; he still hurt.

With her in his arms again, however, he could only think of one objection: it had been too damn long.

She hummed, and the vibration ran from her chest to his and all the way down to his toes.

Their magic centers picked it up and increased the reverberation until they were both quivering with the sound. He held her tighter and kissed her harder. She reciprocated. He barely managed to remain standing.

She broke the kiss by pulling his head back. With a conqueror's smile, she stared into his eyes for several seconds, and he felt her heat warm him to his core. Unlocking her legs from around him, she slid down his body, tormenting him every inch of the way. He supported her until she had her feet under her. She pushed on his shoulders and took a step back.

Where was she going? He reached for her, and the next thing he knew, he was flat on the floor with her on top straddling him. How did he end up here? Surely she couldn't have thrown him, could she? He tried to put his hands on her waist to lift her off, but she captured them, laced her fingers with his, and held their joined hands between them.

Okay, he'd simply push her back.

She didn't move. Back, that was. Instead, she pushed forward until his hands were on the floor on either side of his head.

He struggled a little, carefully. He didn't want to hurt her.

She didn't budge. He struggled harder.

How strong was this woman? She didn't weigh more than a feather and certainly didn't bulge with muscles, yet he couldn't move her or himself.

She grinned—and he could see both delight and determination in her eyes.

"Now, darlin'," she whispered, "we're going to have some fun."

He was in trouble—maybe not too much. At least the imperative hadn't taken over his mind. He was still in control of his thoughts and his actions. He could resist her.

He held that thought for about five seconds—until she lowered her hips to right above the juncture of his thighs and his body, then sank a little lower, and a little lower still. And rubbed herself up and down the length of his rigid cock.

Which, despite the layers of cloth between them, almost took the release it desperately wanted.

What was left of the blood in his head went south in a hurry. The extent of his vocabulary? "Uhhhhhh."

She released his hands and sat back on his thighs. When she slowly, one button at a time, unbuttoned her red shirt, then took it off entirely, he felt his eyes bulge. When she reached behind her and undid the clasp on her oh-my-god-red bra, he was sure his eyeballs stretched out of his head on stalks.

When she slipped off the bra and dropped it to the floor, his hands itched like fire to touch the gorgeous breasts and rosy nipples she'd uncovered. He raised his hands to do so, and she slapped them, took his wrists, and positioned his arms straight out from his sides.

"No. Stay."

He stayed. Her breasts were so tantalizingly close, her fragrance so enveloping, and he wanted so much to touch, to taste. But he stayed.

She put her hands on the neck of his T-shirt, took a good hold, and ripped it right down the middle.

Before he had time to wonder at her actions, she laid herself on him and kissed him again.

This time, for a change, they were flesh to flesh, no barriers. In his dreams, they'd been naked. Those imaginary figments of his overheated libido went up in smoke with the reality of her skin against his.

He revised his estimate of the situation. He was in deep shit.

He had to touch her and prayed she would let him. When he raised his hands and slid them down her back, down her soft, smooth skin to her butt, she rubbed her breasts across his chest. Their magic centers hummed louder.

He was reaching for those breasts when she grasped his hands again and brought them to their previous position. Momentarily bereft, he told himself with the tiny part of his brain still operating that he could move when he wanted to. He'd simply go along with her for the moment. Surely she'd let him touch her again.

With another of those devilish smiles, she sat up and wiggled—it almost killed him—until her skirt was free from between them. She unbuttoned the waistline and lowered the zipper. Gathered the folds in her hands and pulled it over her head.

He almost swallowed his tongue. She was not wearing panties.

His hands jerked of their own accord, but she waggled a finger and said, "Not yet."

After scooting down to his knees, she quickly undid his belt buckle, lowered the zipper, and pulled his jeans and briefs down. He was so relieved to have his throbbing cock free, he didn't even question how she accomplished the feat.

Somehow he lifted his gaze from her body to her face. She was intently studying that jutting part of his anatomy.

Out of the corner of his eye, he saw her hand move toward it, and fear of premature disaster forced the word out of his mouth. "No!"

"No?"

"No." He had to swallow, but he managed to get more out of his dry mouth. "Come here."

She went up on her hands and knees over his body. He put his hands on her waist and drew her down until she was stretched out on top of him, his erection nestled between her legs at the juncture of her thighs. *Oh, God, yes.*

He gathered her close, and this time, *he* kissed *her*.

Good, he was cooperating, Gloriana smiled to herself as she returned his kiss. More than cooperating. An added bonus? Distracting though the man's kisses and caresses and the humming in her center were, she still had her wits about her.

She practically wallowed in the feel of him. His dark blond chest hair stimulated and tickled at the same time. His hands found sensitive spots on her back, especially her butt, she never knew she had. His erection fit perfectly between her legs, and she pumped her hips to rub herself against it. When he groaned, she figured he liked it. She certainly did.

It wasn't enough. She slid her knees to the floor and basically did a pushup to break the kiss and lift her chest. The second she did, he found her breasts with his hands and gazed at them with a half smile while he fondled. Ooooh, much better than having clothes on.

When he lifted his head to lick and suckle, too, the energy that arced through her straight to her womb stunned her. She'd had no clue how exquisitely sensitive her body was, how a touch could excite the core of her being. She arched her back to give him better access. That female part of her in contact with the male part of him started aching. Desire and need rushed through her like a tidal surge, buoying her up and up to light-headedness.

She refused, however, to surrender her ability to think. No matter what, she would be fully conscious. The experience was too good to miss.

Marcus broke their kiss, and she opened her eyes and frowned at him.

"Lift up," he said in a low, raspy voice that sent shivers down her backbone. He put his hands on her waist to help.

She raised her hips, and he looked down, between them, and she did, too. Ah, that's what he wanted. His erection seemed to be reaching for her.

"Yes," he whispered. "Let me in. Please."

Carefully, she positioned her entrance over his broad tip and sank down. As she watched him disappear into her, she could feel her body stretching, accommodating his thickness.

She raised up a little bit and slid down a little farther. And again. He was so hot, so strong, so hard. Oh, how glorious it was, to have him in her. How astonishing. How erotic to watch, to feel.

He groaned, and she looked up. His head was back, his neck arched, and he had a grimace on his face like he was in great pain. He was breathing very hard. Good. She was, too. She wasn't alone in the wonder, the splendor, the sheer exhilaration of making love.

She slid up and down once more, taking him all. If she thought his touch on her breasts had been exquisite, his thick presence in her body doubled, tripled, quadrupled that effect. She felt full and connected. To him and to the universe. It was an act so trusting, so private, so fundamental, so intimate, she could have cried.

She raised and lowered herself again, marveling at the sensations rippling through her—desire, pleasure, rightness, completeness.

When she tensed to rise again, he held her lower body stationary with one hand and used the other to bring her head down for another kiss—a ravenous, devouring kiss. He began to thrust up with his hips.

Their magic centers hummed at a faster tempo.

The combination of kiss, hum, and their connection

stole her breath, increased her heartbeat, and battered at her thought processes. She surrendered to the imperative and to him, especially to him. All she could do was respond in kind, meeting his thrusts, kissing him back, lifting her chest to give him better access to her breasts. Their thrusts grew faster, harder, their kisses hungrier, wilder, until she had to fist her hands in his hair to hold on.

The humming in her body, in his, grew louder, its pulse beating in her ears in rhythm with their movements. Ultimate pleasure beckoned, just out of reach. She felt her muscles tightening, straining, almost there . . .

He added a twist to his hips that brought her nerve-filled nub into rubbing contact with him. The friction created a chain reaction of energy bursts throughout her body and propelled her in a flash into complete ecstasy. She cried out as she convulsed in a long series of shudders and contractions answered by his even more powerful thrusts and explosive release.

After they stilled, he held her tightly for a long moment. With a sigh of pure contentment, she relaxed and laid her head on his shoulder.

She may have dozed or simply blissfully lay there, but when her conscious self reasserted itself, she was still on top of him, and he was caressing her back. She could feel his heartbeat slowly descending from the heights; hers beat in unison. He was still inside of her, and his breath gave a little hitch when she tightened certain muscles.

She raised up to see his face. His eyes were shut.

How had she never noticed how long his eyelashes were?

He opened those light blue eyes with their charcoal rims. At first he stared at the ceiling, but soon focused on her. "What did you do to me?"

"I mated with you."

"Why?"

"Because it was the only way I could think of to get your attention and put you in a position where you couldn't refuse to talk to me. You didn't seem convinced of the soul-mate fact in Chicago. Yet you *know* we are, we *have* to be, or we wouldn't be able to mate. I wanted to make sure you couldn't pretend that instance was some sort of aberration. I also hoped both of us would take part in the process fully conscious—not because the imperative had taken over our minds. I knew everything I was doing—or up until the very end—and I had the feeling you did, too."

"You've accomplished your mission." He tried to push her up and off his body, and she reinforced her strength spell and held him down.

He glared at her, but she smiled and sat up, her hands on his shoulders. They weren't finished yet.

"Let me up."

"No, not until you promise to tell me what you have against being someone's soul mate."

"All right, I promise."

"I mean a real promise, not simply a statement to get me off your . . . uh, front. We really do have to talk about it, Marcus, and come to some agreement if we're to live any kind of life, together or not. I need to understand you and vice versa."

"Did you cast a spell on me?"

"What are you talking about? No, I didn't cast a spell on you. I can't. Remember?"

"How did you overpower me?"

"I'll tell you later. That's beside the point. If you think you're going to deflect me with questions or avoid telling me your reasons, you're wrong. Give me a real promise, and I'll let you up, we'll get dressed and talk. I'm not leaving here otherwise, and I still have some persuasive techniques." To punctuate her statement, she tightened her inner muscles.

He caught his breath, scowled at her, but said nothing.

Honestly, the man was impossible. He was even more stubborn than her brother. Okay, she'd appeal to reason—again. "I'm not going to beg, Marcus. We are soul mates, and if you're going to reject the phenomenon, the imperative, and me, you should explain why. It affects me as much as it does you since I'm going to have to live with your conclusions."

Marcus stared up at her. He tried to ignore his feelings of guilt at her words. Unfortunately for him, she was correct. He owed her an explanation. Distasteful though it was to rehash the past, vulnerable as it made him, and however revealing of his family's life, it was the least he could do. They were both stuck in this mess. He gritted his teeth and said, "Yes, I do promise."

"Start talking."

"Can we get up off the floor and dressed first?"

Although she didn't look happy about giving up her position, she acquiesced. "Okay, just remember, you can't throw me out until I'm satisfied you've told me everything. I'm strong enough to resist being manhandled."

"Fine."

She raised her hips until they came apart—oh, how his cock, momentarily happy and ever hungry around her, regretted that—and scooted back on hands and knees until she could move sideways and sit on the floor. Grabbing her shirt and skirt, she dragged the skirt over her head and slipped into the blouse.

He watched all that loveliness disappear from view before arching on his shoulders and heels to pull up his pants.

She stood before he could help her up, and picked up her bra and purse. "Where to?"

"This way." He led her down to the guest room on the lower level, taking off his T-shirt remnants on the way. He opened the door and stood back. "Bathroom's through there. Towels and soap are in the cabinet."

She walked into the room and turned to face him, but he couldn't gauge her mood. She didn't seem to be triumphant. If anything, she looked apprehensive. All she said was, "Thanks. I'll be out in a few minutes."

"Take your time. I'll meet you upstairs." Forcing himself to move slowly so he wouldn't appear to be fleeing, he climbed the stairs with a measured tread and a heavy heart. He didn't look forward to opening himself up, even to her. Especially to her. A comment his father often used came to him: "Always look the truth in the face, Marcus. It may not be pleasant, but deceiving yourself is worse."

He hadn't been following that advice. He hadn't recognized—hadn't wanted to recognize—the truth of their being soul mates. He knew, however, at this moment, on this subject, he was correct.

CHAPTER
TWENTY-FOUR

I'm going to lose her. The words battered the inside of his skull the way the shower water beat on the outside. Despite his resolve to reject a soul mate, his excellent reasons for doing so, his refusal to perpetuate a recurring cycle of behavior bringing only heartache, the very real chance that he would not have Gloriana in his life after the next hour made him want to pound his head against the wall to stop the pain.

But . . . her seduction replayed itself in his mind, and his body responded. What he would have done if she hadn't let him into her body, he didn't want to contemplate. And when she had, his entire being opened up, accepted her, and gave itself to her.

He had to look the truth in the eye. He'd ruin all her loveliness, her giving nature. Better to make a clean break.

Hell! The conversation was going to be difficult. He shut off the water and toweled himself dry. *Be a man, damn it! Face it and get it over with.*

Dressed again—in different clothes since the jeans he had been wearing still smelled of her and she'd wrecked his shirt—he straightened his shoulders and went down to the living room.

Five minutes later, he paced in front of the windows, wondering how best to begin and cursing himself for his ambivalence. Would she understand? Would she agree with him? What if she did? She'd be gone in a heartbeat. He sucked in his breath as a great hole opened inside him.

No, he had to be strong. His reasons were true and good. Their not being together was in everyone's best interests.

When she came up the stairs, his throat went dry. Rushing into the kitchen, he prepared glasses of ice water and carried them back out.

"Thanks," she said with a brilliant smile that he felt down to his toes.

He waved her to a seat on the couch and remained standing. Better to face the catastrophe on his feet—otherwise, he might end up on his knees.

She took a sip of water and looked at him expectantly. She was so beautiful, so colorful in her red and blue against the neutral colors of his house that he almost smiled—until he remembered his purpose.

He cleared his throat, but still began with a rough voice. "The soul-mate imperative and the whole phenomenon are supposed to never make a mistake. The bond is supposed to make for strong marriages and from that, strong families, for the kind of relationships and feelings I can see in your family. Right?"

She nodded.

"In my experience, the bond doesn't always work that way. Sometimes it goes too far. That's the case in my own family."

She still didn't say a word, only put her glass down, and brought her gaze back to his. She looked puzzled, not angry.

He broke the contact. Somehow the explanation would be easier if he didn't have to look into her eyes. He cleared his throat again, stiffened his back. Damn, telling her, saying it all out loud, was harder than he thought it would be.

"It took a long time for me to figure it out. Here's the gist of it. The phenomenon and the SMI screwed up with my parents. From everything I could find out, and most of it came from people who knew them before they met, each of them was totally focused on a career and had no discernible interest in the opposite sex. The soulmate connection hit them hard when Judith was thirty and Stefan thirty-four. After that, they were still focused on their careers and also on each other—to the exclusion of everybody else."

"What about your grandparents?" she asked.

"They were living at the time of my parents' marriage,

but all died before I was born. I've never understood why my parents had even one child after five years, except for the idea of continuing their bloodlines. Both are only children. I traced my genealogy once. Only children run in my ancestry. All of my forefathers and mothers were quite intelligent, only not prolific." He looked out the windows and pondered his next point.

She didn't let him deliberate long before asking, "No uncles, aunts, cousins, either? I have a bunch."

He shook his head and turned back to face her. "My grandparents had siblings, who had some kind of family falling-out—I remember a reference to my great-grandfather's will being the cause. I believe there are a few distant cousins, although no one ever made overtures to the others." He shook his head and stared down at his feet for a few seconds as he wondered what having other close family members would have been like. Nothing like what Gloriana had, but at least they would have been around.

She must have become impatient with his stopping and starting because she said, "Go on."

He sighed and continued, "At any rate, here I was. Putting this information together with what I can remember of my years before boarding school, Judith and Stefan did little to change their lives because of a baby and then a young child in their house. I had a nanny, and starting when I was five, a tutor. I was precocious and that seemed to please them—when I saw them. I believe I was scheduled for an audience between six and seven in the evening." He heard the bitterness in his voice but decided not to worry about it. She had to understand how strongly he felt.

Evidently she did because when he was silent, she waited a little while before asking, "What happened next?"

"When I was eight, I was sent to a boarding school for gifted children. It was a boys-only institution, and I hated it. Oh, I had an excellent education. On a personal level, however, let's simply say it left a lot to be desired. During school vacations, I either traveled with my parents—and a tutor—and met their colleagues or continued my studies at home with more tutors or at educational camps. I've never been to Disney World, by the way, but I've seen every important museum in Europe." He shrugged, and she gave him a small smile and said nothing.

"I spent my school years trying to live up to my parents' expectations—high grades, difficult subjects, honor rolls, and awards. I was good in sports, but they didn't care about that—mostly they saw athletics as a waste of time better spent on intellectual matters. I played despite their opposition—probably more for the thrill of my slight rebellion than for love of the game."

"Marcus, are you sure they feel that way, that you're reading them correctly?" she asked.

"Oh, yes," he answered. "When I discovered theoretical math and it was clear my magical talents lay there, they were pleased. When I made professor, they were even more satisfied. Their only goals for me that I haven't achieved are to take a position at one of the schools like Harvard or MIT and to win the Fields Medal, the greatest math prize. They've never asked me what my goals are for myself, and they pay no attention to my fiction writing. We don't talk much. In fact, outside of academic subjects and current events, we have little to say to each other, except for their continuous questioning of my career choices and place of employment. It makes for awkward visits."

"What does all this have to do with your decision on soul mates?"

Her expression and tone were neutral. He wished he could tell if that augured well or ill for her acceptance of his explanation. All he could do was tell the truth, and he plunged ahead. "Everything I know of the actuality of soul mates is from my parents—two people so wrapped up in each other and their careers, they had no time for one child, much less more. All they could do was push me to succeed, grant me sparse praise, and present me with role models for success in the academic world. From what they've told me about their upbringings, they parallel mine. I'm determined that I will not force a child to repeat my experience. I will not perpetuate the total concentration on success and pressure on a child to succeed according to his parents' ideals, not his own."

He paced back and forth in front of the windows for

a moment.

She didn't let up on the pressure for him to talk, however. "If you're that determined, why do you think you'll continue their ways?"

"Wait, it gets worse," he said. "I don't *know* how to be a mate. I don't *know* how to share emotions, or even show them, for that matter. I knew they were soul mates, but saw no overt expressions of affection or emotions between them, ever. Hell, I never saw them enough to form a basis for behavior toward and with a mate. I'm a solitary person. I don't *know* how to be otherwise. With everything my parents ingrained in me, how could I be a good soul mate, much less a good father? It will be disastrous for both of us and for our children if I'm your mate. All I know is how to be like them." His center lurched, and a chasm opened inside him. He tried to ignore the empty feeling. He should get used to it. It was going to be with him for a long time.

"How are you absolutely certain they were 'wrapped up in each other' if they never showed it?"

"Because all their practitioner colleagues I met said so. Over and over I've been introduced to someone who knew them during those years and who spoke of their 'double-mindedness' for themselves and their careers. It's famous among their friends." He held up his hands with crossed fingers to demonstrate his point.

"I didn't get that idea at all," she protested. "My parents said they enjoyed their company when they went for drinks and never mentioned even a notion of their being self-centered."

"Among strangers, Judith and Stefan are always guarded and charming. I am, too, for that matter—guarded, at least. When we're simply three together, it's like I'm a spectator or outside the bond. Oh, we converse, but have little to say to each other about things that matter." He gave a little laugh that sounded more like a croak.

"As for soul mates? We've never discussed a potential soul mate for me. Stefan and I had the usual father-son talk about sex and mates when I hit puberty, yet when I brought the subject up later, it was clear he didn't want to discuss it further. My mother has never mentioned the word that I can remember."

Gloriana stared out down at her clasped hands, clearly mulling over what he had told her. She didn't look convinced. He had to make it absolutely clear, and that meant he had to open up even more, talk about what he never spoke of—whether he liked it or not. The emptiness in his chest grew until it seemed to reach the bottom of his soul.

"Believe me, I've spent long hours thinking about it. There are no other logical conclusions I can draw, given the evidence. I will fail as a soul mate and a father. I've seen your wonderful family. I don't have a clue how to be part of a group like yours. You have no concept what it's like living in mine, and you'd hate it. We don't joke or tease or play around. Neither Stefan nor Judith would have joined in with that ridiculous rap song of George's. They'd have thought everybody was either crazy or—one of my mother's favorite put-downs—'common.'

"I envy the way you all hug each other. I can't remember the last time my mother hugged me. I don't think my father ever has. If the debate hadn't been in Boston, they wouldn't have come. They would never have come far simply to provide support like yours did."

"Marcus, there are all sorts of families," Gloriana interjected. "The real questions are, do you love them and do they love you?"

He had to think about that for a moment. Again, he had to look the truth in the eye. He didn't particularly like what he saw, but he told her the truth. "I don't know. I honestly don't. It seems more like it's been a duty on both sides rather than love in our interactions. I've never thought they didn't support me—when I'm pursuing their goals. As for my own goals? They never bother to ask if I have any others."

He held out a hand to her. "Look, Gloriana, I don't want to contemplate what my upbringing did to me or would do to you or our children. I sure as hell don't want to find out I'm correct after we're bonded. You'd hate me, our children would think I'm a lousy father, and our lives would be miserable. You're too lively a person, too vital and energetic to get stuck with someone like me. I can't be what you need. It's better for both of us not to go through the frustration, despair, and finally hatred that would result. Let the SMI attack me. I can take whatever it dishes out. Surely there's a more appropriate, better mate out there for you. You deserve one." There, he'd said it all.

There was a long moment of silence while she stared at him. Finally, she took a deep breath, slapped the couch with both hands, stood up, and glared at him. "Marcus, that's the biggest load of manure I've ever heard of. I've spread better stuff on my petunias!"

He opened his mouth to refute her, but she pointed a finger at him. "Now, you be quiet, and let me have my say. First off, I am not your mother, and you are not your father. I don't act exactly like my mother does, Daria doesn't, either, and Clay certainly doesn't act like Daddy.

"Second, in the old 'nature versus nurture' argument, you're saying we're ruled as adults by the way we're brought up. So what if their nurturing wasn't very good? What happened to conscious free will and your nature? Is their nature truly yours? Are you happy to sit here behind your immaculate walls and keep out the messy world? Or do you want to wallow in self-pity and claim your sacrifice is for *my* own good because you're afraid to face the truth about your own nature or afraid to change?"

A part of him tried not to listen to what she was saying. Another part, several parts, however, loved the way her eyes flashed, the way her expressions made no bones about her reaction to his arguments, and the way she ran agitated fingers through her hair. God, the woman was a fireball.

"That reasoning won't wash," she continued. "Furthermore, let's look at the evidence *scientifically*, the way you're always saying. To date, we have only *your* observations, interpretations, and conclusions, your *knowledge*, and you are hardly a disinterested observer. You have never been in the position of having a soul mate before, am I correct?"

He shook his head, started to speak. She, however, kept going, her voice rising.

"Then, based on one and only one experiment, you don't really *know*, can't *prove*, that you or the relationship will fail, can you? You're basing your conclusions on conjecture, and with your mind-set, you're setting up yourself *and me* for a self-fulfilling prophecy. It's really not about what you *know* here. Sometimes you have to be open to possibilities and to take life on *faith*. Take a *chance*. You want an equation? Here's one you'll like: Me plus You, but You either multiplied or divided by your Family—take your choice, but I like divided— equals No Soul Mate, No Possibility of Happiness, No Life. That's a negative number."

He had no answer for that. Her equation made too much sense.

"You're not even giving the process a chance. I agree, we have lots of differences, yet everything I've been able to learn—from a bunch of observers and people who've actually gone through it—is that the process works those out."

"And if it doesn't?"

"Then we do—as *thinking adults*."

"Look," he said in as reasonable a tone as he could muster, "don't you think I have considered all these factors? Thought of all the counterarguments? I know myself and I know my parents. It's not going to work."

She squinted her eyes and stared at him for a long moment. He waited, ready to refute whatever she might say. Instead, she picked up her purse. "In that case, my self-sacrificing soul mate, we have nothing left to talk about at the moment, do we?"

She was leaving. Despite a certain amount of relief that she wasn't going to argue any more, a stronger feeling of potential loss caused him to say the first thing that popped into his mind to keep her here. "Wait. Tell me, how did you throw me to the ground and hold me there?"

"Oh, that!" She waved a hand nonchalantly. "That was a simple strength spell, *invalescere*. Most women learn it in case they're ever attacked. To put it in your terms, small s is the strength spell you can find in most elementary spell books to channel energy to the muscles. The sub-T is of course my talent, but strength is a universal, low-level spell. The cap L sub s level I use is about at fifty percent to compensate for my size. I dial down the L sub small p, my level, to twenty percent unless I want overwhelming strength. For cap E, I only put a few percentage points of mine into the power/energy part for the same reason. I don't need a ritual or gestures for the spell, because I've made it part of me—that's the *intuitive* side of casting I was talking about. Ditto on items. I'm sure you can figure it out from there."

Before he could ask for further explanation, she stalked over to the stairs and yelled, "Delilah!" The dogs came running up the stairs and followed her to the front door.

He hurried to the door to catch hold of Samson's collar, but the threesome didn't wait for him, and he trailed them to her car. She opened the door and Delilah climbed in. He took hold of Samson before the hound could do the same.

Watching Gloriana buckle Delilah into the harness, he knew he ought to say something, but what? *Convince me I'm wrong? Stay with me anyway? Please?*

She shut the car door and turned to him, stepped close. Since he was bending over to hold Samson, he had to look up to see her face.

Nose to nose, she stared him straight in the eyes. "We're not done, Marcus. While you're in your cold bed tonight, walled up in your castle, think about this." She fisted one hand in his hair and held him still while she kissed him.

The next thing he knew, he'd let go of Samson, wrapped his arms around her, and kissed her back. The way his body reacted, he'd never have even suspected he'd had the most spectacular sexual experience of his life such a short time ago—it wanted more, now. How long they stood there devouring each other, he had no idea, but all too soon, she was pushing on his shoulders. He dropped his arms, and she stepped back. Her green eyes sparkled, her color was high, and her cheeky grin promised trouble.

Without another word, she circled her car, got in, and started the engine. Her radio blared a song, something about "the taillights I may never see again." She roared off and didn't even wave as she rounded the corner. The last thing he saw was indeed the red glow of the taillights of her car.

Marcus sighed and looked down at Samson, who stared back. The hound snorted, shook his head, and trotted back into the house. Even his dog was disgusted with him. Marcus followed, rubbing his breastbone. The hole in his chest had assumed the magnitude of the Grand Canyon.

CHAPTER TWENTY-FIVE

Gloriana thought hard all the way to the farm. She also fumed. She'd wanted to use that strength spell to shake him until all those peculiar notions flew out of his head like the bats from under the Congress Avenue bridge. It was crystal clear however, that nothing she said would make a difference to his foregone conclusions. So, she'd left him to stew before she did him bodily harm. Besides, she needed more and bigger cannons against his walls.

What was she going to do about Marcus? Obstinate, shortsighted, inflexible, infuriating Marcus. Her soul mate. The man she was supposed to spend the rest of her life with. The man who was supposed to be the father of her children. The man with whom she'd had the defining sexual experience of her life.

He'd looked good enough to eat lying there under her on the floor. Perfect. Broad shoulders, toned muscles, blond hair, blue eyes—oh, yes, the way those eyes caressed her and heated her clear to her bones.

Single-minded, self-hypnotized, that's what he was. He'd told himself for so long that he was not soul-mate material that he believed it. She knew better. No man who kissed like that was meant to be alone. He was hers.

How to convince him?

She had to assume that their lovemaking had affected him as strongly as it had her. Deny it though he might, he was still going to want more. She certainly did.

She couldn't, however, ambush him again. He'd be expecting it, and while she did it for the reasons she'd stated, she wasn't going to use that tactic a second time. Lovemaking was something to be mutually enjoyed. Using sex for an ulterior motive or a bargaining chip went totally against her grain.

If she couldn't come up with solutions herself, to whom could she turn for advice? Her parents? No, they'd want to sit down with Marcus and talk him to death. She wasn't going to gain a soul mate because of a guilt trip laid on by them. Daria didn't have enough experience, and Clay would want to zap all Marcus's computers.

There was someone else, however.

"We're going for help," she told Delilah. "You belong with Samson and I belong with Marcus." The dog grinned.

She drove past the turnoff to the farm and headed for LaGrange. Before long she pulled up in front of

Lulabelle Higgins's house.

The old witch answered the door with a big smile. "Glori! And Delilah! I've been thinking about you. Come on back to the kitchen. I can tell from the look on your face that something's happened."

Lulabelle poured Delilah some water and sat down at the table when Gloriana refused her offer of a drink. "First, I have some news about our research."

"The Rhinedebecks?"

"Yes, and it's good news. I called all the Rhinedebeck numbers in the practitioner registry and found his son. He talked to me at length. Evidently, his father had spoken of the help I gave him. After Bill found his soul mate, Gladys Kowalski, again, and she rejected him, I told him to keep trying. He went on a campaign to woo her and change her mind. It worked! They married and had several children."

"Hot damn! Marcus won't be able to use poor Rhinedebeck for a role model anymore."

"Oh, dear. He's still thinking he can defy the imperative?"

"Worse than that." Gloriana told her the story— well, almost all of the story. She omitted most of the mating details. "Then I walked out. I kissed him within an inch of his life to show him what he was missing and drove off. So, what do you think?"

"I think he's been playing with those funny equations of his too long," Lulabelle answered. "His mind is definitely addled. The boy is not in touch with his emotions."

"My conclusions exactly. What can I do?"

"Let me think on it a minute. How about some of my pecan pie?"

"Your special, magical recipe, Lulabelle's Texas Temptation? Sure."

Lulabelle served the pie and poured each of them a glass of milk. She sat down and munched for a few minutes. Gloriana kept quiet as she made her piece disappear.

"All right," Lulabelle said after a few minutes and most of the slice of pie. "I think you were correct when you said he's hypothesizing only on his own observations. For all his attempts to be logical and reasoning, he's thinking much like a little boy here, one who was not much nurtured and who still resents what he perceives as neglect. The behavior of his parents didn't create much of a family bond for him. Lordy, I'll bet you Morgans really threw him. All that love, teasing, informality, sheer family goofiness."

"But how do we get him to change his mind? At least try the soul-mate process?"

Lulabelle smiled, a slight upward quirk of the lips that sent shivers down Gloriana's back. Oh, yes, she'd come to the right place for advice.

"Let's fight dirty," the old witch said. "Let's pull in the other side of that family and see what they have to say. I'm acquainted with a few university folk. Some of them don't have the common sense God gave a June bug, or they live so far into their esoteric studies, they can't relate to the rest of us. Give his parents a call and tell them what's going on."

"Just like that?"

"Of course—as their son's soul mate and prospective mother of *their grandchildren*." Lulabelle assumed the most innocent expression before laughing. "Oh, and another thing. Forscher is of German origin, right? A number of families with Germanic backgrounds live around here. The older generations don't show, what's the term nowadays? Oh, yes. PDA. Public displays of affection. Sometimes not the private kind, either."

Gloriana thought about the idea for a moment. "I'll give him another chance before I call his parents. We'll be in Atlanta next weekend. If he won't talk to me before we leave here, I'll drag him off after the debate and make him listen to me."

"That's fine, dear, there's no rush. Find out also where his parents can be reached. It never hurts to have a backup force in reserve."

✾✺❁✺✾

The rest of the week was an exercise in frustration for Gloriana. If all her soul-mate problems weren't enough, there were the nasty e-mails. From vague warnings of dire consequences, the messages had escalated to outright threats, but were still of indefinite origin—Traddie

or Fomster?   On Wednesday, she hadn't remembered
to mention the escalation in threats to Marcus—funny
thing, she'd been thinking about other matters. She sent
him a note about them on Thursday; of course, he didn't
reply. She also forwarded the messages to Ed and John.

She decided she could use the e-mail problem to
call him, but all she heard was his voice message. She
tried George and Evelyn, who had Samson, and they said
Marcus had gone out of town. They commiserated with
her, relating that they had met the same Forscher stone-
wall when they tried to discuss the situation with him.
Having them on her side was comforting.

Comforting, not helpful.

She actually contemplated reneging on her Friday
commitments and following Marcus to Atlanta, before
deciding to let him stew. If she was going to have faith
in the process, she ought to let the imperative have its
way with him.

At least the SMI was leaving her alone to get a good
night's sleep, even if her dreams were filled with math
symbols.

Finally, on Saturday afternoon in Atlanta, she
looked for, but couldn't find him. He had checked in on
Thursday, and no one knew where he was. She visited
the library, an obvious possibility. He had been there
the day before, rummaging around in the soul-mate archives. The librarians said he looked grim and angry
when he left.

He finally came in to the predebate dinner at the last minute, nodded in general to everyone—except her. He didn't even meet her eyes when he engaged Ed and John in conversation on the other side of the table.

Lily-livered, stinking, yellow-bellied coward. At least he looked as awful as a perfect man could, with bags under his eyes and a slightly pasty complexion. Small compensation for what he'd put her through. She smiled brilliantly at him and received one of his penetrating, concentrated stares back. Out of the corner of her eye, she noticed his body stiffen when she talked to the very handsome Sword, Tom Schmidt, sitting next to her. *Hah, take that!*

On the way to the meeting room, she maneuvered to walk beside him and said, "Can we get together briefly after the debate? I have some news from Lulabelle. Was your research successful?"

He kept looking straight ahead and said only, "Let's get through the event first, okay?"

She didn't bother to answer him, but she wondered what excuse he'd use to get out of seeing her.

CHAPTER
TWENTY-SIX

Marcus took his seat as soon as he climbed onto the stage. He busied himself with his papers and ignored Gloriana. Or he tried to. That was impossible, his body told him. He was aware of her every movement, her every breath—especially her smiles at other men. In the dining room, it had taken all of his control not to throw her over his shoulder and take her where they could be alone—after he punched out Schmidt.

As he sat at the table, his thoughts turned to what he'd learned in the past two days. The results were not encouraging, but he knew he'd been right to get out of Austin early. Staying home wasn't an option when he wasn't sure if he could stop himself from going to her. They'd only make love again, and that would put them much closer to the actual bonding mating, according to all the soul-mate rules. Bonding was the absolute last thing either of them needed. Therefore, he'd dropped off

Samson with Evelyn and George and flown to Atlanta.

His hopes of finding evidence to bolster his conviction to resist and reject, however, deteriorated into discouragement and finally despair flavored with panic. No hard facts about successful mate rejection existed. On the contrary, copious notes, diaries, biographies, letters, and even keepsakes abounded, all proclaiming the wonder and glory of finding and having a soul mate.

Patterns emerged: A woman often didn't take to the idea of her mate at the beginning of the relationship and had to gain trust in the man before she would agree to the connection. A man, on the other hand, usually actively pursued his mate, right from the time he first saw her. Marcus had almost laughed at his discovery. He and Gloriana seemed to be going about the experience backward.

What brought together a woman and a man, what calmed the woman and excited the man, was the *process*. More than simply the lust factor—which aided but didn't foreordain the ending, even for the man—the determining developments were getting to know each other, recognizing the trustworthiness and inherent qualities of the other, coming to realize how interesting the other was, how they fit together on many aspects of life. The sameness in attitudes, beliefs, and opinions helped, but wasn't truly necessary.

What mattered at the heart of the situation was exactly that: *the hearts of the mates. Love.*

He realized as the last word passed through his brain that he was frowning at the audience. He carefully wiped all expression from his face and brought his gaze down to his notes. Neither action stopped his thoughts from returning to his soul mate.

What did he think of Gloriana? She was intelligent, gorgeous, funny, perceptive, straightforward, and downright interesting. They did have things in common besides their dogs—academic careers and running came to mind. They both sincerely wanted to help practitioners improve spell-casting. They'd probably find more in common if they talked about it. Come to think of it, they hadn't really talked about much except the debates and the soul-mate mess.

What about their different ways of doing magic? He'd really like to discuss that subject with her. She'd explained her strength spell in terms of his formula. Therefore, she had to understand part of what he was calling for. In fact, when he thought of her exact words, it certainly sounded like she had actually *used* the formula to cast the spell. Interesting, and potentially significant. If she had, they definitely needed to talk.

For his part in the discussion, exhibit A, the plant she'd rescued from dehydration. He'd bought that little ivy in the supermarket because he somehow couldn't help himself. It had called to him to take it home. Wednesday night, he'd looked on the practitioner Web site for that strength spell of hers. In a spell book for novices, he'd found a plant growth spell, and feeling more than a little foolish, he'd actually tried to cast it on the ivy. That attempt failed, and he wasn't surprised because the book warned that the spell was talent-specific.

He did succeed, however, in finding and casting strength on himself. What a feeling of power and exhilaration had engulfed him when he picked up his couch as a test. He'd also gained insight into calibration for his equation, although exact measurement remained a problem.

If he could learn to cast her spells, maybe she could learn some of his, and, at the same time, he could use her intuitive spell-casting to refine his measurement efforts. He almost laughed at himself for that idea. He might be a theoretical mathematician, but he was becoming a practical wizard.

Maybe, given all that compatibility on all those levels—and the mind-blowing lovemaking—being soul mates with Gloriana Morgan would be more wonderful than the matings depicted in the archives.

Wait. He was forgetting something. Mating led to children.

Glori's children. He could almost see her, round with child, holding a baby, playing with a toddler. He couldn't see himself in that picture. He could never, would never take the chance. Given his experiences and upbringing—probably his very nature, thanks to his parents—how could he be a father worthy of Gloriana's children?

As the enormity of that obstacle struck him, he felt like crying right there in the ballroom. To distract himself from his whirlpool of thoughts, he watched the audience file in. The usual suspects were present. Attendance had grown with each debate, and tonight was crowded with four extra rooms to handle the overflow—and partly to keep combatants separate. Four Swords plus John Baldwin would stand guard in the main ballroom.

Baldwin came onto the stage, motioned to the three of them, and they stepped to the rear with him. The Sword spoke in a low voice. "A few minutes ago we caught one of the people posting the flyers."

"Who?" Ed asked.

"A woman named Bambi Kemble. Have you heard the name?" When all shook their heads, he continued, "She's one of Gordon Walcott's group. She was spitting mad that we caught her, and she spewed a lot of his nonsense. She refuses to identify other posters, of course. The flyers she had in her hands were the milder, vaguer kind, but some of the others we've found tonight talk of 'ridding practitioner life of heretics and evildoers' and repeat the violent threats you've been getting. She claims we can't hold her because all she's doing is exercising her right to free speech. The thing is, she's correct. We're going to keep her until the debate is over, though, no matter what she says."

"Do you think someone will try to disrupt us tonight?" Gloriana asked.

Baldwin scanned the room before replying. "I hope not. Something's in the air, and I can't decide if it's normal excitement or more sinister activity. In addition to the Swords, I've stationed security people outside the room, and we're ready for whatever comes. Oh, and Walcott's here, by the way, hanging out in the THA overflow room. He's quiet at the moment, but if the Traddies disapproved of his outburst, you can't tell it. Everybody's coming up to shake his hand. Kemble said she has no idea what his plans may be, and I wouldn't be surprised if he wanted to speak."

"We'll let him talk as long as he abides by the rules we set after his last rabble-rousing speech. Otherwise, we'll take what comes," Ed said. "Come on, let's get started."

Marcus and Gloriana took their seats again, and Ed called the meeting to order. Marcus studied the audience while they settled themselves. The Traddies were on Gloriana's side of the hall, and the Fomsters were on his, as usual. The middle outnumbered both factions put together tonight, where previously the split had been about equal. When the latecomers were finding chairs, Walcott and two men slid into the room through a side door on the far right. Immediately three people on the front row gave the newcomers their seats and moved to the back. Uh-oh, that maneuver was certainly planned in advance.

Ed was standing slightly back from the table, so

Marcus leaned forward and looked around him to Gloriana. She turned to him at the same time. He glanced at Walcott and raised his eyebrows, and she nodded her head and shrugged. They both faced front again.

The debate began in the usual manner: Ed made his opening remarks, Marcus and Gloriana made theirs, and Ed opened the floor to discussion.

Prick spoke for the FOM, mostly rehashing his earlier statements. At least he called for more research into the equation—while taking credit for most of it. He also proved he'd been listening by incorporating past comments from teaching masters. Well and good, thus far.

Horner rose next, but added nothing new to his "THA call to action." He sounded only marginally more strident in his warnings against the formula than in the past. His side cheered, however, as though he'd brought them to salvation.

They were all becoming more like politicians, giving the same stump speech at town after town. Totally boring and more than a little soporific. Marcus suppressed a yawn and tried not to think about sleep.

A teaching master for elementary magic education made some erudite remarks, a fellow told a story of trying to use the equation and his results, and a woman asked about the possibility of using the formula to cast spells higher than a practitioner's usual level. Marcus didn't think the last was feasible, and neither did the teaching masters present.

He started to doodle on his pad, until he realized he was drawing little flowers and plants instead of his usual mathematical symbols. Shifting in his seat to keep awake, he nonchalantly snuck a peek at Gloriana. She, however, was looking at Walcott, who conferred with one of his fellows.

"Who's next?" Ed asked.

When Walcott stood, a rustle of movement and murmurs rippled across the audience while the usher brought the microphone to him. Marcus saw the Swords come alert at each end of the two main aisles, and Baldwin moved to a position in front of the stage. Walcott took his time, waiting for quiet, before sneering, "Thank you very much for allowing me to speak, Mr. Hearst."

"I hope you remember our last conversation, Mr. Walcott," Ed answered.

"Oh, I do. Indeed, I do." Walcott faced the audience. "Ladies and gentlemen, the last time I spoke to one of these gatherings, I was almost forcibly restrained from speaking."

"Stick to the facts," Ed interjected in a low voice.

Walcott smiled, a small quirk of his lips. When he spoke, his tone oozed with reasonableness. "Almost. Why? Why do some people not want to hear what I have to say? There's a simple answer. Because they aren't interested in the truth about Forscher's 'magic formula.' Because they want to impose their way of thinking, of working magic on the rest of us."

Ed leaned forward, opened his mouth, but Walcott kept talking and gestured at him.

"Mr. Hearst here will say that's not true. That their goal is not imposition of an incomprehensible system or destruction of spell-casting as we love and revere it. I say that it is. I say certain powers within the High Council want us to follow these pied pipers of regularization down a modernistic road to a veritable wasteland of casting."

He held up his hands as if to calm opposition, even though no one said a word. "Those people, and we know who they are, would deny such a plan. Look, even the Fomsters are attempting to placate our concern by calling for research, for testing, for trial. The very members of the FOM who scorned us, who consider us outmoded, old-fashioned, and anachronistic, and who trumpeted praise for the new, modern, and twenty-first-century methods, all of a sudden change their tune and tell us our ways of spell-casting still have merit, should be kept, and will continue."

Walcott wagged his finger at the audience. "Don't you believe it! They are lying to you. They are leading you down a garden path to a cesspool of dark complexity, pernicious modernity, and spell-casting chaos. Those of us who use the old methods will be cast out, useless, unable to cast even a simple *lux* or *flamma* spell without fear of the *spell police* chastising us."

"Walcott!" Ed barked. "We're not forcing anybody to do anything. That's enough distortion and lies for one evening. Your time is up. Sit down."

"Is this what you want?" Walcott boomed into the mike, waving his free hand at Ed again. "To be silenced?"

"No!" someone in the audience yelled from the right.

"To be cast out like the garbage?"

More *no*'s, again from the Traddies.

"To be deprived of your rightful place in the practitioner world?"

"No!" "Never!" "Tell it, brother!" "Amen!" The calls came from the right—and surprisingly from the middle of the hall.

Ed stood, called for order, and told Walcott again to sit down.

"We must fight for our heritage!" Walcott shouted. "Join me, and we will prevail!"

A large number of people in the middle and on the right stood up, cheering and shaking their fists at the Fomsters. Prick's adherents jeered and responded with catcalls. Wads of paper and a few plastic water bottles began to fly between the groups.

The Swords drew their weapons and rushed to put themselves between the Fomsters and the larger middle section. Their blades flashed as they disintegrated the missiles.

Baldwin did not bother with a sword. Instead he took Walcott by the shoulders, spun him around, and forced him into his chair. Snatching the mike from the speaker's hand, he tossed it to an usher.

When the first paper wad flew, Marcus jumped to his feet to go to Gloriana, who had also risen, and they came together behind Ed. Marcus pulled her toward the back of the stage and put his arms around her while security officers entered to help the Swords.

They both watched Baldwin, who pushed Walcott down in the chair again when the tall thin man tried to stand up. The demagogue glared and sat still. The two men were shouting at each other, but the noise from the crowd drowned out their words. Even Ed's shouts for order through his microphone were lost in the cacophony.

People in the center section began to force the missile throwers among them to sit down, and security officers moved in to help. A couple of fistfights broke out, however, then a few more.

The Swords were too occupied with projectiles coming from the Traddies to help with the fights, and Marcus glanced around to calculate the best exit strategy if the situation got worse. The door behind and to their left was the closest. If need be, he'd drag Gloriana out, whether or not she wanted to come. He looked to Baldwin for an indication of the action to take.

In a sea of gesticulating people, flying paper wads and water bottles, and tremendous uproar, the Sword stood quietly surveying the situation as though he was watching a sporting event. After a few moments, he stepped up onto the stage in front of the table. He brought his hands together, and his large weapon appeared, its silver blade bright, with its tip pointing down. Almost non-chalantly, he stabbed the tip into the platform floor.

Booooommmmm!

Thunder shook the room, the crystals in the chandeliers tinkled madly, and Marcus's stomach lurched. The noise and commotion abruptly stopped—except for one group of fighters who still punched and pummeled their opponents.

Baldwin reversed his grip and, blade up, swung his weapon out over the audience, bringing it to a stop pointing at the contentious knot of combatants. One man raised his hand with a bottle of water in it. Crack! A beam of energy from the tip of the sword shattered the plastic and drenched the brawler. Baldwin moved his aim to his neighbor who was cocking his fist.

The would-be gladiators froze. Wide-eyed but quiet, they watched the weapon swing slowly to a neutral position.

Into the silence, Baldwin spoke in a calm, reasonable tone. "Everybody, sit down."

The audience sat. A number of men even lowered themselves to the floor when no chair was nearby.

"Here's what we're going to do. The Swords are going to identify certain persons. Those people will leave immediately through that door." He pointed to one of the exits. "Security personnel will show you where to go from there. If you are selected and do not leave voluntarily, we will assist accordingly. I advise you not to try our patience further. The rest of you sit tight—and find chairs if you're not in one."

The Swords indicated people, mostly Traddies, mostly missile-throwers, with the tips of their weapons. Nobody resisted.

As the rabble-rousers began to file out, Marcus realized he and Gloriana were still standing at the back of the stage and holding on to each other like they were in a windstorm. Trying not to think of how good it felt, he loosened his grip and whispered, "Are you all right?"

"Yes," she whispered and took a step backward. She didn't look at him, only took her seat again.

Marcus did likewise. Ed still stood, arms crossed over his chest.

Baldwin stepped down from the stage and motioned two of the Swords to him. When they arrived, he said, "Escort Mr. Walcott to the security offices, and keep him there."

"See here." Walcott stood and glared down at the shorter man. "You have no right—"

"Oh, yes, I do, Mr. Walcott. Indeed, I do. First, if you think to the contrary, you should read the rules for these gatherings as posted on the Web site and at the doors and printed on the back of the evaluation forms. Second, we told you what would happen if you repeated your incendiary remarks. If you want to resist, however, feel free. I haven't used my stun spell in some time, and your shenanigans give me a great reason." John gave the thin man a smile that promised gleeful and probably painful suppression of even the slightest mayhem.

Walcott scowled, but went quietly with the Swords.

When all the major belligerents—mostly Walcott's followers and a few Fomsters—had exited, and those without chairs had found them, Baldwin turned to Ed. "It's all yours."

"Horner and Pritchart, after we adjourn, come up here with your two most important coleaders," Ed ordered, and he scanned the room. "I'm calling a halt to our debate—or does someone have an important point to make?"

"Yes, I do," Gloriana answered.

"And I," Marcus said.

"Gloriana, you go first," Ed said and sat down.

Gloriana rose and picked up her microphone. "From the gross distortion tonight of what both Dr. Forscher and I have been advocating, I would like to make my feelings and recommendations perfectly clear."

Good, Marcus thought, exactly what he wanted to do.

"When I first spoke of the possibility," she continued, "that Dr. Forscher's equation would be used to teach casting and that we had to beware of forcing it on practitioners, I meant the words to be a warning only. Advice to take precautions against compelling *any* method. Not an expression of reality. Certainly not an indication of a conspiracy.

"Some practitioners have taken my words and twisted

them, made them into a threat that doesn't exist. To the members of the THA, I say, you have taken this idea too far. There is no real split in the community, no division between THA and FOM. On the contrary. In these discussions, we have discovered a broad middle basis, a consensus, for maintaining and building on our current methods. At the same time, we have identified the need to research new spells and new ways to cast them. I call on all practitioners to work together in both endeavors. Thank you." She sat down to scattered applause.

Marcus rose. "I, too, wish to make myself clear. I agree completely with Dr. Morgan. From the beginning I have called for the need to study and refine my equation. The formula is a jumping-off place to explore more casting methods. Some of those methods will be rightly discarded for a variety of reasons. Some may prove useful for the new spells we'll need as our jobs evolve and progress brings new professions we can only speculate about at present.

"I'll admit my hubris and overexaggeration in my remarks about cauldron-stirring and energy-wasting. I believe there is a place for tradition, and I further believe we can combine the old and new in our casting."

He shot a glance at Gloriana, but she was not looking at him. Maybe she would with his next words. He couldn't help smiling while he said, "Let me give you an example. I learned a new spell the other day—an ancient spell, strength or *invalescere*. I taught it to myself from a spell book for novices. Despite the precise directions, I had trouble making it come together. We all know how the new can be confusing. Fortunately, I had some help from a spell-caster who can use not only the old, but also the new. I was able to cast the spell as she explained it by applying the equation. Let me tell you, the exhilaration I felt when I succeeded was totally emotional."

Out of the corner of his eye, he saw Gloriana's head whip around, and he felt her shock as she understood what he'd related. Good, mission accomplished. Now to take on the Fomsters.

"To my mathematical colleagues and others who belong to FOM: You have taken the idea of the new too far. Denigrating, disparaging older, more traditional methods of casting does no good. Many, many practitioners are using those methods, and their spells hold no more or less potency than those cast with the equation. There should be no split among us. Casting is still an individual art—yes, art. To practice magic better and to better the practice of magic, we all need to be involved. I, too, call on all practitioners to work together with the old and the new methods. Thank you." He looked at Gloriana when he sat down, but she was again gazing at the audience.

"Thanks to both of you," Ed said. "Folks, these two fine people have been on the chopping block over this controversy. Let's give them a round of applause."

Ed started clapping, and the audience—even Pritchart and Horner and their cohorts—joined in.

"Our last debate is next Saturday in San Francisco," Ed said when the hall was quiet again. "I suggest to everyone that we use that venue to concentrate on the ways we can blend the old and new, start working on the research and calibration needed for the equation, and take a hard look at the efficiency of our traditional ways. Please, you mathematical types, keep it all in plain English. Thank you and good night."

While the audience filed out, Pritchart, Horner, and their people gathered in front of the stage. Baldwin looked them over and said, "Come with us." He led them all down a side hall next to the ballroom into a conference room with several round tables.

They arranged themselves around a table as they had been in the ballroom. Marcus and Gloriana sat on either side of Ed, with the Fomsters to Marcus's left and the Traddies to Gloriana's right. Baldwin sat in the middle between factions.

Ed looked sternly from Horner to Pritchart and back again. "Gentlemen, I really expected better of you." The two leaders opened their mouths, but Ed continued, "I'm not interested in excuses or blaming someone except Walcott and his band of idiots. Here is a true fact for you to believe: We will not permit such an uproar to happen again. Right, John?"

"Right," Baldwin said. "The next time, people could get hurt. If someone panics and runs into a sword blade, they could be killed. The last thing we need is for somebody to try throwing even the simplest spells. I do have a couple of questions for FOM and THA. Did you have any inkling about Walcott's plans for his inflammatory speech or infiltrating the middle with his troublemakers?"

Pritchart spoke first. "No. Look, to begin with, we were having a little fun with the stick-in-the-mud Traddies. We want them to be intellectually honest instead of all that appealing to emotion. Those guys can't take a joke, and they threw first. We responded to protect ourselves."

Marcus thought Prick sounded self-righteous. It had appeared from the stage, however, that the first missiles came from the right. Horner, on the other hand, looked distinctly uncomfortable when the attention focused on him.

"No, I didn't have any idea what Walcott planned, either," the THA leader said. "I knew, of course, that some of our supporters hold extreme views, but I certainly didn't expect Gordon to become so . . ."

"Rabid?" Gloriana suggested.

"Precisely," Horner said, nodding his head. "I hope you all realize that I and my inner circle had nothing to do with Walcott's words or actions or those of his followers. We totally repudiate them. He's been on the periphery as far as the controversy and the THA are concerned. Yes, he's been important in some of my other projects. Unfortunately we had a falling-out over tactics to oppose Forscher's formula, and he hasn't been to meetings or participated in our planning since before the meeting in Denver."

"The one where he first spoke and the Swords used their weapons?" Marcus asked. Horner had probably not tried to discourage or investigate Walcott, either.

"Yes. After that, he sent me a note to the effect that we were not standing up for our views strongly enough and he wanted nothing to do with us." Horner grimaced. "I expected to have to fight him for THA leadership, but we didn't meet after that."

"As I remember his diatribe," Marcus said, "Walcott said, 'Join me,' not 'Join THA' at the end."

"Exactly," Horner said with a sigh that had to be relief.

"All right. Enough of Walcott," Ed said with a dismissive wave. "John and I will read him the riot act and keep a close eye on him and his buddies."

"There's another matter to discuss," Baldwin said. "These threatening flyers or e-mails to Ed or our two speakers."

"We've written letters to all the High Council members and to you, Ed, and we encouraged our THA members to do likewise. I assure you that we always called for a reasoned approach," Horner said.

Prick snorted. "Yeah, right, as reasoned as you've been in your speeches."

"Watch it, Pritchart," Ed growled.

"No, we haven't written letters or threatened anyone,

either," Prick said. "We figured the decision makers already had their minds made up, and we liked the way the discussion's been going for more spell research in general. Why? What's going on?"

"All three of us have received some disturbing letters and e-mails, and I assume you've seen some of the flyers around the hotel," Ed explained, and Horner and Pritchart nodded. "Those messages have become more and more threatening and vicious over the past two weeks."

"We caught one of the people putting them up, and she's with Walcott's bunch," Baldwin said. "We're back-tracking on the e-mails, but they're originating in public computers in libraries and cafés. We're taking them very seriously, so tell your supporters to cool it in their correspondence. The last thing we need is an escalation to real violence."

"Speaking for the THA, I hope you catch the villains," Horner stated.

"Amen," Pritchart added.

"All right, let's concentrate on the future." Ed looked up from what he'd been writing on his notepad. "Here's what we're going to do for San Francisco, and none of it is negotiable. Traddies and Fomsters, first, get the word out to your people that the debate will be calm and reasonable. Second, you six are to come up with ways to work together, to try the equation, refine it. You will also look at older, more traditional spells and see if they can be made more efficient."

He held up his hand when both sides started to protest. "I'm not asking for a comprehensive study, only an example or two. Split up into couples of a Fomster and a Traddie. Try a spell together. Surely there are enough low-level universal spells that all talents can do. Marcus, what was the spell you used?"

"Strength."

"Okay, start there. How you organize yourselves is up to you. Be ready to report. Talk to your supporters and tell them the new order of things. Encourage looking at the other side. They can protest in writing and in person if they wish, *but we will have no riot*. Make that crystal clear. Any questions? No? Then good night. John, let's go take on Walcott."

Everyone stood, and the Traddies and Fomsters split themselves into groups to talk about their tasks. Baldwin and Ed left.

Marcus turned to Gloriana. She was so beautiful and looked so exhausted that he simply wanted to take her in his arms and hold her. That wouldn't do, however. He had to remember his resolve. He couldn't be her soul mate.

She gave him a smile that lit up her face. "Did you really teach yourself to cast *invalescere*?"

"Yes. You told me how when you put it in the context of the equation. It took me a few tries before I could work it correctly. I learned something about calibration in the process, and I'm pleased with the results. Thank you."

"*I* told you how to use the equation with the spell? *Me? The intuitive caster?* I didn't even realize I had used it."

"Yes, you were specific about power levels."

"I still don't understand how to use the formula."

"I think you do, but you'll have to experiment and decide that for yourself. It may change your whole idea of the process."

"There's something else we have to do first." She looked around before she whispered, "Marcus, we really must discuss what I've learned from Lulabelle. She had news that might make big changes for us, too."

He winced internally at her statement. If they were alone again together, he doubted they'd spend too much time talking, and mating would only make it harder for him to walk away from her—as he must do for both their sakes.

He was pondering what to say when Prick interrupted, "Hey, Forscher, come over here and tell me and Horner about the spell you learned."

"Excuse me, Gloriana," he pleaded, for once grateful to the blowhard. "First things first."

Gloriana watched him walk over to the two men and start talking. Within a minute, they were sitting at a table again, scribbling equations and diagrams. One of the other twosomes called to her, and she went to help them at another table. When she looked back at Marcus several minutes later, his entire group had vanished.

"Where'd they go?" she asked the remaining pair.

"They said something about getting a drink and looking up some elementary spell books," the Fomster said.

"Can you come here when you're finished with them? I don't get how the formula is supposed to work," the Traddie complained.

"Sure," she said. It took all her self-control to stay calm. She'd never find him tonight. He wouldn't be on the plane in the morning, either. Best to help these people and go to bed.

Tomorrow, however, it was time to get in touch with his mama.

CHAPTER
TWENTY-SEVEN

When she arrived home Sunday afternoon, Gloriana hardly stopped to reassure her parents that all was well despite the riot or to do more than give Delilah a quick petting. She'd explain everything to her parents that night at supper. First, she fired up her computer and found the practitioner registry.

Okay, the Forschers were somewhere in Europe. That put them seven hours ahead of her. Two o'clock in the afternoon here, nine o'clock at night there. They would probably be at dinner. No, she couldn't call at this time. Nobody wanted to be interrupted while eating, and if they were in a restaurant or with friends, real conversation would be out of the question.

E-mail was the solution to the problem. She'd hope that Judith Forscher would check her e-mail first thing in the morning. If she had no answer to her message tomorrow, she'd call, no matter what time it was there.

Composition of the message took a while, but she finally put together a note to send. She read it over, checking for typos.

Dear Judith,

It is imperative that we speak at your earliest possible convenience. You see—and I'm sorry to have to spring the news on you by these impersonal means—your son and I are soul mates. We only discovered it recently.

Given our first meeting—over the spell-casting controversy—neither of us expected such an outcome. There is, however, no mistake here. We are, in fact, soul mates.

Marcus first denied the facts vehemently. He is determined to reject the phenomenon and me. He claims that he could not possibly be a good soul mate or a good father to our children, your grandchildren.

Would you please call me as soon as possible at one of the numbers under my name at the bottom of this message. Either my home or the cell phone number is fine. I will be home tonight after 10 p.m., my time, or 5 a.m. tomorrow, Monday, your time. If that isn't convenient, send me the best time to call you. Do not worry about waking me up. I'm looking forward to discussing the situation with you.

Thanks,

Gloriana

There. That sounded urgent enough and not overly emotional. It raised questions while offering no answers. The zinger about grandchildren should get Judith's attention, and stating only the bare facts left lots to her imagination. Gloriana copied the message from her word processing program to the e-mail screen and hit *Send*.

Nothing to do now except wait and discuss the situation with her parents over dinner.

The next morning she woke up at two, and at three, and at four. At five, she said to hell with it and got out of bed. When Delilah whined for a run, Gloriana let her out into the fenced backyard. The dog gave her a dirty look before going out the door. Too bad, she wasn't budging from her house.

Gloriana first checked her e-mail. No word from Judith. She made herself some breakfast and was on her third cup of coffee, jotting down the points she particularly wanted to make, when the phone rang. At last.

"Hello, Gloriana. I hope it's not too early," Judith said to her hello.

"Oh, no, of course not." Gloriana overcame a small feeling of panic, almost wishing for a moment she'd taken up her parents' offer to be a party to the conversation. No, this she had to do on her own. "Thanks for calling promptly."

"Stefan and I are extremely happy to learn that you're Marcus's soul mate. As you can imagine, we've been wondering when he'd find his. I was beginning to despair, in fact. You'll be perfect for him. You're intelligent and beautiful and come from a good family. We were very impressed by all the Morgans at the Boston debate."

Gloriana could hear nothing except joy and warmth

in Judith's voice. "Thank you. It's gratifying and encouraging to have your support."

"Why on earth is Marcus rejecting you? How?"

"He says he's not opposed to me personally. He simply maintains that he doesn't want a soul mate, at all, period. Ever."

"How do you feel about him?"

His mother certainly asked the hard questions. "I'm drawn to him more and more—when I don't want to shake some sense into his head. I don't think I'm in love with him yet—or he with me. We haven't had the time alone to get to know each other. I'm willing to give the process a chance, however. He's not."

"What are his exact reasons for his recalcitrance?"

Gloriana took a deep breath. There was no use in sugarcoating them, not if she wanted to get Judith on her side. "They are twofold. First, his upbringing, and second, his genes."

"What? He's blaming his father and me?" Judith paused, then continued, "Tell me everything, please."

"Here's the story," Gloriana said, not surprised at the astonishment she heard in the questions. As requested, she laid out all the details, referring to her notes and making new ones while she talked.

"That's the situation," she finished.

Silence on the other end of the line.

After some seconds, she asked, "Judith?"

"Oh, I'm here, dear, a bit shocked, a little sad, and

really quite alarmed. To think Marcus had these feelings and ideas all along. He never said a word. I've suspected something wasn't quite right between us for the past couple of years, and I'm sorry to say, I put it down to his overworking. He's always driven himself, but for him to think we want him to live up only to *our* expectations . . . or that we don't love him . . . or that he's flawed in some way . . ."

There was another little silence, and Gloriana didn't try to fill it. She'd told Judith all she knew, and the woman needed to think it through. The pain she heard in Marcus's mother's voice made her want to cry, though.

Finally Judith spoke again and with a firmer tone. "I think I see where all his thinking is coming from. Gloriana, don't you worry. It's our problem to correct. Stefan and I will straighten Marcus out, and I'm sure he will return the favor—about a number of matters. I only wish it had come to light long ago, and we have to accept full responsibility for why it did not. We simply went along with his saying everything was fine. Thank you for telling us. I'm sorry to have put you in a difficult position."

Gloriana wished she wasn't in her position, either, but thought it better not to voice that opinion.

Judith didn't wait for a comment. "I have a good idea of what you've been facing with my son. Marcus takes after his father, and they are both stubborn. When faced with incontrovertible proof, however, they do change their minds. I'm going to talk to Stefan as soon as we hang up. I know we can get to the bottom of the matter quickly. We'll let you know what happens with our son—or Marcus himself will. Once again, we're both overjoyed you and Marcus have found each other. Please give your parents our regards."

"I'll do that. Is there anything in particular you want me to do or tell Marcus?"

"No, I think we'll surprise him. I'd let him stew if I were you. And," she chuckled, "let the imperative work on him, too."

"Judith, I think we're going to get along fine," Gloriana said with a chuckle of her own.

"We'll talk soon. Good-bye."

"My regards to Stefan," Gloriana said and hung up the phone.

She slumped in her chair, exhausted and relieved. At least their talk was over and had gone pretty well. Part of her would have liked to talk longer with her future mother-in-law. *Mother-in-law!* Yikes! At least Judith had taken her report seriously.

All she could do was wait and see what they did and hope they could get through to their stubborn son where she had failed. They, and the phenomenon, had their work cut out for them.

In the meantime, she supposed she should get back to work after the weekend away. First, check her e-mail. When she saw what awaited her, she wished she hadn't

opened the program. Numerous messages about the debate filled her in-box almost to capacity. She opened a
few and discovered a disturbing trend. The subject lines
often gave no clue to the contents, and while the vast majority applauded the outcome, a distinct few made vile,
vicious, violence-threatening attacks on her, Marcus, Ed,
the High Council, and whoever else wanted a reasoned
study and discussion.

Gloriana immediately called Ed and told him of her
messages. He had also received the attacks.

"Send them all to John," the editor said. "He has
some of his people working on them. Have you heard if
Marcus received threats?"

"No, we haven't spoken." She wasn't going to elaborate on that.

"Okay, I'll call him."

"Any word from Walcott? How did the discussion
with him go Saturday night?"

"Nothing from him personally. He had control of
himself when we talked to him after the debate. Claimed
he couldn't help it if people chose to take action because
of our high-handed refusal to let him state his opinions.
Smug bastard."

"How serious are these threats? How worried do I
need to be?"

"The prime instigators seem to be Walcott and
Kemble. While many people are sympathetic to the
Traddies' view, very few of them are actually following

the extremists. John thinks it's basically the two of them causing an uproar. Thus far, it's only talk and these letters, and we're watching them closely. Just in case, keep an eye out. If you feel threatened in any way, tell John, and we'll assign a Sword to you."

"I'll be glad when the last debate is over," Gloriana said with a sigh.

"We've done good work, but I will, too."

She said good-bye and put down the phone. Thinking about what Ed had said, she decided to tell her parents about the threats. She herself wouldn't worry about them. She'd be at the farm all week, they could confine customers to the store areas, and strangers stood out, especially around the greenhouses where she'd be working.

By Wednesday afternoon she'd done most of the work she had planned for the week and was feeling restless. Oh, a few more threats had come in, and a couple were extremely rabid, but all else was calm.

Except for her. She felt itchy, restless, and generally discontented. There'd been no word from the Forschers, parents or son. What was she going to do for the next few days?

The last debate would be in San Francisco, a city she'd always loved. She talked it over with her parents and decided she'd go there the next day. She had friends to visit, she wanted to discuss some botanical issues with colleagues there, and she could use the downtime. Staying in Austin, she'd only obsess over Marcus—or she'd give in to impulse and go see him, and neither act would accomplish anything. Not in the long or short term. Besides, the imperative was leaving her alone, so she ought to take advantage of the lull and prepare herself for seeing him on Saturday.

She made the arrangements and flew out early on Thursday.

CHAPTER
TWENTY-EIGHT

Thursday morning while he drank his second cup of coffee and read the paper in his living room, Marcus congratulated himself on the amount of work he'd accomplished since he returned from Atlanta—he'd evaluated an article for a professional journal, proofed one of his appearing in the next quarter, written a chapter in his novel in progress, and sent the rabid e-mails to Ed and John. The threatening messages had given him pause, but their origin and their specific details were still too vague for him to worry much. Let the Swords take care of it.

Best of all, he'd succeeded in blanking the soul-mate situation out of his mind.

Oh, sure, he had a couple of bad moments—when he'd gotten a country music station by mistake on the car radio and heard a plaintive ballad that sang of deep loneliness and loss when the loved one had left and wouldn't be back. Something about not loving as often as he should have and asking for one more chance.

No, that didn't describe him or his problem. He quickly changed the station and tuned his mind to another subject.

He'd had the usual erotic dreams about her and had woken up aching.

And the damned imperative gave him sharp jabs if he saw something that reminded him of her, like a dark-haired woman at the grocery store or a profusely blooming plant.

To top it all off, the little ivy, while thriving with a new leaf, did seem to give him reproachful looks from time to time. No, that last part couldn't be possible. He certainly wasn't communing with plants now.

He looked at his watch. Time to get back to work. He was putting down his coffee cup when the doorbell rang.

Who on earth would be here so early? Gloriana? When her name crossed his mind, his hand holding the cup lurched, and the coffee splashed on the table.

No, it couldn't be. Samson wasn't going crazy. Standing by the stairs with his ears pricked, the hound was watching the door, but not moving.

Marcus put down the cup, threw the paper on the coffee table, got up from his easy chair, and stalked to the door. Whoever it was, he'd get rid of them quickly. He jerked it open, not bothering to look through the peephole first.

"Oh, my God. What are you doing here?" burst out before he could control himself.

"Don't stand there gawking, Marcus," his father said. "Are you going to let us in or not?"

"Thank you, dear, and close your mouth," his mother said as she breezed past him after he stepped aside.

Marcus closed the door—and his mouth—and followed them into the living room. Stefan leaned down to give Samson a pat before taking one of the easy chairs, and Judith made herself comfortable on the sofa.

"Is something wrong? What's happened? You're both all right, aren't you?" he asked, certain a catastrophe had struck. Why else would they have come here all the way from Europe? They didn't look like their usual immaculate selves. Instead they were rather rumpled and travel-worn—and something else below the surface. Anger? Sadness? He couldn't tell.

"We're fine," Stefan said. "Sit down. We need to talk."

"What about your conference, your appointments?"

"What we have to say is much more important," his father answered.

"Would you like some coffee? Water?"

"No, dear," Judith said. "We'll have some later, perhaps. First things first."

Uh-oh. Those words always preceded a discussion he didn't want to have. Marcus lowered himself into the chair closest to his mother. He remained stiffly upright.

"I had a long talk with Gloriana on Monday," Judith

said. "We know she's your soul mate, and we are thrilled and happy that you've found your mate at last. She's perfect for you."

"Damn fine woman," Stefan put in. "Lots of talent and intelligence. Pretty, too. You couldn't do better."

Marcus didn't say a word. He could all too readily imagine how that conversation with his soul mate had gone. Reminding himself that he was an adult and had valid reasons for his stance on the matter, he waited for their comments. He crossed his arms over his chest and looked from one to the other.

"She told us you're rejecting the mating, however," Stefan continued, "and she's told us why. I'll admit, your reasons have caused both of us a great deal of confusion and some heartache. We decided to come to you. We need to discuss the situation face to face and try to stop you from making the biggest mistake of your life." His father leaned forward and pointed a finger at him. "Marcus, you are excellent at studying facts and making the correct decisions about all manner of problems, but, son, you're coming to the wrong conclusion here."

Marcus still said nothing. His father didn't like interruptions, especially not those contradicting what he was saying. They were very much alike in this—and in many other aspects, like needing proof before changing their minds—a thought that bolstered his confidence in his determinations. How could they refute him? Hadn't he lived it?

"That is our fault," Judith said. "We never sat down and talked to you about soul mates, the reasons for our actions, or our feelings."

"Quite frankly, we never thought we needed to." Stefan rubbed his hand over his face—a weary gesture. "I guess we took it for granted that you'd understand us the way we understand each other."

"Also, neither of our families ever talked much about what has become so important here or showed their affection for each other in public," Judith said, "so I think we perpetuated their practices without considering the consequences, indeed without realizing we were doing so. We're here to clear the air. Therefore let's start at the beginning—your beginning. I can't tell you how overjoyed we were when we found out I was pregnant."

"Damn right," Stefan added. "We'd wanted a child as soon as possible after we married. It simply took a little longer than we originally planned."

He hadn't been an afterthought or a bloodline issue. Marcus's heart beat faster while their words began to sink into his brain. He stopped himself from smiling, however. Better to hear the whole story before rejoicing. He did relax enough to uncross his arms.

Then he noticed his mother's hands clasping and unclasping in her lap. He'd never seen her make such a nervous movement before. And his father was fidgeting, and Stefan never fidgeted. The discussion seemed to be harder on them than on him. Or was it about to get worse, much worse for him?

"I don't think we ever told you," Judith went on, "but your birth was a difficult one for me, and it took some time to recuperate. We brought in nurses for a while, and after I got back on my feet, we continued with a nanny to help with you. You understand the demands of academia. Our careers were taking off, and like many women at that time, I was trying to 'have it all.' That left little spare time for either of us. We made it a point to eat breakfast together with you every morning and dinner every evening and tried to work in some playtime. Also, one or both of us tucked you in at night. Do you remember any of that?"

Marcus shook his head, but he wasn't sure if it was because he didn't remember or because he didn't believe her. She had to be telling the truth. His mother never, ever lied. Images of his parents laughing and cleaning his ice-cream-smeared face and of them reading a bedtime story flashed through his mind, too quick to grasp and study. Were the pictures real? Or merely wishful thinking?

"Of course, he doesn't remember. Most of that was before he was five years old," Stefan said with a shake of his head before he smiled broadly. "By God, how bright you were, Marcus. When we had you tested, you scored higher than either of us had, and we were no slouches. That's when we brought in a tutor. Remember Toby Feldman?"

Marcus nodded. Oh, yes, he remembered his tutor. Feldman had been in graduate school at the time, and very different and more outgoing than his parents. Much more fun. Marcus had hated it when Feldman graduated and went off to teach—and Marcus found himself in . . .

"We knew we had to send you to a good school that would challenge you, and Silberkraft Academy seemed perfect. We had no idea that you were miserable there," his mother said with a catch in her voice. "Why didn't you tell us?"

"I don't . . ." Marcus started slowly. The tears glistening in Judith's eyes gave him a moment of panic. He'd never seen her cry, and he prayed she wouldn't now. He cast around in his mind for the reasons he never told them of his misery. "I guess because . . . when we were together on vacations after I started boarding school, there never seemed to be time to talk. *Simply talk.* We were always going somewhere, meeting somebody, seeing something. We talked about my grades or what I was studying, but you never asked if I liked it."

"What was the problem? Why didn't you like it?" Stefan asked. "We both loved our boarding schools. We thought you would, too."

"Oh, the classes were all right, and I had some good teachers, and I enjoyed learning," Marcus answered. "Since I placed three years ahead of my age level, however, I was always in classes with the bigger kids. I wasn't even in a residential house with boys my age because the school wasn't organized that way, but by grade level. The older kids . . . well, let's simply say, they weren't always as friendly as they might have been. Those my age called me a freak because I was smarter than they were. I spent most of my time alone studying when I wasn't with tutors. The only place I was in my age group was in sports, because teams were determined by age, weight, and height." He wasn't about to tell them about the hazing he'd also endured there.

"Besides," he concluded, "what could you have done about it? Sent me someplace else? It might have been worse. Look, don't worry about that. It's in the past. Over and done with."

"That may be," Judith said, "but it's all affecting your future. I'm doubly sorry we didn't, as you say, simply talk. Those years were frantic, both of us chasing professorships or prizes or publication or something, while trying to fit in time to be together with you. You're correct, there was no time *to simply be*."

She gave him a sheepish look. "I have to confess something also, Marcus. You scared me a little."

"Me?" He couldn't stop his voice from rising or his eyebrows lifting toward his forehead. "I scared you? How?"

"By being male. No, both of you hear me out. I never told you, either," Judith said, pointing at Stefan when he laughed. "I was never totally comfortable around boys, or later, men. Remember, I went to an all-girls school. The few men I saw were stuffy old teachers who didn't have an ounce of sex appeal among them. The only boys were those in a neighboring school who were rowdy, rude, and, after a certain age, probably rapacious, or so I feared. When I went to undergraduate college, again solely women, I ignored all males. That may have partly been the soul-mate phenomenon at work, but the result was the same. I repeated the pattern when I was in graduate school and again when I started teaching."

She smiled at his father and suddenly looked much younger. "Then I met Stefan. What a revelation! We were soul mates, with all that term implies. I learned more about men in our first three months together than in my entire life before that. My relationships with other men, however, remained the same—friendly but distant. And here you came along. A boy! What was I going to do with a boy? How do you talk to a boy? You were rowdy and rambunctious, of course, and interested in things that were foreign to me, like trucks and cowboys and space aliens.

"After a while, just as I thought I was making progress with you, it was time to send you to school. The years simply flew by and suddenly you were a teenager and didn't want to have anything to do with us. On vacation, I felt like we were dragging you around against your will. I counted it a success if we heard a whole sentence from you, much less a paragraph. The only people you wanted to talk to, thank goodness, were the ones to whom we were introducing you and who shared your interests, which didn't coincide with ours. You grew up, of course, and we could talk about adult subjects, and I was comfortable again."

"Have I lived up to your expectations, accomplished your goals? Are you proud of me?" Marcus asked and crossed his arms again, bracing himself for the answer.

"Of course, you have," Judith said. "We both could not be prouder of you. Some of our colleagues are tired of us telling them about your latest achievements. Your equation is stunning, a real contribution to spell-casting. Why do you even have to ask?"

"Because you don't tell me so. All I hear is how you want me to publish more, to take a position somewhere else, to meet *your* goals. I think you've said 'good job,' your highest praise, to me eight times in my life, Stefan. What do I have to do, win the Fields Medal?"

"I didn't think we had to tell you," Stefan said, looking both puzzled and somewhat defensive. "I thought we were showing you. Otherwise, we certainly wouldn't have introduced you, especially as a young boy, to all our friends and colleagues, or gone out of our way to put you in contact with the leaders in so many disciplines. Man, I really enjoyed watching their faces when you started asking questions. You knocked their socks off." He grinned, then frowned.

"As for heaping more praise on you? Frankly, I was apprehensive too much of it would go to your head.

Nobody likes a show-off or an overweening ego in a young man, even a brilliant one. The last thing we wanted was for you to end up like that Pritchart fellow."

"What about my meeting *your* goals?"

"What do you mean?" Judith asked.

"Like publishing more, like teaching at an Ivy League school? What about *my* goals, the ones I set for myself?"

"Oh, Marcus, I thought those *were* your goals."

"No, those were the ones you set for me, not the ones I set for myself. We've never discussed goals from my perspective. Neither of you ever asked what I wanted to do. You always told me."

"Ah, I see where you're coming from," Stefan said, his frown clearing. "All right, what are your goals?"

"To make whatever advances I can in my field and in magic, to teach my students and help them learn as well as I'm able, to continue to write my science-fiction books, and *to live my life as I see fit*."

"Those sound commendable to me," Stefan stated. "Oh, by the way, I enjoy those novels of yours."

"You read them? Why didn't you tell me?" The discussion was becoming one surprise after another. First, they actually wanted him, and second, his father read his books. What next?

"The subject never came up."

"Of course, it didn't. I wasn't about to ask since I thought you disapproved of my writing them because you never said a word. Why go looking for criticism?"

The real question was, why did he have to ask? Why hadn't Stefan said something? He opened his mouth to ask those very questions.

"Hold it, you two," Judith interjected, holding up both hands before he could say a word. "We're missing the main point here. Let's agree that none of us can read the others' minds and that we need to discuss *everything* from this point forward and to give praise when it's due. No matter what our parents did, Stefan." She gave him an emphatic nod.

"Let's stipulate that as parents we should have talked *with* you more, instead of *at* you, Marcus. I think we both assume the professorial demeanor too quickly—heaven only knows how frustrated I become when your father starts 'dictating' to me as if I were one of his students. But I don't let him get away with it. I never thought you would take his statements like commandments. All right, does everybody agree on these points?"

The two men nodded. Marcus kept himself from smiling in triumph. No more guilt or frustration over not living up to their goals. They were recognizing him as an adult at last. He was almost floating with happiness, when her next words brought him back down to earth.

"And you, Marcus," she continued, "might have told us how you've felt about school, goals, and your novels and probably other things. Even if males in general don't discuss feelings, it would have helped if you'd raised the question about goals and whose they were, and we should have asked. On the other hand, you've certainly gone your own way successfully, and we're very proud of you."

She looked from him to his father and back. "The most disturbing discovery of your situation for me is that we have fallen into a pattern over the past years of not discussing the really important parts of our lives—our family, our hopes, our dreams, our successes and failures. We've been simply existing on the surface, but not sharing deeply. No wonder we haven't been communicating. Do you both agree?"

"Yes, Judith," Marcus murmured and shot a glance at his father who also said, "Yes, Judith."

"That brings us back to the real reason we're here," Judith said with a smile that boded trouble. Here came his biggest problem. "You have a soul mate. You're trying to reject both her and the phenomenon. According to what you told Gloriana, you're doing it because you don't know how to be a mate or a father, you don't know how to show affection for a mate, and you were afraid you'd treat her and possible children as you think we've treated you. You think you can't be loving, and, I suspect, you think that you aren't loveable. Am I correct in those statements?"

Marcus managed not to wince at her statements. His mother always could get right to the core of a thesis. He'd never consciously thought about not being loveable, although he supposed it was part of the mix. His parents had certainly given him cause to think so. He looked to his father to see if he wanted to add a comment, but Stefan only raised his eyebrows in question. He turned back to his mother and nodded in the affirmative. "Essentially, yes."

"Son, I have news for you," Stefan stated. "*Love* is the most important thing there is, the most ancient magic, the basis of the soul-mate bond and the resulting family bond. We love you, completely, wholeheartedly, unreservedly. We haven't said that enough to you, and I apologize. We haven't taught you to say it back to us. My parents didn't teach me, either. Your mother did, at least to her. I'm not sure when we stopped saying it to you—probably when you were a teenager. New rule: whoever says it first, the other has to say it back." He looked back and forth between Marcus and Judith until they had each agreed.

"Furthermore, Gloriana loves you, and not because of the imperative. Judith said your soul mate's love came through right over the telephone line, even though she doesn't acknowledge it yet. She's probably denying it to herself for protection if you follow through with your rejection. Why on earth would she have tracked us down and told us about you if she didn't?" Stefan shook his head. "I swear, you two need to work on your communication like the rest of us do."

"As for your ideas about soul mates, children, and all that blather"—Judith waved a hand in the air—"*of course* you don't know how to be a mate or a parent. *None* of us did until we met our mate, got married, and had children. Oh, you can read books galore. When faced with the actual mate or child, however, your education, training, or upbringing on that subject . . . it simply flies out the window. Trust me, you will learn quickly how to show affection."

"I second that," Stefan stated. "Your mother scared me to death when we met. The feelings that bombarded me practically left me in a coma when I was alone. When with Judith, however, simply being in the same room and not even touching . . . let's say I was stupefied no longer."

Marcus looked at his mother, who was *blushing*. His father's words took on a deeper meaning, and he looked at his hands when he felt his face heat. Too much information.

"If you're as smart as I think you are," Stefan went on, "you'll come to your senses and go to Gloriana and make up, not only for the time you've wasted, but also for putting that woman through a bunch of hoops she shouldn't have had to jump through. You have to have faith in the process. The phenomenon doesn't make mistakes. You've never given us cause to be disappointed in you. Please don't start now."

"I agree," Judith said and turned to his father. "I think we've covered our main points here, Stefan."

"I can't think of any others, either."

"Marcus, we'll leave you to think about everything we've said and your desires and needs," she said and stood up. "In your usual fashion, you'll need to go over and over all we've said in your brain until you accept it. Your father and I have a reservation at the Driskill Hotel. We're going there to get some rest. The flights were not conducive to sleep."

Marcus stood automatically when his mother did. "Wait . . . we still have things to talk about. I have questions about everything."

"We'll talk more when you've resolved your most important problem and made peace with Gloriana," she told him. "Now, give me a hug. It's been too long. I think you stopped hugging me when you went through those horrible teenaged years. Come to think of it, that's when we stopped talking, also."

"But . . ." No, it was the other way around—she had not wanted to hug him or had not wanted him to hug her. Or something like that. He didn't get to voice his opinion, however, because she was giving him a fierce embrace, and he was returning it. And it felt sooooo good. He shut his eyes tight to make the burning sensation in them go away.

"I love you, Marcus," she said, drawing back to look into his eyes.

"I love you, too," he answered and saw the tears in her eyes that must mirror the ones in his.

"Good boy," Stefan said, and, as soon as Judith

released him, he pulled Marcus into his arms and pounded him on the back. "I love you, son."

"I love you, too," Marcus said through a suddenly tight throat.

"The women are correct here. They usually are when it comes to feelings. You get together with Gloriana, and everything will be a lot clearer."

Marcus walked them out to their car and exchanged more hugs. While he watched them drive away, he rubbed his forehead. The revelations of the past hour had made him woozy. He looked down at Samson, who had accompanied them to the curb. The hound grinned and yodeled.

CHAPTER
TWENTY-NINE

What just happened here?

His head spinning, Marcus went back into his house and stood looking down at the chairs and sofa grouping, replaying the conversation in his head.

His parents had come in like a double tornado and obliterated his complete theory and ideas about himself, his relationship with them, and their whole family . . . what was the term? *Family dynamic?* Yes, their entire family dynamic, all blown to hell and completely reorganized. His new understanding was going to take some getting used to.

What had he been thinking previously? About looking truth in the eye?

They'd certainly done it. Talk about seeing something from the other's point of view. He knew they were telling the truth, and not simply as they saw it, but as it actually happened. How to decide what to do? His mother was correct; he did go over and over problems. That was his mathematical process, and the answer usually appeared like . . . well, like magic once he'd looked at it from all viewpoints.

He plopped down on the chair he'd been sitting in. Samson came over and put his head on Marcus's knee, and he rubbed behind the dog's ears. "What do you think, boy? Have I been a total idiot, or what?"

Samson shut his eyes and leaned against him.

How pathetic he was. On the other hand, to hear the words *total idiot* out loud certainly drove his predicament home. Maybe, instead of living in his head all the time, it would help to actually verbalize his thoughts. Only the two of them were here, and if it didn't work, nobody would witness his failure, and Samson wouldn't talk.

"What I don't understand is how I could have been so wrong-headed about my family. Where did I get all those ideas? I hardly remember anything before going off to school. Although . . . Come on, boy, let's go downstairs."

With the hound following, Marcus went down to his office and over to the corner farthest from his desk. He knelt next to the floor-to-ceiling shelves and perused the bottom shelf. "Yes, here they are, my copies of *The Hobbit* and the Belgariad series. And look here . . . Elric . . . and Thomas Covenant . . . and Narnia. Oh, here's Philip Pullman I found in my twenties."

He picked up a few of the dog-eared books, took them to his desk, and sat down while Samson sniffed around the books and the shelves. When he leafed through them and read passages, he could *hear* his father's voice saying the words. Yes, they'd read them together, every night, until he went to Silberkraft.

"Oh, my God. I was totally wrong." He closed the book he'd been looking at and tossed it onto his desk. He pointed a finger at the hound. "But not about everything, Samson. I wasn't wrong about there never being time to talk about inconsequential things—how I liked school, for example. Even Judith agrees with me on that. I certainly wasn't wrong about being miserable."

He nodded at the correctness of those statements and added another. "Was that really inconsequential? It was to them, I suppose, since they couldn't imagine me not enjoying myself. But it sure wasn't to me."

Samson curled up in the corner and yawned.

"Yeah, I'm boring." Marcus turned to stare out the window. He didn't see the hills unrolling before him, however. Instead he saw the family trekking through Europe. "What do I remember of those vacations? Lots of traveling, one museum after another, my parents always working, and I got to meet all kinds of cool people who were interested in cool subjects. Somewhere in there . . . Judith and Stefan became almost like strangers—friendly but not people I could talk to. Not people who would understand what I was going through. Not people who cared."

He rocked back and forth, forcing his thoughts past the

wall he'd erected in his mind against the long-ago pain.

"Was that around the time I was really hating school? I must have been about thirteen? Oh, damn, it was, and I was too embarrassed about my inability to stand up for myself to tell them how I was being bullied or ignored." He ran his hands over his face as the memories surfaced. "They were and are always sure of themselves. I wasn't when I was around them. They had many friends. I had none, and I was so lonely. And I knew it was my own damn fault."

He crossed his arms over his chest, took a deep breath, and released it. "But was it? If I'd been one of the older students, how would I have felt about me? The kid who made higher grades and the teachers called a genius? I'd have ignored me, too. The bullies were truly sick, evil people."

He slumped in his chair until the injustice of the situation made its way into his brain, and he thumped a fist on the chair arm. "Damn it! That's not right. I was a kid, for God's sake. Where were the teachers while I was going through hell and obviously having problems? Why didn't my parents try harder to talk to me? Why didn't they have some idea of my misery?"

All sorts of events, comments, and people paraded through his mind. It had to be what an amnesiac experienced when his memories returned—fascination with what it showed him about himself, and terror about what he might learn. He blocked the humiliating images with a shudder that shook his whole body.

He still had no answer to his questions. For whatever reason, the adults hadn't known, didn't ask. His parents didn't have a clue what he was going through. He had decided then they never would understand and all he could do was survive till college. He'd been right about that. He was merely one of a bunch of really smart kids at MIT and actually had competition for the first time in his life. Even better, nobody bullied him, and he'd even made a few friends.

He had always taken it for granted—or from Stefan and Judith's brainwashing—that he'd teach in a university. He hadn't settled on his major until his sophomore year at Silberkraft when he'd discovered higher math. By that time, the non-talking pattern had been set.

As for praising him? His parents may have been proud of him, and certainly they introduced him to their circle of friends and colleagues. Why didn't they express that pride, whether or not he got a big head from the praise?

A vague recollection surfaced of his mother telling his father to stop acting like a know-it-all professor with his family. It had never registered until her comments today what that meant. Judith understood that Stefan seldom asked, but usually told people what to do, what conclusions to come to, how to solve their problems. She'd never, however, run interference for him with his father, and Stefan had never changed his behavior toward his son.

She'd shocked the hell out of him when she said he frightened her. The woman who had an answer for everything, who could make graduate students and assistant professors quake in their boots with the lift of an eyebrow. She'd never understood men, or boys, and hadn't realized how, when he was a little kid, he looked up to his father, took every word as gospel, and strove to make him proud.

So, he'd grown up and tuned both of them out.

It had been his own damn fault that she'd stopped hugging him.

Or had it?

"No," he said, facing his desk again. He must have said it with more force than he realized because Samson woke up with a start and stared at him.

"No," he continued more softly. "It's not all my fault. It's half theirs. What a screw-up. Okay, where do I go from here? Whatever or whoever's fault it is, the past is the past. I'm a grown man. It's time to get over my childhood. Even if it does take some getting used to. I'm glad we're talking again. All we can do is go on from here."

But, where did *he* go?

Right to the person who had brought him and his parents together.

His mate.

What a revelation that nobody knew how to be a mate before they met their own. Judith had certainly set him straight about his thinking—if it could be called that—on the soul-mate situation and his ability to be one. So had Gloriana—and in more forceful terms.

Gloriana.

His soul mate.

What was he going to tell her? How was he going to explain? He tried saying things out loud. "You were right and I was wrong? I was demented? All those things I told you about my parents and my upbringing? Most of them lived only in my head? They really do love me? I'm not too bad, actually?" He couldn't stop his voice rising at the end of each sentence, making what should have been statements into questions.

Samson cocked his head and listened.

Should he beg? "Please be my soul mate? Please take me back, let me in, let me be with you, let me . . . love you?"

Damn, that was all worse than pathetic. It was pitiful. Samson even agreed because he came over, whined, and put his head on Marcus's knee again.

"Well, boy," he said as he rubbed the dog's head, "it looks like both of us are surrounded by strong females. Delilah probably takes after her mistress, and I'm between my mother and Gloriana."

Samson's ears perked up at the sound of Delilah's name, and he grinned.

"Yeah, I know." Marcus's center seemed to perk up also at the thought of her mistress. They both had it bad. He still had a problem, however. What was he going to do about Gloriana?

No, wait, that wasn't the first question he should be asking. The first was, *what did he want?*

Gloriana. He wanted her. He needed her.

Love. He wanted her to love him. He wanted to love her and show that love every way he could. If what they'd been through was any indication, the physical part of loving would be mind-blowing.

Children. The outcome of physical love. He wanted to have children with her. Plural. No more of this only-child business like his ancestors.

It All. He wanted *It All*, everything the soul-mate phenomenon promised practitioners. A bond for life.

He'd hurt and confused her terribly, he could see that now. How could he get her to talk to him? Would she?

Of course, she would. She was still his soul mate.

He sat there, mulling over approaches and petting his dog. He'd probably come off as a pompous idiot to Gloriana, and more than one time. Still, he'd like to salvage a little of his pride if possible. He wouldn't grovel. Not unless he absolutely had to.

But . . . he could ask for help. If he maintained that he really didn't know how to be part of a family or how to have a soul mate, what if . . . what if he asked her to teach him how? She'd watched her brother and sister and their mates. She'd been part of a big family. She had the experience and must have the knowledge.

Oh, yeah. He liked that idea. He'd bet money that

she had no clue that nobody knew how to be a mate beforehand. They could learn together, and that would put them on equal footing. He'd have some control. Over himself, hopefully. She was definitely a force of nature, uncontrollable by anybody—and he liked it that way.

He would institute his family's new rule about saying "I love you." Since his parents had started that practice, he wanted to hear it more and more.

Did he really mean it where Gloriana was concerned? A fierce little jab in his solar plexus accompanied the thought. "Oh, all right," he said to his magic center. "Your damn process takes some getting used to. It's all so damned new. Yes, I love her. Yes, she's my soul mate."

His center hummed, and warmth and joy spread out from it. Marcus had to grin. It appeared his thinking process was working—the solutions were coming swift and certain like they always did.

Samson gave a yip and looked at him as if to say, "What are you waiting for?"

"Good point." He reached for the phone and the file with her numbers. Why hadn't he put her on speed dial?

Two minutes later, he frowned at the phone. She wasn't picking up at any location. Not at her campus office, not at her condo, not at the farm, and not on her cell phone. He looked at the file again—ah, here was the number for her parents.

Alaric answered. "Hi, Marcus, how are you?"

"Fine. Listen, I don't mean to be rude, but I'm in a

little bit of a hurry. Do you know where Gloriana is? I can't get her at any of her numbers."

"Yes, she's gone to San Francisco. Left this morning."

"Already?"

"She said something about wanting to get out of town to somewhere she could think with no interruptions. If you don't mind my asking, how are you doing? Have you solved your soul-mate problems yet?"

Damn, she'd told her parents. He really didn't want to talk about it with his prospective father-in-law. Oh, my God, *his father-in-law*. Marcus gulped and said, "No, and that's what I want to discuss with her."

"We had a nice talk a little while ago with your parents."

"They called you?"

"They're coming to stay with us for a couple of days after they sleep off their jet lag. We're going to watch the Webcast of the debate together."

Marcus could practically hear Alaric grinning. It was one thing to realize he was about to have in-laws. Then to find out the two sets of parents were going to be staying together? God help both him and her. "Thanks for the info, Alaric, I—"

Alaric interrupted. "Marcus, you go get that girl of mine. You two need each other. Everything will work out, you'll see. Remember, being soul mates just gets better all the time."

"Uh, thanks, I'll keep that in mind. Thanks for the

information."

They exchanged good-byes, and Marcus hung up the phone.

"Guess I need to check the airline schedules," he said while he booted up his computer. Maybe she'd sent him an e-mail about her plans.

None of the e-mails listed her as the sender, however. He clicked on the oldest in the list to see what it was.

> *WE'RE NOT GOING TO LET YOU DESTROY MAGIC!*
> *RENOUNCE THE FORMULA!*
> *RETURN CASTING TO THE PEOPLE!*
> *OR YOU'LL BE SORRY!*

Didn't these people ever get tired? He tried the next one.

> *LET GORDON WALCOTT SPEAK!*

At least the message was short. One more and he'd send all with an address he didn't recognize to the Swords.

> *YOU AND THE WITCH ARE TO BLAME FOR IT ALL.*
> *AND YOU AND THE BITCH WILL PAY FOR IT ALL*
> *WITH EVERYTHING YOU HAVE AND ARE.*

*WE'LL SEE YOU IN HELL BEFORE WE
LET YOU WIN!*

Uh-oh. That one sounded more serious. He quickly
went through several more, and the anger and vitriol
grew. He opened the latest message.

*REPENT AND RENOUNCE YOUR
PERNICIOUS FORMULA!*
*If you do not use the forum in San Francisco to repudi-
ate that horrible and degrading equation, you and that
traitorous witch will be sorry. We will fight you and
the High Council conspiracy in every way we can, using
every method available to us. A warning of our power
will be waiting for you at the next so-called debate.*

THE FORCE FOR TRUE MAGIC

A cold shiver went down Marcus's back when he
read the words. He hadn't thought it possible, but the
evil in the words leaped off the screen as if it was alive.
The message was no joke. He reached for the phone and
punched the button to speed-dial Baldwin.

"John, this is Forscher. Where are you? Do you
have access to your e-mail? I'm sending you a message
that was sent to me overnight. It looks serious."

"I'm at my computer," Baldwin replied. "Send it
and stay on the phone."

"Okay, forwarding." Marcus hit the button. "I

found out from her father that Gloriana's on the way to San Francisco early today. I don't know if she's received the same message."

"Damn. I'm still in New York. Ed and I are flying out there later. You caught me before I left for the airport. Ah, your message has arrived. I guess we can thank the gremlins of the Internet for moving it through so quickly."

There was a moment of silence while Baldwin read the message. "I see what you mean. It is the first communication with real action threatened. I agree, we have to take it very seriously. I'll call our people in San Francisco. Most of the team is there already. We'll put someone on Gloriana and double-check all the meeting rooms."

"Good," Marcus said. "I'm going to try to get out there as soon as possible."

"Okay. Check in at the Sword office when you get there. If we're not there yet, talk to either Steve Alioto or Fergus Whipple."

"Whipple? He's going to be there? You're certainly pulling in the big guns, aren't you?"

"Believe it or not, the most powerful Sword alive asked to join us. It seems he's a big fan of Morgan herbs and spices—and your formula."

"Great. I'll look for all of you there." Marcus said good-bye and set about finding a plane reservation.

CHAPTER
THIRTY

Marcus was in luck. A flight out in the afternoon would put him in San Francisco about six in the evening. He packed and dropped off Samson with Evelyn and George, telling them he'd explain everything when he returned. On the way to the airport, he changed stations on the radio and found that country-western one again. The male singer asked if he could trust her with his heart. Good question. He was about to find out.

At seven thirty that evening the limo dropped him off at the San Francisco HeatherRidge on Nob Hill. He checked in and sent his luggage to his suite. He called Gloriana's suite when she didn't answer her cell, but no one answered there, either. That left the Swords as a source of information. They would be able to pinpoint her location.

"Ah, Forscher," a giant bear of a man with flowing white hair and beard greeted him as he walked in the door. He radiated magical power and looked like a well-fed Gandalf. "I'm Whipple. Glad to meet you. You've done wonderful work with your equation. I'm having a great deal of fun with it. We'll talk about it later."

Feeling somewhat like a kid standing next to a legend, Marcus shook the large hand of Fergus Whipple, a wizard of such power that he was rumored to be off the level chart. "I'm honored to meet you, Mr. Whipple."

"Call me Fergus. This is Steve Alioto. John told us you were coming and sent a copy of that threat."

"Security officers and the rest of the Swords on the team have been scouring the building since John called. So far, we've found nothing out of place. Of course, we can't go into the private condos," Steve said.

"Where's Gloriana?" Marcus asked.

"We don't know," Fergus answered.

"What?" An icy fist took hold of his stomach. "She's supposed to be here."

"She's checked in, and her things are in her suite, but she's not in the building."

"Have you tried her cell phone?" The ice was growing, down to his gut.

"Yes, and we called her parents," Steve said. "They told us she had planned to visit with some friends. The doorman saw her get into a car with some people yesterday. She had a small bag and a backpack, and she was laughing and hugging them. There's no reason to think harm has come to her. The parents gave us names and a couple of phone numbers. We called and got only answering machines. When the Morgans asked why we wanted the information, we simply told them Ed wanted to rehearse early tomorrow."

"That's all fine, but . . . that was yesterday. What about today?" Marcus stopped himself from yelling at the man, took a deep breath, and regained some control. Steve had done the best he could. She was probably all right. The ice retreated a bit. "Sorry. It's been a long day."

"Let's go get some dinner," Fergus said. "We're doing what we can to find her, you need to keep your strength up, and I want to discuss your formula."

"Fine," Marcus acquiesced, and they headed for the restaurant.

Later in his suite, Marcus tried Gloriana's cell again, but all he got was her voice mail. He decided against phoning the Morgans. They had promised to tell her to check in with the Swords if she called.

He ought to be on cloud nine. The dinner with Whipple had been one of those occasions he'd remember for a long time. Not only did Fergus understand his equation, he had actually used it and come up with calibration methods that might translate into ways lower-level practitioners could cast with it. To have a warlock of Fergus's level, talents, and reputation on his side could make a powerful impact on those who were ambivalent about the formula.

Worries about Gloriana, however, kept him from

enjoying the triumph. They also kept him from sleeping much. In the morning, he checked out the ballroom and the overflow rooms with Ed and John, who had arrived late last night. Afterward he went back down to the Sword office and hung out there.

Still no Gloriana. No call. No nothing. Where was the woman?

At eleven thirty, Ken Livingstone, the general manager of the HeatherRidge, came in with a serious look on his face. "We've had a bit of vandalism," he reported. "Housekeeping went into your suite, Dr. Forscher, and found it a shambles."

Everybody hurried to the tenth floor and into Marcus's suite. Someone had thoroughly ransacked the rooms. Feathers and foam billowed from cut seat cushions and pillows, the bedsheets were in tatters, and Marcus's clothes were in a pile with a sticky substance smelling of cleaning chemicals all over them. "FORCE FOR TRUE MAGIC" was spray-painted on one wall. Steve immediately left for the security offices to see if the hall cameras had recorded the vandal's entrance.

"Thank God, I had my laptop and notes with me," Marcus said after surveying the damage and tamping down the anger rushing through him.

"We'd better check Gloriana's suite," John said. "Did Housekeeping look in over there?"

The head of Housekeeping and the maid, who were waiting outside the suite, said that no one had been in the other suite yet. Standard procedure was to clean his first, then the rooms across the hall.

When the maid opened the door to Gloriana's suite, the same sort of destruction greeted them. Baldwin walked in first and told the others to stay back while he and Fergus checked out the rooms. He was about to move into the bedroom when Fergus stopped him and pointed to the door. A thin thread stretched across the threshold.

The Swords ordered everyone back to Marcus's rooms while they searched. Within minutes they returned. "Two booby traps," John reported, "one behind the door and the other in the bathroom. They look to be smoke bombs. We defused them, and Fergus is taking them to the Swords' training facilities in the sub-basements. It's okay for you to come in, but be careful where you step."

When Marcus entered her suite and took note of the viciousness of the destruction, cold dread seeped from the icy lump that started growing in his stomach the day before. The devastation was definitely worse here. The vandal had ground broken glass into the carpets, smashed the bathroom mirror, and ripped Gloriana's clothes to shreds. Thank God she hadn't been here.

"All right," John said after a thorough perusal of the scene. "Here's what we're going to do. Livingstone, you and your people take care of these rooms. Move Forscher and Morgan to other quarters, ones we can keep a very close eye on."

"We'll replace their clothing also—the basics by tonight and anything else they need tomorrow," the manager stated. "They'll be ready for the debate. My apologies, Dr. Forscher. The HeatherRidge will take care of all expenses. I'm deeply sorry and embarrassed that you have suffered such an indignity and crime."

Baldwin's cell rang, and he answered it. After he hung up, he said, "That was Steve. The cameras show someone in a housekeeping uniform with a maid's cart going into both rooms, Gloriana's at a quarter to ten and Marcus's thirty minutes later. The 'maid' kept her face hidden behind a pile of towels or cleaning equipment, but we're checking other views on other floors and the elevators to see if we can find her."

"Too bad I didn't stay in my room this morning," Marcus said.

"She simply wouldn't have come in," John answered. "She went into Gloriana's room first, and I doubt you would have heard her. Doing such damage doesn't make much noise. We're fortunate she didn't start a fire. That's not all the news. Shortly after we came up here, a cabbie delivered a small overnight bag and a backpack with Dr. Morgan's name on it. It contains her laptop and a change of clothing. There was an accompanying note from her saying to put it in her room and she expected to be in about three if Ed was looking for her."

"That's it?" Marcus asked. "No idea where she is?"

"No. The concierge asked the cabbie where he got it,

and he said he'd picked up both luggage and lady at a residence close to Golden Gate Park. He dropped the lady off in Union Square and brought the bags up here as she instructed. He thought her getting out in Union Square was a spur-of-the-moment decision on her part because he had to change his route to go there. She looked and sounded fine to him. Seemed to be in good spirits and tipped him well."

Marcus let out a whoosh of relief, and his anxiety lessened—a little.

The Swords and Ed trooped downstairs to see the video, leaving Marcus and Livingstone to make a list of his clothing and toiletry needs. Marcus managed to keep his mind on the task, but once he finished, all he could think about was Gloriana. There was no use his going out to search for her; she could be anywhere.

Damn it, where was she?

He paced and fidgeted around the Sword offices until John and Fergus took him aside. "What the hell's the matter with you?" John asked. "Trust me, we have things under control. A couple of Swords are out looking between here and Union Square, but she's probably shopping."

"You see, here's the thing," Marcus answered. "We've recently discovered we're soul mates."

"Ah." A huge grin spread over John's face.

"Congratulations!" Fergus shook his hand and pounded him on the back.

Marcus looked around nervously. "Can we keep that

to ourselves, please? We're still getting used to the idea."

"Sure. We don't need more uproar, which there will certainly be if the two sides find out," John said. "In the meantime, take it easy, will you? Take your laptop into the back office and see if you can get some work done, or read a book. Livingstone said he'll be by before long to show you your new rooms. When Gloriana comes in, we'll bring her right to you."

What choice did he have except to comply? He went into the back office where there were several desks, sat at one, booted up his computer, and pretended to be working. Mostly he played mindless computer games.

Where was that woman?

CHAPTER
THIRTY-ONE

On a beautiful summer day, Gloriana looked out at the Golden Gate Bridge from the cable car Hyde Street turnaround at Fisherman's Wharf. The orange bridge stretched to her left and a tall-masted ship rested at anchor to her right. A few fat seagulls waded in the shallows of the bay, but didn't bother her. The savvy birds knew she had no food for them. It was blessedly cool, a wonderful contrast to the heat of Texas. She breathed in the slightly salty air and, for the first time in days, felt alive.

Until she'd finally relaxed with some old friends last night, she hadn't realized how tired she was—tired of the debates, tired of running at home to get everything done, tired of being cooped up in the various Heather-Ridges. She hadn't seen one bit of the cities she'd been in except on the rides to and from the airports.

She was so tired of the entire soul-mate situation. Neither Judith nor Stefan had called. Oh, they may have sent her an e-mail. She'd stopped looking at her messages—too many contentious people and the increasing number of nasty comments were getting very old. There was nothing she could do about Walcott or his cohorts. She'd let the Swords handle the mess.

So, she'd stolen some time for herself, first with her friends and by herself before she had to be back at the HeatherRidge. She'd purposefully never turned on her cell phone except to check her messages, and she'd ignored the ones from Marcus. If he had something to tell her, he'd have to tell her to her face. No playing phone tag, no games. Her phone was off, and the freedom that came from being unconnected was surprisingly exhilarating. She was her own boss, unfettered by the tyrant of technology.

She probably ought to tell someone where she was, but she couldn't bring herself to do so. She turned around in a circle—only a few people were in sight, and they were all walking away from her. How anyone could be following her, she couldn't imagine. They would have been pretty obvious.

After poking around the fancy stores on Union Square, she'd walked with all the tourists over to the cable car, bought a day pass, and taken the Powell & Hyde line up to the top of Russian Hill. From there she'd walked down the stairs on twisty Lombard Street and around to the Cannery and Ghirardelli Square. The shops, however, held nothing to attract her attention, and she took a few minutes here by the bay to relax.

Time to get moving again. She found the end of the Powell & Mason cable car line and rode it to Chinatown.

She wandered down Grant Avenue, but nothing caught her eye in the souvenir and jewelry shop windows. Thirsty, she stopped for an iced mocha in a Starbucks outside the Chinatown gate and put her feet up for a few minutes. Wow, was she glad she'd worn her running shoes. The blocks were long and some very steep. She finished her drink and looked at her watch.

Oops, it was already past three. On the other hand, she was in no hurry. Ed and John would probably be at the HeatherRidge already, but she didn't really want to eat dinner with them—or talk about the debates. She told herself she didn't care where Marcus was. No, she'd go back, have a nice shower and a nice dinner, and go to bed.

She left the coffee shop and started back for the cable car on Powell. It was really the simplest way back up the hill—and the most fun. She was waiting for the light when she spied a blond male head across the way. Was that? No, certainly not. The man turned around. It wasn't Marcus.

The sight put her soul mate right back into her head. What was she going to do about him? Being passive and simply waiting grated on her nerves and her disposition. What choice, however, did she have?

When she reached Powell Street, no cable car was

in sight. Thinking about Marcus was making her blood churn, and she started walking north along the line. She didn't like waiting for man or machine.

Damn the man for being so stubborn.

What if, despite his parents, and the SMI, and her parents, and her arguments, he held fast to his refusal to be anyone's soul mate? In that case, no one else would ever be hers.

She still wanted a family. Would he consent to giving her a sperm donation? That way she could be artificially inseminated. He wouldn't have to deal with them—he could even pretend they didn't exist.

No, that probably wouldn't work, either. Her parents might go along with the idea, but his would be mad as hell at him and would demand to have a place in the lives of their grandchildren. Besides, every time she looked at the kids, she'd think of their father.

All the anger and frustration boiling inside her was making her walk faster. She had already reached California Street. Nob Hill loomed above her. She looked down the California cable car line. No car coming there, either; she had no choice except to climb the steep incline, and she started up the Fairmont Hotel side of the street. Halfway up, she was breathing hard. Damn, she needed to do more climbing or step aerobics or running in the hills. Her flatland legs weren't used to such mountains.

To distract herself from the effort, she concentrated on her major problem. What were her conclusions for her contingency plans? No, rephrase that. What was her one, singular, solitary conclusion—her only course of action, or should it be inaction?

She had to wait and trust in the process. Marcus would have to come to her. In the meantime, she hoped the imperative was plaguing the devil out of him. In sympathy, her center hummed.

After stopping at the top of the hill to catch her breath, she walked slowly past the reddish-brown Pacific Union Club and across Sacramento and into the HeatherRidge. She had gotten no farther than ten feet inside the lobby when John Baldwin and a huge man with a white beard swept her up.

"Come with us," John said, practically dragging her into a hallway behind a door marked *Staff Only*.

They marched down a corridor and into a set of offices.

"What's going on?" she asked as alarm and excitement brought an adrenaline rush. "What's the matter? Who's he?" She pointed to the bearded man.

"Somebody wants to talk to you," John answered, "and this is Fergus Whipple, one of our Swords."

"Pleased to meet you," Fergus said and grinned from ear to ear.

"Likewise. But . . ."

Before she could say another word, John opened a door and pulled her through it. "Here she is," he said.

"Glori!"

And Marcus had her in his arms so tightly she could

hardly breathe.

"Oh, God, I was damned worried when I didn't know where you were," he murmured.

Caught up against his body in the tight band of his arms, she tried to make sense of what was happening. Her heartbeat began to calm down when no immediate threat appeared, and then their magic centers aligned and began to hum. Oh, it felt so good. She almost relaxed while her body began to heat.

When she realized the Swords were still in the room, however, she squirmed to put some distance between them. The last thing she wanted to do before them was lose control to the imperative. But she couldn't budge him, even when she wiggled and muttered in his ear, "Marcus, let go."

Finally, he put his hands on her shoulders and pushed her to arm's length, scowled, and shook her gently. "Why didn't you turn on your cell phone, woman? Do you care what you've put me through?"

Gloriana stared at him. What she'd put *him* through? Had he gone insane?

Realizing he was slightly crazed and probably over-reacting, Marcus stopped shaking her and pulled her close again. It was impossibly difficult to let her go. Gloriana remained still only a few seconds before wriggling. She was right to do so. His center was vibrating, and his blood beginning to heat . . . and he knew where that would end up if he didn't separate them. Calling on every ounce of his ragged control, he stepped back and took a deep breath. "You don't know what happened."

"No, evidently I don't." She twisted to look over her shoulder at John and Fergus, who were watching with big grins. "All right," she said, aiming her eyes back at him, "somebody tell me."

"Let's sit down," Fergus said.

Pulling chairs from behind the desks, they all took seats, Gloriana's several feet from his.

Marcus dragged his chair next to hers. She looked at him with a wary expression, but he didn't care. He had to be close to her.

"Have you seen the threatening e-mails that came in on Thursday and today?" John asked.

"No, I stopped looking at them," she replied with a shrug. "I figured you all were getting them, too."

"There have been a couple saying a 'warning' would be waiting at the next debate," John continued. "We scoured the building and found nothing of a suspicious nature. However, this morning, while Marcus was down here with us and you were out, someone trashed both your suites."

"Oh, my God." She put her hand on her chest and sat up straight, clearly shocked. "What'd they do? Did anyone get hurt? What about my clothes?"

"No one was hurt. The vandal ripped up the upholstery and sheets, poured a mix of shampoo, hand lotion, and cleaning products over your clothes after slashing some into pieces, and spray-painted 'Force for True Magic' on the walls. The worst part is that she left behind two booby traps—smoke bombs. If you'd set them off, you could have been badly burned." John went on to explain about the fake maid and their failure to discover who she was.

"That bitch! And you can't find her?" she asked. "What is the Force for True Magic?"

"Walcott's group," Marcus answered. "They have a Web site up, calling for the defeat of the equation. They're lashing out at both of us for being parties to the 'conspiracy' they claim exists."

"We have to assume the vandalism is their handi-work, also, although we can't prove it yet. Walcott is incommunicado, and the Web site contains no threats directed at you," John said.

"Did you have anything of value in the rooms?" Fergus asked.

"No, but damn"—she hit the chair arm with her fist—"I really liked the blouse I planned to wear tomor-row. I'm carrying the few pieces of jewelry I brought. My laptop—oh, that reminds me, did my stuff make it here okay?"

"Yes, it's in your new suite," John answered.

"Are my clothes wearable? I don't want to appear nationwide in these jeans." She waved a hand at her clothes.

"The head of Housekeeping went through the pile

and salvaged what she could, and they're being cleaned," Marcus said, thinking she looked fine in her Morgan Farm shirt. "She also noted your sizes and brands and bought some basics. If you give her a call, she'll be happy to help you shop for whatever you need. They're doing the same for me. The HeatherRidge is picking up the tab because of the lapse in security."

Gloriana slumped in her chair, and Marcus watched the emotions play across her face while she processed the information. After sitting silent for several moments, she rubbed her forehead, took a deep breath, and lifted her gaze to John. "Okay. We go on from here. Anything else? Are there changes in the program for tomorrow?"

"Essentially, no," John said. "One other point. The damage in your rooms was worse than in Marcus's. No slashing of his clothes, for example. Therefore, we want you to take some precautions. Don't go anywhere alone, even in the hotel, and that applies to both of you. We'll have security with you if you go out. Otherwise, the de-bate goes on as scheduled."

"All right. If you don't need me," she said and stood up, "I'll check on my clothes. Buying a new blouse or dress purchases can wait for tomorrow. Where do I find the head of Housekeeping?"

"Her name is Bonita Williamson, and her extension is 4854," John said.

"Thanks." Gloriana picked up the phone on one of the desks and dialed. When she had Williamson on the line, she thanked her for helping and said she'd call the next morning about shopping. After she hung up, she said, "Bonita said she's put some things in my new room. Where is it?"

"I'll take you up," Marcus said, marveling at the way she controlled herself despite being shocked and probably furious. He still wanted to hit someone—preferably the culprit. He grabbed his case and ushered her out.

"If you'll give me the key and room number, I can find the room," she said when they had exited the Sword offices.

"Neither of us is to go alone, remember?" he answered. Besides, no way was he letting her out of his sight. They had to talk. He was about to burst with what he wanted to say, and if he didn't get her alone soon, he'd probably blurt it out in front of everybody. Man, wouldn't that go over well?

She made no comment, only nodded. Neither said a word as they walked to the elevator. He saw people in the lobby pointing them out, but no one tried to approach them. When the elevator doors shut, he took the key cards out of his pocket and swiped one in the special slot for the penthouse level. He handed the other to her.

"They put us on the top floor. There are only a few suites up there and access is limited. The locks have also been reprogrammed. The floor's halls are under constant surveillance, and Housekeeping staff will go in pairs. If

unauthorized people do get up there, they'll be trapped."
He scrutinized her while he talked. From the tightness
of her mouth and eyes, he could see the stress of the situation beginning to take its toll. "Are you all right?"

She sighed and leaned against the elevator wall.
"When I came in, I was feeling pretty good. I'd had a nice
walk and seen some of the city. I was looking forward to
a leisurely dinner and a good night's sleep. I come back
to find out my clothes and hotel room are trashed. All
my plans for a quiet evening are out the window. How
'all right' I am is open to question. I'd really like to get
my hands on these jokers—or better still, toss them to
a flesh-eating plant, if there was one big enough." She
smiled grimly. "Did they destroy your computer?"

"No, I had my laptop with me." He held up the case
to show her. "I'll pick up a shirt and suit tomorrow."

The elevator stopped and they exited into a small
lobby with a short hall and only a few doors. He led the
way to one of them, but hesitated and faced her before
putting the card in the slot. "Uh, there's one thing . . ."

She only raised her eyebrows in question.

"The hotel is booked solid. Looks like the debate is
popular. They had to put us together in the same suite."
Her eyes squinted and her lips thinned with suspicion, so
he rapidly said, "It's a one-bedroom suite, and the couch
is large enough to hold me . . ."

"But? I know there's a 'but' coming."

He cleared his throat. "From a protection standpoint,

it's probably a good idea to have both of us in one place, but . . . it's the Soul-Mate Suite."

"The Soul-Mate Suite? Like the Bridal Suite?" Her voice rose with each word. Then she muttered something about the SMI playing a joke. She ran her card in the slot, pushed open the door, and walked quickly into the opulent set of rooms.

He knew what to expect, and thank God, it wasn't a frilly, frou-frou kind of place with all the lace and idiotic "romantic" stuff you might expect. Instead, the Soul-Mate Suite was tastefully decorated in what he considered a "traditional" style of comfortable furniture and rich colors.

He followed as she went from the living room with its view that stretched from the Golden Gate Bridge around to the financial district into the bedroom with its enormous, gold and light blue, velvet-covered bed. She stuck her head into the bathroom, cocked her head at the whirlpool tub built for two, and rolled her eyes when she came past him back into the living room.

On the dining table were boxes and bags with the names of clothing stores. Gloriana rummaged around in a couple of the bags, although she didn't pull out any of the contents. "My goodness, they certainly went all-out. My clothes were not this nice."

"Glori, we need to talk," Marcus said.

She froze with her hand in one of the bags and looked up at him with a big green, slightly suspicious gaze. "Do we have something to talk about?"

"Yes. Why don't we sit down? This is probably going to take a while."

CHAPTER THIRTY-TWO

Gloriana slowly took her hand from the bag but didn't move otherwise.

It was clearly up to Marcus to begin. He smiled, hoping it came across as a friendly one and not a grimace, raised his eyebrows, and held out his hand in the direction of the grouping of sofa, easy chairs, and low table. "Shall we sit?"

She nodded, went to one of the chairs, and sat, her hands primly in her lap.

He sat in the other chair. He'd been hoping she'd go to the couch where he could sit close enough to touch her. Under the circumstances he'd take what he could get—he had to. He was damned tired, however, of being on the opposite side of a coffee table from her.

"My . . ." He had to stop to clear his throat. The enormity and risk of what he was about to say almost overwhelmed him. It was as if he stood on a precipice overlooking a vast ocean of uncertainty and insecurity that reminded him all too much of his teenaged years.

Go for it, Marcus. He breathed deeply and jumped off the edge. "My parents came to visit me on Thursday."

She blinked. "They came to your house? All the way from Europe?"

"Yes. They said you had called them and told them we're soul mates."

"Yes, I did. It seemed the only way to get you to address our problem in a realistic manner and not like a . . ."

"Jackass?"

"That word will do." She said the words without inflection—no anger, no teasing.

He paused, but she said nothing, only waited with a neutral expression for him to continue. She wasn't going to help him one iota, and he couldn't blame her. She'd been correct—he had to speak. "I'm glad you called them. We had the most important and illuminating discussion we've ever had."

Again, not a word. Not a flicker of what was going on in her brain showed on her face or in her eyes. The woman would be a killer poker player.

He took heart from the fact that she hadn't refused to talk. He was still in the air after his leap and hadn't hit bottom yet.

Leaning forward, he rested his elbows on his knees, looked at his hands, then back at her. "I learned that I've had a number of misconceptions about myself and them. These ideas started when I became a teenager, and for a variety of reasons on both my part and theirs, the errors grew and compounded themselves into a stalemate. I was pretty insufferable as an adolescent, and my father has certain . . . habits of speech. Let's just say he's the typical know-it-all professor, and I took his suggestions as orders. Anyway, between the demands of their careers and my absence in school, we didn't talk much, even when we were together. The result? We grew apart, far apart."

He stood, came around the damned coffee table to stand before her a couple of arms' lengths away from her chair. If he crashed, it would be on his own two feet. Or something to that effect.

"Between the two of them, they effectively showed me the errors in my thinking and in my judgment. What they said dovetailed with your views and reinforced my research findings—that the *process* of the whole soul-mate experience is what's important and needs to be trusted."

Although she still didn't speak at his statement, her lips played with a slight smile. He glanced at her hands—ah, there was her reaction. Her fingers were so tightly entwined that her knuckles were pale. She was as nervous as he was.

Emboldened, he pressed on. "So, I've come to thank you and to ask your forgiveness and your help. First, thank you from the bottom of my heart. You gave me back my parents. If you hadn't forced the issue, I don't think that we'd ever understand each other or have been able to reforge our family bond."

"You're welcome." Her small smile grew a little wider, yet her hands didn't relax. He was still in the air, still with an uncertain landing.

"I ask your forgiveness for my being thickheaded and for putting you through misery. I ask your help because . . . because . . ." As he came to the crux of the matter, he seemed to be falling faster, not floating at all, but plummeting downward. All his rehearsed words flew out of his head, and in utter panic of crashing, all he could say was, "Oh, damn, Glori, I still don't know how to be a mate or part of a big family like yours or even part of my small one. I'm not sure how we get to know each other. Will you help me learn? Will you be my soul mate?" He held out both hands to her in hope and supplication.

Her smile vanished when she broke eye contact. She still didn't say a word, she simply sat, staring in an unfocused way to the side, and he almost died in those seconds of silence. Finally, she stood up and looked him in the eye. Her hands were still tightly clenched, and he braced himself for whatever was to come.

"What do you want, Marcus? What do you truly want out of life?" she asked softly.

Oh, good. He had the answer to this particular question nailed. "I want you, I want love, I want children, I want a family. Most of all and first of all, because everything else comes from it, I want you—in my heart, by my side, in my bed, in my life. I want *It All*."

Her big green eyes shining like darkened emeralds, she stared at him, and a bolt of pure fear hit his stomach. Was she going to say no? The hands he was still stretching out to her quivered; he held them steady by sheer force of will.

"Fun . . ." She cleared her throat, began again. "Funniest thing. When I asked myself that question, I came to the same answer." And the sweetest smile lit up her face.

She put her hands into his, and he pulled her into his arms and hugged her fiercely. Relief washed over him, followed by sheer exhilaration. He was doing better than floating. He was flying.

As their bodies met, their centers aligned. The hum was a deep, satisfied, all-encompassing purring he felt in his bones. He drew back, intent on a kiss, but stopped when she raised her eyes. Tears glistened in the green, and one slid down her cheek.

"Hey, what's wrong?" He wiped the tear with his thumb and licked the salty drop from it.

"I can't help it," she answered, her voice wobbling slightly. "I was so afraid you were going to reject *me*, reject *us* again."

"No, I may have been slow to accept reality, although with you and my parents working on me, I've become a very fast learner."

She frowned, and the tease was back in her tone

when she said, "It certainly took you long enough."

He had to hear the exact words. "Is that a yes?"

"Yes, Marcus, I'll be your soul mate. Will you be mine?" Her voice didn't tremble even one little vibration.

"Oh, yes, Glori, definitely."

He wasn't sure who moved first, but suddenly they were kissing, their centers were humming, and their hands were holding on tight. Heat began to build, his heartbeat increased, and his breathing did, too.

His mind began to fog. *No, the damned imperative was not going to take him over again.* He beat back the attempt with an effort. Determined to control his own lovemaking, he separated himself from Gloriana.

"Wait," he panted.

"What for?" Her hands were in his hair. She tugged, but he resisted.

In a swoop, he picked her up in his arms and started walking to the bedroom. "This time, we're going to make love in a bed."

CHAPTER THIRTY-THREE

Gloriana was glad he was carrying her. She was so weak from relief and his kiss that she doubted she could stand. She could, however, take advantage of the situation. Being carried gave her access to a part of him she usually couldn't reach, and she kissed his neck and nibbled on his earlobe while he walked into the bedroom. He tasted and smelled wonderful—a combination of chemicals, she knew in her mind, but a potent, arousing mix to her nonintellectual body.

"Stop that," he growled and squirmed, but she ignored him and gave his neck a smacking kiss.

By the side of the bed, he lowered her quickly to her feet. Her legs seemed strong enough to hold her, and she pulled his head down for another of those kisses. He seemed happy to oblige, and within seconds their centers were humming again. While their tongues tangled, she began unbuttoning his shirt. She'd been delayed long enough. He was her mate, and she wanted him *now*.

"Wait." He broke the kiss as he captured her hands and held them to his chest. "We're also going to take it slow. We're going to realize all those fantasies plaguing my dreams."

She stared up into his light blue eyes. Where had she ever gotten the idea they were icy and disapproving? His gaze was so hot and deep, he could be seeing into her soul. She wet her lips. His eyes dropped to follow her tongue and rose again when she asked, "What fantasies?"

"We'll start with me undressing you." His smile promised untold pleasures, and his low raspy voice sent prickles of excitement racing through her blood.

"What do I do?"

"Enjoy." He pushed her jacket off her shoulders and down her arms to fall at her feet. After a small kiss that left her wanting more, he pulled her Morgan Farms shirt out of her jeans and up over her head.

"Nice," he murmured, running his fingers down her straps, over the swell of her breasts to meet in the middle of her chest at the bottom of the deep V of her lacy bra. As his fingers neared her magic center, the hum, which had receded to a low presence in the background, increased in volume and intensity.

She felt her eyelids grow heavy and lethargy creep through her body, but she forced her eyes to remain open, her mind to work. She needed to see his reactions to her. She was determined to be conscious of every single moment.

Although she wished he would go faster, she'd humor him for the moment. *Fantasies* sounded interesting.

He reached behind her, unhooked her bra, and slid it down her arms. Staring at her bared breasts, he licked his lips and murmured, "Oh, Glori, you are beyond beautiful."

She shivered when he cupped, weighed, and kneaded her in his hands. Her breasts seemed to grow heavier, fuller. Her nipples tightened into dark red buds when he ran his thumbs over them. Once, twice. On the third, little zings of energy ran down her nerves straight to her womb, and she grasped his hands to hold them in place.

As he fondled her, he smiled again, looking like he'd discovered treasure. When he lifted his hands away, she tried to press them back, but he captured hers instead and brought them up to his shoulders.

"Hold on," he said and knelt, put his hands on her breasts again, and continued playing. With his tongue, he gave each nipple a flick, a light caress that almost brought her up on her toes as the zings increased in power, and she had to grab tight to his shirt for an anchor. The hum grew louder.

"Let's get the rest of your clothes off."

He removed her shoes and socks, unbuckled her belt, unzipped her jeans, and helped her step out of them and her panties. Leaning back on his heels, he surveyed her body with a look combining desire, need—and total possessiveness. *Mine!* his expression proclaimed.

She found it impossible to be embarrassed or shy

about her nudity in front of him. On the contrary, his gaze was so hot, so exciting, so adoring that she almost wanted to strike a "come get me, big boy" pose.

In fact, she was determined to return the favor. Neither had had the chance to see, really appreciate, the other during their last two oh-so-fast encounters. She wanted to see him, also. And touch, and explore, and more.

She gave an exasperated sigh. Going slow was incredibly frustrating. Her whole body was tingling, demanding to be skin-to-skin with his.

He reached for her, but she seized his hands. "My turn for a few of my fantasies. Stand up."

He looked startled, but he complied. She finished unbuttoning his shirt and pushed it off his shoulders.

Oh, nice. She ran her hands up his muscled chest, through the curly blond hair, over his flat nipples, down his breastbone. The hum, which had lessened, resumed and increased. She kissed his chest right above his center, and he gasped and she jumped when energy flashed between them.

She glanced up, and his head was back, his jaw clenched, his hands in fists at his sides.

"Are you all right?" she asked, her voice as raspy as his had been. "I felt a jolt, too."

"Don't stop," he grated.

She helped him out of his shoes and socks before she focused her attention to his belt buckle, then his pants where his erection was straining against its confinement.

Slowly she lowered the zipper. His pants dropped to the floor, revealing his briefs, tented with the strength of his arousal. She placed her hands on his waist and slid her fingers under the elastic waistband.

He sucked in his stomach and put his hands over hers. He whispered hoarsely, "No."

She froze and raised her head to look at his face. He wasn't smiling. Instead, every muscle was taut, strained, like he was holding on to something as tightly as he could.

He grimaced. "Let me."

She nodded and stepped back, and he stretched out the elastic and took off the underwear. When he straightened up, she ran her gaze up and down him. His body was that of a runner, lean, rangy, not an ounce of fat, and his sex rose powerfully from its blond nest of curls. The man really was perfect, and in sheer admiration she said, "Oh, Marcus, you are too gorgeous."

He laughed, a strangled sort of chuckle, turned quickly, and stripped back the covers on the big bed.

His backside was gorgeous, too. She couldn't resist putting her hands on him.

"Hey!" He jumped about half a foot, whirled around, and swooped again, picking her up and tossing her into the middle of the big bed.

She laughed, bounced, and struggled to sit up, but he was hovering over her in a flash, braced on his arms and knees, one leg between hers.

"Slowly," he whispered, and, coming down on his

left elbow, he lowered his body slightly to the side of hers, anchoring her to the bed with his thigh between her legs.

The man radiated heat, and, hot though she was, she needed warming. As she reached for him, this time he caught her hands, manacled them together in his left one, and stretched her arms above her head.

"Patience," he murmured and kissed her.

More than a little disgruntled at being restrained when she wanted badly to touch, she resisted and kept her lips together—for a moment. When he ran his tongue along their seam and simultaneously slid his free hand down her side to her hip, then upward to settle over her breast and play with its nipple, she gasped as her body stiffened of its own accord.

Her inhalation gained him entrance into her mouth, and he kissed her deeply. And deeper still. Until she was only conscious of his mouth on hers, their tongues dueling, his fingers fondling a breast grown increasingly sensitive, his alluring scent filling her nostrils. The hum from their centers oscillated in time with the blood beating in her ears and the thrusts of his tongue.

He dragged his mouth from hers, pressed kisses down her neck, over the vein throbbing there, and down to her breast where he swirled his tongue around her hard and aching nipples. When he suckled, waves of heat rippled through her, and she squeezed her eyes shut to concentrate on the sensations, so much stronger than their last time on his living room floor.

Lack of sight, however, seemed to intensify the ache, now compounded by a fierce longing and rampaging need, as she concentrated entirely on her breasts and his actions. He roamed from one breast to the other, and she arched her back and pushed against his mouth, searching for relief.

When she didn't find it, she moaned and began to move, twisting and turning against his hard, rigid body. Her captive arms strained against his hand, and her free leg rubbed and lifted against his, but nothing brought even temporary relief.

"Easy," he murmured against her skin.

Easy? More like torture. The aching traveled from her breasts to between her legs, and grinding herself against his thigh didn't help, even made it worse. When the throbbing went from merely discomfort to torment, she protested with a wordless cry.

He must have realized the tumult she was undergoing because he slid his hand down her ribs to her hip and nudged her back, away from him. When his fingers settled in the curls at the apex of her thighs, he ceased his attention to her breasts and said in a raspy, gravelly voice, "Open your eyes."

When she did, her gaze met his—concentrated, intent, scorching. Hardly any blue showed around the black of his iris. It was the look he'd given her from the moment they met—only multiplied by a thousand. It seared her soul.

He used his thigh to open her legs wider, and his hand cupped her, explored her hidden folds. Each sliding caress along her slick swollen flesh brought a tiny bit of relief. Mostly it intensified her need for more—more stroking, more pressure, more . . .

"Marcus," she groaned, pushing against his hand below and against his hand above.

"Glori," he whispered and slid his wet thumb over her nerve-filled nub.

As shock waves ran upward through her body, he thrust one finger into her core. It felt so good, and she contracted her inner muscles around him, held him tight. When he began to stroke in and out, she arched and worked her hips to match his movements. When he rubbed and flicked that most sensitive spot also, every muscle in her body tightened. She grew even hotter, and she hauled in air as though she was running up a huge hill.

Inside her, pressure began to grow, pushing her harder against his hands, arching her back in a deeper curve. The blood beat faster in her ears, and her body began to vibrate from the hum of her center.

His eyes still bore into hers; it was impossible to look away. She saw raw need behind the lust, powerful desire within the heat, and the sight doubled and tripled her own.

The pressure built and built in a long crescendo. She was beyond consciousness except for what she saw in his eyes and what she felt in his touch. Greater and greater her excitement built, faster and faster her hips moved, her lungs worked. Until finally, finally, she went blind as long shudders wracked her, and the release seemed to throw her to another dimension.

Panting and limp, she focused her eyes to find him still gazing at her, but with definitely a look of sheer satisfaction. He'd released her hands, and she reached to pull him into a kiss. By the time he raised his head again, both of them were breathing hard.

Marcus gazed at her for a long moment before lifting himself up and over her and kneeling between her legs. He leaned down to kiss her again softly and had to smile against her lips when she languidly ran her hands from his hair, over his shoulders, and down to his arms.

Good. His instinct had been correct: bring her to a small measure of satisfaction to slow her down. She had finally stopped fighting him, stopped trying to rush to completion. While satisfying in one sense, their first and second lovemaking episodes had left much to be desired—especially the opportunity and the time to touch, to caress, to savor, to delight.

If she was going to teach him how to be a soul mate, he could teach her the joys of slow lovemaking. From all the evidence, she had a much harder job than he did.

At the moment, however, waiting, holding back was practically killing him. His blood was racing through his body, his cock was throbbing with its pressure, and if he didn't get inside her soon, he knew he'd spontaneously combust.

Patience, man, patience.

He stopped kissing her lips and moved down her body to her delectable breasts, where he feasted until she was moaning and moving restlessly again.

"Marcus . . ."

He raised his head and met her eyes. The green was softer than he'd ever seen. "Yes, Glori . . ."

"I want to touch you," she whispered.

Her words caused his cock to twitch. It wanted her to touch, too. If he was going to explode, however, it would damn sure be inside her. It was an effort to speak. "Not yet. I want to be in you when I come."

Her eyebrows went up, and an *O* formed on her lips. She must not have realized the effect she had on him.

"We have a mating to accomplish first," he said. He braced his upper torso on stiff arms and positioned himself at her entrance between her bent legs. "This one's for keeps. Watch."

She raised her head and he bent his, and together they watched themselves joining. She raised her legs to grip his hips, while he slowly pushed in, all the way to the hilt. It was the most erotic thing he'd ever seen, and the heat, and wetness, and grip of her sheath took his breath.

A perfect fit. She was perfect, made for him and he for her.

The hum increased in volume and intensity when he looked back into her eyes. Hardly any green showed, yet what did gleamed like emeralds.

She brought her hands to his chest on either side of his breastbone and said, "Touch my center when I touch yours."

"Why?"

"Because it will complete the circuit."

Her words didn't make much sense, but he did what she asked. He transferred his weight to his left arm and placed his right hand directly over her center. Hers was directly under his breastbone.

"On the count of three," she said. "One. Two. Three!"

And lightning struck, a bolt of magic power that fused them together.

Energy swirled around them, through them, in circles, from hand to magic center to where they were joined below and back up. Under his hand, he could feel her heart beating, matching his rhythm.

The hum dropped an octave, pulsated in sync, increased in volume. Their bodies heated even more, straining for a goal just out of reach.

It wasn't enough.

He came down on his left elbow, took her mouth in a deep, hot kiss. Another road for the circuit opened through that connection, and energy surged, oscillating between them.

Everything—heartbeat, vibration, energy level, temperature, tension—increased yet again; they had to be incandescent from the surging power.

It still wasn't enough.

Move! He had to move.

He pulled slowly part of the way out of her torrid depths and thrust slowly back in. A second time. A third. Each time she squeezed her inner muscles as he withdrew, welcomed him in on the return.

It was seduction of the highest order. It was heaven. It was home.

The energy, the beat, the heat, the hum, all spurred him on, and he began to move more rapidly, with greater and greater force. He thrust with his tongue and his body, powerful driving lunges that almost raised her off the bed. She gripped his hips tighter with her legs and rose to meet him.

The hum accelerated, deepened into a roar, the drum beat faster and faster as he coiled and recoiled, withdrew almost all the way and plunged back in. His world compacted to them alone, the rhythmic thrusts of his cock and his tongue, her answering responses—and the transcendent energy coursing through them.

They were melting, fusing, becoming . . . becoming one.

Climax came with a lightning bolt of energy and a bone-vibrating clap of thunder in a simultaneous storm of contractions that seemed to last forever. When it subsided, the tempest left behind great wonder, enormous elation, and ecstatic bliss.

And utter exhaustion.

Marcus managed to gather enough presence of mind to hold on to Gloriana and roll to put her on top, sprawled across him. For a while, only the sound of their breathing broke the silence.

After a few minutes, she lifted her head. She blinked lazily and whispered, "Wow."

He nodded. "I agree. Wow."

She slumped back down and wiggled until she had aligned herself to him, centers parallel and touching, his cock right between her folds. She stretched one arm up on the pillow next to his head and rested her own head on it. He idly rubbed her back and let his mind go blank. They both dozed.

※❋✻❋※

Some time later, Gloriana stirred. Their magic centers still hummed—more of a purr, really. His hands, which had been holding her hips, began to move up and down her back in a light caress. She raised her head. His blue eyes were looking straight into hers out of a solemn face.

"Hi," she said, wondering what his expression meant. Surely the man wasn't reverting to his past behavior.

"Hi to you, too." He smiled, turned it into a grin, and hugged her fiercely, rocking them from side to side.

She hugged him back and returned his grin.

"Oh, Glori, I love you so."

"I love you, too, Marcus." The words, both from

him and her, sent thrills down her spine. She kissed him to seal the pact.

After they recovered from that, he said, "That had to be a bonding mating. There was enough magic energy between us to levitate the building."

"I have no idea what I had been anticipating, but the reality was stupendous. Daria and Francie were right when they said it was transcendent. When you said this time was for keeps, their words came back to me. Touching centers seemed the thing to do."

"It certainly was." He gave her another hug and a kiss. When they surfaced for air, he asked, "What next?"

"What time is it?" She stretched to see the clock. "Oh, it's going on eight. I had planned a leisurely dinner, as I remember. What about something to eat?"

"Room service," he stated and grinned. "Then we can practice mating again."

CHAPTER THIRTY-FOUR

A shower first involved some creative uses of soapy hands and more "practice" and delayed them until they barely had time to don the plush robes the HeatherRidge provided before the food arrived. After they'd shooed the waiters out, Marcus looked over at his mate—*his mate*—and grinned. He was simply so damn happy he was giddy.

"My goodness," Gloriana said, surveying the huge dinner. "Steak, lobster, everything from soup to nuts. Oh, look at the scrumptious dark chocolate dessert. We didn't order all this, did we?"

"No," Marcus answered with a laugh. "I was going to tell you but I got distracted by the sight of you in the shower. When I called them, Room Service said Fergus had taken care of ordering for us and asked when we wanted it delivered."

"Why would he do that?"

"Look, here's a note." He picked up the envelope leaning against his wineglass and took out a card. He read it aloud.

Dear Gloriana and Marcus,

Enjoy! If your first days as soul mates are like mine and my Bridget's were, you'll need to keep up your strength.

Fergus.

"He knows?" She didn't look happy at the revelation.

"Yes, I told him and John." Her frown said he'd better explain, and he continued, "When we couldn't find you, I got a little anxious, I guess. They asked why, so I told them."

"I hope they'll keep the news to themselves."

"I asked, and they will." He brushed away thoughts of John and Fergus to concentrate on what was before them. He picked up his knife and fork. "I'm starved. Let's eat."

They both ate like they hadn't seen food in a month.

After dessert, Gloriana leaned back and patted her stomach. "I'm stuffed. I don't remember eating this much even when I've been casting spells all day."

"Me, either. Must be that expenditure of magic energy." Marcus took a last swig of coffee. "Speaking of spells, we haven't figured out the other benefit of bonding—the possible change in magic potential."

"So, let's see. Here's my old level twelve," she replied. She cast her red lightball and took it up the levels to an indigo sphere with a few higher violet swirls. "Now I'll push it."

The violet curls increased in number, size, and color intensity until the ball was almost totally violet with only a tiny bit of indigo showing.

"I think that's a level thirteen," Marcus said. "Let me try."

He cast his sphere in the same manner she had, bringing it up from red to his old level of eleven, an indigo ball with a few lower bright blue swirls. "Something feels different . . ."

He focused his energy in his center and projected it outward to the glowing globe. As the blue melded into the indigo and violet appeared, the well of power in his center expanded like it never had before. He poured on the power until he could find no more within him. In front of him floated a sphere identical to hers.

"That looks like another level thirteen to me," she said. "That's great! A two-level increase in power. My research said that much augmentation is rare. How do you feel?"

He rubbed his center. "I'm fine, I think. When I started pushing higher than my old level, it felt like my center inflated and more and more energy cascaded in. Man, I can't wait to try the higher-level math spells."

"Oh, you're right. I didn't think that far ahead. What fun we'll have learning new ones, and the power increase will help my plant growth spells."

Marcus looked at her, and the sight of her animated face, her thoroughly mussed hair, and her sparkling eyes tossed all ideas about spells out of his head. He rose, came around the table, and pulled her up into a hug. "Looks like a successful mating to me!"

He was luxuriating in the sheer feel of her in his arms and thinking they had to get out of these thick robes, when she stiffened and tapped him on the shoulder.

"Marcus, turn around," she said in a low, wondering tone.

He leaned back to look down at her, but she was gazing toward the table. Keeping one arm around her, he pivoted—and froze, staring in amazement.

The two spheres they had left floating over the table had drifted to touch each other, and while he watched, they began to merge—and grow. A low hum reverberated in the background.

"I'm not doing a thing to my sphere," she whispered.

"Me, either," he whispered back.

When the two globes had joined completely, the resulting orb was twice the size of one of the originals and totally violet.

"Are you still supplying power?" he asked. "I had mine on automatic pilot."

"Yes, so did I. I usually don't even think about cutting maintenance energy until I don't need it."

"Cancel your spell on three. One, two, three."

With a little "Bink!" the lightball vanished.

"Cast yours again," Gloriana said, the excitement in her voice matching his exhilaration at the discovery.

They cast, the balls appeared, and with no compunction from either, drifted together and blended into one. The hum returned, a low thrum in the air.

"Marcus? Do you feel something in your chest?"

He glanced down at her. She held a hand to her magic center. He concentrated on his. "It feels like there's even more power in it than there was a minute ago when I cast the first *lux* and all that energy rushed in. I thought when you bonded, the enhancement took place, you rose in level and acquired more magic energy, and that was it. The way I feel now, my energy is still increasing. What's going on? "

"I have more energy, too, all of a sudden, but I didn't feel a rush. The energy is simply there for me to use. Furthermore, the hum is back, and if we can go by the colors, that combined, totally violet ball is a higher level than we are individually. Maybe there's more to our enhancement than we realize."

"I've got an idea," he said. "Let go of each other."

They separated, and the hum disappeared, although the larger sphere remained and did not change color.

"My center went back to its former enhanced state," she said.

"Mine, too."

"Isn't that the damnedest thing?" she said. "I wonder

what it means. We have to show that to somebody. Lula-belle, of course. Who else might know about it? I found no reference to blending lightballs in my research."

Marcus looked down at her as she rattled on about research. The merging of the two spheres had had a definite effect on him—or maybe he was simply in a "merging" mood himself. The last thing he wanted to do at the moment was talk about lightballs, so he silenced her in the most effective way he knew how.

When he raised his head some minutes later, their robes were open, they were skin to skin, both of them were panting, and she had been moaning. "Come on, woman," he murmured. "Let's do some coalescing and fusing of our own."

CHAPTER THIRTY-FIVE

Saturday night Gloriana tried to keep her face expressionless as she looked out over the place she least wanted to be—another HeatherRidge ballroom filled with contentious people. She'd much rather be back in the Soul-Mate Suite with Marcus. They'd been apart for only a couple of hours today—shopping for new clothes to wear tonight—and it had seemed like an eternity.

Now, here she was, and there he was at the other end of the table. *Her soul mate.* There had been times she wondered if they'd make it to the mating. What had she decided? Trust in the process. It—with the help of his parents—had proved true.

They'd talked about nothing and everything in between their lovemaking. What they'd been like when they were young, how to get along in a family with siblings, how they'd decided on their talents and professions, what they liked and disliked in movies, books, food, music, art. The time had been like one long date where they got to know each other as they hadn't had the opportunity to do while running from one debate to the other.

Once Marcus relaxed and lightened up, he'd turned out to be a lot of fun. Oh, he still had a touch of stiffness, but he was learning to tease her back, and lo and behold, the man was ticklish!

He was also a generous, caring, wonderful lover. Now she understood why Daria went around with that fatuous, smug, blissful look on her face. Gloriana rubbed her cheeks to stop her own lips from curling upward.

She rested her chin on her hands and focused again on the audience. The very last debate. Hallelujah!

Ed was talking to John and Fergus. At least he was blocking her view of Marcus. Even glancing at each other was getting them in trouble. At lunch the editor had taken one look at them and said, "I'm certainly glad you two finally got together."

When asked what he was talking about, he'd said, "Soul mates, of course. It stuck out all over you from the beginning."

She had only been able to shake her head at his announcement. Marcus managed to mutter something about keeping it quiet, and Ed had agreed. The editor had grinned like W^2's circulation had doubled and warned them that rumors were flying after someone discovered they were in the same suite.

All they had to do was survive the last debate, and she and Marcus could go home and back to their normal lives—as normal as it could be getting used to having a soul mate. They'd called their parents at the farm and notified them that they'd come to a satisfactory conclusion. Her mother immediately started planning a party on Sunday and told Marcus she'd invite George and Evelyn and they'd bring Samson. Gloriana wasn't sure she was looking forward to the get-together. She was still coming to terms with the reality of Marcus and a soul mate, period, and the two of them could use some downtime.

Uh-oh. A flurry of activity by one of the doors brought Gloriana back to the present. Gordon Walcott and Bambi Kemble walked into the room with a swagger that dared anyone to take exception. The two fanatics took seats in the middle section on the aisle closest to the Traddies. Several of the THA supporters on the right pointed them out to others, yet didn't look happy about their presence. Word had gotten around about the vandalism and its possible perpetrators. Walcott denied participation in the stunt, but it looked like he had lost ground with both the middle and the THA. The woman sitting beside Kemble made the man next to her scoot over a chair so she could move away.

Fergus walked up the aisle and said something to Walcott, who only glared and shook his head. The eight Swords took their places, one standing directly in the aisle and slightly behind Walcott.

After all the preceding anxiety-causing events, the debate went smoothly. Ed announced the agreement by the THA and FOM to study both the formula and conventional methods of spell-casting. The High Council would be setting up study groups, and everyone should watch W^2 and the practitioner Web site for details. Prick and Horner reported on their attempts at casting by each method—some success, certainly worth pursuing—and each called for more study of the formula and tests of older procedures. Horner managed to put in a comment about the THA making sure there'd be no backsliding on the agreement, no rush to the future. Prick, of course, smirked and looked down his nose.

She and Marcus, practically alternating sentences, asked all practitioners to study magic methods together, reiterating that nobody was losing a thing by studying. Ed urged those with strong opinions not to tear the community apart.

Members of the audience had their chance to speak, and almost everyone who did told of their agreement with the end result of the debates. Gloriana began to think they had finally reached consensus when there was a stirring in the right middle.

Walcott stood in the aisle and took a microphone from an usher. Kemble came to stand behind him. The Swords became even more watchful, and the audience seemed to hold its collective breath. With an admonition to "watch it," Ed recognized the man.

"Would you look at the lovefest we have here? Let me offer a counterpoint," Walcott said in a totally calm, rational-sounding voice. He pointed at the FOM and continued in the same tone, "You people are crazy. Mindless followers of the new and sensational. You will burn in hell."

The hair on the back of Gloriana's neck rose at the contrast between his reasonable tone and his venomous words. The enraged glitter in the tall man's eyes disturbed her even more. Capping her sense of foreboding was his physical appearance. Although he had been thin before, the Walcott standing before them was almost cadaverous, his eyes more sunken, his pointed nose sharper. His skin was so translucent she could almost see the skull beneath it. Give him a robe and scythe, and he would be Death personified.

Walcott turned next to the THA. "As for you, you are unthinking philistines, sycophants, joining a cause but remaining with it long past its usefulness or its degeneration into the very enemy it was fighting against in the beginning. Worthless, every one of you."

He smiled benignly toward the audience in the middle. "And then there's you—stupid, ignorant fools willing to go along with the rest of the herd to the slaughterhouse. Sheep. You're little better than sheep."

The middle audience shifted in their seats. Fergus moved down the aisle from his position near the stage and stopped about fifteen feet from Walcott, who ignored him and kept speaking.

"These so-called debates have been nothing but a sham. As proof, look at our two debaters." Walcott pointed, first at Marcus, next at Gloriana. "We were led to believe they were complete antagonists, especially that Dr. Morgan was a true guardian of all that is right and good in spell-casting. Now they're calling for us all to work together on their heretical formula. Blasphemy."

Gloriana frowned and braced herself for his next words, sure to be a personal attack.

Walcott spread his hands and assumed an expression like he was laying out the only logical conclusion. "It's all been a ruse, an illusion. How do we know? Because of what was revealed today. Forscher and Morgan are soul mates. Yes, that's right, *soul mates*. How could they possibly disagree with each other? Furthermore, it's clear that the member of the weaker sex has been under her futurist soul mate's command all along. What else could we expect from a woman?"

An indefinable ripple of noise and movement blew through the audience. Did they agree or disagree? Facial expressions gave Gloriana no clue.

"I warn you," Walcott said, his tone becoming sharper, more strident, "the Force for True Magic will not agree to or abide by a takeover of our casting methods. We will do all in our power to stop it. I proclaim all of them, the instigators of this farce, the THA, and the FOM, to be traitors to what should be the cause of all practitioners—the preservation of our magical heritage. Beware, for they will bring destruction! We of the Force for True Magic will fight them! Follow me or be doomed to perdition!"

He tossed the microphone to Fergus, spun around, and stalked out of the room, with Kemble on his heels. Nobody in the audience moved.

Ed stood. "Does anyone else have something to say?"

A cane waved in the middle of the Traddies.

"I recognize Mrs. Bernice Shortbottom."

Looking like she was about to burst, whether with excitement or indignation Gloriana couldn't tell, Mrs. Shortbottom waited for the microphone to reach her. When she had it, she exclaimed in a voice that bounced off the walls, "*Soul mates?* You two are soul mates?"

Gloriana felt the heat rising in her face and shot a glance at Marcus, who shrugged. "Yes, ma'am," she answered, "we recently found out."

Mrs. Shortbottom beamed. "Oh, that's sooooo sweet. Best wishes to both of you. I attended the first of these debates, and if you and Dr. Forscher can get along, especially as soul mates, after all the arguments and contention, there's hope for us all. Hip hooray for love!" She began to clap, others joined her, and before long, everybody had risen in a standing ovation.

When the applause subsided, Ed laughed and said, "A fitting end to these proceedings. Watch W^2 for later developments in the research and study. Thank you all for coming."

After the audience filed out, Gloriana, Marcus, Ed, and the Swords met as usual.

"What's the matter with Walcott?" Ed asked. "He looked like death warmed over."

"Something's wrong," Fergus answered. "I'm picking up strange vibes."

"Me, too. Almost like . . . well, never mind," John said with a frown. "We're going to keep an eye on him, and everybody be careful a while longer. I hope he turned off possible followers with that crazy speech."

"One good thing resulted from it, at least," Ed interjected with a grin. "Everybody's together on the soul-mate question."

Gloriana felt herself blushing again and quickly changed the subject. "We're leaving early tomorrow morning, so we won't be around if Walcott decides to take out his anger on someone."

"If you have a problem with anyone, let us all know," John said. "We're still investigating the vandalism, and if Walcott's behind it, we'll find out. If we prove it, the High Council may want to censure him for his trouble-making. These actions certainly go against every code of practitioner ethics."

CHAPTER
THIRTY-SIX

Sunday afternoon, Marcus and Gloriana walked off the plane in Austin and straight into the arms of their parents. There was more hugging in the next few minutes than he had seen, much less been a part of, in years—no, forever—Marcus reflected as he extricated himself from Antonia's exuberant embrace. He did have to admit, it had all felt damn good.

Alaric drove Gloriana's car home, and she rode with Marcus to the farm. When they left the airport, she asked, "How are you? You looked a little overwhelmed back there."

"I'm all right. Not used to so much family, I guess."

"Brace yourself. Mother said the Houston four and George and Evelyn are here."

He couldn't help but sigh.

She laughed. "We'll plead jet lag, and maybe they'll

let us leave early."

"That won't work, either. George will tease us about wanting to go to bed, and *not* to sleep, and he'll probably tell us some interminable story about when he and Evelyn met."

"Oh, I didn't think about that. Clay will be obnoxious, too, especially since he'll be getting back at me for teasing him when he and Francie got together."

"I'm still staying the night, right?"

"Of course. I'm really glad I have my own house. We'll have some privacy."

"Do you have something planned for the week?" he asked, an idea forming in his mind.

"Nope, only catching up. Why?"

"Why don't I go home tomorrow, do what needs to be done there, and come back out for a couple of days? I've been thinking about the magic-potential results of our mating and the equation, and I'd like to try some experiments. What you told me enabled me to learn the strength spell, and we could start with it. Maybe we can work on calibration, also."

"I'd like to do more with our lightballs, too. Let's show them to everybody and see if they merge again."

He laughed. "I can't wait to see the look on George's face."

"And on Clay's," she snickered.

In the living room after dinner, they each cast *lux*. Everybody congratulated them on their magic-level increases. The lightballs, however, sat there in the air, not moving. Marcus looked at Gloriana, who was standing by the fireplace, and raised his eyebrows.

She frowned, but her face cleared, and she sat down next to him on the sofa and whispered, "Put your arm around me. We were touching when they merged before."

He did, and the spheres started moving—and merging and humming.

Several people made exclamations, and George and Clay came over to the orbs for a closer look.

"What the hell's going on?" George asked.

"What's with the hum?" Clay poked the merging balls. "Ouch!"

"What happened?" George asked, and he brought his finger close to the object. A tiny spark jumped to his finger. "Ow!"

Marcus grinned at Gloriana, who winked. "We didn't try that," he whispered.

"We're not moving the balls. They're on maintenance as far as our energy is concerned. We don't know what's causing the merging or the hum—or the resulting larger ball," she told their audience. "We didn't show it to anyone in San Francisco, either. I'm hoping Lulabelle might have heard of such a development."

"Be careful with the thing, will you?" Clay asked, studying his finger.

"Oooh, poor baby," Gloriana smirked. "George, no comments from you, either. We'll tell you when we find out the cause."

Marcus leaned back and relaxed. Everything was going to be fine. Gloriana could handle all the family stuff. She would protect him.

                    ≈✦✧✦✦≈

On Tuesday morning, Gloriana and Marcus were sitting down in her kitchen to try out some spells when Marcus's cell phone rang. John was on the line, and Marcus put the phone on speaker so they both could hear it.

"We've got the goods on Walcott," John said. "Kemble ratted on him to us, and the High Council's going to censure him. Bambi confessed to being the one who wrecked your hotel suites, on his command, of course. She got angry when he began to treat her like an underling instead of a partner, and she finally realized he wanted absolute control of everything, not only spell-casting. She got scared when he started threatening to put a stop to our plans—and to you."

"What should we do?" Marcus asked.

"Sit tight. According to Kemble, he's still out here in California, and we've sent Swords to pick him up. She's telling us some disturbing facts about him, but he doesn't like to do his own dirty work, and after his last performance, his few supporters left him. We doubt he'll try another threat or action before we can bring him in."

"We're both at the farm," Marcus said.

"Good. Stay there, and we'll inform you when we have him."

They thanked John, and Marcus clicked the button to end the call. "I guess all we can do is carry on."

"Fine with me. We have enough to think about." She spread out the spell books she had put on the table. "I found these in Mother's attic. Clay and I used them growing up. Daria certainly tried to use them, but the only spells she can throw are on herself and after their mating, on Bent."

Marcus picked one up and leafed through it. "Let's see. Looks like basic, low-level, universal spells. We have strength, speed, levitation—I could never do that—and a few illusions like putting a ball or box around yourself. Oh, here's some arithmetic ones for addition, subtraction, multiplication, and division. I can already cast those."

"Me, too," Gloriana said. "Let's try one we don't know. I've never managed to levitate, either."

"The instructions say to choose a small, lightweight object. The weight of the object you can lift will depend on such variables as your power, your level, and your talent. Of course." He shook his head and returned to the directions. "Concentrate on the object, transfer some of your energy to it, visualize it rising, and activate the energy. I assume the transference and activation are like lighting a candle. The key words are *levo* or *levare*."

She took a sheet from a notepad and ripped it into

several strips. "Okay, here's some small pieces of paper. They should be light enough to start. You go first. I'm more used to manipulating actual objects than you are. I can make a vine twine around a trellis, for example."

"Here goes nothing." He accessed his magic center, where the increased amount of power he found still thrilled him. Concentrating as though he was casting *flamma*, he transferred the energy, saw in his mind's eye the paper floating in the air. "*Levo!*"

The paper rose about an inch off the tabletop.

Before Marcus could congratulate himself, however, it burst into flames.

"Oh, damn!" Gloriana grabbed a dish towel off the counter next to her and covered the paper to put out the fire. "What happened?"

"I was concentrating energy like I do for *flamma*. I guess I forgot to make the energy cool, not hot." He shrugged, then had to grin. "At least I did get the paper off the table. You have to give me that."

She looked down her nose at him after she wiped up the ashes. "This, Dr. Forscher, is what I meant about the 'messiness' of magic." And she laughed.

He made a disgruntled face at her and pushed a piece of paper in her direction. "Your turn."

Within seconds, she had the paper floating about three inches above the surface. "I'm going to put it on maintenance like a lightball."

She slid her body around in the chair and away from

the table. "What's it doing?"

"Sitting there. I'm going to try again," he said as she faced front.

Soon his paper was floating next to hers. "Let's try moving them."

They floated the papers around the room for a couple of minutes. "That's like moving a lightball," she said after the papers were sitting on the table again.

"How about something heavier?"

She rose, went over to the couch in the living room, and brought back a thick magazine. "Here, and it's not breakable."

Neither of them could budge the heavier object. The most either achieved was to make the cover flutter.

"I guess we reached our limit," Marcus said and nudged the magazine with a finger to make sure it hadn't glued itself to the table. "Our talents don't run to more than lifting a feather. No matter. The only thing I ever really wanted to levitate to bring it to me was the TV remote."

"What if . . .?" Gloriana was staring off into space.

"What?"

"I've been thinking about our merged lightball that shows a higher combined power than we have individually. Maybe we're not going about the process right."

"Okay, let's try a combined effort." He scooted his chair around next to hers and put his arm around her. "Concentrate and activate on the count of three. One, two, three."

They cast simultaneously, and all of the pages rif-
fled up and down as if through a reader's fingers, but the
magazine itself didn't move.

"More power," he said, mentally reaching into his
center and feeding energy steadily to the book.

The object sluggishly rose, a wobbling movement
that stopped about four inches up. A slight hum droned
in the background.

"Okay," she said after a few seconds, "I can feel my
energy flowing toward the magazine, and that's normal.
What's weird is, I can feel yours, too."

He studied his power output and its target, then
hers. "You're right. I can almost 'see' another stream
coming from you."

"Can we combine energy, so there's only one
stream?"

"Good idea. Our power combines in the big lightball. Why not here?" At the suggestion, his center
seemed to perk up and gather his increased energy into
a tight formation. "I'm going to try to direct my energy
to you. See if you can channel all of it toward the book.
One, two, three."

She jumped slightly. "Oh. I can feel your surge.
Wow, what a feeling. I'm tingling all over. If I can increase the power . . ."

The hum grew in volume, and the magazine rose
another two inches. Marcus fed more energy to her, and

the book elevated another inch.

"I'm cutting power," Gloriana said after about thirty seconds. "Constant output is exhausting, and I can feel my power quantity diminishing."

Marcus ceased his energy projection also, and the magazine fell with a small thud. "How do you feel?"

"Tired but exhilarated. It was easy to combine our energies. Made me feel like I could cast almost any spell with that amount of power behind me."

"Power . . ." An idea was suddenly hovering in the air, right before his eyes. What was he seeing? He stared at the magazine for a moment. What had she said about power quantity? The answer practically hit him in the head. "Oh, it's been right there in front of us from the beginning."

"What? What are you talking about?"

"We've been going about calibration all wrong. Think about energy and the amount you have. I've been assuming, as I think others have, that we needed to specify exactly how much power to apply to a spell. What if we don't have to assign a finite value? What if we don't have to say, 'expend X amount of ergs or dynes or amps or volts or some other specific measure'?"

The rightness of his questions resonated inside him, exactly like the solution to an equation did, and he eagerly followed them to the next logical step. "What if . . . What if each practitioner defines his amount of power for himself? When I pushed my *lux* to a higher level after our mating, what I've always considered to be the 'well,' the container, of power in my center expanded like crazy. I could actually feel it grow. What if we think of our energy resource like a well or a box or another sort of container?"

"Oh, that's interesting," she said, and he could see the idea take hold in her mind. "Since a person's amount of power is finite and varies by level and individual, and you know or can feel intuitively how much you have, how much you're using, and what's left, then . . ."

He grinned at her in triumph. "We can speak in generalities, percentages, instead of absolutes. That woman at the first debate asked how much a cup of power was. You don't have to work according to someone else's scale. It's your cup. You used percentages to describe your casting process for strength when you explained it to me. I used them, measuring against percentages of my own cup when learning the spell, only I didn't realize it."

"Aha!" She poked him in the chest.

"What?"

"See, you do use intuition in casting! You can't do it all by the numbers."

He thought about that, looked at her grinning mouth, and kissed it. "I surrender. You're right."

"So are you. I'm thinking these days in formulaic terms. I have all these math symbols and ideas in my dreams."

"That's funny. I'm looking at plants more carefully.

I even tried to cast a growth spell on my ivy plant before we mated. Didn't work, but something—my intuition?—compelled me to try it."

"Looks like the soul-mate phenomenon is merging more than our lightballs—maybe our talents, too. Why don't we head for some plants and try out some spells?"

They spent the day in a greenhouse full of herbs working on casting and energy sharing—with only mixed success. When he was directing energy, Marcus couldn't make a plant grow, even in combination with Gloriana. He could and did push some of his mathematical spells to his new level. She, however, could cause even greater growth when channeling the energy from him.

Antonia came out to see what they were up to, and after trying a few spells, she became enthusiastic for the idea of a power well of the practitioner's making.

Her mother also noticed something—when the two of them were casting together, concentrating on the same object, and touching each other, their individual spell auras coalesced into one. Usually practitioners couldn't see their own auras, which stuck close to the caster's body, while family members could. In their case, however, neither Marcus nor Gloriana could see each other's aura, even though Antonia said the combined aura extended some inches from their bodies.

Although the aura combination made sense, given the energy sharing and their merged lightballs, where it might lead was another question to which they had no answer. Furthermore, Marcus had no idea how that fact or the reality of it might be incorporated into the equation. He'd expected the need for a number of equations, but it looked like the amount would grow exponentially.

Man, spell-casting got more and more complicated, the deeper they investigated it.

CHAPTER
THIRTY-SEVEN

As they were leaving the house for dinner, another call came from John. "I don't think you have to worry about it, but Walcott left for Texas. He could be simply going home to Waco. He's found out about the censure, and if he has any smarts at all, he'll go to ground and not stick his head up. We're on our way in a High Council plane to pick him up and deliver him to the council for their actions."

"Do we need to do something actively?" Marcus asked.

"No," John replied, "Keep an eye out and call if he shows up. I suggest refusing to talk to him. He's only going to spew more of his usual rantings."

"Okay," Gloriana said. "We'll throw him off the property."

Marcus and Gloriana relayed the news to their parents at dinner, and everybody agreed to be on watch.

Other than that, what could they do? So they turned to their attention to their spell-casting ideas. Soon light-balls and mathematical and physics equations were flying around the room.

After dinner, Gloriana sat back and watched the interplay. Marcus's parents had certainly loosened up under her family's influence. Stefan and Alaric were comparing the differences between displaying computations in the air—Stefan's and Marcus's method—versus highlights on paper as Alaric did in his auditing. Judith and Antonia were using glasses and bowls for visual aids to determine "well size."

She, however, was pooped, and Marcus was looking somewhat tired, so she announced, "I've had enough casting for one day. Y'all keep going. I need to check on something at my jungle."

"I'll go with you," Marcus said.

The parents said good night and quickly resumed their spell discussions.

"Do you really have to check on the jungle?" Marcus asked as they walked to his car. "And thanks, by the way, for getting us out of there."

"Yes, I do need to check on a setting. One of the pumps has been acting up. I meant to do it earlier, but we got involved in the spells. By the way, where are the dogs? I haven't seen them since before dinner."

"They're around somewhere, I'm sure. The last time I saw them, they were headed in the direction of your house. I'll drive by there first."

They got into the car and started down the road. Gloriana snuck a glance at him. He'd certainly relaxed over the past few days. Oh, he remained intense when he looked at her, thank goodness. She still got a thrill from exchanging gazes. He and his parents appeared to be mending fences and making up for lost time, although she thought he might be still on the lookout for disapproval.

One indication of his relaxation was his changing the car's radio station. Thank goodness. George Strait was preferable to that jazz he usually had on—although she was beginning to develop an appreciation for it. Yet another change in her thinking and preferences.

She was wondering idly what other alterations, besides those already identified, the phenomenon was making in both of them when she realized he was singing along with the radio. The station was playing "Can I Trust You With My Heart." There was a song she could relate to. She started singing, too, and he reached for her hand, brought it to his lips, and kissed the back of her fingers.

The song ended as they came to her house. He slowed the car, and they saw Samson and Delilah lying together on the welcome mat. The dogs looked up and didn't move otherwise. "Okay, they're fine," he said and pointed the vehicle toward her jungle.

Once through the two doors and inside the glass structure, she turned on the dim, ground-level lights that outlined the path through the growth.

"Whoa, spooky," he said, looking up. "I can barely see the treetops and only because the moon's shining through the glass. I'm glad you don't have man-eating animals in here."

She laughed. She'd forgotten that he hadn't been in the jungle in the dark. "Only Sassy's lurking on his branch. Remember Clay's toy? The control room is over here."

She led him around one bend and behind the trees and bushes on the outer wall side of the computerized python's clearing. She hit the switch when they entered, and the bright illumination was jarring.

"I suppose I could have cast *lux*, but to be honest, I'm tired of casting," she said. "The only other bright lighting in the building is at the cabana. I wanted to leave the rest as jungle-like as possible."

"You certainly did that. If you hadn't showed me, I'd never have found my way here, light or no light," he replied and pointed to an object on the table. "What's that?"

"What? Oh, that's the remote control for Sassy."

"Can I try it?" He picked it up.

"Sure. I'll be finished here in a couple of minutes."

He picked up the implement and went back into the plant area. When she completed her adjustments, he reappeared.

"I played a little too vigorously, I'm afraid, and he slithered so far he fell off the branch. Where's a stepladder?"

They put Sassy on his perch and the ladder and

remote control back in their places. When she shut off the lights in the control room, she said, "I need to check the connection in back of the cabana, and we're done."

They followed the path around two more bends to the open area. She flicked the switches on a post holding up the palm-frond roof to turn on the waterfall and pool lights and manipulated the dimmer until only a soft glow illuminated the cabana. She went behind it and checked on the pumps residing inside their cabinetry while he walked around, looking at the waterfall and the plants.

When she came out of the pump room, he stepped up onto the cabana deck.

"What's this plant?" he asked, pointing to a pot with a small, fuzzy-leafed, purple-blossomed plant on one of the small tables by the double chaise. "Why isn't it out with the rest of them?"

"That's an African violet I rescued from one of my friends. It doesn't like much water. I was taking it to another greenhouse but forgot it when I got sidetracked by the pump the other day . . ."

Her voice trailed off as she looked at him and her mind took off on a different tangent entirely. It was still hard to believe that he was hers. She had no problem being absolutely certain she was his, but the reverse continued to surprise her. When he returned her gaze, she could feel the pull between them. The last thing she wanted to talk about at the moment was plants. They were alone here. Why not take advantage of it?

Swinging her hips more than usual, she sauntered over to him and ran her hands up his chest and around his neck. He immediately put his arms around her and pulled her close.

Pitching her tone low and sultry, she asked, "Ever made love in a jungle?"

"Not till now." His blue eyes twinkled, and he bent to scoop her up.

"Uh-uh." She took a step backward and gave him a mock frown. "My jungle, my rules."

"Glori, Queen of the Jungle, huh? Okay, command me, my queen."

His grin melted her insides, and she hid her reaction and looked him up and down. "You have too many clothes on for a jungle. Take them off."

"Down to what? My underwear?"

"Down to the skin." While he followed her commands and she stripped off her own clothes, she walked around in back of him and watched the interplay of his muscles and bones. Damn, he was so perfect. She sent a little thanks to the soul-mate phenomenon for its gift.

When he was down to nothing, he moved to face her. She stopped him with her hands on his shoulders. "Just stand there."

She ran her hands down his back and squeezed his butt. He stiffened, and she noticed his hands clenching. She slid her hands around his waist to his front and up his chest. Under her touch, his muscles hardened even more. Her movement brought her breasts into contact with his back. He must not have realized she, too, was naked, because he inhaled sharply. She kissed his back between his shoulder blades, once, twice, three times, and rubbed her front over his back.

He raised his hands, probably to capture hers, until she tapped his chest and said, "Not yet."

When she dropped her hands to his waist and lower still to run fingers through his springy curls, finally to hold his erection, he hissed and threw his head back. Through her cheek pressed against his back, she could feel his heartbeat increase.

The hum started, pulsating in her eardrums, and her blood heated as her heart speeded up to match his.

It wasn't enough. She had to be closer.

She moved her hands to his hips and turned him to face her. His gaze was intense, and every muscle in his body was steel hard under her fingers. Happily, he was still playing by her rules.

"Lie down," she ordered, and he lay on the chaise. She followed and straddled him, bracing herself on her hands and knees to lean down and kiss him. His hands came up to cup her breasts, and the familiar zings flashed from her nipples to her womb when he fondled them. The hum increased in tempo and intensity as she lowered herself until he was inside her all the way.

As she looked into his eyes, the playful ideas she'd had when she began this game evaporated like water in the Sahara before the heat in his gaze.

He pulled her down into a kiss that transformed in the time of two heartbeats from warm to hot to blazing to incandescent.

Her control slipped, then fell away altogether, when his touch grew more urgent and she began to move up and down on him. He changed his grip from her breasts to her hips and thrust in counterpoint. Their magic centers aligned and met with each thrust. Within seconds, they were pounding together. He added a twist of his hips that increased her frenzy until her world consisted of him and her and the deep, sonorous hum and swirling magical energy. They strained together toward . . . toward . . . an explosive, prolonged merging . . . until finally, nirvana.

Sometime later he stirred first, and she raised up on her arms again. He smiled and tucked her hair behind her ears. "Glori, you simply blow me away."

"The feeling is mutual, or couldn't you tell? To be absolutely clear, I love you very much."

"I love you, too, Glori." He said the words very seriously as if to be sure she understood. He shook his head and rolled his eyes. "To think, I wanted to reject it all. God, what an idiot I was."

"Nah, in the end I wouldn't have let you. I don't know what I'd have done, but it would have been something." She gave him her evil little-sister smile.

"Oh, I'm sure of that." He laughed and gave her a hug. "Listen, I could stay right here forever, but if we don't get up soon, we never will."

She groaned and looked at her watch. "It's going on midnight. Let's get moving."

They rose and started dressing.

"Now, that's peculiar," he said a minute later.

"What?"

"The African violet. It wasn't that big or had that many flowers when I first noticed it."

She came over to take a better look. "You're right. How on earth . . ." She felt the leaves and the soil and counted the flowers. It had almost doubled in size. She measured the distance from the chaise to the table with her eyes. The answer she arrived at caused her to gasp. "Oh, my God, Marcus. We did that. We must have. It's our combined spell aura. The magical energy, the hum—the plant must have been inside our spell-aura diameter, and that caused it to grow."

He stared at her. "Antonia said our aura only extended a few inches."

"We were certainly merging our bodies, and energy was flowing through both of us. The combined aura must be growing in the process like the bigger lightball."

"Okay, if you're correct, we've yet to see what else the soul-mate phenomenon has done to us." He waved at the chaise. "What we went through here was almost as powerful to me as the bonding experience."

She nodded. "For me, too."

"We were expending a great amount of energy,

much more than previously, so it stands to reason our aura could have expanded. But how did the plant grow without a specific spell to guide it or push it or whatever?"

"I don't know." She spread her hands in helplessness and shook her head. "Oh, man, we have to get to some teaching masters or somebody who can help us find out what's going on. First the merged lightballs, next the ability to learn spells previously outside of our usual talents, after that to merge energy, and now an output of energy that causes results without our intervention."

"Or maybe it's your subconscious casting spells you've already learned, like the plant growth one," he offered. "I agree, we need to get to the bottom of it, no matter what. Not right now, though. It's too late to do that tonight."

"Then let's go home." She switched off the cabana lights. Hand in hand, they walked the dimly lit, winding path to the entry.

"Someone's coming," Marcus said, looking out through the glass of the inner and outer doors.

"Who?" She did likewise. A car was coming down the road.

A big white Cadillac pulled up next to Marcus's car. Under the light above the outer door, Gordon Walcott got out.

CHAPTER THIRTY-EIGHT

"What's he doing here?" Marcus whispered as he watched Walcott reach back into the car and come out with an object—a gun, a semiautomatic, from the looks of it. "Oh, shit. John was wrong about him. Come on, we need to get out of here."

"There's no back door. When we bring in a tree, we have to remove sections of the wall. That is the only way out, and the glass in the walls is too thick to break easily. The front door is locked, and"—she manipulated the lever on the inner door—"so is this one."

"That won't hold him long," Marcus said, pulling her back into the jungle.

"Wait. Let me turn off the path lights." She flipped the switch. "Take my hand."

"What about a phone? Can we call our parents?" he asked as she led him quickly through the darkness.

Walcott began to beat on the outer door and shout,

"Forscher! Morgan, you witch! I saw the lights. I know you're in there. The time for retribution has arrived, traitors."

"There's no phone out here," Gloriana said. "Mine's in my purse in your car."

"Great, and mine's at your house because I didn't think I'd need it."

Walcott started banging on the door with something metal, and a crash of breaking glass told them he'd made it through the first door.

"Damn," Gloriana said. "I hoped the wire reinforcement in the glass would hold longer than that."

"If we can sneak past him, we can make a run for it, but he'll probably follow us. I don't want to lead him to our parents."

"Me, neither."

Walcott started beating on the inner door.

"We've got to get the drop on him somehow," Marcus said when they stopped in front of the control room. "Start the rain. That'll slow him down."

"Here's something to use as a weapon," she said, stepping around the corner and opening a door in the outer side of the room. She pulled out a machete and a crowbar.

He hefted the machete. "Good."

She went into the control room and started manipulating the pump mechanisms by the glow of the LED displays. "It will take a few minutes to fully charge the system."

"Get it started. I'll create a diversion to slow him

down. Give me the remote, too."

She handed it to him. "Be careful, Marcus. I love you."

"I will, and I love you, too." Funny, the words got easier to say, and hearing them became more pleasurable every time. He couldn't stop to think about that at the moment. He had to do something to protect Gloriana. The glass broke on the inner door with another crash. He felt his way into the thick bushes close to Sassy's lair.

"Where are you, you bastards?" Walcott yelled. "You're destroying magic and I'm going to stop you if it's the last thing I do."

Marcus heard Walcott cursing, but he didn't seem to be moving. A little blip of green light glowed through the leaves from a location by the door, and the path lights came on.

"Aha, got you now," Walcott called. He appeared at the opening from the path into Sassy's clearing. A green lightball bobbed in the air beside his head.

The color of the ball didn't help to penetrate all the green around it, however, and Marcus sneered silently at the seventh-to-eighth-level son of a bitch. Walcott didn't even realize what a perfect target the globe made.

If the man would come a little closer . . . Marcus hit Sassy's power button. A flash of red light from the python's eyes showed the snake was working.

Holding the gun out with two hands like they did in cop shows, Walcott advanced slowly into the clearing.

"You must come out and face the consequences of your lies," he said in that calm conversational tone he'd used back at the debate. "You'll never get away from me."

Marcus gauged his distances carefully. When Walcott reached the point directly under the python, Marcus started the toy moving. Sassy dropped right on the thin man's head.

"Yaaaagh!" Flailing his arms and almost hitting himself in the head with the gun, Walcott knocked the snake off his shoulder. When it lay on the ground wiggling, he shot it two times, then once more. His ball of light had disappeared in the excitement, and he recast it after he stared at the toy's remains for a few seconds.

A loud "CLICK" in the ceiling above the clearing brought his eyes up.

And the rain came down in a deluge like Gloriana had upended a huge bucket.

The woman herself appeared at Marcus's side and tugged him down to say in his ear over the thunder of the rain, "Are you all right? I heard shots."

"Yeah. He shot poor Sassy, though. He's so agitated, he can't seem to hold his lightball together. If it weren't for the gun, we could take him down easily."

"The flood will only last a few minutes. I've got an idea. Let's lure him into the next narrow portion of the path. If we can get him close to the vines there, we might be able to use our combined power to ensnare him."

Marcus thought about that for all of a second. It was

likely the only chance they had. Walcott might decide to start shooting, and who knew what might happen when bullets started flying. At the moment, the man was revolving in a circle in the clearing, holding his free hand like a visor over his eyes to try to see through the rain. The other held the gun in a ready position. The lightball had disappeared again, probably washed away.

What about a frontal attack? No. It would be difficult, if not impossible, to get through the undergrowth quickly enough to tackle him before he could shoot, and throwing the machete wasn't a sure way to disarm him. Using one of them as a decoy wasn't acceptable; no way would he expose Gloriana to a madman. Furthermore, sneaking past him to run would only lead him to their parents. It was either her idea or an unacceptable alternative. "Okay, let's go for it."

She pulled him out of the bushes, across the path leading from the clearing to the cabana, and into the thickly growing plants on its other side. The path narrowed to less than three feet, but the planted area between its loops was broad and supplied plenty of cover. They squeezed in between a good-sized tree and a big-leaved bush. The tree offered some protection if Walcott tried to shoot, and, while they were effectively hidden, they had a clear view of anyone on the path itself.

Pointing to the overhanging limbs and the vines climbing a tree trunk barely visible across the way, she said, "Those right there."

He put his arm around her and pulled her close. "Start casting. I'll try to get him coming in our direction." He felt the hum begin when their centers aligned.

"Hey, Walcott!" Marcus yelled as loud as he could. "Go to hell!"

The fanatic shouted something back, although Marcus couldn't make out the words through the rain. Marcus bellowed epithets once more, calling the asshole every name he could think of.

He shut up when Walcott stuck his head around the corner of the path next to a big elephant-ear leaf. The idiot had *lux* going again at a yellow fifth level, and its puny light was swallowed up by the dark and the downpour.

As suddenly as it had started, the rain stopped.

Only dripping water, Walcott's heavy breathing, and the spell hum broke the silence. If he would only come forward a few more feet . . .

Marcus started sending energy to Gloriana. He could feel their hearts beating in unison, their centers working together, the magical power of her spell reaching out from them to the vines on the other side of the path. She had been correct about their auras; energy flowing between them charged the very air. He only prayed the auras weren't visible somehow to Walcott.

The dim lights reflecting off the wet leaves and the idiot's feeble *lux* spell only marginally improved visibility. Walcott advanced a step at a time, the gun out in front of him. He looked like a bedraggled skinny rat, his thinning hair plastered to his skull, sharp nose almost twitching as if he was trying to smell them.

Marcus saw a couple of vine leaves on the tree trunk wiggle. One tendril, then another, reached out into the open space. Hanging from an overhead tree limb directly over the path, a larger one as thick as his thumb began to sway and grow longer.

Walcott took two more steps, stopped, spun around, and whirled again toward his previous direction. His lightball rushed frantically to follow him, but his movements were too quick, and it almost hit him in the head. Cursing, he shoved it aside.

Marcus held Gloriana tighter, and she, with her arms around his waist, gripped his sodden shirt in her fists. Their magic centers were circulating power like they had when they'd bonded—and the energy flowing between them was growing exponentially by the second. He sank into his power well, drew forth about half of it, and sent it mentally to hers. She threw it immediately into her spell. The hum dropped an octave, intensified.

Walcott shook his head and took a hand from the gun to rub his ears as he stepped forward two more paces—right next to the tree vines and directly under the hanging one. Before he could put his hand back on the gun, a tendril from the tree tapped him on the back of his head.

He jumped and looked around wildly. He must

have decided the threat would come from one end of the path or the other because he backed up to the wall of vines. The whites of his eyes showing even through the gloom, he shot glances to his left and his right.

Despite what appeared to be his growing apprehension, Walcott spoke in that earlier oh-so-reasonable tone when he said, "Come out, come out, wherever you are. You can't escape me."

Marcus would have laughed in derision if he'd been able, but the spell and swirling energy absorbed all his attention. Glori was gathering more power and flinging it at the vines. He poured more into her well.

As she took his energy, she directed it to one place, and the hanging tendril lashed out at Walcott and knocked the gun away. Before the man could move, Glori changed the direction of her power flow to the green wall behind him. The vines at his back snaked forward to wrap around his arms. Walcott began to struggle and shout, but the plants held him tight and encircled him more densely. His lightball flashed up through green into blue before disappearing altogether.

"You can't do this to me!" Walcott screamed as he fought. "I have powers. I'll crush you. I'll smear your blood from one end of your damned jungle to the other."

"Cut the energy," Gloriana whispered. "The vines will hold him."

She ended the spell, and Marcus was glad they were

holding on to each other. The cessation of energy flow made him slightly dizzy, and it took a few seconds to regain his equilibrium. They hadn't moved, however, when they heard several people yelling their names and the dogs adding their calls to the din. The humans sounded like John, Fergus, and their parents.

CHAPTER THIRTY-NINE

Gleaming blades drawn, the two Swords came around the bend, two bright silver lightballs floating in the air above them and dissipating the darkness. They stopped in their tracks to stare at Walcott, who was still shouting a stream of invectives, although he had ceased struggling against the confining greenery.

"Marcus! Gloriana!" John shouted as Alaric joined the two men.

"We're here," Marcus said, not really surprised when his voice came out in a croak.

Keeping a grip on each other, he and Gloriana emerged from the bushes. He still wasn't sure either of them could stand alone. Walcott subsided when he saw them and sagged against his restraints.

"What happened? Are you all right?" Fergus asked.

"We're fine. Wet, and a little tired," Gloriana answered in a weak tone.

"This wild man wanted to kill us. His gun's around here somewhere," Marcus said.

"Here it is." Alaric picked up the gun on the edge of the path.

"Hold on to that," John said while he studied the ensnared Walcott. "It certainly looks like you handled him. We tried calling you once we found out where he was headed, but all we got was voice mail."

"We don't have our phones with us," Gloriana said.

"I switched ours to the answering machine so we wouldn't be interrupted at dinner," Alaric put in.

"No matter," Fergus said. "Alaric, why don't you tell Stefan and the ladies that Marcus and Gloriana are all right. We must settle something here with Walcott before we do anything else, and we need to ask our newest soul mates some questions."

"Will do," Alaric answered. "The ambulance has arrived, and we've managed to get the dogs in our car before they cut themselves on the glass."

"Please tell the medics to stand by and ask Hal to come in."

Alaric nodded and left.

"Ambulance?" Marcus asked, noting that, despite the calm, the Swords had not sheathed their weapons. "What's going on?"

"Did Walcott throw a spell on you?" John asked. "Get close enough to touch you?"

"No," Marcus said, and Gloriana shook her head.

"Good. We don't have to worry about decontamination," John said. He spread his hands apart, and his sword dissipated. "You see, Kemble told us that Walcott has some kind of crystal or stone he uses to focus. He's had it only three weeks, and when he pulls it out, she gets a queasy feeling. It's time we saw that item. You two stay where you are. Ready, Fergus?"

The big Sword nodded, and his blade glowed brighter as he raised it. "Ready."

John approached Walcott, who began to struggle again, but feebly. Baldwin held up his hands in front of the thin man's chest for a few seconds, nodded, and removed Walcott's tie and unbuttoned his shirt. When John spread the shirt open, he said, "Looks like we were correct."

Marcus watched as John lifted a chain over Walcott's head. At the end of the loop dangled a dime-sized, yellowish crystal with streaks of green—a half-sharp-edged, half-semi-melted crystal—in a silver wire cage. It looked like a distorted lump of vomit to Marcus, and it gave off a foul odor and an even more fetid wave of magic power. He kept his arms tight around Gloriana, and she held herself more closely to him.

"What you see here is a genuine evil magic item," Fergus said. "Feels like only a level two or three from here. We surmised that something besides magical fervor or a true disagreement with the sides in the debate was driving Walcott, especially once he started using threats and then violence. He'd never behaved like that previously. We haven't learned how he obtained it yet, but we will."

A stocky white-haired man came around the corner carrying a big, pentagon-shaped suitcase. Baldwin introduced him as Hal Thomas, a member of his Defender team. Hal said hello, set the case down, and opened it.

"What do you think, Fergus? Destroy it here?" John asked. When Fergus nodded, John turned to Gloriana. "What's below the building? Particularly this path? Concrete? Dirt?"

"Dirt and rocks," Gloriana said. "Some plumbing pipes. The pipes are mostly along the walls, and there are none under the path."

"Good. With your permission, we're going to destroy the item. That's our procedure when we find one small and weak enough for the two of us to handle. Doing so should not harm you, your greenhouse, or the plants. Is that all right with you?"

She looked up at Marcus and smiled. "As long as we can stay to watch."

"Yes," Marcus said. "I want to see destroyed what's given us such grief."

"Okay. We usually don't allow 'civilians' to watch. I see no problem, however with making an exception here, seeing what he and it put you through. Stand over there"—John pointed to a spot several feet away—"and once we start, don't move, no matter what happens. Understood?"

"Understood," Marcus and Gloriana said together.

"How do you feel?" Marcus asked when they reached their designated spot.

"Exhausted, but, hot damn! It worked. The merging of power and spell actually worked. I know our auras expanded. How about you?"

"I feel like I've run two marathons to the top of Mount Everest and back."

"I'm sure I've lost weight, and my legs feel like rubber. We'll get something to eat soon. That should help."

They fell silent as they watched the Swords and Defender set themselves up. Hal spread out a black cloth blanket on the path and placed the suitcase on it. From the case he took a platter and a shallow bowl, both of clear crystal. He closed the luggage and placed the platter on it and the bowl on top of the platter. After making sure everything was aligned precisely, he left in the direction of the door.

John held the pendant directly over the bowl and cast a spell. The wire cage bent and opened, and the crystal fell into the bowl.

Gloriana made a growling sound, and Marcus grunted when a fist of nausea hit him in the stomach.

"Feel that?" Fergus asked. "Sort of a sickening wave? That's one of the signs of an evil item, and it's easy to spot. Walcott was smart enough not to wear the thing at the HeatherRidge. Too many Swords and Defenders are ultrasensitive. We'd have stopped him immediately."

Hal came back with two emergency medical technicians from the ambulance, who took up position by Walcott. "These guys are from the medical facility in the HeatherRidge," he said.

"What's with the crew?" Marcus asked.

"Destruction of an evil item usually knocks out its user," Hal answered. "Destroying the larger ones can kill whoever's been under its control. Yes, in reality the item does control the practitioner, although it tricks the person to think he's doing the controlling."

"Walcott said something about 'having powers,'" Gloriana said.

"An item can contain certain powers and talents and can confer them on the user, even make the practitioner think he's invincible. Looks like we're good to go. We're going to lay down a shielding pentagon to contain any problems. Still, don't move from your spot."

Hal walked over to a position between John and Fergus but about a step farther away from the case. He pointed at the ground. A glowing pentagon etched itself into the path around the men and sent shimmering walls up to the glass ceiling.

The Swords stood opposite each other about a blade's length from the item in the bowl between them. The silver lightballs hovering above winked out. John drew his weapon, and its silver blade shone. Fergus had never ended his spell, and his sword, now a dark blue, changed color through violet into silver and then into a silver-laced gold. The light emanating from the weapons made the area as bright as day.

A hum, much deeper, fuller, and more resonant than the ones he and Gloriana had produced, vibrated through the air. The hair on the back of Marcus's head stood up when he felt the potency of the magical energy swirling around all of them. He couldn't help making a swift calculation. If each rise in level signaled an exponential rise in power, the amount displayed here staggered him. Furthermore, Hal was standing with a hand out to each Sword, and a faint glimmer of spell aura surrounded the three men and the object in the middle. Marcus could swear the Defender was sharing power with them like he and Glori had between themselves.

The Swords raised their weapons and brought them down to point directly at the blob of evil. "One, two, three," Fergus said softly. On the "three," laserflike beams shot out from their tips and converged on the object.

"One, two, three," Fergus said again. John's blade intensified with a whoosh into a silver-whipped gold while Fergus's turned pure gold. The beams from the swords burned white where they met the crystal. Soon a white light surrounded the crystal and pressed in on it until the white was almost too bright to look at.

Walcott began to moan and struggle against the vines. The Swords held their positions for another five minutes.

Marcus didn't know if it was an optical illusion, but the item seemed to be rocking, first in one direction, then another, trying to evade the sword beams. He was wondering if the crystal could escape, when, ZAP!

The deformed crystal disintegrated into a small heap of ashes.

Walcott howled, a long, mournful cry, and collapsed, only held vertical by the vines around his arms and torso.

The Swords sheathed their weapons, bringing darkness back to the jungle. Hal cast several lightballs to illuminate the scene, and the medics began to extricate Walcott from his vine prison.

"Hal," John said, "if you'll take care of the item's remains, we'll see Gloriana and Marcus back to the house."

"Come on, you two," Fergus said, making shooing motions. "There are some people who want to see you, and I want to hear how you caught the bastard with those vines."

Once outside, Marcus and Gloriana were enveloped by their parents while the dogs danced attendance. Stefan drove them in Marcus's car to Gloriana's house to change into dry clothes and back to the big farmhouse, where Antonia and Alaric hustled to fix food to replenish their energy. Only when they had eaten would her mother allow them to tell what had happened.

After hearing the tale, Fergus spoke up. "I believe I've heard of another one or two couples like you, so different originally, but so very compatible at the end. I've never seen such a merged lightball before, however. As for merging and exchanging magical energy, Defender teams do it all the time. It's still a rare talent."

"From what you've told us," John interjected, "I doubt you're candidates for the Defenders. The merging talent usually manifests itself quite early, and it appears you can only utilize it when in physical contact. Defenders don't need contact. But it won't hurt to have you tested."

"What will happen to Walcott?" Alaric asked.

"That depends on how or if he wakes up. When an item is destroyed, the person it was controlling usually lapses into unconsciousness and often a coma. What he'll be like when he wakes up depends on how powerful the item was, how long it controlled him, and how far into evil he had gone. I think Walcott will be in one of our nursing homes for quite a while. Most of those who succumb to an evil item lose some brain and magic functions when it's destroyed. Some have even lost the ability to cast spells altogether. We take good care of them, but they're broken people and seldom live long. The evil simply wears them out."

There was a moment of silence while everyone absorbed the information. Marcus was searching for some new subject to dispel the gloom created by it when his mother asked to see a drawn sword. She'd never seen one up close.

While the parents discussed Fergus's weapon, Marcus glanced over at Gloriana. She looked ready to drop. "Let's go to bed," he said. "It's after two."

She yawned and nodded. They made their good-byes, collected the dogs, and went home, straight to bed.

CHAPTER FORTY

Gloriana woke and opened her eyes to get her bearings, but didn't move otherwise. She had no idea what the time was, except it was still dark. She wondered if she'd slept more than an hour. Not that it mattered. She was perfectly comfortable where she was. She luxuriated in the feel of Marcus's arm around her, the rise and fall of his chest under her cheek, the thump-thump of his heartbeat matching hers.

She had to smile at the wonder of having a soul mate, and she turned her head to give him a little kiss.

His arm tightened around her, and his other hand came up to cover hers on his chest. A deep voice rumbled, "You're supposed to be asleep."

"So are you. I didn't mean to wake you."

"You didn't. I woke up several minutes ago and was lying here thinking."

"About . . .?"

"You. Me. Us. How astonished I am to be here with you. How grateful I am that you didn't give up on me, despite my pigheadedness."

"Funniest thing. I was thinking along the same lines. The astonishment, not the other. In the beginning, we were so far apart."

"Yes, in about everything except attraction for each other." He ran his hand up and down her back again, and she wished she could purr.

"It's a good thing we're soul mates," she said. "I don't think we could have ever resolved our magic differences if mating hadn't changed us. Leaving magic aside, we're going to have enough trouble, adjusting to each other."

"Trouble, what trouble? We love each other, our lovemaking shakes the earth, the dogs get along. Everything else is simple."

She sighed. "Just like a man. If the sex is good, nothing else matters."

"Of course." He patted her on the bottom.

"Smug, that's what you are," she retorted. "Well, I guess if you can learn to live with my clutter, I can learn to live with your penchant for austerity."

"And if you can learn to live with my jazz, I can handle country-western. Deal?"

"Deal."

"As for the magic, I expect we'll have lots of fun working out our combinations and permutations, adding what works, subtracting what doesn't, multiplying and dividing as necessary. You can help me figure out what the asterisks are."

Math? The man was worried about *math* while they were lying there naked? She lifted her head to frown at him. "Asterisks? What asterisks?"

"Remember the formula? I didn't use regular multiplication symbols because something else seemed to be happening between the elements of the equation to result in the finished spell."

"Oh, *those* asterisks. That's simple. Lulabelle explained the key thing about spell-casting to me long ago. When you get right down to it, nobody really knows how we focus energy and get results. We simply can. That's the *magic* part."

He groaned and pulled her around on top of him. As their centers aligned, the hum started. He found her lips in the dark and gave her a little kiss. "I guess there's only one thing to do."

"What?" she asked as she made herself comfortable and rubbed herself against him.

"We'll take some of your magic"—he ran his hands down her back and kneaded her backside—"and some of my magic"—he rubbed his erection along her rapidly dampening folds—"and merge." He slid into her all the way.

"I have a new equation for you, Dr. Forscher," she said as desire grew within her. "My magic *asterisk* your magic, equals *our* magic."

ANN MACELA
THE
OLDEST KIND
OF MAGIC

Daria Morgan is a magic practitioner, one of a group of people who uses magic and spells to do their everyday jobs. Her job: A management consultant.

John "Bent" Benthausen is a CEO who, despite every improvement in product and production, can't get his bottom line out of the Red Sea. He needs a management consultant.

With her special gifts, Daria gets right to the heart of her employer's problem—crooked employees. Crooked, vicious, employees who are now out to get Daria. Those are just Problems One and Two.

Problem Three: There is an ancient force, an irresistible compulsion, called the soul-mate imperative. It's known throughout the practitioner ranks for bringing together magic-users and their mates in a lifelong bond. And it won't be happy until the participants surrender to the inevitable . . . the Oldest Kind of Magic . . .

ISBN#9781932815436
US $6.99 / CDN $9.99
Paranormal Romance
Available Now
www.annmacela.com

ANN MACELA
DO YOU BELIEVE IN MAGIC?

According to lore, an ancient force called the soulmate imperative brings together magic practitioners and their mates. They always nearly fall into each other's arms at first sight. Always . . . or so the story goes.

But what happens if they don't? What happens when one mate rejects the other—in fact won't have anything to do with him? Who doesn't even believe in magic to begin with?

Computer wizard Clay Morgan is in just such a position. Francie Stevens has been badly hurt by a charming and good looking man and has decided to avoid any further involvements. Although the hacker plaguing her company's system forces her into an investigation led by the handsome practitioner, she vows to keep her distance from Clay.

The imperative has other ideas, however, and so does Clay. He must convince Francie that magic exists and he can wield it. It's a prickly problem. Especially when Francie uses the imperative itself against him in ways neither it, nor Clay, ever anticipated.

ISBN#9781933836164
US $7.95 / CDN $9.95
Paranormal Romance
Available Now
www.annmacela.com

R. GARLAND GRAY
DARKSCAPE
THE REBEL LORD

Lord Lachlan de Douglas, a noble warrior lord, is heir to a Clan of Ancient Earth. Bold, rebellious, possessing strength and passion, he defends his clan from annihilation against a wretched war of masked vengeance and treacherous shadows. Until one day, a sudden horror alters his being, condemning him to a world of private anguish and torment.

Kimberly Kinsale, a diplomat's daughter, is a rare beauty motivated by honesty and integrity. Serving as a lieutenant in an elite combat fighter group aboard a war ship, she governs her life by the intrigue and lies of her commanding officer. A moment of lunacy and folly, a secret revealed, and Kimberly stumbles upon an unspeakable deception.

Now she must decide. Maintain her loyalty, or betray her Clan and ship for a Douglas enemy lord who can prove the truth--never knowing the battle for justice will take her through Lachlan's nightmare, a rage so deep, a suffering grounded in shame and pride, even when peace shines in sight.

For theirs is an unexpected passion, born in the fires of a shared need and desperate struggle. Kimberly must fight the sinister legacy of the matrix robots and trust the handsome enemy lord with her life, her heart, and her very soul. But as time slowly runs out, even an exquisite love may not be enough for salvation.

ISBN# 9781933836485
Mass Market Paperback / Sci-Fi Romance
US $7.95 / CDN $8.95
DECEMBER 2008

Amy Tolnitch
A Lost Touch of Magic

Veiled by the mists of the highlands are tales of beautiful, magical, and sometimes dangerous worlds. One such realm, Paroseea, dwells hidden within the stone walls of a medieval fortress, Castle MacCoinneach. Yet danger has escaped paradise and stalks the halls of Castle MacCoinneach seeking vengeance, patiently waiting for the return of the fallen laird.

You must return.

Those words, uttered by the ghost of Padruig MacCoinneach's beloved sister, send him back to the highlands and a life he forswore. To save his remaining sister and aid his clan, Padruig will do anything. He never expected that he would have to marry his ally's daughter, whom he deems both a reckless child and a potent temptation.

You are the price.

With these callous words, Padruig destroys a fantasy Aimili de Grantham has long nurtured, created from her memories of Padruig himself. A cool, dismissive stranger has replaced the golden man of her dreams, a stranger she must wed. Worse, the fey part of her senses that evil lurks in the shadows of Castle MacCoinneach, and she has nowhere to turn.

One true laird and one of fey blood.

Strangers they may be, but Padruig and Aimili are destined to join together to defeat a force beyond their imaginings. It will take trust, faith, and most of all, love to save themselves, their clan, and discover . . . A Lost Touch of Magic.

ISBN#9781934755518

US $7.95 / CDN $8.95

Paranormal Romance

DECEMBER 2008

www.amytolnitch.com

LYNDA HILBURN

Denver psychologist Kismet Knight, Ph.D., doesn't believe in the paranormal. She especially doesn't believe in vampires. That is, until a new client introduces Kismet to the vampire underworld and a drop dead gorgeous, 800-year-old vampire named Devereux. Kismet isn't buying the vampire story, but can't explain why she has such odd reactions and feelings whenever Devereux is near. Kismet is soon forced to open her mind to other possibilities, however, when she is visited by two angry bloodsuckers who would like nothing better than to challenge Devereux by hurting Kismet.

To make life just a bit more complicated, one of Kismet's clients shows up in her office almost completely drained of blood, and Kismet finds herself immersed in an ongoing murder investigation. Enter handsome FBI profiler Alan Stevens who warns her that vampires are very real. And one is a murderer. A murderer who is after her.

In the midst of it all, Kismet realizes she has feelings for both the vampire and the profiler. But though she cares for each of the men, facing the reality that vampires exist is enough of a challenge…for now.

ISBN#9781933836232
US $15.95 / CDN $19.95
Trade Paperback / Paranormal
Available Now
www.lyndahilburnauthor.com

Angel Unaware

ELIZABETH SINCLAIR

Dora de Angelo was never supposed to be an angel. Her soul was placed with the angels instead of the mortals and, as a result, she has never fit in and has an undying wish to be a mortal. Maybe that's why she is one of the most inept angels Heaven has ever had the misfortune to employ in the Celestial Maintenance Department.

Finally, Dora is sent to Earth. For the three weeks prior to Christmas she must help a mortal family, and return to Heaven on Christmas Eve. During that time, she must help a man find his faith in family again and his ability to trust in love. Dora must also help a little girl become a child again and get past the guilt she feels for the death of her parents. Doing so, Dora finds more than just a challenge to her questionable angel skills.

Dora loses her wings. But she gains something she has always wanted with all her heart. She also finds her family…and discovers love. And hope for a future she's only dreamed of …

ISBN#9781933836317
US $7.95 / CDN $9.95
Paranormal Romance
DECEMBER 2008
www.elizabethsinclair.com

For more information
about other great titles from
Medallion Press, visit

www.medallionpress.com